MELISSA ANNE

A Different Impression

A Pride and Prejudice Variation

Contents

Acknowledgement

I express my sincere gratitude to Ann, my immensely helpful Beta reader. Your input and support have been invaluable, and I appreciate the time and effort you have invested. Thank you for being a part of this creative journey.

Also, to all of those who read it as it was being developed and provided feedback: thank you! I appreciated the feedback and comments, and suggestions, as they frequently helped me know where to go next.

Thank you to my husband, Brian, and my children, who allowed me to ignore them while I worked.

Jane Austen, of course, created most of the characters and have helped so many find inspiration in creating new happily-ever-afters for our beloved couple. Like so many before me, I love helping Elizabeth and Darcy find new roads to their happiness.

One

The Assembly

"Come, Darcy; I must have you dance." Charles Bingley, the newly arrived tenant of Netherfield Park, chided his friend who had accompanied him to the assembly that night. "I hate to see you standing about in this stupid manner."

"Bingley, you insisted that I come, and I informed you before we left your home that I would not dance tonight, so leave me be," his friend, Fitzwilliam Darcy, stated. "My head aches, yet had I stayed behind, your sister would have insisted it was her duty to stay. Since that seemed the worse fate, I grudgingly came along, but I told you I was not in a mood to dance."

"Darcy ..." Bingley started.

"No, Charles," Darcy cut him off. "Had you told me there would be a dance tonight, I would have delayed my departure from London until tomorrow. I am here to help you learn to manage an estate, as you requested, and for no other purpose. Despite her efforts, Miss Bingley will never be my wife; I will not risk her attempting to compromise me by remaining alone in her company."

"Darcy ..." Bingley tried again to cajole his friend.

"No, Bingley, go and return to your latest "angel" and her many smiles," Darcy stated abruptly. "Leave me be to hold up the wall. I will be in a better humour when I have rested and my head no longer aches. I am tempted to call for the carriage to sneak out of this damned assembly, return to your estate, and sleep; I would if I thought I could do so without it being noticed.

Bingley grumbled but finally walked away, returning to the blonde woman he had met that night. Since Bingley met a new angel every other month and typically lost interest just as quickly, Darcy rarely paid them much attention.

Darcy had not noticed the lady sitting just behind him and had not attempted to whisper, as Bingley would have never been able to hear him over the music. So, when he glanced around him and their eyes met for a moment, each coloured slightly, clearly aware of the conversation that had been overhead.

"I am sorry your head aches," Miss Elizabeth Bennet said softly, standing and moving infinitesimally closer. "I know we have not been introduced, so forgive me for speaking, but I have some headache powders in my reticule that might help." As she spoke, she took out the packet and handed it to him surreptitiously.

"Thank you," he said, without looking at her, taking the small packet she offered.

"I did not mean to listen to your conversation," said she,

"but I could hardly avoid it either. I do apologise."

"It does not matter," he said, somewhat abashed, but quickly realised he honestly had not minded that she overheard.

She started to walk away, mindful of the impropriety of speaking to the gentleman when they had not been formally introduced. His whispered, "I hope to speak to you again soon, miss," took her by surprise, and she turned to smile at him. Her rather brilliant smile entranced him, making her features very striking. "Perhaps I can entice my friend to introduce us later," he offered as she began to walk away.

"Ask your friend to have my sister do the honours when their dance is over," she threw the comment over her shoulder as she walked away, hoping the brief *tête-à-tête* had been unobserved by the crowd, particularly by her mother. Looking around, it seemed her mother's attention had been on Jane's progress on the dance floor with Mr Bingley, so she approached Charlotte Lucas and began to chat about the assembly. Charlotte, who was older than Elizabeth and considered to be "on the shelf" by many in the neighbourhood, was a good friend, despite the seven-year difference in their ages.

They spoke teasingly of the dance, and Charlotte remarked on how taken their new neighbour seemed to be with Jane. "He is captured by her beauty, to be sure," Charlotte told Elizabeth. "If she wants to catch him, she will need to encourage him."

"Catch him?" Elizabeth cried. "Is he a fish to be caught? Surely you would not truly expect Jane to behave in such a way. You know she is shy."

"Marriage is a chance regardless," Charlotte returned. "Better to know as little as possible of your potential partner in life before securing him. Longbourn is entailed, which makes an advantageous match that much more important for you and your sisters. If he is interested, she should show that she returns his interest so he will quickly marry her and secure the future for all of you."

Both women fell silent, with Elizabeth settling for sending a sharp look at Charlotte as she did not know how to respond to such a comment. The song ended, and Bingley and Jane began approaching their location. Starting to feel slightly better for the kindness bestowed on him, Darcy also began to move that way. Elizabeth noticed his approach, having kept an eye on the handsome gentleman since their brief conversation. Jane and Bingley were grinning at each other, and upon realising others were watching them, both coloured slightly. Charlotte and Elizabeth shared an amused look at the pair.

"Thank you for the dance, Miss Bennet," Bingley said. "Here are your friends – would any of you ladies care for a glass of punch?"

All three women nodded and offered a quiet "thank you" as Bingley moved to walk away.

Spying Darcy approaching, Bingley immediately turned back to the ladies and began the introductions before his friend could decline: "Ladies, might I introduce you to my good friend, Mr Fitzwilliam Darcy of Pemberley in Derbyshire? Darcy, meet Miss Jane Bennet, Miss Elizabeth Bennet, and Miss Lucas."

Darcy bowed, and the ladies curtseyed. "It is lovely to meet you all," his deep voice murmured. Then, abruptly, he turned to Miss Elizabeth and said in his clear, deep voice, "Miss Elizabeth, are you free for the next dance?"

Bingley looked shocked, given his friend's earlier declaration that he would not dance. Elizabeth hesitated briefly and gazed into his eyes briefly before softly replying, "Not the next, sir, but I am free the one after that."

"Then might I have the honour of your hand for that set?" he asked. Then, seeing her nod and Bingley's shocked expression, he spoke again as if suddenly aware of himself. "Miss Bennet, Miss Lucas, might I also claim a dance with each of you?"

Both ladies answered in the affirmative, with Miss Lucas accepting the dance that was about to begin while Miss Bennet accepted for the next to last dance for the evening.

When the opening chords of the new dance played half an hour later, Mr Darcy held out his hand to Miss Elizabeth. Both felt the brief spark of … was it electricity? … when they touched and started slightly. Despite their gloves, each felt the warmth from the other's hand and a brief sensation of … something. Darcy realised it was the same feeling he felt when he saw Pemberley after returning from a time away – a sense of belonging and homecoming. It was an incredible feeling, making him pay closer attention to his partner than was his wont.

"Thank you for agreeing to dance with me," he whispered as he led her toward the line.

She smiled up at him, "I thought you did not mean to dance tonight?"

"I did not, yet somehow could not help myself after our brief conversation earlier," he admitted, with a quirk of his lip that might have been the beginning of a smile. "I found myself wanting to become more acquainted with you."

She looked at him archly, contemplating how to respond

as the dance separated them for a moment. When it brought them back together, she asked gently, "Is your headache better?"

"Remarkably so," he admitted, with that sardonic half-grin again.

She looked back at him archly. "Was the headache invented to excuse bad behaviour?"

"Whose bad behaviour, Miss Elizabeth?" he asked. "Could it be someone else's poor behaviour that caused my head to ache?"

"Ahh, well, I cannot deny that the actions of others have occasionally affected my own disposition – particularly some members of my own family." Now it was her turn to quirk her lip at him. "And a time or two, I have developed a sudden headache to avoid an uncomfortable situation."

"So," he arched a look at her, "are you prone to this sort of dissembling?"

"Dissembling?" she cried. "You would not be attributing to me what you are doing yourself."

"No, my head honestly did hurt earlier," he said gravely. "Between avoiding unwanted attention and … ah … worrying over another situation, my head was aching rather badly when I entered the hall. But I found myself presented with a temporary reprieve, and it has lifted my spirits."

"Hmmm, unwanted attention," Elizabeth laughed. "What a problem to have, sir."

"You have no idea," he remarked dryly. Then he continued, speaking softly, almost to himself, "Surely you heard the gossip when my friend and I entered tonight. Most women see the material things marriage to me could offer them – the grand estate and my income – few would bother to look past that to the man I am. So many, it seems, desire to be 'Mistress of Pemberley' and chase the status it would bring." He frowned, glancing at her as though he had not meant to say that part out loud. "I am merely tired of being chased."

She looked at him, catching his eye and seeing the sad look contained in it. Their eyes maintained their contact for a moment before the dance separated them.

When they came back together, she offered a whispered apology, "I am sorry the Meryton gossips began to speculate about you and your friend the moment you entered. Unfortunately, my mother and the other ladies here will speculate and talk about any single men who enter the neighbourhood, as we seem to have a shortage of available gentlemen in our town. Therefore, as soon as you appeared tonight, several mothers sought to claim you for their unmarried daughters – my own mother being among the worst of them."

"That is not exactly unique to a country town," he replied, seeking to reassure her. "The mothers of the *ton* are equally adept at gossip and matchmaking; in fact, many are rather proficient at it."

"Still, it must be difficult to be judged on one's wealth," she asserted, adding more softly, "… or the lack of it."

They were both contemplative while the dance separated them. As they returned to each other as they followed the dance steps, she offered a lighter topic, "This topic is much too deep for a dance, sir. So, I will change it and ask, how do you like Netherfield Park, Mr Darcy? It has been some years since I have been there, but I remember it being a lovely home, although the previous owners seriously overlooked the library. Will your friend remedy that?"

Darcy laughed, "I have only had a brief glance, but I would

agree that the library has been very neglected. Unfortunately, I am not sure that Bingley or his sisters will do much about that particular room, although I will encourage him to do something about the neglect if only to aid me during my stay here."

"Are you here to offer advice on the furnishing of the rooms then," she asked lightly.

"Bingley asked me to come here to tutor him on the running of an estate since my father trained me since I was a boy," he stated. "I inherited my own estate more than five years ago, and he knows the work I have put into managing it. Bingley hopes to purchase an estate eventually, and Netherfield was ideal for learning it."

"How good of you to help," she mused, then added, "I am sorry that you lost your father at such a young age."

"Wha…" he faltered. "How could you possibly know that I have lost my father?"

"You said you inherited five years ago and spoke of him teaching you in the past tense," she stated clearly. Then more softly, she added, "and your eyes when you spoke of him were sad, as though you miss him greatly."

He looked at her sharply for a moment, uncertain of how to proceed, and then softened his gaze when he recognised the true look of sympathy in her eyes. Most women would not have picked up so much from his conversation except as confirmation that he was single and wealthy. Few women he had encountered among the *ton* would have even considered offering sympathy for any loss, much less one that occurred five years ago. He considered these thoughts as the couple made their way silently through the dance.

Quietly, she said to him, "I am sorry to have reminded you

of your sorrows. Do you have other family?" she asked.

"A younger sister," he nearly bit out, his mind still in turmoil whenever he thought about her. "My mother is also gone; she died when Georgiana was four."

"How old is she now?" she asked.

"Just fifteen," he replied. "I am more than ten years older than she."

"I am truly sorry for both of you," she murmured. "As much as my mother often pains and mortifies me, I cannot imagine her or my father being gone from my life. Nor can I imagine how difficult it must be to have the responsibility of caring for a much younger sibling. My sisters are all close to my age, but I cannot imagine being responsible for them. It must have been much more difficult as not only did you have to see to her, but you also had the care of your estate and your tenants dropped upon you as well."

"I share her guardianship with my cousin, Colonel Richard Fitzwilliam," he hesitated. "Neither of us are all together ... certain when it comes to raising a young girl on the cusp of womanhood." Darcy was still astounded that this woman seemed to think of his estate not in terms of its wealth but in terms of the responsibility it carried.

"I imagine that would be a challenge, sir," she remarked. "Having no brothers, I can only imagine how difficult it would be to guide someone if I had no notion of what they were experiencing."

"Tell me of your family, Miss Elizabeth," he said, abruptly changing the topic. "You have a mother and a father, and I have met your older sister."

"I am the second of five daughters," she offered with an arched brow. "My father's estate is called Longbourn, which is adjacent to Netherfield Park. You met Jane, the eldest of us, and then there are Mary, Catherine, and Lydia after me. My mother has declared us all in desperate need of husbands as quickly as possible, so all five are out at once. Lydia is far too young to be out, at just barely 15, but Mama would not hear of her waiting, and Papa simply chooses to follow the path of least resistance." Her tone at the end was equal parts bitter and mortified.

"Why do you all need husbands as quickly as possible," he inquired with a look of surprise in his eyes.

She threw him a look, but when he appeared genuinely interested and not challenging, she sighed and said, "Papa's estate is entailed. None of my sisters may inherit, so a distant cousin will instead. Mama constantly bemoans the entail and worries that when Papa, who by-the-by is perfectly healthy, dies, this cousin will throw us out into the hedgerows to starve."

He looked surprised, "Have you no other family?"

"Yes, an uncle here in Meryton, who is a solicitor, and my uncle Gardiner is in trade in London," she said, continuing to watch him closely to see how he responded to this news. "Both have assured Mama they will take care of her and us when and if the time comes, but Mama does not hear it. I think she prefers to view herself as ill-used due to the entail."

"But you said your father is well?" he asked.

"Yes, he is hale, but Mama is … she prefers to … oh, I do not know how to explain this," she said. "She fancies herself nervous and does not deal well with things she does not understand. I am sorry … I should not be saying any of this to you." Her face turned scarlet as she realised what she was revealing about her family to someone she had just been introduced to that night.

The dance was ending. He took her hand and placed it on his arm as he escorted her back to her sister and his friend. "I am glad you confided in me," he said quietly. "I enjoyed speaking as openly as we have. By chance …" he hesitated briefly, "by chance, might I claim another dance with you tonight?"

"That will incite speculation and gossip from my neighbours," she pointed out. "My mother will be the worst of all, and she will crow about the forthcoming 'engagement' that a second dance must surely indicate."

"I find myself not caring about the gossip it may raise," he replied, watching for her reaction.

"You will not have to live with it, sir," she said pointedly, then agreed. "If you do not care, then I can bear it, but I will have you know the only dance I still have open is the last."

"Perfect," he said, genuinely smiling at her, revealing his dimples.

"He is beautiful when he smiles," Elizabeth thought, again colouring at the direction of her thoughts.

When they arrived back beside Bingley and Jane, the four spoke together for a time before Jane was claimed for her next dance. Bingley claimed Elizabeth for their dance while Darcy stood and reluctantly watched them go knowing he would have to until the last set to dance with Miss Elizabeth again. Charlotte was free for this set, so they enjoyed the punch and easy conversation while watching the dancers.

* * *

One person in the room was decidedly unhappy about the

turn of events. Caroline Bingley had been rather annoyed when Mr Darcy told her in the carriage that he would not dance with her, and then to see him dancing with these local women made her quite angry. Charles appeared taken with Miss Jane Bennet, which was bad enough, but Mr Darcy making a fool of himself over her younger sister was not to be borne. She knew no one else in the room was as well-dressed or well-suited to Mr Darcy as she, and she was confident that no country chit would replace her as the future Mistress of Pemberley. As she watched Darcy dance, she determined to do something to force him to realise it.

Louisa Hurst saw all these thoughts on her sister's face, especially after Darcy began to dance with Elizabeth Bennet. She had repeatedly warned Caroline that setting her cap at Mr Darcy would never bear fruit. She and Charles had both told Caroline that Mr Darcy would never offer for her, but Caroline ignored them all. Finally, Louisa whispered to her husband, who stood nearby, that they would need to watch Caroline carefully while they were at Netherfield.

"You may want to speak to Mr Darcy and warn him," Louisa told her husband. "He has often told Charles that he would not offer for her even if she were compromised, but he should be careful anyway. Perhaps advise him that having his valet sleep in the same room would not go amiss while he is here."

"Darcy should not have to go to such lengths to avoid her," Hurst replied. "Charles needs to send her away."

"I am afraid he will not do that until after she has done something to ruin herself," Louisa worried. "Nothing we have said to her has kept her from repeatedly throwing herself at him, despite his obvious lack of interest. I just hope that whatever she does will not ruin the rest of us along with herself."

"Let us start by taking her back to Netherfield before she does something we will regret," Hurst suggested. "Perhaps you could feign a headache?"

"If you could let Charles know our plans," Louisa told him. "I will collect Caroline. Let him know we will send the carriage back for him."

Hurst moved closer to the dancers and motioned to Charles to join him when he could. Louisa moved to Caroline and told her, "I am not feeling well. Mr Hurst and I are returning to Netherfield, and I need you to accompany me."

"I am not leaving until Mr Darcy asks me to dance," she pouted. "This is his second dance of the night – it would be rude for him not to dance with me."

"He told you in the carriage, after your many hints, that he was not going to dance with you tonight," she advised. "If you are waiting for him to ask, you will be here long after the assembly has ended."

"I will not leave this early in the evening. There are still plenty of dances left," Caroline stubbornly refused.

"If I leave, you will stand or sit here alone for the rest of the evening," Louisa pointed out. "You will not bother speaking to anyone, and they will continue to avoid you due to the scowl on your face. Do you really think that will be better than returning to Netherfield early? Besides, Charles wishes to establish himself in this area as the master of his estate, and your behaviour will do him no favours."

"I do not want to step foot in that awful place ever again," Caroline complained. "I am returning to London tomorrow, and you will all have to join me there. Charles cannot possibly stay here without me, so the impression he leaves on these people will hardly be worth considering!"

"Well, then, let us go ahead and return so we may begin packing," Louisa complied.

Both women headed toward the front of the building. Louisa requested their carriage to be brought around while they retrieved their wraps.

Hurst joined them as the carriage was being called, telling his wife, "I told Charles we would send the carriage back for him and Darcy."

Caroline smiled in the darkness. *"What if the carriage did not return for them?"* she thought. *"They will have to walk back to Netherfield in the dark. Charles has been so disobliging, and Darcy refused to dance with me. It would serve them both right for their ill use of me!"* She determined that she would tell the servants to return the carriage to the stables and do so without Hurst noticing as soon as they returned.

Hurst noticed her smile and wondered what she was going to attempt. He did not say anything to Louisa but was determined to watch her closely to see what she would try.

At Netherfield, Hurst descended from the carriage first and handed out his wife. Caroline refused his hand when offered and followed behind them slowly. She dropped something along the way and stopped to pick it up, calling to them to go on ahead of her. Hurst continued but kept watch to see what Caroline would do. When she thought they were inside, she spoke to the coachman, who was obviously surprised by what she said to him. When he noticed the coachman heading toward the stables instead of turning it back toward town, Hurst looked at his wife and told her what he suspected.

A moment later, Caroline came inside, looking very pleased with herself. The three separated – the ladies to their rooms and Hurst to the library, claiming he needed a drink before bed. He snuck out a different door and went to the stables. There, he saw the horses being unharnessed and the carriage put away. He sighed and asked a groom to saddle three horses. He told the groom to ride one and lead the other two to the assembly rooms to await Bingley and Darcy. He hoped they wouldn't mind riding back – it would be far better than the walk that Caroline had clearly intended for them.

That task complete, he realised he might be better off speaking to Darcy's valet himself than relying on a message. He asked the housekeeper, Mrs Nicholls, where the keys to the guest rooms were kept and for the location of Darcy's room.

Hurst went to Darcy's room, where he found his valet. "Marston?" Hurst said to the man.

"Yes, sir," the valet replied. "What can I do for you?"

"I have not spoken to Darcy yet, but it may be in his best interest for you to sleep down here rather than upstairs," Hurst stated bluntly. "Caroline is in a fury, and I worry what she may try."

Marston smiled blandly. "I appreciate the warning, but Mr Darcy had already asked that I do just that, and I already have a cot set up in the dressing room. Most of the time, when we stay in a home where an unmarried female lives, Mr Darcy requests that I stay close. However, since the last time your family was at Pemberley, any time we are in the same house as Miss Bingley, Mr Darcy not only locks all the doors and has me sleep near but also moves furniture in front of the door to block the entrance."

Hurst grinned at this. "Good man, Marston. I am glad to know Mr Darcy has you watching out for him."

"Good night, sir," Marston replied impassively. He knew why the furniture went in front of the door. Darcy took extraordinary steps to avoid being alone with Miss Bingley, and his valet wondered why the master continued to subject himself to it.

Two

Caroline Makes a Colossal Mistake

Back at the assembly rooms, Darcy had enjoyed himself as he would never have believed he could at an assembly or ball. He had been unusually sociable and had taken advantage of the many opportunities for conversation that evening. Sometimes he, Elizabeth, Bingley, and Jane talked together; other times, the couples spoke just to each other. Other members of the community had also joined them at times, but for much of the evening, the four were together.

The dance was coming to an end, and Bingley and Darcy danced the last set with their preferred Bennet lady. As the last dance finished, Mr Darcy quietly asked Miss Elizabeth, "Might I call on you tomorrow?"

She blushed prettily and looked at him with a question in her beautiful eyes. "As much as I would like to agree, sir," she breathed, "you do not know my Mama. As much as I love her, if a gentleman called on me the day after an assembly, she would rush to conclusions and have us, in her mind, married within the week. You also danced with me twice tonight; a call tomorrow will make it a certainty in her mind. It will cause much talk."

He was stunned by her words. He had encountered many matchmaking mamas and coquettish daughters who would have liked nothing more than to rush to assumptions and gossip about his intentions. This lady, with nothing flirtatious in her manner, had been truly sincere and interesting. She drew him out of himself and was interested in more than just his status. Inheriting so early, Darcy had had multiple encounters with unscrupulous and mercenary women. Too many women only wanted what they could get from him.

This lady, however, was warning him away from calling to prevent gossip and speculation. She was truly a jewel among women. "I do not know that I would mind such speculation," he whispered in response.

With a glance, she murmured a soft, "Then, I would be delighted, sir. But do not say I did not warn you." And she smiled at him in such a way that he was wholly and utterly lost.

Joining the ladies outside and helping them into their carriage, Bingley and Darcy were surprised their carriage was not yet ready. Glancing around, Darcy noticed the groom and horses and moved Bingley toward them.

"Mr Hurst sent me with the horses after Miss Bingley ordered the carriage horses unharnessed," the groom stated.

Bingley and Darcy exchanged glances. "Why would she not send the carriage back as we requested?" Bingley wondered.

Darcy thought the same but reflected on how angry she

had been when he had ignored her at the dance. He knew she desired Pemberley – not him, but his estate and his wealth – and he despised her for it. The only reason he maintained any sort of relationship with her was because of his close friendship with Bingley. He had never told Bingley about the incident at his estate last summer, but perhaps he had better. He knew Marston would sleep in his dressing room and do what he could to minimise the risk of compromise within his chambers, but outside his chambers, he still had to worry. He determined he would talk to Bingley that very night.

They mounted the horses and rode silently back toward Netherfield. Conscious of the groom's presence, Darcy did not want to broach the subject, but as they approached the house, he roused himself out of his reflections to suggest a nightcap in Bingley's study.

"Bingley, there is something I need to talk to you about when we get to the house," Darcy said to his friend. "Do you still have some of that brandy Richard smuggled in from France?"

"That sounds ominous," he said. "It is late, and you are asking for liquor and a chat?"

Darcy sighed. "It is serious," he replied, glancing at the groom. "The brandy will just make it easier, although whisky would work as well."

Bingley gave him a searching gaze but, like Darcy, glanced at the groom and wisely held his tongue.

Soon, they arrived at the house, dismounted, and headed into the study. Bingley poured them both a glass. Darcy took it, sipped, and stared into the fire for several minutes before speaking.

"Charles," he began, then stopped. After a moment, he

started again. "This summer, at Pemberley, your sister attempted a compromise. I did not tell you about it because I hoped, after what I said to her, she would put aside her … her … well, her obsession with me, well, not with me really, but with the idea of becoming Mistress of Pemberley." Here he paused, taking another drink and looking over at his friend.

"She was in my bedroom, naked in my bed, when Marston entered the room before me. He quickly sent her away before she realised I was there and warned her never to attempt anything like that again. The next day, she approached me at breakfast to complain about my valet's high-handedness with her. I told her then, in no uncertain terms, that nothing she did would ever induce me to marry her. It was the day you were leaving, so I did not see a need to discuss it further.

"I hoped, after all this time, she would have dropped her obsession, given what I said to her then, but after tonight, I am not sure she has. Coming here was a mistake – I worry she will try something again, something more public and harder to prevent."

Charles looked shocked at this. "Why did you never tell me?"

"She was embarrassed," Darcy paused at that and tried again, "well, most likely furious when I spoke to her that day," Darcy told him, remembering the brief conversation. "Bingley, it was not something I wanted to remember. I hoped not to have to relate the story to you because I intended to avoid her long enough that she would marry someone else."

Again, Darcy paused, looking at his friend's face. "I truly am sorry I never told you; I should have. But I arrogantly believed I handled it in the best way; I see that I was wrong."

At that, Bingley jerked his head up, "You are admitting to

being both arrogant and wrong in the same conversation," he exclaimed, shock rolling off of him.

That took aback Darcy – both the words and the apparent surprise of his friend. "Surely, I have confessed to being wrong before, Bingley?"

"You do tend to think you are right, Darcy," Bingley told his friend. "You rarely speak unless you are absolutely sure about what you are going to say, and typically, people listen to you because of this. Even at Eton, you rarely were wrong, and after your father passed, well, let me say that you became even more used to people listening to you and making decisions for others.

"Do not get me wrong, Darcy, you typically do know what to do, and most people do listen to you to their benefit, but I am not sure I have ever heard you admit to an error in judgement."

"Many people depend on me," Darcy justified. "I cannot afford to make mistakes in judgement. However, I do try to make amends when I realise that I have made a mistake."

"But do you acknowledge those mistakes and apologise like you just did to me?" Bingley asked. "Or do you try to 'fix' the situation without publicly admitting to the wrong?"

Darcy stopped at that. This conversation was taking a decidedly different turn from where he had intended it to go, but it made him consider several other actions he had taken recently. Darcy knew he rarely changed a position once he had made up his mind because he typically thought through every decision meticulously and carefully.

As he considered decisions, he thought about the ones that were most weighing on his mind. He thought about Georgiana; he had made several errors in judgement there, not that Bingley was aware of that situation. On his way to Netherfield, he considered again what he had been thinking about – he needed a wife, and Georgiana needed a sister. But not one of the artificial women of the *ton*. Not one like Caroline Bingley.

His mind wandered back to the assembly. He typically hated assemblies and dancing, and meeting new people. He had enjoyed meeting Miss Elizabeth Bennet. She was intelligent, witty, and completely charming. Not a classical beauty, like her older sister perhaps, but stunning in her own right. Her eyes, those flashing, challenging, articulate eyes, captured him like none before hers ever had.

After several minutes of reflection, Darcy interrupted the silence that had descended on both of them: "Bingley, if you think I have rarely made errors in judgement, I have another confession that might surprise you."

He related his error in judgement about George Wickham. He admitted to his best friend how he had chosen, along with Colonel Fitzwilliam, not to tell Georgiana about the perfidy of the man she had known as a child and how that decision had almost led to her ruin. How Georgiana was heartbroken, too young to understand how any man could be so ruthless and finding it so difficult to trust almost anyone now. How she had been shy before, but now it was almost painful for her to even speak in company, particularly to strangers.

"I believe I need a wife," Darcy finished. "One who can help draw Georgiana out; one who can help draw me out and to help me find humour again in life. Richard told me that I have become an arrogant, depressing bastard, and now you say the same. That is why, as much as I need to stay far away from Miss Bingley, I find that I really do not want to leave

Meryton just yet.

"I want to get to know Miss Elizabeth Bennet better. Tonight, I found myself speaking more to her than I have ever spoken at a country assembly before. I felt comfortable with her. I think I could fall in love with this lady. You fall in love with a new 'angel' every other month, but this is the first time I have felt this way about a woman. I have been in society for nearly a decade, and this is the first woman I have ever even remotely considered as a possible wife."

Bingley was shocked again by Darcy. He had never heard his friend admit to so much ... or even allude to having these types of feelings toward a woman. It seemed strange, but he also noticed that some of the tightness that typically showed on Darcy's face appeared to be a bit more relaxed – just a little, but noticeable nonetheless.

Bingley knew that Caroline would make it difficult for Darcy to court or get to know any other woman while she was nearby. He wondered if he could get Hurst to take his sisters back to London for a while. His Aunt Edith could come and serve as hostess for him so he could host some of the families from the neighbourhood.

"If I had known about the incident with Caroline last summer, I am not sure how I would have reacted," Bingley finally acknowledged the beginning of the conversation. "However, first thing tomorrow, I am going to request that Hurst take Caroline and Louisa back to London. I will make them believe we will follow along in a day or two if my sisters seem reluctant, but we will get Caroline out of this house. Take precautions until she is gone – lock your door, have your valet sleep with you, whatever you think it will take. She was unhappy with you tonight – I think she was trying

23

to force us to walk home, but Hurst caught on to it somehow and sent the horses."

There was a light knock on the door. Both men were startled, but Bingley called, "Come in."

Marston, Darcy's valet, stepped in the door. "Sirs, forgive me for the interruption, but please come with me. I think you both need to see this."

"What is it, Marston?" Darcy asked, perplexed by his man seeking him out in this way.

"Please come with me to your room, sir," Marston replied. "It will explain itself when we arrive."

With that, both men followed Marston quietly up the stairs. As they passed the hallway to the family wing, Hurst came out of his room and quietly joined the group. They walked to Darcy's room, where a soft light flickered inside. The servant's door was ajar, and Marston directed them to walk into the dressing room. From there, they could see into Darcy's bedroom, where on the bed lay Caroline, obviously waiting for Darcy to appear. She was barely dressed in a flimsy night rail that left little to the imagination, even from a distance.

The men withdrew from the dressing room and gathered in the hallway. Charles, his face red, was furious at his sister. Darcy was also livid, but Hurst and Marston displayed mild amusement.

Charles was the first to speak. "What could either of you find remotely amusing in this situation?" he bit out.

Hurst spoke, knowing the valet would not. Hurst laughed, "Surely, you see how foolish she is in this. You have told her; Darcy has told her; Louisa has told her; we have all told her, over and over again, Darcy will never marry her. Yet twice now, she has been found in his bed, stark naked or practically so, and twice she will have been rebuffed for it. She is a fool to keep at it."

"Foolish, yes, but … wait, you said twice," Bingley was shocked. "Did you know about the first attempt in Pemberley?"

"Aye, Louisa knew about it and told me after we left," Hurst admitted. "I was surprised Darcy did not say anything to you, but I believed he must have said enough. But, of course, for most women, it would have been enough."

"I would like to think that most women would not deliberately set out to compromise a man by getting into his bed naked," Darcy said dryly. "Although enough try other sorts of compromises to achieve a similar end."

"That is one more reason you should marry that girl from tonight quickly, Darcy," Hurst commented.

Hurst laughed at the look of shock on both their faces. "She did not stop ranting about her in the carriage on the way back. She attempted to get back at you both for your interest in the lovely Miss Bennets by forcing you to walk back from town. I saw what she was up to and let her succeed in not sending the carriage back and sent horses for you in its place. She did not know I knew about her plan."

"Hurst," Bingley began suddenly, "would you be willing to take Caroline and Louisa to London tomorrow? Just until I can make some other arrangements for Caroline. After this, she clearly cannot be trusted to stay in the same house with Darcy, and we cannot get him married unless we stay close to the object of his desire." Bingley winked at Hurst and then looked at Darcy, catching the slight smile that flitted across his face.

Hurst, who also caught the grin that passed over Darcy's otherwise dour face, told his brother-in-law he would escort the ladies back to town first thing in the morning. "Well, that is settled; let us get to bed," Hurst said, all too jovially for three in the morning.

The four men looked at each other. Darcy was the first to speak, "Who is going to wake Caroline and tell her?"

Three pairs of eyes swung to Bingley. He walked to Darcy's door – the one leading to the hallway – and jerked it open. Before anyone could see what was happening, he slammed it shut, and they all heard a small feminine squeak. Then, they heard Bingley roar, "What the hell do you think you are doing here, Caroline?"

Hearing that, the remaining three men scrambled away – Hurst seeking his own bed and Darcy and Marston seeking to be anywhere but there.

Marston directed Darcy upstairs. "There are several empty beds in the servant quarters, sir. And one benefit is that you will not be caught alone," he grinned at his employer.

"Thank you, Marston," Darcy replied, grinning in return. "At this point, I think any flat surface will do. Fortunately, I doubt Miss Bingley would be able to find the servant's quarters."

Three

Meeting on Oakham Mount

Despite the late night, Darcy woke early. Marston had collected riding clothes for him from his room, and Darcy quickly dressed before heading out to the stables. His goal was to stay far away from the house this morning until Miss Bingley was far away. As he saddled his horse, the grooms either were not awake yet or were needed elsewhere this morning, and he thought about Miss Elizabeth. He wondered if Bingley's aunt could come to serve as hostess and if Bingley would be willing to invite both Georgiana and Richard to join them. With Miss Bingley gone, he knew his sister would be far more inclined to visit, and he would like her to meet Elizabeth. He smiled as the thought that Georgiana would thrive with Miss Elizabeth as a sister flitted through his mind.

Darcy rode across the fields, enjoying the cool but still beautiful late autumn weather. He came to a fence, perhaps the boundary between Netherfield and Longbourn, and slowed to inspect the fence. He and Bingley would need to inspect all of the fences soon, but a quick check of this fence would help him form an idea of how well the estate had been maintained. The fence was in good order, but he noticed a couple of areas in the fields that may have drainage issues if it rained very much.

In the distance, he saw a small hill and remembered that Elizabeth had mentioned walking to a high spot often. Oaksomething, he thought. He wondered if that was the spot she had mentioned. While not as high as the peaks in his native Derbyshire, it looked like a fair prospect, and he set out toward it. If he were lucky, Miss Elizabeth would have walked out this morning as well, and he would encounter her. However, it was probably much too early for her, especially after an assembly that had lasted until midnight.

As he moved in that direction, he saw signs that others were awake and moving about. He saw some tenant farms in the distance, wondering if they were tenants of Longbourn or Netherfield. Elizabeth had mentioned to her sister something that needed to be done for one of the tenants on their estate. That was another reason she would make a remarkable Mistress of Pemberley; she already knew what was required of the wife of an estate owner. His own mother had done much for their tenants during her lifetime, and Georgiana was slowly taking over some of those duties. However, she lacked the necessary guidance to take on the role fully, and she was still young.

He approached a little-worn path leading to the top of the hill. Oakham Mount was what she had called it, he remembered. His horse started up the trail, and Darcy saw something moving through the woods. He was almost at the top when the path he was on joined another one, and Elizabeth came out of those woods just ahead of him. He was momentarily stunned by her sudden appearance and the rush of feeling that swept through him at the sight.

"Good morning," he called out when he regained his senses. "I would not have expected you to be out this early."

"Mr Darcy," she turned to him, smiling at his greeting. "Good morning to you as well. I am often out walking this early – the rising sun makes it hard to stay abed, irrespective of what time I found it."

An image danced quickly in Darcy's mind of Elizabeth in his bed. He shook his head to clear it and noticed that Elizabeth seemed to shy away from being too close to him.

He started to dismount but wondered if that was the best choice. While she smiled at him, she had not taken any steps forward and seemed to be eyeing him a bit warily.

"I had thought of joining you," he said to her, "but I do not wish to make you uncomfortable with my presence."

"It is not your presence making me uncomfortable; it is him," she said, indicating his large horse.

"You do not care for horses, Miss Elizabeth?" Darcy inquired.

"Horses make me nervous," she admitted softly. "I was nearly trampled as a child and have been leery of the beasts since."

"Let me tie him to this tree over here," he offered. "I do assure you, he is a gentle thing and would appreciate any attention you would be willing to bestow on him. I do hope you will let me introduce you to him one day soon."

"I will consider it," she said, still wary of the big horse. She was less suspicious about the man but not wholly at ease with coming across him like this.

"I did not expect to see you out so early this morning," she said when he started back in her direction.

"Nor I you," he said, smiling softly at her. "You mentioned the view from here last night, and since I typically ride in the mornings when I am in the country, I thought to begin my inspection of Bingley's estate. No one at Netherfield was awake yet, and I had assumed the same to be true at Longbourn."

"My father is also an early riser," Elizabeth stated, "although he's rarely afield this time of day. Typically, he is already in his library reading or going over the accounts. He prefers to ride out later, if at all. My sisters and I often walk to check on the tenants, but they will not accompany me until after breakfast."

"That is good of you," Darcy said. "My mother did that as well; my sister Georgiana has begun learning to make tenant visits with Pemberley's housekeeper and my steward, although I believe there are many things that Mother did that she is not learning due to the lack of a true mistress of my homes." His look turned slightly contemplative at this thought.

"Tell me about Pemberley, sir," Elizabeth said, changing the topic away from his potential wife. "I cannot wait to visit Derbyshire and its environs ..." There, Elizabeth paused, blushing slightly as she realised what it must sound like to him. She did not dare to glance at his face but quickly rushed ahead. "I have heard of the area for years from my aunt by marriage – she grew up in the town of Lambton, and I had a letter from her yesterday inviting me to go north with her and my uncle this summer. They plan to visit the Lake District with a stop in her home town to visit some acquaintances who still reside there. I am most anxious to travel with them on this trip."

Darcy found himself inordinately pleased at the idea of Miss Elizabeth visiting his home and idly wondered if he would be the one to take her into that district. "Lambton is just five miles from Pemberley," Darcy exclaimed, his face lightening with her explanation. "Pemberley has been in my family for generations; I believe Derbyshire to be the loveliest county in England. If you enjoy this prospect, I am sure you will find many lovely ones that are equal to or surpass this view."

"My aunt claims the same," Elizabeth stated, risking a glance upwards at him, "and I hope one day to see for myself how it compares to Hertfordshire. Aunt Madeline has sung the praises of Derbyshire and the Peak District so much that I cannot wait to explore it thoroughly."

"If you enjoy walking, you will enjoy visiting both areas," Darcy told her. "While Hertfordshire is everything lovely, the Peak District and Derbyshire are very different from the southern parts of England. Undoubtedly, you would enjoy traipsing through the moors and traversing the heights. Mam Tor is a particular favourite of mine and a place I have often visited."

"That does sound wonderful," she enthused. "I have rarely had the opportunity to travel – aside from once- or twice-yearly jaunts to London to visit my aunt and uncle. Papa hates to travel nearly as much as he hates town, and he absolutely refuses to go except for rare trips to Hatchards or another bookseller. He would never leave his library if that were

31

a possibility, but alas, he suffers through visiting with the steward and his tenants when absolutely necessary." This last was said archly with the slightest hint of criticism for her lackadaisical father.

"I spend much time in my library as well; at least, I do when I am not in my study dealing with business. Unfortunately, business takes up far more time than I would like at times," Darcy said, noting Elizabeth's tone and wondering about it. "It is my favourite room in the house – the work of generations of Darcys. If I am home when you visit Lambton, I would love to show Pemberley to you.

"Might I inquire after the maiden name of your aunt?" Darcy asked. "I wonder if I am acquainted with her family if any of them remain in Lambton. And perhaps her approximate age."

"The family left the area some years ago," Elizabeth said. "Her maiden name was Thornton, and I believe, while her father was alive, he owned some kind of shop in Lambton. She may be a few years older than you – but since I am not certain of your age, that may be inaccurate. She celebrated her birthday a few weeks ago and was five and thirty."

He smiled at her wit. "She is seven or eight years older than I, and I vaguely recall the Thornton family from my youth. He was a milliner, perhaps, or was it a bookshop?" He trailed off, trying to recall details from many years ago.

"I think my aunt mentioned that he may have owned both at one point," Elizabeth said. "But when he died, his widow sold both establishments and returned to her family in London. My uncle had already established his business by then, and they met when she visited his warehouse one day with her brother. Her brother invested with Uncle Gardiner, which led to them being in company often. It was not long after this that they became engaged."

"Gardiner, you say?" Darcy questioned. "That name sounds familiar. Doesn't he own several warehouses – Gardiner Import/Export?"

"Aye, that is his business," Elizabeth acknowledged.

"Then I met him not so long ago," Darcy said thoughtfully. "A very savvy businessman and quite well-off, I would dare say. Bingley and I met with him about some investment opportunities. I was impressed with his liberal ideas and was very pleased to partner with him on a venture or two. I hope we will have a long and prosperous partnership. I found I liked him very much. Will you be travelling with his family?"

Elizabeth nodded. "Uncle Edward is one of the best men I know and, yes, a savvy investor. I have invested small amounts of my allowance with him over the years," Elizabeth winked. "He and my aunt are a well-matched pair, and we were thrilled when he married her eleven years ago. Now, they have four children, and both Jane and I adore visiting with their family."

"How often do you visit them?" he asked.

"Jane or I often accompany them to London after Christmas for a few weeks, and occasionally we will visit in the autumn. One of us has frequently visited when my aunt has had her lying in to help with the other children. Last year, we had planned to stay with them for the entire Season, but my aunt's confinement interrupted those plans," Elizabeth smiled as she said the last. "Part of me thinks a Season would be entertaining, but I would not want to stay in town all those months. I would miss the country far too much. Although I very much enjoy the dancing, the musicals, and the theatre, I hate not having the freedom to walk in London as I do here."

At that, Elizabeth noted the sun's position. "I am afraid I must return home, sir; my family will wonder where I am."

"Might I escort you home?" Darcy inquired.

"Heavens, no!" Elizabeth exclaimed. "Mama would have a nervous fit if I returned home with a gentleman after an early morning walk. I already warned you what would happen if you called – you do not still mean to do so, do you?" she grinned at him unrepentantly.

"I would like to, but not if it causes you any discomfort," he remarked kindly. "Perhaps I could delay Bingley until tomorrow?"

"If you would," Elizabeth said. "While both Jane and I will miss your company, Mama would be a sore trial if you both appeared so quickly after last night. Besides, many ladies in Meryton will call today as they always do to discuss last night's assembly."

Darcy arched an eyebrow at that. "What is there to discuss? You were all just together last night?"

Elizabeth smiled at him archly. "Your sister is not yet out, am I correct?" At his nod, she continued, "Part of the fun of an assembly, at least in Meryton, is the gathering afterwards amongst all the ladies of the district. We speak of dresses and lace, who danced with whom … " Here she stopped briefly and looked at him in that impertinent way she had, "and about newcomers to the neighbourhood."

With that, she darted back into the woods, smiling broadly as she heard his loud laughter follow her.

* * *

Elizabeth arrived home to a mostly empty dining room. Her father, she supposed, had already eaten breakfast and was ensconced in his book room. Mary was sitting primly at the table.

"What have you been doing?" Mary asked pertly.

"I took a walk, as I do most mornings," Elizabeth calmly replied.

Jane entered the room serenely, followed by the boisterous Kitty and Lydia, who immediately began discussing the most pressing *on-dit* from last night. "The militia is coming to Meryton," Lydia cried. "In a month, we will be dancing daily with the officers."

"The arrival of the militia in Meryton will not result in daily opportunities to dance," Elizabeth corrected. "They will have duties to attend to."

"Besides," Mary said, "we have duties and responsibilities here at Longbourn that cannot be neglected."

"La, I will dance every day when the militia comes," Lydia proclaimed.

"Where do you think these dances will be occurring, Lydia?" their father asked as he wandered into the breakfast room to inquire about the noise therein.

"Wherever there are officers," Lydia announced laughingly.

"Lydia!" Elizabeth and Jane admonished.

"What is so wrong about wanting to dance?" Lydia turned to ask her sisters. "Just because you two are prigs who think flirting is beneath you does not mean that I should not do it. I fully intend to be the first sister married."

"The first sister married?" Papa exclaimed. "How do you think to manage that?"

"I intend to catch an officer," Lydia told him proudly.

"And how exactly do you plan to 'catch' one?" Papa asked, narrowing his eyes at Lydia dangerously.

Oblivious to her father's growing ire, Lydia gaily retorted, "Mama told me that if a lady accepts a kiss from a gentleman, it is as good as an offer of marriage. I intend to accept a kiss from the best-looking one."

"You are more foolish than I could have ever dreamed, Lydia," he said. "If this is the nonsense your mother spouts, you have little chance to improve here. I wonder what is best to be done ..." he trailed off, considering. "Lydia, go to your room and stay there until I call for you. I do not want to hear any more from you until you have learned some sense."

After ordering a servant to escort Lydia to her room and lock her in, he departed to his book room to consider what he should do about his youngest daughter.

Four

Caroline's Banishment

D arcy returned to Netherfield after a circuitous tour of the estate, entering the breakfast room to find it fortunately empty. He asked a footman nearby if any of the family had been down to break their fast.

"No, sir, no one has been down," the footman replied.

Darcy looked around and saw nothing on the sideboard. Just as he started to ask the footman about it, a harried maid entered the room.

"Oh," she cried. "Can I get anything for you, sir? Miss Bingley said none of the family would be down to breakfast this morning."

"Coffee, please, and a roll or two," Darcy requested. "Tell the cook not to go to too much trouble; I will be happy with whatever she has available." He stopped, then spoke again. "Can you have someone bring it to the library in fifteen minutes?"

"Yes, sir," the maid said, then curtsied and hurried off.

Darcy headed upstairs to quickly change into fresh clothes and met Bingley on his way down the steps.

"Have you already had breakfast, Darcy?" Bingley asked his friend.

"When I returned from my ride, the breakfast room was empty, and a maid informed me that your sister told the housekeeper no one would require breakfast this morning," Darcy told him. "I asked her to send coffee and whatever she had prepared to the library. Join me?"

"I told Caroline yesterday morning you would most likely ride out this morning and would want breakfast afterwards," Bingley complained. "I do not know why she would have told the housekeeper not to have food ready."

"Can you really not guess, Charles?" Darcy asked.

Bingley looked sheepish for a moment. "She still does not believe you will not marry her. She believes that since we all found her in your bed, you are somehow honour-bound to her. I am afraid that if I send her to London, she will spread gossip – no matter how I try to restrict her. We argued for ages last night."

"Then I will leave," Darcy said. "I will stay at the inn for a day or two – you and I are expected to call at the Bennets tomorrow, Charles – then I will return to London until you decide what to do about your sister."

"Where did you sleep last night anyway," Charles asked him.

"In the servants' quarters," Darcy replied.

"The servants' quarters?" Bingley was shocked.

"I have slept in less hospitable lodgings," Darcy replied. "Other than being a bit cool, they were in good shape."

"Darcy, in just four and twenty hours, I have learned a great deal about you that I never knew," Bingley replied, shock lacing his statement.

"We have known each other long enough; little of what I have confessed should be that shocking," Darcy replied with a groan. "It cannot be that far-fetched to learn that I can sleep in a servant's bed without complaining, and I know that in the ten years that we have known each other, I had to have apologised before."

"Perhaps, Darcy, but I do not remember an apology where you admitted to a lapse in judgement," Bingley said. "You have always seemed to know exactly what to do."

"Bingley, my father died when I was two and twenty and just barely out of Cambridge," Darcy replied seriously. "From that point on, for every moment of the last five years, I have had to be confident and sure of myself. Even before he died, I was always taught to look at every situation from a variety of different angles and have rarely made snap decisions. If I have made few errors in judgement, it is because I have been trained, from an early age, to carefully weigh every decision I make to see how it may impact a variety of people. Each day, hundreds of people depend on me and my ability to make decisions carefully and, I hope, wisely.

"As the master of an estate, even one the size of Netherfield Park, which is of a decent size, you will need to learn to do the same. Decisions you will make about the estate can have far-reaching impacts. Of course, you already know this to a point – dealing with some of the inventions and business decisions you have made. However, as the master of an estate, your decisions have an even greater impact."

Bingley studied his friend. He knew that Pemberley kept

Darcy busy and that since inheriting, he had far less time for frivolity than many of his peers. Moreover, he knew Pemberley was well run and employed many people – both those who worked in the house and the tenant farmers. But he had never really imagined himself in Darcy's position, with so many people dependent on him and relying on him to make good decisions.

For the first time, he began to wonder if purchasing an estate was really the best path for him. If he could not make solid decisions regarding Caroline, could he make those decisions for tens or even hundreds of people who were depending on him? Could he seriously consider taking a wife if he was not prepared to even stand up to Caroline?

A maid came in with the tray of coffee and breakfast items. Apparently, someone had seen Bingley join Darcy because the tray contained two coffee cups and plenty of food. Hurst followed the maid into the room.

"What are you going to do about Caroline?" Hurst asked, helping himself to a roll from the tray. "Miss, can you bring another coffee cup and some more coffee?" he asked the maid before she could walk out of the room. She curtsied and walked out of the room, closing the door behind her.

Bingley looked at his brother by marriage. "What do you suggest, Hurst? Taking her to London seemed like a good idea, but she kept insisting that she had to marry Darcy since we found her in his room. She even claimed he had asked her to come, but I told her I knew that was a lie."

"If we allow her freedom in London, she will continue to spread that story to ruin Darcy's reputation – and will destroy her own," Hurst said. "Not many folks will believe her, particularly not those who know you well, Darcy. Nor will those who know Caroline best." Hurst bit out a laugh at that.

"My family would deny any stories Miss Bingley tried to spread about me," Darcy acknowledged. "They know I have avoided your sister as much as I can and have always said I would not marry her. Bingley, I know you know that I value your friendship, but I have never sought your sister's company. If necessary, I will write to them to inform them of what has transpired so they will be prepared to combat it. But, Bingley, I will not acquiesce to this and will take whatever steps necessary to prevent her from forcing me into a marriage I do not want."

"I know, Darcy," Bingley sighed. "Caroline was always determined to accompany me whenever she thought I might be in your company. I have given her too much freedom and allowed her to bully me too many times. Last night was the final straw. I have got to do something about her behaviour and her unreasonable expectations. Most of London would laugh off her accusations about you, but she would make herself unmarriageable in her attempt to ruin you."

All three men were silent for a moment. "Your aunt in Scarborough … would she let Caroline stay with her for any length of time?" Hurst asked.

Bingley thought for a moment, "Caroline hates Scarborough," he began thoughtfully. "There is little society there, and my aunt does not go out much. She would, hopefully, help Caroline realise how selfish and mercenary she has become." He trailed off, then straightened and looked sharply at Hurst.

"Hurst, would you and Louisa support me if I were to send her there?" he asked his brother-in-law.

"Bingley, Caroline is a menace, and I am tired of putting up with her," he said. "I will do whatever I can to help you, especially after what she tried last night. Louisa is also fed up with her and was utterly horrified when I related the events of last night to her.

"If you will arrange it, Louisa and I will escort Caroline to Scarborough today," Hurst decided. "I will tell them both to start packing right away, and we should be able to leave by noon. Bingley, you will need to send an express to your aunt alerting her of our coming. And make sure it is legible, please!"

Thus agreed, the three gentlemen went about their business. Charles went to his study to write a note to his aunt and another to his solicitor to prepare to turn Caroline's fortune over to her. Hurst went to make the arrangements for a departure before noon that very day. Darcy retreated to the library with his correspondence; already, several letters had arrived for him to deal with. He ensured a footman was standing nearby and instructed him that if Miss Bingley attempted to enter the room, he was to follow her in and stay, no matter what the lady may say. Fortunately, he was undisturbed for several hours and completed his business. He was sitting in front of the fire with a book when Bingley entered.

"It is done," he sighed. "Caroline argued until the end, but Hurst forced her into the carriage and threatened to beat her if she did not leave off her yelling."

Darcy sighed. "I know she is your sister, Bingley, but I am exceedingly glad to know she will no longer continue to pursue me while I am here. I want you to know that I will cut her if she ever approaches me again. I have written a letter to Lady Matlock informing her of what Miss Bingley attempted last night. If she tries to spread any stories, Lady Matlock will be able to counter them."

Bingley nodded sadly. "I do understand, Darcy. What she may not realise is that anything she says will only serve to ruin her own reputation. It is well known that you merely tolerate her presence due to your friendship with me, and most are aware of her reputation as a shrew. Few would find fault with you for anything she may say, and most will assume she made the overture."

Darcy agreed. "So, Bingley, we are a bachelor's establishment for now. What will we do? Begin your lessons in estate management, or did you have something else in mind?"

"What would you say to luncheon first, Darcy, then a ride around the estate where you can tell me all I need to know." At the raised eyebrow, Bingley revised his statement. "Fine, then, you can begin telling me a tiny bit of what I need to know about running this estate, despite the fact that it pales in comparison to the wonder that is Pemberley. The housekeeper must know that my sisters are gone, and I probably should speak to her about our plans for the coming weeks. I also have a few more letters to write, but I would prefer to wait until after we ride."

The gentleman agreed and proceeded to carry out their plans for the afternoon. That evening, after dinner, they gathered in the game room to play billiards, having thoroughly enjoyed the rest of the day. After arranging for an early morning ride to view some areas of the estate they had not been able to see that day, they spoke about the ladies of Longbourn they intended to call upon the following day.

Five

A Second Meeting on Oakham Mount

The following morning, Darcy headed out for his early morning ride toward the hill where he had met Miss Elizabeth the previous morning, hoping to encounter the lovely woman once again. As luck would have it, he did encounter her as he reached the hill.

"Good morning, Miss Elizabeth," he called, dismounting from his horse and tying him off before arriving at her side.

"Good morning, Mr Darcy," she replied. "It is another lovely morning, although I expect that to change soon."

"Why do you say that?" he wondered.

She laughed. "November tends to be very wet here in Hertfordshire, although we rarely get snow. With luck, I will be able to continue my early morning walks for another few weeks, but soon, the rain will likely prevent it."

"Ahh," he said. "So, when it rains, what do you do for

44

exercise?"

"Pace and drive my family quite mad," she teased. "I do read quite a bit when the weather is bad, but I ... I need to get out and walk frequently. I am not afraid of a little mud on my dress, although my mother does not understand my need to walk out so often. I simply cannot sit still and sew for days on end; I need to be outside and moving."

"I understand the feeling, Miss Elizabeth," he said. "I ride nearly every morning and sometimes walk through Pemberley, especially when I need to work out a problem. Somehow moving helps me to think better. There is a well-worn path in my study both at Pemberley and at my house in London."

"Exactly – none of my family understands this need to move, especially when I am concerned about something," she replied eagerly. "Something about the movement helps me to ... I do not know ... think better. I fidget if I do not walk, which annoys Mama nearly as much as my walking."

Darcy laughed at the picture. "I have been told I was often reprimanded for fidgeting in my formative years, and I know that I drove my tutors quite mad before I went to school," he told her. "I eventually learned to deal with the need to move in public, although I still pace frequently in my study as I am working out a problem."

"Mama complains about her nerves when I pace," she laughed. "So, I must always be careful to do it away from her."

The two continued to chat for several more minutes, and Darcy attempted to coax Elizabeth to greet his horse. "I brought an apple to share with Erebus if I can convince you to meet him today."

"Erebus?" she inquired. "The Greek personification of darkness?"

He looked at her in surprise. "You are familiar with Greek mythology?"

"Aye, as my father does not restrict my reading, I have read nearly every book in his library. He has treated me as he would a son, and we regularly discuss history and philosophy, as well as literature," she replied. "When I would visit London as a child, my uncle would frequently hire masters to tutor me in languages and the sciences. He encourages my reading by sending me books that he hopes to discuss with me when I visit."

Darcy nodded, impressed with the apparent breadth of her knowledge. "Will you meet him then?" he asked.

Elizabeth considered for a moment and then cautiously nodded. Darcy offered his hand, which she took as he led her to the tree where he had tied off his horse. Neither was wearing gloves, and that same jolt of electricity struck them both once again as it had at the dance, flooding each with a sense of belonging. They continued to hold hands as they approached Erebus, and Darcy introduced his horse to her with a level of seriousness that caused her to laugh.

The laugh did what he intended and dispelled some of her nervousness. She greeted his horse with a level of equanimity and, following his lead, curtsied to the horse in greeting before reaching out toward his nose, allowing him to smell her, before moving her hand to caress his neck. "Good morning, Erebus," she cooed. "You are terribly big, but I do hope that we can be friends. I have never been friends with a horse before."

Erebus nuzzled Elizabeth's hand, pushing her to pet him

more, and she laughed. She turned to look at Darcy, smiling broadly. "He is a lovely animal. I assume his name is because of how completely black he is?"

Darcy smiled back, his heart swelling with happiness at the sight of Elizabeth with his horse. "Yes, I have never seen a horse as black as he; and my father thought Erebus an appropriate name."

"Your father named him?" she asked.

"He purchased him as a gift when I reached my majority and informed me of his name on that day. This was the last gift he gave me before he died," he said, his eyes sad as he remembered the day his father had presented him with Erebus. "He had told me that day I would begin intensive training to be the master when I graduated from Cambridge and that I needed a horse for that role. He intended for me to begin to take over for him that summer, but he died before my training could begin. I had learnt a great deal from him already, but it has taken several years for me to feel confident in my role. I never expected to inherit so soon ...." He trailed off, lost in his thoughts.

She removed her hand from his horse and placed it on his arm. "I am very sorry for your loss, Mr Darcy," she whispered.

He placed his free hand on top of hers and looked down at her. Their eyes caught, and they stood staring at each other for several moments. "Eliz ... Miss Elizabeth, would you, that is, I realise that we have only just met, but I would very much like to court you. But ... if you feel it is too soon ..." Once again, he trailed off, uncertain how to continue. He closed his eyes and shook his head, although he did not remove his hand from hers.

"Mr Darcy?" Elizabeth asked. "Are you well?"

He sighed, lifting her hand from his arm and bringing it to his mouth for a kiss. "I do not mean to rush you, Miss Elizabeth, but I would like the opportunity to get to know you better. We have only met and spoken three times over as many days, and I hope we can continue our acquaintance and perhaps deepen it into something more."

Elizabeth considered him cautiously for a moment. "I will enjoy getting to know you better as well, Mr Darcy, and I … I am … pleased to know the direction of your thoughts. Perhaps for now, it is best that you pay a formal call or two on me at home before we enter into a courtship. You have not yet been exposed to my family, and you may change your mind when you get to know them better."

"So, you would like me to renew my request in a few days?" he asked.

She laughed a little. "Perhaps we could give it a week before you speak to my father. It might be best if you meet him once, at least, before you request permission to court me," she teased lightly.

Darcy groaned. "I had forgotten that bit," he complained, laughing at himself. "Will I meet him today when I visit with Bingley?"

"Perhaps, although it is more likely he will remain in his book room," she told him. "I will encourage him to greet you both. He was rather angry with Lydia yesterday because of something she said and has presently banished her to the nursery. Since both she and Mama are protesting this, I do wonder how long it will last." She paused and scowled. "I love my family; they are my family, and I know I would miss them if they were gone, but they are … difficult. Mama is loud and silly; my two youngest sisters are loud and silly and far too flirtatious. Jane and I do what we can, but I admit I am terrified for you to meet them. If you cannot tolerate them, it is best you do not begin to call. I will not hold you to your request for courtship."

He brought her hand to his mouth for a kiss. "I will tolerate them, and I will remember what you have said about them. Perhaps the banishment to the nursery will last and have an impact," he said hopefully.

She blushed and smiled softly at the kiss on her hand but sighed at his words. "One can hope," she replied. "I worry that Mama will override him or that he will simply give up. However, he was sufficiently angry at the comment that it may spur him into action."

"Perhaps I could offer a hint to your mother about all her daughters being out. While my Aunt Catherine is a busybody, I have heard her advise her friends that having too many daughters out at once confuses us poor simple males and makes it too hard for us to make a decision," he teased.

She laughed. "Please ensure I am listening when you have that conversation with her," Elizabeth replied. "I would love to see how she responds to that. If you can attribute it to some titled lady, that would make it even better."

He grinned broadly. "She is the daughter of an earl who married a Baronet. She retains the courtesy title and is Lady Catherine."

Elizabeth nearly cackled at that addition. "Aye, please be sure to include that piece of information. I cannot wait to see how she will react." She looked at the sky. "It is getting late," she began.

"Yes, and I will not offer to walk you because I know you will decline," he replied. "But I will see you at your house with

Bingley this afternoon, and I will meet your father. Does he play chess?"

She grinned. "He does, and since he can no longer be assured he will defeat me, he would likely welcome a challenge from a different quarter."

"You play chess?" he inquired with a raised brow.

"Aye, Papa taught me when I was, oh, I think seven or eight," she responded, smiling broadly. "I beat him for the first time when I was 15, and then by 17, I was beating him nearly every time. My Uncle Gardiner also plays with me occasionally, and we are evenly matched. A friend of his, Lord James Fitzwilliam, I think, came in one day as we played and was astounded when I won. He challenged me to a match and won, but we have played once or twice since, and I believe we are tied now."

"You played chess against Lord James and won?" he asked, amazement creeping into his voice.

"Aye," she said uncertainly, unsure how to take his comment. "Do you know him?"

He laughed. "He is my uncle," he replied, not noticing her reaction. "I will be writing to tell him I met the girl who beat him in chess. He is rather good, and I have only defeated him once or twice. I cannot wait to tell him what I know. When might we play?"

She eyed him cautiously. "You would be willing to play chess with me?" she repeated.

He grinned. "I will look forward to it. And I do hope that I can watch the next time you play Uncle James."

She laughed and began to walk down the hill toward her home. "It can be arranged, sir," she called as she walked away.

Darcy laughed to himself as he mounted his horse and rode

back to Netherfield. He owed his uncle a letter and wondered what he would say when he told him about the girl he met. He decided then that it did not matter what her family was like; he was going to marry Elizabeth Bennet.

Six

Mr Bennet Takes Control

Mr Bennet was not in his book room that morning. Instead, he was upstairs outside the nursery arguing with both Mrs Bennet and Lydia about their ideas on 'catching a husband.' Mr Bennet laid down the law about flirting in general and basic comportment around men.

"Lydia is just barely fifteen, Mrs Bennet, and far too young and immature even to be considering marriage at this point," Mr Bennet stated. "She will remain in the nursery until she demonstrates some sense, and if you continue to protest, I will hire a governess for *both* of you. Kitty will join Lydia until she demonstrates better behaviour as well. You will also stop spouting such foolishness. A girl who accepts a kiss from a gentleman she is not engaged to is not engaged but is a fool and, if caught out, is likely ruined along with all her sisters. You are encouraging your daughter to ruin herself and her sisters and likely ensure you end up in the hedgerows when I die. Those who might help you will be unable to if Lydia ruins the entire family with her loose behaviour."

Mrs Bennet's jaw dropped open as though she had never considered the idea. "Mr Bennet," she began in a calm, for her, voice, but then she could not find the words to complete her sentence. Instead, she began to cry; Mr Bennet led Lydia into the nursery and led her from the nursery to her bedroom, pausing to lock Lydia back in.

Once Mrs Bennet was in her room, Mr Bennet spoke to her, slowly and carefully explaining what would happen if Lydia were permitted to continue as she was. Not once as he spoke did she call for her salts or mention her nerves as she listened to his explanation. He explained again what she should already have known – what would happen to the rest of the family if one of their daughters were ruined and how the rest would be ruined by association. They also discussed the arrival of the militia, that not all militia officers were reputable, and how unlikely it was that any of them could afford a wife.

Through it all, she remained calm, and when he was finished, she cried. He allowed Hill to tend to his wife and then went to find his daughters. Perhaps the same sort of careful explanation would also work on his younger daughters.

* * *

An hour later, he left the nursery frustrated and angry at his recalcitrant daughter. He realised that hiring a governess to teach Lydia would not be enough. She remained locked in the nursery, and he had ensured the window was locked, and there was no other way for her to escape her room as she had threatened. Kitty would not join her sister in the nursery but was no longer out and would be engaging in some kind of instruction for several hours a day from now on. He would write letters inquiring about a governess or companion for Kitty and a school for Lydia – or perhaps a convent. He was not in a good mood when he went downstairs.

Shortly after luncheon, two visitors were announced. He had just finished his fifth letter of the day, a task he had rarely undertaken and was ready for the distraction of visitors. Mr Bingley introduced him to his friend, Mr Fitzwilliam Darcy. He felt Mr Darcy's eyes on him and became aware that the gentleman was taking his measure. That made Mr Bennet suddenly pay more attention to the conversation and begin to probe a little deeper. He was aware that his wife had determined Bingley was for Jane, but Mr Darcy had not been mentioned aside from his having danced with several ladies, including both Jane and Lizzy. Bennet wondered if he were there to be of aid to his friend or if he had a different purpose in mind.

After speaking for a few minutes to the gentlemen, he invited them to join the ladies for tea. He apologised for his wife's absence but reported that she was indisposed and that his eldest daughters would be pleased to act as hostesses in her stead. Bennet watched as both gentlemen immediately jumped to attention and led them to where Jane, Elizabeth, and Mary were sitting with their sewing. He asked his eldest daughter to request tea for their company and allowed the gentlemen to sit. He noted that Bingley immediately gravitated toward Jane but was surprised when

Darcy immediately sat beside Elizabeth. From the looks that passed between them, he decided that this would be the couple to watch.

The six engaged in casual conversation, although Mary contributed little. Mr Bennet engaged with Darcy and Elizabeth, who were discussing Greek mythology, and learned that Elizabeth had encountered Mr Darcy that morning and had been persuaded to meet his horse, Erebus, which caused Bennet to raise an eyebrow at his daughter. Once tea was served, Darcy asked Bennet a question about his estate, and the three discussed the advantages and disadvantages of crop rotation and what grew well in this area. Since Darcy was to advise Bingley on running Netherfield, he had several good questions and was surprised at how often and how well Elizabeth contributed to the conversation.

"Since Papa was not blessed with a son, he raised me to assist in nearly all matters," she said at one point in the conversation. "Despite the fact that the estate is entailed, it has served both of us well for him to instruct me in this. This was likely born of my inability to sit still for more than five minutes as a child. Papa eventually found it easier to teach me what he was doing instead of fielding my many questions." All three laughed at this as Darcy envisioned a brown-haired little girl following her Papa, peppering him with dozens of questions.

When a younger sister was mentioned, Bennet had an idea. "Mr Darcy, I find I need a governess or a companion for my daughters, particularly Catherine, and am considering school for my youngest. Do you have any connections that might aid me in my search?"

Elizabeth and Darcy looked at each other in surprise. Darcy

recalled what she had said about her youngest angering her father and considered the implication. Slowly, he replied, "My aunt might have some ideas about a companion, but the type of school you are looking for would determine the types of inquiries we make."

"I have written some letters on my own, including to my brother in London, Edward Gardiner," Bennet said and sighed heavily. "I am afraid that Lydia will need a school where there is a strong hand and few opportunities for misbehaviour."

"My aunt may have some suggestions as I know the daughter of a friend of hers had an ... incident and had to be sent away afterwards," Darcy related. "It is a common enough problem among all levels of society, and I can imagine several schools would cater to more ... difficult students."

"Thank you, sir," Bennet said. "I would welcome your help."

Darcy nodded and then grasped for a new topic. "Did you say Edward Gardiner is your brother?" he asked, recalling the conversation about that man with Elizabeth. "I met a man by that name a few weeks ago about an investment that turned out to be an excellent opportunity. I was rather pleased with the encounter and hope to continue my acquaintance with the man."

Bennet looked surprised. "Yes, he has done well for himself. He keeps after me about investing, but I have put him off. Perhaps ... perhaps the next time he asks, I should reconsider."

"It was an excellent opportunity, and I believe it has already borne fruit," Darcy replied. "I intend to continue to invest with him as I am able and have the funds to do so."

Elizabeth added a comment. "For years, I have been

investing small bits of my allowance with my uncle as well," she told him. "It is not much, but my little bits have done well over the last ten years or so since I started."

Bennet looked surprised. "You have been investing with Gardiner?" he asked.

She looked self-conscious as she replied. "Aye, I saved a few pounds from my allowance each quarter and gave it to our uncle whenever we would visit him. I have invested something like fifty pounds at this point, and it has more than doubled."

"That is impressive, Miss Elizabeth," Darcy interjected. "Doubling your investment is always propitious."

"Darcy!" Bingley cried, having overheard a small portion of the conversation. "You are the only fellow I know who uses words of four syllables when only one or two will do."

"Propitious has only three," Elizabeth teased. "Unless you referred to his use of 'impressive.'"

Darcy laughed. "Try again, Bingley. With Miss Elizabeth around, you will not be able to insult me nearly as easily," he teased his friend, causing Bingley's mouth to drop open in surprise. This caused the rest of the party to laugh even more.

"Why is your friend so surprised at your tease?" Elizabeth asked quietly.

"Would you believe it is not something I often do in company, particularly among those with whom I am not well acquainted?" Darcy suggested, leaning forward to nearly whisper in her ear. "I believe it is your influence, Miss Elizabeth." His voice was low, and the way his breath touched her ear felt almost like a caress. Elizabeth shivered in response, and Darcy grinned when he noticed.

"Mr Bennet," he began, changing the topic once again. "Miss Elizabeth happened to mention this morning that you play chess. Would you be interested in a game? If not today, perhaps later this week?"

"Did she mention that she also plays?" Bennet inquired.

"She did," Darcy acknowledged. "I hope to challenge her for a game at some point, too."

"I would like to see the two of you play before I accept your challenge, sir," Bennet stated. "Perhaps if you and your party could join my family for luncheon after church on Sunday, we could have a game or two."

"I believe that could be arranged. The Hursts and Miss Bingley left us yesterday, and Netherfield is now a bachelor's establishment. Unfortunately, we will not be able to return your hospitality, but I believe Bingley, and I would enjoy the company on Sunday," Darcy replied.

"What made them leave?" Elizabeth inquired.

"The countryside did not agree with Miss Bingley, and it necessitated a return to town, although she will soon be returning to their family home in Scarborough. The Hursts hope to return before Christmas, but Miss Bingley will reside with an aunt for some time," Darcy stated candidly.

Elizabeth raised a brow, and he made a motion to indicate there was more to the story. Bennet watched the exchange and realised that these two were already communicating without words. He was saddened by the realisation that his favourite daughter would be leaving him much sooner than he liked.

Sooner than anyone would have liked, the two gentlemen realised it was past time for a polite call to end, and they needed to take their leave. Reluctantly, they stood to depart, and after a brief exchange between Elizabeth and Jane, they were invited for dinner the following night. This invitation was accepted with alacrity, and the invitation for Sunday luncheon was also repeated for Bingley's benefit.

Bingley apologised that he could not return this hospitality, but such protestations were waved away. After an extended leave-taking, the gentlemen departed, and Bennet remained in the drawing room with his daughters, surprising them all.

They were even more surprised when he spoke. "Girls, I have had a frank conversation with your mother and sisters, and, as of right now, Kitty and Lydia are no longer out. Lydia, in particular, will need new gowns that reflect this status, but as she is presently locked in the nursery, what she wears will matter little. I have asked my brother Gardiner and Mr Darcy to help me find a school for challenging students that will accept Lydia as a student. Kitty will be under the supervision of a governess or companion, and Mary, I believe you will also benefit from such a person. Until then, I would like Jane and Elizabeth to spend time with Kitty daily to provide some instruction on comportment and etiquette. You two have benefited the most from your Aunt Gardiner's instruction, and I realise that has been lacking for Kitty and Lydia. Kitty needs to learn the importance of behaving with propriety and respectability and to follow the example of you two rather than Lydia.

"Mary, you will join me in my book room after breakfast each morning. You will read the texts I assign you, and we will discuss them together. You have read and studied Fordyce long enough; it is time to branch out into other authors and subjects. I hope to acquire a music master for you and will ask Gardiner to allow you to visit soon to take advantage of the ones that can be found in town."

All three girls nodded but looked around the room in shock, unsure of what else to say. They had all been present in the breakfast room the day before and knew what Papa had said to Lydia, but to see him take such decisive action was … surprising, to say the least. After years of ignoring them, they would never have expected their father to take such drastic action with their family.

Bennet must have realised how surprised the girls were by his pronouncements. He excused himself to his book room, where he began to study the account books to find the funds for all these changes. He also wrote one last note to request Mr Darcy visit him the following morning to discuss Longbourn and some ideas for increasing its profits.

Darcy received this note just before dinner and found himself rather surprised at the content. He wondered if Elizabeth was as surprised as he was at the changes her father was making and began to wonder precisely what Miss Lydia had done or said to warrant such an extreme reaction.

Seven

Advice is Sought

❦

Once again, Darcy and Elizabeth met on Oakham Mount. "I received an interesting note last night, Miss Elizabeth," Darcy said immediately upon seeing her.

Elizabeth arched her brow, and he laughed, recognising this as a signal that he should continue. "Your father wrote asking me to visit today to discuss ways to increase Longbourn's profits. My first thought was that he realised sending your youngest sister to school and hiring a companion for your sister would be expensive, and he needs to find the additional funds to provide for these. Still, most of what he needs to do, or what I assume he will need to do, will require at least a small initial investment and will take a year or two to have an impact."

Elizabeth made a face. "He has clearly decided to take charge of his family. He overheard Lydia remark that Mama

61

had told her the way to 'get a husband' was to let him kiss her," Elizabeth rolled her eyes at this but continued on. "His reaction was to lock her in the nursery and declare her no longer 'out'. When Mama protested this action, Papa sat her down and calmly explained what would happen to all of us if this were discovered. He explained to her that militia officers would make poor husbands, as most of them cannot afford a wife, and that a girl labelled as a flirt could effectively ruin all of her sisters, which would result in none of us being able to marry. She was indisposed all of yesterday as she thought about what he said, and when she joined us for dinner last night, she was rather quiet and withdrawn and completely unlike her normal self. It was a pleasant meal, and Mama did not react when Papa informed her that you and Mr Bingley are coming to dinner tonight and luncheon on Sunday."

Darcy smiled. "Are you pleased by all these changes?"

Elizabeth laughed. "I am inordinately pleased," she told him. "I just pray it will last. I always wished Papa would do something to ease Mama's worries. He could have made more of an effort with the estate years ago; I know Uncle Gardiner has encouraged him many times to do more about the estate and my younger sisters. I am very relieved he is doing something before they do any harm to themselves or our reputations."

He took her hand in his. "I am, too," he whispered as his eyes flicked to her lips.

She took a small step back. "Mr Darcy, the lesson we have learned here is that women cannot allow men to kiss them until they are formally engaged."

"Marry me, Elizabeth?" he asked, winking at her.

"No, Mr Darcy," she replied in the same teasing voice he

had used. "I agreed to a courtship yesterday, and I would like to know you at least a week before I agree to bind my life to yours."

He chuckled. "It was worth a try. When may I speak to your father about our courtship? I think he already suspects there is something between us."

"He was rather pointed in his questions after your visit," Elizabeth agreed. "I believe he saw the chess game between us on Sunday as some sort of gauntlet."

"Interesting courtship ritual," he rejoined. "If I defeat you, I win your hand; if I lose, I must court you first."

She arched that eyebrow, and again he thought again about kissing her. Granted, he thought about it frequently regardless, but that particular look practically begged to be kissed. "I would be unwilling to make that bet if I were you, Mr Darcy. In fact, I would be unwilling to make any wagers on such a game. What happens if you lose? You quit your efforts to court me?"

"No, Elizabeth, I do not think I will quit courting you until I have you at the altar. And, although I have never been married, based on my parents' marriage, I think the courting continues even after that," he told her, lifting his hand and lightly touching her cheek. "I look forward to the day I can kiss you, Elizabeth," he breathed.

She sighed and swayed toward him. He sighed and lightly touched her forehead with his lips and immediately retreated. "Once we are openly courting, we will need to stop meeting like this," she lamented.

"Oh, aye," he sighed. "I have enjoyed having this time with you."

They stood there silently for a minute, standing a little too close but not touching.

"My sister will arrive later next week," he said after a moment. "My cousin, Colonel Fitzwilliam, my sister's other guardian, will bring her to me."

"I look forward to meeting her. You said she plays the piano?" Elizabeth replied.

"Yes, she is rather talented," he breathed.

"Perhaps she and Mary will become friends. Not that I do not want to befriend her as well, but, well … I imagine I will also be spending time with you. I believe she will find Mary good company," she said in a rush.

He chuckled lightly. "I understood what you were saying, Elizabeth."

She arched that eyebrow at him again. "You are making awfully free with my Christian name today, Mr Darcy," she teased.

"Oh, forgive me, Miss Elizabeth, I did not realise…" he trailed off when he saw the bemused look on his face.

"I truly do not mind, Mr Darcy; it is just that I cannot return the favour," she told him.

He understood her meaning. "Ahh, well, my given name is Fitzwilliam, but no one calls me that except my Aunt Catherine. Fitzwilliam is also the surname of my mother's family, so when she yells out Fitzwilliam, two or three heads always pop up. She refers to me that way, but she also calls my cousin Colonel Fitzwilliam by his surname, and my other cousin, the Viscount, also goes by his surname. My friends call me Darcy, and my sister mostly calls me Brother. A long time ago, my mother called me William. I … you could use that name, if, if you would like."

"William," she repeated, trying it out. "Are you sure you

would not mind me using that name?"

"No," he whispered, swallowing tightly as he brushed an imaginary hair from her face, lightly caressing her face as he did so. "I would very much like it if you were to use that name." His voice was rough as he spoke.

She smiled gently. "Thank you, William," she said.

He drew in a deep breath through his nose to regain his equilibrium. "You are dangerous to my composure, Elizabeth," he told her. "I struggle to keep myself under good regulation when I am in your company."

Elizabeth took a step away. "We should avoid these situations," she replied shakily. "We should not be alone out here."

"I know," came his reply. "But I also do not want to stop."

She sighed. "I will see if Jane or Mary will begin accompanying me on my morning walks. That would make them more proper. Perhaps Bingley could join you as well?"

"I will see. Bingley is not one for keeping country hours. He is far too accustomed to the late hours of town," Darcy told her. "I prefer rising with the sun. I cannot imagine sleeping the day away while my tenants work in the fields."

"That is a rather admirable trait," she said.

"It is what my father did and his father before him," he replied. "It is the way of the Darcys. We are merely stewards of Pemberley, and our role is to do what we can for the land and the people who depend upon us. Our task has always been to make the land better than it was when it was given to us, and I hope that is what I am doing."

Elizabeth reached out a hand to touch his. "That is an incredible legacy, William. It is a legacy of which you should be very proud."

He clasped her hand in his larger one once again. "I look forward to the day I can show you Pemberley, Elizabeth."

"Is it a foregone conclusion that you will someday show me Pemberley, sir?" she asked, the look on her face teasing.

"It is," he said. "I do not intend to give up until I have convinced you. Should I ask again?"

She blushed. "Do you frequently flirt like this with women you have known less than a week?" she asked, feeling a little shy.

"Never," he stated confidently. "I have never acted this way with anyone else. I did not even know I could flirt, nor was I aware I was doing so. Remember Bingley's shock yesterday when I teased him?"

"Aye, and you said it was infrequent, particularly in company," she replied.

He smiled. "I said it was something that you seem to have brought out in me. I do not know why, but I feel lighter and happier when I am with you. My father has been gone for five years; for those five years, I have carried the weight of Pemberley and the Darcy legacy. It does not feel as heavy when I am near you, and I feel more like the man I was before that weight descended on me."

"You are terribly persuasive, sir," she said.

"What happened to William?" he asked.

"You are terribly persuasive, William," she repeated quietly.

"I want to kiss you, Elizabeth," he said softly but stepped back rather than closer, keeping her hand firmly gripped in his. "It is time for me to depart, I think. Tomorrow, one or both of us should bring along that chaperone. I am not nearly as persuasive as I would like to be, but it is indeed for the best."

"You are, but I am doing my best to resist, especially after seeing my father take such extreme steps to preserve my family's reputation," she replied, also taking a step away from him but still not relinquishing his hand.

"Marry me?" he asked again, his eyes bright and his manner clearly teasing.

"Not yet, William. I will see you at Longbourn later today," she told him, grinning at him while taking one more step back with their hands still clasped but stretched between them.

"I still have your hand," he teased her.

"I have not given it to you yet," she replied.

"You will," was his reply, making her smile.

She gently tugged on her hand, and he released it reluctantly. "Soon, William."

"Not nearly soon enough, Elizabeth," he whispered.

The two parted and made their way back to their homes. A few hours later, Darcy arrived at Longbourn and asked to see Mr Bennet.

"So, Mr Darcy, Lizzy tells me you inherited your estate five years ago when your father passed away. Is your mother still living?" Bennet inquired pleasantly.

"No, sir, she passed away many years ago, not long after my sister was born," he replied. "I have been master of my estate for five years now, and we have raised its profits by nearly twenty per cent in that time."

"Really," he said, genuinely interested now. "What did you do to affect such a change?"

And so, Darcy and Bennet began an earnest conversation about steps to take at Longbourn that could have an equal impact. Bennet had thought the request a clever ruse to get the young man into his office so he could learn more about him, but he ended up with more than he expected. As they talked, they sketched out a specific plan to increase the profits of Longbourn to allow Bennet to invest the profits for his daughters' and wife's futures. With the plan outlined by Darcy and a minimal investment on his part, Bennet came to believe it was possible to increase Longbourn's profits by a significant amount over the next several years.

"So, Darcy, you have done me quite a turn. What can I do for you in return?" Bennet teased.

"You could give me Miss Elizabeth," Darcy replied seriously.

Bennet gulped. "Explain yourself," he demanded of the younger gentleman, displaying outrage as he intentionally misunderstood Darcy's meaning.

"I want to marry your daughter, sir," Darcy told him earnestly. "Most likely, I would have had this same conversation with you regardless, but since you asked what you could do for me, I thought it would be good to let you know my intentions. Since that night at the assembly, I have been impressed by your daughter, and even though we have only known each other for a few days, I already know that I want to marry her. I will give her as much time as she needs to be comfortable with the idea, but when I leave Hertfordshire, I intend to take her with me."

"You are very confident," Bennet observed.

"I am well known for making a decision and sticking with it. I am not impulsive. I am deliberate and methodical. Yet, nearly as soon as I met Miss Elizabeth and saw the small kindness she bestowed on another, I knew I wanted her as my wife, as the Mistress of Pemberley. I made that decision in an instant, I think, and I will do whatever it takes to win her," Darcy contended.

"Why her?" Bennet probed.

"When our hands touched that night at the assembly, I felt something I have never felt before – and I love her," Darcy said, his voice assured and confident.

"Does she love you in return?" Bennet asked.

"I have not asked her that," he admitted. "I intend to give her the time she needs to know that for herself.

Bennet shook his head. "Love is a fleeting emotion. There is no guarantee it will last."

"Perhaps in some cases, but I do not believe what I feel for her will be fleeting. Not only do I love her, but I also admire her strength and respect her for her wit and intelligence. My wife will be my partner in all things, and from my few conversations with her, I think she is more than capable of being that. Her kindness recommends her. She is intelligent; our conversations yesterday confirmed that. I think we have similar interests, although I do hope to coax her into learning to ride, as that will be a necessity for her on my estate. I know she loves to walk, and Pemberley has many paths to walk, but it is very large, and she would more easily traverse it if she could ride," Darcy said to him.

"I make no promises, nor will I force Lizzy into a marriage she does not want," Bennet said. "She needs to understand what marriage to someone like you will mean."

"What do you know of what marriage to me will entail?" Darcy countered.

"My wife told me the rumours that circulated about you that first night at the assembly," he replied. "You own half of Derbyshire; you are worth ten thousand a year; you are arrogant and above your company."

"My income is above ten thousand a year, although I will not share the exact amount until the marriage settlement is prepared. Pemberley is large, but I am not sure it encompasses half of Derbyshire, although it is one of the largest estates in the region. I am sorry I was perceived as arrogant at the assembly, and I know that I was in a poor mood when I first arrived, but before the night was over, I danced with several of the local ladies, including two of your daughters. I also danced with Miss Elizabeth twice that night and spoke to her whenever she was not dancing," Darcy countered.

"I will not give my consent for you to wed Lizzy for at least a month. You should court her first, and I insist on at least a month before I will agree. I know you two met yesterday morning on Lizzy's walk, and you should avoid being alone with her again. It would not do to have her reputation damaged while I am trying to prevent one of her sisters from doing the same. You may call on her, and you may take chaperoned walks together. No letters, no touches, nothing that goes outside the bounds of propriety. I expect you to act the perfect gentleman, sir." Bennet demanded.

"I agree," Darcy immediately complied. "I have a younger sister, and I will court Miss Elizabeth as I will insist the man who one day courts Georgiana will do. Georgiana will come to stay at Netherfield next week with her companion and my cousin, Colonel Richard Fitzwilliam, who is her other guardian. I requested that he bring a couple of riding horses, and I wonder if I might have your permission to teach Miss Elizabeth to ride at Netherfield. Her sisters may accompany her, although my sister will also be there."

"That is fine, but keep in mind you should not be alone with her," Bennet insisted. "Nothing to endanger her reputation, not even a little bit of gossip."

"No, sir, nothing to incite gossip other than what will naturally occur due to the news of our courtship," Darcy agreed.

Bennet scowled as the young man took his leave. He had not thought things would move this quickly, and he did not like it. He wanted to utilise this man's expertise, but he did not like the cost.

Eight

A Courtship Begins

Darcy entered the drawing room and saw that Bingley had arrived. Immediately, he sat on the sofa next to Elizabeth and spoke quietly to her. "Do you think we could walk in the garden with your sisters chaperoning?" he asked.

"If you suggest the walk, I feel certain Mama would not object," she replied in a whisper.

"How long has Bingley been here?" he asked next.

"About fifteen minutes," she replied.

He nodded and then stood. "After spending so long in Mr Bennet's study speaking of business, I think I would enjoy a walk. Bingley, ladies, would you care to take a turn in the gardens?"

Bingley and the two eldest Bennet daughters quickly agreed. As Elizabeth had not yet spoken to either of her sisters about meeting Mr Darcy the last three mornings, neither was aware of the connection between the two. Mary elected to practise on the piano instead of accompanying the two couples, so they headed outside. They quickly divided into pairs, and Elizabeth and Darcy lagged behind the other two allowing both couples the room to speak privately.

"I told your father of my intention to marry you," he blurted out.

She stopped and looked at him. "You did what?" she asked incredulously.

He looked slightly sheepish. "We were speaking of his plans to increase Longbourn's profits. I think he could increase the yield by a significant amount and increase the profits by at least fifty per cent in the next few years," he began, and she just continued to look at him with that raised brow he had begun to adore. He took a deep breath before continuing. "Anyway, he thanked me for my help and asked what he could do for me in return. And ... and, well, I blurted out that I would accept your hand in return. I realise it was not my best moment, and I probably should not have said it in that moment or in the way I did, but since this morning, I have barely been able to think of anything else." He was slightly flushed as he said this, and Elizabeth could tell he had not intended to embarrass her.

She grimaced slightly. "What did he say?" she asked.

"He told me I must court you for at least a month before he would agree to my marrying you," he replied. "I did not tell him I had already requested a courtship from you and that you had agreed. I did not say anything about our meetings at Oakham Mount. However, he did warn me that I should not be alone with you and that I should conduct myself in a gentlemanly manner and follow the rules of propriety."

He pondered the discussion for a moment. "I do not think he likes me as a suitor in some ways. I believe he might be concerned about my wealth and my place in society, as well as how you might fit into it."

Elizabeth nodded. "Papa does not think much of London and most members of society. Quite frankly, I am amazed that he has asked you for suggestions on increasing Longbourn's profits since he has never been interested in doing so before."

"I believe he is finally aware of how he has injured your family with his lackadaisical attitude toward the estate," Darcy replied. "Seeing how utterly foolish his wife and daughter have become has shocked him into action; at least, that is what he said to me earlier. He wants to increase the estate's profits so he might ease your mother's worries about the entail by investing the extra and ensuring he can afford a school for Miss Lydia and a governess for Miss Catherine. He seems to realise that his youngest two daughters, in particular, need guidance that their mother cannot provide, and he has not bothered to provide."

"He said as much to you?" she asked, seeing him nod in reply. "I am in shock. Jane and I have spoken to him for years about the need to do something about my youngest sisters, and he did nothing. Finally, he heard one of Lydia's ridiculous statements and realised the potential for injury to the rest of us if she continued unchecked. I am grateful you arrived at just the right time to provide advice and assistance."

He squeezed the hand that lay on his arm. "There was one other thing I said to your father that I think I need to tell you, too," he stammered, feeling nervous. "I, um, when I was speaking with your father, when I told him that I wanted to marry you eventually, I, um, I told him how I feel about you. I, uh, just realised I have not told you yet, and, um, well, I wanted you to hear it from me." He paused and took a deep breath. "I do love you, Elizabeth," he said in a rush. "I know it is early in our acquaintance, and I realise you may not feel the same about me right now."

Pressure on his arm made him stop. "I do care for you very much, William, and while I am not yet ready to say I return your sentiments, I think that if we continue as we have, I will be in love with you before long. We, well, you said that we have at least a month of courtship before we can take any further steps, but will you settle for me telling you today that I care for you very much and, when I do feel I return your love, I will tell you immediately."

He could not stop the grin. "I realise we have only known each other for a matter of days and will gladly settle for knowing that you care for me. And, yes, whenever you are ready, please, do not wait to tell me what you feel."

She smiled and squeezed his arm to her chest a little. "And, William, if you," she sighed, "if you change your mind, if you realise you spoke too soon, tell me as soon as you realise it."

"Why do you think I would change my mind," he asked, looking down at her in concern.

She sighed deeply. "I have always known that Jane is much prettier than I, and my appearance is less than fashionable. I am impertinent and challenging and not at all what most men would prefer in a wife. I have always expected to be a favourite aunt for my sister's children."

"Why would you think any of that?" he asked, incredulous at her perception of herself.

She shrugged. "I know Mama exaggerates my faults, but

I grew up with most of the men in the neighbourhood, and they have no interest in me. I am too smart for most of them, or so they have told me, and everyone knows that Jane is the most beautiful girl in the county. When we have gone to London and attended balls and the like, she has always garnered far more attention than I."

"The men you have encountered thus far have all been fools, although I should not complain too much since that has left you available for me," he stated. "Elizabeth, you are stunningly beautiful and, to me, at the very least, are ten times prettier than your sister. I love that you are intelligent and are willing to challenge me. One reason I have always avoided women of the *ton*, those like Caroline Bingley, is that I could contradict myself five different times in the same conversation, and they would agree with every statement I made. I like you because you think and are willing to express an opinion. I do not want a wife who will hang on my arm and agree with me; I want one who will be a partner and make me think more deeply about things and one who will aid me as I run our estate. If you agree to marry me, you will be my equal partner in all things."

"You will have the final say, though," she stated.

"Aye, but that is only because someone must, and you will have the final say in managing our homes and staff," he agreed. "When I need your help with the estate, or you need mine with the household or tenants, we will work together to come up with the best solutions. I hope you will participate with me as a partner when we marry."

Elizabeth considered this. "No matter how many times you ask me, Papa will not give your permission for us to marry until next month," she reminded him.

"And we will marry as soon as possible after that," he whispered in her ear, the warmth of his breath playing with the curls that hung there. "I love you, dearest, loveliest Elizabeth."

She blushed profusely. "You, sir, are ... something. I am not even certain what to call you. Are you a flirt? A rake?"

"A man in love?" he suggested.

She smiled. "Fine then, a man in love."

"With you," he murmured.

"With me," she repeated softly, her voice showing her surprise mixed with pleasure at the sentiment. "We need a new topic," she said after a moment. "What books have you read recently?"

He laughed at her segue into a safer topic but allowed it, and the two discussed several books they had read in the last little while. They shared similar tastes in books, but there were several he had read that she had not. He offered to allow her to borrow them and promised to bring them when he called the following day.

"You intend to visit again tomorrow?" she asked archly.

"Of course," he replied. "I will come every day unless you tell me to quit. And even then, I will attempt to persuade you to allow my visits. I want first your love and then your hand in marriage. And I will not settle until I have acquired both."

"You are persistent, sir," she told him, repeating an earlier conversation.

"William," he reminded her.

You are persistent, William," she repeated, ignoring his satisfied grin. "And perhaps a tad too confident."

"I am confident I will win you, Elizabeth. You are already falling; you just need a little more time," he told her.

"You have a month, William," she teased, emphasising the use of his Christian name, and then she laughed at him again.

Seeing that Bingley and Jane were ready to return, the two couples went back inside for tea, and the gentlemen stayed to visit for another half hour. They took their leave then, although they would return in a few hours for dinner. As they rode back to Netherfield, Darcy began to acquaint Bingley with a few important facts about the estate.

* * *

The three eldest Bennet daughters joined their parents and the gentlemen for dinner. Kitty and Lydia were prohibited from joining, which was mentioned a few times during the meal. Mrs Bennet seemed to be weakening on her agreement to send Lydia to school and hire a governess for Kitty after Mr Bennet told her they would need to economise to pay the expenses of both.

This discussion allowed Mr Darcy to mention to Mrs Bennet his aunt's advice about too many daughters out at once. "My aunt, Lady Catherine de Bourgh, insists that too many daughters out at once will confuse potential suitors. When a man has too many options, he may struggle to decide. When he is presented with fewer options, he has less to consider and ultimately can make a decision much more easily."

Elizabeth easily detected the glint in his eye as he spoke these words, but Mrs Bennet was unaware and answered him seriously. "Truly, Mr Darcy?" she asked, her eyes twinkling with mischief. "Are most men so easily distracted?"

Darcy attempted to hold back a laugh. "I have often found

that too many choices can confuse matters," he acknowledged.

Mrs Bennet continued to think about what the gentleman said and remained quiet for some time after. It was only during the dessert course that she spoke again. "Mr Darcy, what does your aunt say about the education of girls?"

"She takes a firm stance on all girls being educated," Darcy said, knowing this to be only partially true. His aunt had a firm stance on everything but actually thought little of most girls being educated as, in her opinion, only girls in the highest levels ought to be taught. "I have heard her advise many ladies on the importance of hiring a proper governess for daughters and ensuring that all daughters display proper decorum in public. I believe she would applaud your and your husband's efforts to ensure your daughters' futures."

Once again, Mrs Bennet considered these words. When the ladies left the table, Mr Bennet used his sardonic wit on the gentleman, in awe of his accomplishment in persuading his wife but resenting him at the same time.

"So, Mr Darcy," intoned Mr Bennet, "I believe if I were to hand Longbourn over to you, you would do infinitely better than I in managing both my estate and my family. Is there anything you do not do well?"

"I am sure there are many things, sir," Darcy replied. "While I am competent at managing my estate, there are many things I either do not know how to do or do not do well. No man can master everything, but I have striven to do well those things that I must do."

"You are well-spoken, at least," Bennet said dryly.

Darcy could only nod in response, not certain if any reply would please the man. As he did not want to give him a reason

79

to deny his request later on, he did not want to antagonise him as Bennet was clearly trying to antagonise him.

Bingley asked a question just then and spared Darcy further attention for a time. Darcy observed the gentleman, trying to understand the antipathy he felt from Elizabeth's father.

When the separation of the sexes came to an end, Darcy and Bingley joined the ladies while Bennet retreated to his book room once again. Each man gravitated to his chosen lady and sat beside her. Mary joined the conversation with Darcy and Elizabeth while Mrs Bennet began a conversation with Bingley, praising Jane to the skies. Neither Jane nor Bingley was able to speak to each other much as her mother dominated the conversation for most of the remainder of the visit.

Mrs Bennet appeared oblivious to the other couple in the room, so focused was she on gaining Bingley's attention for her favourite daughter. Elizabeth noticed, and, although she was pleased to avoid the attention herself, she felt sorry for Jane and Mr Bingley.

Eventually, it was time for the gentlemen to depart, and they bid the ladies farewell. Mrs Bennet encouraged Jane to show Mr Bingley to the door and frowned when Elizabeth also stood. She protested, but Elizabeth claimed the need to show Darcy to her father's study to take his leave.

Standing in the hallway, Darcy took Elizabeth's bare hand in his to bestow a lingering kiss on it. Elizabeth shivered at the touch, causing him to grin once again. "Is it too soon to ask you again, my dear?" he whispered teasingly, causing her to blush once again. He found he enjoyed every one of her blushes very much. Continuing to hold her hand as he moved to board his carriage, he kissed it once again before finally releasing it.

Nine

Another Suitor Intrudes

T he following morning found Elizabeth dragging Jane along with her to Oakham Mount while a bleary-eyed Bingley accompanied Darcy. It did not take long for the two couples to separate, although they kept in sight of each other. Jane and Bingley were quiet and complained somewhat about the other two forcing them to rise so early, but they found enough to discuss to keep them occupied.

Darcy and Elizabeth found conversation easy, discussing various topics of interest to each of them. Darcy shared some of the ideas he had discussed with her father the previous day about improving the estate, and Elizabeth was pleased by the suggestions. She had recommended a few of these ideas to her father herself as she and Jane frequently visited the Longbourn tenants and frequently shared needs she observed during these visits or during her walks.

Elizabeth asked questions about Pemberley and Derbyshire, having heard about it from her aunt, and she had many questions for the gentlemen about the district she hoped to soon visit with her aunt and uncle.

An hour passed in this way until, finally, Jane requested to return home. The gentlemen offered to escort them there, and Jane readily accepted the offer of assistance as she was already tired from having walked so far that morning. All four chatted together, each lady on the arm of her preferred gentleman, with their horses trailing behind. When they arrived at Longbourn, Darcy and Bingley began to mount their horses to return to Netherfield. However, Mrs Bennet had spied the group from her window and hurried downstairs to invite them to join the family for breakfast.

Kitty had been allowed to join the family for the meal but was unusually quiet, occasionally speaking to Mary or Mrs Bennet while studiously avoiding speaking to either gentleman. Mr Bennet seemed displeased with their company, but as Elizabeth and Darcy had been accompanied by Jane and Bingley, he found he had no good reason to complain. When breakfast was finished, he asked both gentlemen to accompany him first to his study and then to ride the estate with him to discuss improvements.

Darcy readily agreed to the invitation, and Bingley, who would have preferred to remain in company with his 'angel' rather than riding an estate not his own, reluctantly agreed. Bingley had been less than interested in riding out to view his own leased estate and was becoming wary of making such a purchase the more Darcy spoke on what ownership entailed. Since owning an estate was required for him to become 'landed', and fulfil his father's dreams for him,

Bingley thought he should consider simply hiring a steward to deal with the many responsibilities Darcy was explaining.

The harvest was nearly done, and Darcy and Bennet spoke together about the yields and the plans and preparation for the coming year. On Darcy's recommendation, Bennet would plant a winter crop in an effort to increase the profits of the estate. It was an experiment, as Darcy was more familiar with farming in the north, although he assisted his aunt's estate in Kent each spring and managed his satellite estates in Scotland and Yorkshire. He also had a smaller farm in Kent, not far from his aunt's estate, but it was a horse farm and did not grow crops.

Bennet had not ridden out on his estate very often of late, although he had enjoyed doing so in his earlier years of managing it. As he rode, he realised he had missed spending part of his day riding and talking with other gentlemen in recent years. Since Lydia was born, he had taken less and less interest in the estate and its doings, and he was beginning to realise this was the source of many of the problems within his family. His sense of … shame, perhaps … was uncomfortable, but he wondered if he was willing to do what was necessary to restore the estate. It brought in two thousand pounds a year, although when he had taken it over, it had brought in three. He wondered if it was truly worth the effort, but then he looked over at the young man with him and realised that Darcy was far better a man than he ever would be. This thought bothered him a little, but he was torn between dislike for this man and envy for the will and dedication that made him so much better.

These thoughts translated to a look of deep contemplation on his face, and Darcy, recognizing the look, wisely stayed quiet as they rode. Bingley, however, rarely recognized the signs of contemplation in others and chatted amiably about everything he noticed and asked questions that Bennet answered tersely. Darcy added his own thoughts when he could, but being unfamiliar with the estate and the area, he was able to add little. Eventually, even Bingley realised that Bennet was distracted and stopped asking questions, leaving the rest of the ride mostly silent.

Arriving back at Longbourn, Bennet invited the men into his study for a discussion and a drink. Darcy agreed, and although Bingley would have preferred to visit with the ladies, he followed.

"So, Darcy, what did you think?" Bennet began once they were all seated.

Darcy thought for a moment before he responded. "It is a good estate. I expect the winter crops will be a good additional source of income for you, but I did not notice anything that gave me pause," Darcy replied. "I imagine a few of those fields to the north are prone to flooding if it rains too much, but I cannot imagine that is much of an issue."

Bennet nodded at the observation. "You are correct about those fields. My steward has suggested adding a draining field there to alleviate that problem."

"I did not see any livestock on our tour," Darcy observed. "Do you keep any?"

"We have a few head of cattle and some sheep and pigs. Not many, and most belong to the home farm to provide my family and our tenants with milk, butter, and cheese. We either sell the wool or our tenants use it, and we slaughter a few pigs a year as necessary. Of course, we keep a few chickens, as do some of our tenants, both for the eggs and for the meat," Bennet related. "We have not considered keeping animals for anything beyond our own needs."

Darcy nodded in acknowledgement. "That is wise, sir. I raise a great number of sheep in Derbyshire, but that is because much of the land there is less arable than your estates. My family has raised sheep for centuries, I believe."

It was Bennet's turn to nod, and the talk continued in this vein for an hour or more, during which Bingley said little. When the maid came to announce luncheon, an invitation was extended to the gentlemen, who readily accepted. Afterwards, Elizabeth mentioned she had a need to go into Meryton, and Darcy volunteered to accompany her along with Bingley and Jane. Mary was asked to join, but she declined. After gathering their things, the four set off to town, walking in pairs.

Darcy and Elizabeth were ahead of Jane and Bingley this time, as both were accustomed to taking brisk walks. They spoke easily as they walked, and, once again, their conversation was wide-ranging, leaping from topic to topic as they found several mutual interests and debated varying viewpoints. Soon, however, they discovered Shakespeare, and they laughingly discussed their mutual enjoyment of that author. Elizabeth, who dearly loved to laugh, preferred his comedies, but Darcy, who was far more serious in nature, tended toward his histories and tragedies.

"Have you attended one of his plays during a stay in town, Elizabeth?" Darcy asked her as they neared town.

"My aunt and uncle were able to procure tickets for Macbeth last spring," she replied. "I thoroughly enjoyed the experience, although it seemed that many attended for reasons other than to enjoy the play. It was very well done, and I would love to attend another if I have the chance."

"Perhaps you can persuade your father to allow you to travel to town before the Christmas holidays, and we could attend a performance or two," he suggested.

She looked at him inquisitively. "Is this another attempt to convince me, sir?" she asked, her eyebrow raised as she teased.

"No, Elizabeth," he said seriously, not giving in to her teasing. "Your father was correct; you deserve to be courted properly. If we were to become engaged within days of our meeting, it is possible that people would think I have compromised you, and I have no wish to endanger your reputation in such a way. Although I do still wish for that eventual outcome, I will not pressure you."

She smiled at him softly. "I did enjoy your teasing me, William, and I feel that I know you better than is normal after just a few days of knowing each other. But it probably is best that we court publicly for some time before announcing anything more permanent," she told him.

He sighed and brought his free hand up to caress the one lying on her arm. "Your mother seems to be unaware that we are courting. I see her pushing Bingley toward Jane, but she has not done the same to me," he observed.

She immediately slowed and grimaced slightly. "That is because she cannot fathom my ever being courted, particularly by one such as you. I feel certain that in her mind, you are far too important to desire a 'headstrong, obstinate girl' like me, and she often tells me that I am far 'too intelligent and clever' to ever be able to attract a man. I do not fit into her idea of what men are seeking in a mate. Since you are worth more than Bingley, being richer, I confess I am surprised she is not attempting to push Jane toward you. If Lydia were still permitted downstairs, she would surely be trying to convince you to sit with her," Elizabeth said. "By not mentioning our courtship, I also limit her effusions, which I am sure will be excessive. Between that and her questioning my suitability and worthiness, it has seemed best to keep it to myself for now."

Darcy frowned. "Are you serious?" he questioned. "How can she not see how completely suitable you are? How can she not see how very special you are? I have known you mere days, and I value you considerably and believe you to be my ideal match. Although I have promised not to press, you must know I am entirely serious in my desire to marry you after an appropriate period of courtship so others might see how much I admire you."

She brought her other hand up to lay on his. "Thank you, William, but my mother does not seem to be able to understand me. In her mind, men all want a woman like Jane. She does not think I am beautiful and thinks I should be demure and silent, sitting quietly with my sewing instead of walking all over the estate or even visiting the tenants. I should not read as much as I do, nor should I express my opinion as freely as I do. All of these traits somehow make me less 'ladylike', and the fact that my father has taught me as he would have taught a son makes me ... less worthy, I guess."

"All things I find admirable about you, Elizabeth," he told her. "I do hope you do not listen to your mother. And I neglected to mention how very lovely you are, my dear, and, at least to me, you far outshine your sister."

She blushed and hugged the arm she held. "Thank you, William," she whispered. As they had arrived in town, they separated slightly, returning to a more proper distance for a couple newly acquainted. They slowed to allow Jane and Bingley to catch up, and the four walked down the high street of the little town. Elizabeth directed the group first to the book store, where she picked up a book her father had ordered and another for herself that had been ordered several weeks before. Next, they visited the milliner, where Bingley and Darcy waited outside for the ladies to make their purchases of muslin and ribbons. Jane also purchased several ribbons, as requested by her mother. After those tasks were completed, the group walked through town for a little longer, speaking to several people in town before finally turning back toward Longbourn.

As they walked home, they encountered Charlotte and her brother, John, walking toward Longbourn. Both ladies greeted their friend enthusiastically, and she, in her turn, introduced her brother to the two gentlemen. He had missed the assembly due to an errand in town for Sir William and had not met them before now. He eyed them carefully, not liking the way that Darcy was standing too close, in his mind, to Miss Elizabeth, who he quite considered as his. He had proposed to her when she was five, and he was ten, and she had told him then she was much too young to consider marriage. At the time, he had laughed with her but still believed that he would make the proposal again someday when she was ready. Mr Lucas had always been certain of her acceptance since he had laid claim to her fifteen years before, even though he had never mentioned the idea again.

The two decided to accompany the group to Longbourn since they were already going that way, and Jane issued an invitation for them all to join the family for tea once they arrived home. As Elizabeth was holding William's arm, Lucas could do little to separate them and grudgingly offered his arm to his sister as they all set off toward Longbourn.

Mrs Bennet lit up when she saw John Lucas accompanying Charlotte to the house as she also thought John to be a good match for Lizzy since her second daughter certainly could not aspire to anyone higher in her mind. She scowled when she saw the pairings; while she did not want Charlotte to marry either of the residents of Netherfield, she did not want "that rude Mr Darcy" to scare away John Lucas or to deter him from proposing soon.

The group entered the house and quickly settled themselves around the large room. Mrs Bennet scowled once again when she noticed that Mr Darcy continued to sit next to Lizzy, confused by the man's actions. Surely such a great man as he could not possibly be interested in *'that wild, unladylike girl'*, she thought. John Lucas was to be her husband; he was all she deserved. She certainly would not marry better than her beautiful Jane.

Mrs Bennet remained frustrated throughout the tea. All her efforts to get Lizzy away from Mr Darcy and nearer to Mr Lucas had been for nought. While Lizzy had engaged everyone in conversation, she had focused particular attention on Mr Darcy, conversing with him frequently and about things that others in the group did not seem to understand. More surprising to that lady was the fact that the attention appeared to be reciprocated.

"This will not do," she muttered to herself as she watched all in the room. She attempted to engage Mr Darcy in conversation herself and to pull him to her side, but again, this ploy was unsuccessful. After some time, all the visitors began to rise to depart, and Mrs Bennet made one last attempt to get Lizzy to speak to Mr Lucas privately.

"Lizzy," she called loudly, "be sure to escort Mr Lucas to the door. You know you missed him at the assembly, and he has not been able to speak to you as I am certain he wishes to do. Please accompany him out."

Elizabeth rolled her eyes surreptitiously, and Mr Darcy smiled at her reaction. He did not like Mrs Bennet's pushing his Elizabeth toward another man and knew he needed to make his own suit more obvious to the matron.

"Might I tell your father of our courtship to make it formal, dearest?" he whispered into her ear, causing several occupants of the room to scowl at the familiarity. "I confess I have noticed your mother's less-than-subtle efforts to push you toward another this afternoon."

She grimaced. "I had hoped you would not notice but realised that was unlikely. I hope you know I have never been interested in him. He has never been more to me than the brother of my friend. We played together when I was younger, but once he went to school, we saw each other only rarely. He has been finished with school for the last couple of years at least and has never paid me any special attention. I am not sure why Mama felt the need to push him at me today."

He nodded in reply, but others conspired to separate them as the guests began to move around the room to take their leave. Lucas took Elizabeth's hand and placed it on his own arm with a smirk at Darcy, not noticing the scowl on the lady's face at his possessive action. She attempted to pull her arm away, but he held tightly to it. Not wanting to make a scene, she attempted to hurry him out the door by encouraging others to accompany them. However, Mrs Bennet continued in her attempts to isolate the pair, and Lucas, sensing his opportunity, pulled Elizabeth toward the hallway. Darcy was delayed by Mrs Bennet and could not immediately follow without being rude.

As quickly as he could, though, he extricated himself and followed the pair into the hallway. He watched Elizabeth attempting to pull her hand from Lucas's and heard her demand its return.

"Lucas," he stated in a stern voice, laying his large hand on that man's shoulder, "the lady has asked you to release her. You should comply." Lucas dropped Elizabeth's hand, and she moved infinitesimally closer to Darcy's side.

"What is it to you?" Lucas demanded angrily. "She is to be my betrothed. We will marry before Christmas, and I will not allow you to toy with her."

Elizabeth gasped. "I have never agreed to marry you, John Lucas, and I have no intention to do so now. I do not know why you would spout such nonsense."

"I proposed to you when I was ten and you were five, Lizzy; surely you remember," Lucas insisted. "I have always known that we would marry someday."

Elizabeth thought for a second. "Mr Lucas, I remember nothing of the sort. And a proposal when I was five, and you were ten is hardly binding, regardless of what we may have said then. Now release me and end this delusion. I will not marry you."

"Delusion," he cried. "What can you mean?"

"You proclaimed us engaged, sir, which is decidedly not true, regardless of what may have been said when we were children," she protested. "Are you attempting to force my hand by ruining my reputation unless I agree to a proposal offered fifteen years ago? You do realise that spreading the rumour that we are engaged could result in my being labelled a jilt when the wedding inevitably never occurs. You have no right to such a claim."

"But Lizzy," he pleaded, "your mother and I have spoken many times of my plans to marry you."

"Strange that you have never said a word to me of these plans," Elizabeth said coldly. "I have no intention of being forced into an unwanted marriage, especially not with a so-called gentleman who conspired with my *mother* behind my back. When I marry, it will be to a man who respects me enough to speak to me about his wishes and who will then go to my father, as is appropriate in such a situation. One who would plot behind my back is not a husband I would ever want."

"Do you really expect this fop to offer for you, Lizzy?" Lucas taunted. "Your mother knows you cannot do better than me. Mine is likely the only proposal you will ever hear, at least the only honourable one. This one," he pointed toward Darcy, "only means to lead you on and take advantage of you before returning to town. He will never marry you."

Darcy nearly growled his displeasure and took a menacing step forward. Only Elizabeth's hand on his arm prevented him from demonstrating his anger at the slights of both himself and Elizabeth. Fortunately, Mr Bennet had emerged from his book room, having been alerted by Mrs Hill of the need, and had entered the hallway in time to hear Lucas's offensive words.

"Lucas, you are no longer ten. It is inappropriate for you to refer to my daughter in such an informal way. She is

Miss Elizabeth to you unless she or I grant you permission to address her otherwise," Bennet began sternly. "And do I rightly understand that you are attempting to win my daughter's hand by slighting her and the man she is courting? He, at least, has made his intentions known by speaking to me, her father, as is the custom, and not her mother, who lacks any authority over who my daughter marries. And as for Elizabeth not being able to do better than you, I sincerely doubt that to be true.

"Now, Mr Lucas. I think it best if you depart my home right away. I will inform Miss Lucas of your need to leave with some haste and that you will not be waiting for her." Mrs Hill was standing behind the group with Lucas's hat and coat in her hand, and she promptly handed the items to him.

Lucas began to depart when Darcy spoke. "I would recommend that you not repeat to anyone your belief of an established engagement to Miss Elizabeth. As I have spoken with her father and requested a formal courtship of the lady, which has been accepted, it would be my pleasure to challenge anyone who impugns her honour in any way. I will overlook your slight to myself ... this time." The threat in his tone was evident to all those gathered in the hallway.

Looking back at the three people standing there, Lucas nodded and hastily departed. Bennet invited the remaining two into his study for a chat about what had transpired before he arrived in the hallway. Following that discussion, he thanked Darcy for his efforts on his daughter's behalf. He began to wonder if it would be best to remove Elizabeth from Longbourn for a time to allow Mr Darcy to court her without interference once he informed his wife that she was not to make any promises on their daughter's behalf.

Ten

The Courtship is Made Public

T he small group returned to the sitting room a few minutes later, and Mrs Bennet looked up, expecting an announcement. She frowned when it was only Darcy who returned with her husband and Lizzy, and she wondered what could have happened to Mr Lucas. Perhaps he had already left to share the news of their engagement with his family?

She opened her mouth to speak but was forestalled by her husband. "I have an announcement," he said, and Mrs Bennet beamed, knowing what was to come. Once Elizabeth was engaged to Mr Lucas, surely Bingley would want to request at least a courtship with her Jane since one engagement often led to another. She was not listening to the rest of the announcement and was surprised when all in the room began to congratulate Lizzy and that other man, that Mr Darcy.

Mrs Bennet made her way to her husband. "What is happening, Mr Bennet?" she asked.

He looked at her with an arched eyebrow. "How did you miss my announcement of your daughter's courtship when you were standing in the room?" he inquired.

"My mind wandered," she replied. "I was thinking of all the things I will need to do in planning for the wedding between Lizzy and Mr Lucas."

He eyed her sharply. "Why would you be thinking of such a thing?" he said. "Mr Lucas has never once spoken to me of an interest in Lizzy, and I have just agreed to another's request to formally court her. In fact, I believe that she will need to go to London to conduct this courtship since I am no longer certain you are capable of overseeing it."

"Who is courting Lizzy, Mr Bennet, if not Mr Lucas?" she asked. "How can you allow her to be courted before my dearest Jane?"

"You would have married Lizzy to Mr Lucas before Jane was being courted or married," Bennet pointed out to his wife. "Have you not seen the attention being bestowed upon Lizzy by an eligible gentleman? He has been courting her under your nose for days."

Mrs Bennet gaped. "You cannot mean … surely you are not telling me Lizzy is being courted by Mr Darcy?" she cried.

When Mr Bennet nodded, she began to sputter. "Why … why would he be courting Lizzy? Mr Darcy is so much richer than Mr Bingley, and she is nowhere near as pretty as my Jane … Although Mr Bingley has been paying such marked attention to Jane … And Jane is ever so much more beautiful than Lizzy …" her thoughts began to trail off as she seemed to be thinking of how to transfer Mr Darcy's interest onto Jane.

"Mrs Bennet, cease this unfounded speculation," her husband's voice hissed in her ear. "It makes you appear mercenary and foolish, and you will frighten away both of our daughters' suitors with such nonsense. Could you not consider that perhaps Mr Darcy is courting Lizzy because he finds something admirable in her, even if you do not? I have never realised until just now how little you think of our second daughter. I am ashamed of myself for not taking more notice of my family until now. You have taught our youngest daughters to be foolish, and you have slighted and ignored those of whom you thought poorly. Things will be changing from this moment, Mrs Bennet. I suggest you go now and congratulate your daughter and her suitor. Once that is done, excuse yourself to your room. We will speak before this day is done."

Mrs Bennet did as directed and offered tepid congratulations to the courting couple. Elizabeth felt the slight and knew her mother had only done so because her father had insisted. She had heard her mother's words to her father, as she had not attempted to be quiet, and she knew Darcy had as well.

After Mrs Bennet left the room, Darcy and Bingley once again made to leave. Elizabeth walked Darcy toward the door behind Jane and Bingley and softly apologised for her mother's words. He noted the slight evidence of tears pooling in her bright eyes and sought to comfort her.

"Elizabeth, please do not be offended, but I think your mother is a foolish woman who cannot understand you as you are so unlike her. Your father has observed how he has done little to aid her or your younger sisters in their education, and this appears likely to change in the near future. Regardless of what your mother says or believes, I know what I want, and that is you," he whispered. "Nothing will change my mind about that, so please, do not let her worry you, dearest."

"You are too kind, William," she whispered in return. "Forgive me if it takes me some time to believe you and not be affected by what she says of me. I have heard it all for many years. Are you sure you wish to court me knowing what a foolish mother I have?"

"Then allow me to convince you of your worth," he murmured in her ear. "Your father mentioned something about allowing you to go to London for a month or so. He seems to think I could court you more effectively there."

"We would not have the freedom of our walks in the country," she replied. "And surely it is too soon for you to leave your friend. Are you not here to teach him how to run an estate?"

"That was the intent, although Bingley has proven an unwilling student," he sighed. "But please know that it is an option to go to London, especially if it becomes too difficult for you here."

"Thank you," she replied. "I will let you know. Perhaps in a few weeks, I can go, and maybe then it will be time to begin my trousseau." She winked as she said the last, and he brought her hand to his lips to kiss before turning it over and pressing a second kiss into her palm.

"That, my dear, is a wonderful idea," he said, then releasing her hand, he mounted the waiting horse and rode away to Netherfield.

The following day was Sunday, which meant Elizabeth

was unable to walk out early in the morning, and Darcy had been unable to persuade Bingley to rise early. Since they were now formally courting, and due to Lucas's actions the previous day, Darcy had every intention of demonstrating his preference for and connection to Elizabeth publicly at church, where all could see it and know she was his.

The gentlemen from Netherfield arrived at church early and stood in the yard awaiting the Bennets. Darcy observed Lucas there as well, seemingly waiting for the same person he was. Soon, the Bennets arrived, and Darcy rushed forward to greet Elizabeth, immediately offering her his arm, which she gratefully accepted.

Lucas appeared on her other side, where Jane stood, and he waited for Bingley to claim her so he could take Elizabeth's other arm and pull her from Darcy. He was surprised when Bingley did claim Jane's other arm, but the two ladies did not separate until after they entered the church. The four spoke for several minutes in the churchyard until it was nearly time for the service to begin, preventing Lucas from engaging the group.

Jane released Bingley's arm when they entered the church, as they had no understanding, and walked to her family's pew. Darcy continued forward with Elizabeth and only released her arm when they arrived at her family's pew. Such attention was not missed by those in attendance, and they were subsequently curious to discover what it all meant.

Therefore, when the service was over, and Darcy once again waited to escort Miss Elizabeth, many whispers followed them. Mrs Bennet was heard crowing about the fact that Mr Bingley and Mr Darcy had visited her home several times since the assembly and had much to say about the potential of a match between Jane and Mr Bingley, only adding the courtship of Elizabeth and Mr Darcy as an afterthought and openly speculating on how soon it would end. The neighbours, who were used to Mrs Bennet's frequent disregard of her second daughter, discussed amongst themselves what they had witnessed between Elizabeth and Darcy that morning and were much more positive about the possibility of a lasting attachment and not the one between Jane and Bingley.

Darcy and Elizabeth studiously ignored all of the attention and, after speaking to a few of Elizabeth's friends, began walking toward the Bennet home with Jane and Bingley. Mr Lucas had intended to interfere with the couple, but Mr Bennet put a stop to that. When he saw Lucas's attempt to approach his daughter, he stopped him and quietly warned him about what had been said the day before.

Lucas was not happy about this but retreated quietly enough afterwards, having noted the way Darcy had glared at him as they left the church. Lucas felt it was in his best interest to simply wait for Darcy to leave town and then, when Elizabeth was heartbroken, convince her to marry him.

Bingley and Darcy escorted the ladies to their home and were happy that they had an invitation to lunch. Darcy looked forward to another opportunity to spend time with Elizabeth and was looking forward to challenging her in chess after the midday meal. This had been discussed several times between them, and both were looking forward to the match.

The rest of the Bennets had arrived home in the carriage ahead of the two couples and were already gathered in the drawing room when they arrived. Jane and Elizabeth escorted the gentleman into the house, and greetings were once again exchanged. It was not long before the meal was announced.

Luncheon was a pleasant enough meal. Elizabeth and Darcy engaged Mr Bennet in conversation about books and chess while at the other end of the table, Jane and Mr Bingley spoke almost exclusively to each other, with Mary and Mrs Bennet occasionally joining in. Kitty, who had attended church that morning, had been permitted to join them for the meal, although she would return upstairs after. She listened to the conversations on either end of the table and found she had little of worth to contribute to either.

This thought made her wonder if the idea of a governess was more of a boon than she had earlier believed, especially as she had begun to wonder if she were better off since she had been removed from Lydia's influence. Her other sisters had paid more attention to her since Lydia had been locked in the nursery, and she had observed how Jane and Lizzy's behaviour was so different from the way Lydia and their mother normally behaved.

Kitty returned upstairs after luncheon and picked up the book her father had given her the day before. It was a book of poetry, and, as she paged through it, she found several poems that proved interesting. Later, she attempted to draw, something she had always enjoyed, but Lydia had mocked her for it, and she had not attempted it very often, except in private. She wondered if her father would be willing to hire a drawing master if she asked him.

Downstairs, the family, along with Darcy and Bingley, gathered in the drawing room for conversation. Bennet's presence in the room led Mrs Bennet to act in a more subdued manner, as did the absence of Kitty and Lydia from the family party. The conversation was a continuation of that at the meal, although, on occasion, it broadened to include everyone gathered in the room. Mrs Bennet found a little left out since she had little to contribute to the discussion when it did not include neighbourhood gossip, ribbons, or lace.

Soon, however, Darcy reminded Bennet and Elizabeth of his promised chess match with Elizabeth. The game lasted a considerable amount of time before Elizabeth managed to place Darcy in checkmate, but it was a near thing. She grinned broadly at him when the game was over, and he grinned back, feeling a measure of pride in the challenge. Her smile dimmed when she heard her mother's whispered reprimand for not allowing him to win. "No man likes a woman who is smarter than he, Lizzy," she whispered harshly. "You will never catch a man beating him in men's games like chess."

"Madam," Darcy said, drawing himself up to his full height. "I admire Miss Elizabeth because she was not willing to let me defeat her and because she is capable of challenging me in this and other areas. I do not know where you got the idea that men want foolish wives, but I assure you, men of quality do not, and many of my acquaintances would prefer a wife with whom they can share an intelligent conversation. By beating me in chess, Miss Elizabeth has shown herself as more deserving of my attention, not less. I believe my biggest challenge will be to convince her that *I* am worthy of *her* attention."

Mrs Bennet sputtered before slumping in her seat and then calling loudly for salts. Bennet shook his head sadly before helping his wife from her seat and escorting her upstairs. "If you will excuse me, sirs, my wife has taken ill, and I will need to escort her to her room to rest. She will not be joining us again this afternoon."

Once again, Mrs Bennet was left shocked at her husband's actions. He had never responded so when she had been overtaken with nerves in the past, and, frankly, he had never bothered before to sit with them when they had guests. Most Sunday afternoons, he was firmly ensconced in his book room while the ladies of the family sat. She began to be concerned about his behaviour and what it may mean.

The three ladies and two gentlemen collectively sighed as they shook off the effects of Mrs Bennet's hysterics. Although they invited Mary to join them in a stroll, she declined, so the remaining four retreated to the garden for a short walk in the warmth of the afternoon before returning for tea sometime later. Mr Bennet eventually returned after explaining once more to his wife the potential effects of her behaviour that day and reprimanding her for her continued disparagement of Lizzy. He warned her that going forward, such behaviour would be penalised with a reduction in her pin money.

After taking tea together and one more game of chess between Darcy and Elizabeth, the gentlemen departed just as the sun began to set. Both felt that it had been an enjoyable day, and Darcy felt his courtship was proceeding well. He did not relish the idea of Mrs Bennet as his mother-in-law, but given her behaviour toward Elizabeth, he wondered how frequently Elizabeth would desire to be in the company of her mother. He hoped the steps Bennet was taking would help the two youngest and even, perhaps, Mrs Bennet, but rather doubted that Mrs Bennet would change. Both he and Bingley had noticed that Miss Catherine, called Kitty within the family, had behaved better that day, which made them look more positively at the potential of her being a credit to the family when she re-entered society.

Eleven

Lydia Attempts to Escape and Ends up at School

Lydia watched the gentlemen leave from her window of Longbourn. Since Thursday morning, she had been locked into the old schoolroom, and meals had been delivered on a tray with a maid and a footman in attendance. That had begun at dinner on Thursday when Lydia had attempted to push her way from the room and had spilt her entire meal on the maid. Mr Bennet had been angry and had forced Lydia to help clean up the mess. The following morning, two people arrived to deliver the meal, one to guard the door while the other brought in the food. Lydia had been rather hungry by that time since her father had not allowed a replacement meal to be brought up after she had spilt the first.

Her father had visited after breakfast each morning to give her an assignment and instructions for the day. He brought her a book to read so they could discuss it and threatened her enough that she would not dare to damage it. The previous day, she had attempted to refuse to clean up her mess, and the look in his eye when she stomped her foot at him had her rethinking her defiance. She was accustomed to her mother giving in to her demands and her father ignoring her, but something made her realize that he would not be easily manipulated. Lydia had determined if she could just stick it out for a few days, surely no more than a week, he would become bored with his efforts and allow things to return to the way they were.

So, she assisted the maid as she cleaned the schoolroom, or at least she pretended to, and did not rip up the book her father had given her as she was tempted to do. She attempted to read the history book she had been assigned but was largely unsuccessful, as the book was not interesting to her. Lydia did not like reading or learning; the only things she really enjoyed were flirting with the boys in the neighbourhood and resewing bonnets to fashion them to suit her. Even though she did not like to work on her bonnets, or anything else, or very long, as she preferred to always be doing something, sitting quietly to sew was not very much fun.

On Sunday, her father did not visit until well after luncheon. He brought Mama with him, and the two joined forces to plead for Lydia to be returned to the family and allowed to be 'out' once again. He firmly denied this request.

"Mrs Bennet, Lydia, as I have explained to both of you, Lydia has no business being out. She is too young and too immature to be out in society," Bennet told them both. "Mrs Bennet, I would like for you to explain to our youngest daughter how you were wrong to tell her that kissing boys or men is acceptable. Please explain to her what is appropriate behaviour for a young girl who is not yet out."

"Whatever do you mean, Mr. Bennet?" Mrs Bennet asked, having forgotten their discussion from earlier in the week.

"Lydia believes that the quickest way to 'catch a husband' is to allow a man, particularly an officer, to kiss her. She believes, based on what she had heard from you, that kissing will lead to an engagement and that officers are eligible suitors," Bennet explained, his patience already waning.

"What is wrong with that?" Mrs Bennet asked.

"Mrs Bennet, have you forgotten everything we spoke of earlier this week? Officers, particularly those in the militia, are not eligible since most of them can barely afford their own food and lodgings on their pay. Unless they receive a generous allowance from their families, they have very little to live on until they reach the rank of Colonel or higher. If Lydia were to marry an officer, she would live without any servants or nice clothes and would be responsible for cooking and cleaning in whatever lodgings her husband could afford for them. Not only that, but living with an officer will mean 'following the drum' and moving from town to town. There would be little pin money available for ribbons and dresses or any of the other furbelows you waste your money on," Bennet explained bluntly.

He fixed his youngest daughter with a hard look. "And this all assumes that the man is honourable and does not take more than just a kiss. Or that he offers for you after taking such a liberty. A real lady does not allow such liberties before she is engaged, at the very least. Even then, liberties should still not be allowed, particularly certain ones, until after one is wed. Mrs Bennet, what does your daughter know about appropriate behaviour with men? What have you taught her? That is, if you have ever taught her anything beyond flirting," Bennet said disgustedly.

"Lydia, I will see you in the morning when we discuss your reading. I expect you to have it completed by then," he told her as he stood to exit. "Mrs. Bennet, it seems we need to have yet another conversation, although I believe sending Lydia to school and hiring a governess for Kitty will be best since what is appropriate behaviour for young ladies appears to be beyond you."

He led Mrs. Bennet from the room and locked the door on Lydia. Bennet heard something crash against the door and called through it. "I will expect your pin money to pay for whatever you broke, Lydia. And you must clean it up if you intend to be served dinner."

Mrs. Bennet gasped at the treatment of her favourite child and attempted to berate her husband. That lasted only a moment before he fixed her with another hard look, and she immediately stopped speaking. "Mrs. Bennet, I will remind you that I am the head of this family. I have failed you and our daughters, but I intend to remedy that. I do not know if Lydia can be corrected, but I will not allow her to taint the rest of our daughters with her misguided and foolish behaviours. You must see that Lydia is headed for ruin if she continues unchecked?"

"I do not see it, Mr. Bennet. I do not know what you speak of or why you find it necessary to be so harsh on my dear Lydia all of a sudden," she moaned.

"I am being harsh on our youngest so she does not ruin our family. She has not learned proper behaviour, and you seem incapable of teaching her the correct way to behave," Mr. Bennet said. "She will go to school soon to see if her behaviour can be amended."

Mrs. Bennet moaned and complained for several minutes about the unfairness of such an action. Once again, Bennet stopped her complaints with a glare. "I am beginning to wonder if hiring a companion for you would not be better than hiring one for our girls. Mary will improve with wider reading and perhaps by hiring a music master. Kitty has already improved by being away from Lydia and observing her elder sisters. Some education would benefit her as well, but she might do well by simply visiting Mrs. Gardiner since that is where Jane and Lizzy learned proper comportment. That might be an option in the spring," he concluded.

"Whatever would I do with a companion, Mr. Bennet? Oh, why are you so cruel to me? Oh, my poor nerves," she moaned.

"Mrs. Bennet, enough of your hysterics," Mr. Bennet commanded. "I have had enough of them, and such displays will no longer be permitted. You must learn to control yourself."

She continued to whine and complain about her ill-treatment, and finally, Mr. Bennet left her alone. However, he also commanded Hill and their daughters not to sit with her and commiserate over her perceived poor treatment. Bennet was determined to no longer allow his wife to disrupt the household in this way. Perhaps the idea of a companion for his wife was not such a bad idea.

***

Later that night, a ruckus outside woke Bennet and several others. Lydia had broken her window in an effort to escape. She had tied several dresses and petticoats together to make a rope to get to the ground, but it was far too short, and she was dangling more than ten feet in the air and was currently attempting to enter through a window on the first floor. This window happened to be in Elizabeth's bedroom, and she had raised the alarm before she attempted to grab Lydia and bring her back inside.

Bennet was livid when he stepped into the room just as Elizabeth dragged Lydia in through the open window. Several of her dresses had stretched, and the seams in a few places were starting to pull apart. A servant went up to the third floor to recover the rope at that end and used boards to cover the window. A severely chastised Lydia was returned to the nursery with far fewer dresses than she had before, and Bennet was determined the girl would be placed in school somewhere within the next fortnight.

Elizabeth recounted these events for Darcy the following morning when she and Kitty met him at the top of Oakham Mount. Neither Jane nor Mary would be persuaded to go, but Kitty had appreciated being asked and having Bennet's approval to venture outdoors for a time. Bingley did not accompany Darcy either, so the couple walked and talked while Kitty sat and attempted to draw the landscape.

After some time, Darcy and Elizabeth sat next to Kitty to admire her drawing. Darcy, surprisingly, was able to offer Kitty some advice to improve her drawing and related that he had attended a few sessions with his sister when he had hired a drawing master for her. He suggested that when Georgiana arrived, the two might sit together to discuss techniques. His sister was by no means an expert, but she enjoyed drawing and had enjoyed the benefits of masters on several occasions.

Darcy accompanied the ladies back to Longbourn, where he was invited to join them for breakfast. When they arrived, they all went into the breakfast room and served themselves from the buffet. Mrs. Bennet was still abed, but Jane and Mary were at the table already. Jane looked disappointed that Bingley had not accompanied the walkers, but Darcy quickly volunteered the information that he would join them later that morning. Truly, Darcy was too early for proper calling hours, but he desired to spend as much time as he could in Elizabeth's company.

Darcy and the four Bennet ladies ate and talked about a variety of different subjects as they ate. The five of them discussed art, music, and books, although Elizabeth and Darcy dominated most of the conversation, with the rest adding bits as they were able. Darcy appreciated how intelligent Elizabeth was and how well she was able to discuss and debate with him. He looked forward to a lifetime in her company, certain they would always have plenty of conversation. He also liked how she deliberately steered the conversation to allow her sisters to contribute and noticed the way she was able to put others at ease.

When the group was nearly finished with their meal, Bennet joined them and was surprised to find Darcy at the table sitting beside Elizabeth. He frowned slightly but did his best to hide it before he recalled that he needed to speak to Darcy about a school for Lydia and a governess or companion for Kitty and someone else for his wife.

"Darcy," Bennet began after a few minutes, "will you join me in my study after breakfast? I wanted to speak to you about one of the things we discussed last week. Have you heard anything from your aunt about schools or companions?"

"I have, sir," Darcy said, patting his coat pockets and looking for a letter. "I received a letter from her Saturday evening and forgot to bring it with me yesterday. She did have some recommendations. I am ready to speak whenever you are."

Bennet stood from the table. "Well, let us begin now if you are ready. Lizzy, I will return him to his courting before too long," he said, causing both Elizabeth and Darcy to blush and Elizabeth to scowl at him. He laughed, and the two gentlemen exited the room.

Bennet recounted the events from the previous night, not surprised to learn that Elizabeth had already discussed portions of the story with Darcy. "My wife is incapable of educating Lydia properly, which makes me consider that Jane and Lizzy turned out so well because they stayed with the Gardiners frequently during their formative years. Mrs. Gardiner likely had more of an influence on them than my wife has had. And Mary was ignored by her mother and attempted to follow her own moralistic path; I have her reading Shakespeare instead of Fordyce. It has been interesting to hear her thoughts.

"Kitty and Lydia have been influenced too much by my wife, although Kitty seems capable of learning to modify her behaviour. Just these few days of being separated from her sister seem to have made a difference, and I wonder if hiring a companion for all my girls would be the best idea. Lydia must go to school; there is no question about that. She needs structure she will not get at home. The only one I am uncertain about is my wife. I do not know what to do about her at all."

Darcy took a deep breath and considered the problem briefly, uncertain about advising a man old enough to be his father. "Sir, if I might suggest an idea…" seeing Bennet's nod, he continued. "I agree that Lydia must go to school. I think that your next youngest daughter might benefit by spending some time in London with your brother and sister there. You say that your oldest two learned from her example, so separating Miss Kitty from her mother and other influences may have a positive effect on her. She is close in age to my own sister, who has been learning from a drawing master this autumn. If Miss Catherine were in London, she could attend lessons along with my sister, who would be a good companion for her as well, and it would be someone her own age from whom she could learn proper comportment. You could still hire a companion for Longbourn, but she could focus her time and attention on your wife for now instead of your daughters."

Bennet considered this for a moment. "You would not be concerned about Kitty negatively influencing your sister?" he asked.

"Georgiana has a companion that would prevent that, I believe," Darcy said. "With Mrs. Annesley supervising their interactions, I am not worried about her learning bad habits."

"I think it is a good idea," Bennet said. "Give me a week to work out all the details, and maybe Lizzy will wish to accompany her sister to London for a week or so as well."

The two spend some time discussing schools for Lydia. When Darcy left the study, Bennet spent the next hour writing letters to two of the schools Darcy's aunt had recommended while Darcy joined the ladies in the drawing room.

***

It took a rather tumultuous fortnight for a place to be found in a school for Lydia. Darcy's aunt, Lady Matlock, had recommended a school in Northampton that was unlike many other schools in that it operated year-round and allowed students to be enrolled in the middle of a term.

Several letters went back and forth by express, and Lydia was accepted into the school.

It was an unusual school in that it was designed for young ladies who had misbehaved in some way, providing more structure than other schools for its students. It required the girls who attended to be responsible for themselves and for chores around the school. Lydia would not only be required to attend classes, she would be responsible for keeping her room clean and neat, and there was no maid to take care of her hair and clothes. The girls were allowed very little free time, at least at the beginning, as that freedom would be earned by behaving as expected. If a girl misbehaved, she would be punished by performing additional chores or having privileges revoked.

The school was also isolated and several miles away from villages or towns. It was a great privilege to be permitted an afternoon away from school, and it would be months before Lydia could possibly earn it. Students were required to write letters home a minimum of once per week which were read before they were sent until the girl earned the trust of the headmistress.

Naturally, Lydia was unhappy about the prospect of attending any school. When her father described the school and its rules, she immediately protested. However, no amount of protest would prevent her father from taking her, and on the first of November, Lydia boarded a carriage with her father to begin the two-day journey to the school. Her father established her at the school, told her to do a good job and learn as much as she could, and gave her into the keeping of the headmistress to be educated.

Twelve

Engaged

~~~ ❧❧❧ ~~~

C hanges continued to take place at Longbourn while Lydia was confined to the nursery until she could be sent to school. Bennet had written to the Gardiners asking them to allow Kitty to visit through at least Christmas. He suggested that Lizzy might join her if it was agreeable to the Gardiners. Elizabeth sent additional letters to the Gardiners during this time, describing her courtship with Mr Darcy and the changes being made at Longbourn since her Papa had decided to take an interest in his family. Elizabeth was pleased with the changes, although a small part of her wondered if her Papa would maintain these changes or if he would eventually lose interest. She admitted that he was taking a far more active role than she had ever imagined. However, she wondered if he would eventually return to what he had been.

Elizabeth expressed these same concerns to Darcy one

morning as Kitty chaperoned them to Oakham Mount. Kitty had continued to go with her nearly every day since the morning Mr Darcy had complimented her drawing and suggested the possibility of lessons. She was determined to draw a picture of the landscape from that point. She debated whether to include Lizzy and Mr Darcy in it and present it to them as a wedding gift. Kitty, who was frequently able to watch their courtship advance by leaps and bounds in these early morning walks, was fairly certain that a wedding between the two was inevitable, although no formal announcement had been made.

Much of Meryton was aware of Darcy and Elizabeth's courtship and silently encouraged the couple while waiting for the courtship to reach its inevitable conclusion. Knowing how much Lizzy disliked gossip of any kind and seeing the same in Mr Darcy, few would discuss the circumstances in her presence, but there was much speculation in private. Everyone noticed that at any public event, the two almost immediately would gravitate toward each other and converse to the exclusion of all others. They also observed how well-matched they were since they often spoke in ways that most others could not understand their conversation.

John Lucas watched bitterly and wondered if he had acted sooner if he would have won her, or if she would have talked circles around him and, in the end, merrily rejected his proposal. Even he had to admit that the pair were well-matched, and he could not in any way compete with Darcy. It had little to do with the material possessions of either gentleman. Resigned, he acknowledged that Lizzy would have never encouraged him, and had Mrs Bennet not promoted the idea, he likely would not have given marriage to Miss Elizabeth much thought.

On the morning Mr Bennet was to depart with Lydia, Darcy and Elizabeth were again watching the sunrise at Oakham Mount, having managed to sneak out of their respective houses without anyone else being aware. Whether this was arranged purposely or not, neither was quite sure. Still, Darcy had decided his time of waiting for Elizabeth had ended.

"My dearest Elizabeth," he said as he moved to embrace her from behind as they stood and watched the sun rise over the hills of Hertfordshire. "You know I love you dearly and want nothing more than to make you my wife, do you not?" At her nod, he continued. "Might I ask … do you, I mean … could you love me in return?"

She sighed happily and turned around in his arms to look him in the eye. "Oh, William, I do love you so. You have shown yourself to be a truly admirable man in the last month, and I do not think I could have stopped myself from loving you in return. You have demonstrated your care and respect for me in many ways in this month of courtship."

He leaned down and let his lips touch hers in a brief kiss. "Marry me, Elizabeth? I know I have asked before, although it was first offered in jest, this was always my intention toward you. I told you on the second, or perhaps it was the third day of our knowing each other, that I wanted to marry you, and your father made me promise to court you for a month. That month is over, and I know that I love you even more now than I did the first time I asked you."

She smiled at him and reached up to caress his cheek. "Yes, William, I would be delighted to marry you. But I will confess, I do not want our wedding to be what Mama will try to make it become. She will want us to wait to marry until spring and will want a large, elaborate wedding. I do not want to wait months and months and have to endure months of her wedding planning. I would prefer a far smaller and far simpler wedding than Mama will insist upon planning."

"You are suggesting we have a short engagement then?" he asked, grinning. "I will certainly not object to that plan. How soon would you like to marry?"

"Do you think we could marry before Christmas? Is that possible?" she asked shyly.

"Would it make you happy if I were to insist upon it? So your mother will think I insist on a short engagement period rather than you?" he asked. "I would certainly be content with marrying before Christmas, and I think it could be easily arranged. Do you still want to go to London next week as we have planned? You mentioned before that you would like to shop for your trousseau there."

She sighed. "Aye, I think that is an excellent plan. Papa leaves today, and you should ask his permission when you visit this morning. Then, we can leave for London in a day or two to begin my shopping."

"Would you like to spend Christmas in London or at Pemberley, dearest?" he asked her quietly.

"Oh, definitely Pemberley," she said. "I do so look forward to seeing it after all you have said about it. And we could take Kitty with us so she and Georgiana could entertain each other."

"Or we could allow our sisters to stay in London with a companion," Darcy suggested.

Elizabeth shot him a look. "You would leave your sister alone for Christmas, William?" she asked.

Darcy sighed. "No, I would not, despite how much I might want to," he said, then continued to consider. "So, we could marry as soon as the banns can be called – at the end of this month – and then you and I could go on a short wedding trip before we take our sisters to Pemberley for Christmas. Or we could simply go on to Pemberley and have my aunt and uncle escort Georgiana and Miss Catherine when they return to Matlock for Christmas."

"Would they be willing to do that?" she inquired.

"I believe they would," Darcy replied. "We could introduce them to you and your sister when we visit."

"We can discuss this further with my father before he departs with Lydia," she suggested. "We should each return to our home, and then you can pay a visit to Longbourn before my father departs."

Darcy agreed, and after one final kiss, they separated, each to their own home. Elizabeth snuck back in without anyone realising she had left. Quickly changing into a more appropriate dress for receiving callers, she called the maid to fix her hair and descended the stairs to the dining room for breakfast.

Bennet was sitting at the table with Mary and Kitty when she came down. Jane was still upstairs, likely preparing for their expected callers, as Bingley had visited nearly as frequently as Darcy. However, that gentleman had not yet declared himself or asked for a courtship. He had announced a day or two ago that he was planning for a ball near the end of November, but that still depended on his aunt's willingness to come and act as hostess for him.

Jane had just joined them when the two gentlemen were announced and invited to join the family for breakfast. The invitation was readily accepted, and the conversation at the table was lively. Soon enough, however, the meal ended, and Mr Bennet rose to depart. Darcy's voice stopped him. "Mr Bennet, might I speak with you for a moment before you go?"

Bennet knew what was coming – he was in some ways amazed that Darcy had managed to restrain himself for the full month as he had insisted. Therefore, when Darcy requested his daughter's hand in marriage, he did not even toy with him as he would have a month ago. He readily agreed to the gentleman's suggestion for a short engagement and simple wedding. The older gentleman suggested Darcy acquire a common licence and only notify Mrs Bennet upon their return from London. It was quickly decided that Darcy would escort Elizabeth and Kitty to London in two days, and they would remain there for a week.

Nearly as soon as it was all decided, the two gentlemen left the study to announce the engagement to the family – all except for Lydia and Mrs Bennet. As expected, they were all pleased for the couple. The plans were shared – a wedding within the month, a trip to London for Elizabeth and Kitty in a few days, and Mrs Bennet was not to know until everyone had returned. Bennet expected to be home within a week, and Darcy, Elizabeth, and Kitty would return a day or two later.

Bennet retrieved Lydia from her room, and the two departed for her school. Bingley proposed a walk, which was readily agreed to by all but Mary, who chose to stay home and practice on the pianoforte. Kitty accompanied Darcy and Elizabeth for part of their walk, and he spoke to them about his sister. He told them Georgiana was terribly shy, and he intended to bring her to Netherfield when they all returned from this foray into London so she could attend his wedding and get to know her new sisters better.

They walked into Meryton and visited a few shops as they had done before. Kitty joined Bingley and Jane on the return trip, and Elizabeth and Darcy lagged behind the others. "Dearest," he began, "your father suggested I obtain a common licence so we may marry before the end of November. Bingley intends to hold a ball on November twenty-sixth, and I wondered if you would like to marry before or after that event."

"If the ball were after the wedding, where would we stay until the ball was held?" Elizabeth asked.

"That was what I wondered as well," Darcy admitted. "I confess I would prefer not to stay at Netherfield for any length of time after our wedding. I selfishly would like to have you to myself after our wedding."

She smiled at him. "I think I would prefer that as well. Might we marry on the twenty-eighth of November? The ball could serve as an engagement celebration of sorts and would please Mama, but then we can have a much quieter wedding and breakfast two days later."

"And depart for London afterwards," he stated before checking to see that no one in the other group was paying them any attention. He immediately leaned down and kissed her quickly. "I cannot wait to make you my wife, dearest Elizabeth."

"And I cannot wait to be your wife, William," she responded, standing on her tiptoes to press a kiss to his lips.

Looking around, Darcy pulled her off the road and behind a tree, kissing her deeply and passionately, leaving them both breathless when they finally stopped. "I love you, Elizabeth," he whispered as he attempted to catch his breath.

She leaned against his chest and listened to his still rapidly beating heart. "I love you too, William," she whispered back. "We will go to London in two days, and then, in less than four weeks, we will be married."

Despite the temptation for more, Darcy settled for a brief kiss before the couple returned to the road and continued to make their way toward Longbourn, where they continued to make plans and speak of the amusements they would partake of in London.

Thirteen

Visiting London

〰️〰️〰️

Two days later, Darcy, Elizabeth, and Kitty made their way to London accompanied by a maid to maintain the propriety of their travelling together. The ladies were to stay with the Gardiners, and Darcy was looking forward to meeting Mrs Gardiner as she hailed from Lambton. Darcy knew her husband and had rather liked him, so he was predisposed to like his wife as that lady was Elizabeth's favourite relation.

The introductions went smoothly despite Mr Bennet's letter announcing the girls' intention to visit not having reached London. Mrs Gardiner welcomed them gladly, always pleased to have Elizabeth visit, however unexpected. Although she had heard much of Darcy courting her niece over the last month, she was slightly surprised at the news of the engagement. She congratulated both her niece and Mr Darcy and mentioned to Darcy her slight acquaintance with his father and mother from her time in Lambton.

Darcy was inordinately pleased with this mention of his parents. As they had both been gone for many years, he always enjoyed hearing stories about them, even from one who had only a remote connection to them as Mrs Gardiner did. He invited them to dine at Darcy House the following night so they could all be introduced to Georgiana. Then, far too soon for both Elizabeth and Darcy, he departed for Mayfair to acquaint his sister and cousin with his engagement.

To say Georgiana was pleased with this news was an understatement. When he announced his news to his sister, she squealed her excitement. "I am to have a sister," she proclaimed. "When might I meet her? Is she in London? When will you marry?" She asked these and several other questions in quick succession, not allowing her brother the opportunity to respond.

Darcy laughed, which was surprising enough to cause Georgiana to quit her rapid questioning. "You are happy, Brother?" she asked her final question and then waited for him to answer.

"Very happy, Georgiana," he replied. "Elizabeth has accepted me, and I could not be more pleased to make her my wife. We will marry before the end of the month. You will not have one sister, but five, although it is unlikely you will meet Lydia any time soon as she is at school. I believe she will return home before the summer."

Georgiana was surprised to be reminded that she would acquire not only her brother's wife as her sister but the others as well. "I had forgotten about the others. Tell me about your betrothed and all of her sisters."

He laughed. "You will meet Elizabeth and her sister Catherine, called Kitty, tomorrow evening. I have asked them to join us for dinner, and I hope you will accompany both ladies on their shopping trips this week. I will call on them at Gracechurch Street in the morning, and if you like, you might accompany me to meet them even sooner." At Georgiana's nod, he considered another matter. "Georgie, would you like to introduce Elizabeth to your modiste tomorrow or the following day? Since the letter to her relations announcing their arrival went awry, I imagine no arrangements have been made for her to begin her trousseau. She will need a great number of dresses and things for town as Mrs Darcy as well as warm attire for Derbyshire. Although there is scarcely enough time, if you help her place the orders now, everything should be ready before we go to Pemberley."

"Oh, I will send a note first thing in the morning," Georgiana said. "Will you include one to add her to our accounts?"

Darcy nodded, realising this was not something he had considered before that moment. He wondered what arrangements Mr Bennet may have made for Elizabeth's purchases since he had left almost immediately after approving their plans. In the morning, before the ladies began their shopping, he would need to speak to Mr Gardiner to see what steps needed to be taken to ensure the ladies could shop to their heart's content.

* * *

Darcy's considerations were all unnecessary. Gardiner had already considered the lack of planning on Bennet's part and had spoken to his wife about what was needed.

Gardiner's warehouse would provide the material for all of Elizabeth's clothing, and Mrs Gardiner's customary modiste had been able to arrange an appointment that very morning. Georgiana was invited to accompany them on the outing, and Darcy was summarily left alone with Mr Gardiner.

Although Darcy would have preferred to remain with his betrothed, he could not, and so the gentlemen removed to Mr Gardiner's study, where they discussed the marriage settlement and other arrangements. Knowing Bennet's desire to increase the dowries of his daughters, Darcy elected to refuse Elizabeth's portion leaving the funds for her sisters. Gardiner acquainted him with Elizabeth's own investments, which amounted to a little over a thousand pounds. She had done well, saving her bits and bobs for so many years, and Gardiner had added to it when he was able to do so, which had helped it reach that amount. Darcy intended to leave it under Elizabeth's control and made a notation on the draft of the marriage settlement of the fund and his intentions regarding it.

Gardiner was rather impressed at the breadth of the marriage articles. Included within were arrangements for children, both sons and daughters, for Elizabeth should Darcy predecease her, her settlement – thirty thousand pounds to start – and her personal income, also known as her PIN money. In addition to this, she would receive a quarterly allotment for her clothing that was separate from the money required for the several households Elizabeth would manage as the mistress. Darcy had his home in London, and, of course, there was Pemberley, as well as a smaller estate in Scotland and homes in Bath and Lyme. His annual income was well over twenty thousand pounds from these properties and his investments, making Elizabeth's settlement easy to manage without her dowry.

The settlement had been drafted by Darcy's solicitor even before he had proposed and needed few adjustments. He fully intended to acquaint Elizabeth with all its particulars and asked Gardiner for permission to do so when the ladies returned. Gardiner agreed to this request and was appreciative of the obvious respect this man had for his niece.

Once the marriage settlement was reviewed, the conversation drifted to business and the success of the investments Darcy had already made with the gentleman. From there, the conversation moved along to the changes in the Bennet household. Elizabeth had told of these in her letters to her aunt, and they had discussed them the previous night after dinner, but Darcy had a different perspective on the situation, not being a member of the family.

"Quite frankly, sir," Gardiner said, "I am amazed at my brother doing anything about his family, and I wonder what, if anything, will aid my sister. Bennet would have done well had he attempted these measures twenty years ago, but my sister's behaviour is ingrained. Sending Lydia to a school will at least keep her away from embarrassing the family so readily, and I am amazed at the changes I see in Kitty already. It seems all she needed was a separation from Lydia and some time and attention from someone with sense. I am glad she will be joining your sister and receiving some lessons from an art master. I have offered for years to bring her to London for just that, but Bennet has always refused my request."

"Mary is much improved as well, or so Elizabeth says," Darcy added. "I am not certain what she was before, but Elizabeth seems to think that separating her from Fordyce has significantly improved her." He laughed as he and Elizabeth had discussed that particular author and what they both thought about his strictures several times. While not all the man said was bad, some of his lessons on how "proper young ladies should behave" were ridiculous. Elizabeth preferred to discuss Wollstonecraft and her Vindication of the Rights of Woman, which was far more in line with her thinking and, to be honest, with his.

Darcy remained in Gardiner's office until the ladies returned several hours later, surprising both. "I did not know you intended to remain all afternoon, sir," Elizabeth said archly after greeting him.

"I did not," he replied, standing quickly and walking toward her at the door of the study. "Your uncle and I began conversing and apparently have lost track of time."

She smiled at him. "I have often had the same happen to me, most often in your presence," she said softly.

He smiled back. "I am glad to have seen you again," he replied near her ear, causing her to shiver slightly as his breath caressed it.

"You will see me at dinner tonight, sir, at your home, even," she teased.

Darcy took her hand in his and brought it to his lips. "Soon to be our home, dearest," he whispered.

The sound of a throat clearing reminded them they were not alone. "We should join the others for tea. I do not doubt that my wife will have ordered it almost as soon as she arrived home," Gardiner said to the couple. "After tea, Mr Darcy, you may meet briefly with Lizzy to discuss the settlement unless you prefer to wait."

"Elizabeth, it is up to you if you would like to review it now or later. I would like you to review it before I present it to your father upon our return to Hertfordshire," he told her.

"I am not in need of refreshment, Uncle," Elizabeth said. "Might we stay here and begin?"

Gardiner looked between the pair before nodding. "I will leave the door open and will be back to check on you after I have had my own tea," he said. He left the room, leaving the door cracked open behind him.

Still standing, Darcy and Elizabeth quickly momentarily sought each other's embrace. "I have missed you, William. Your sister is charming, but I found myself wishing you could have accompanied us to the shops," she told him.

"It will not be long, my love," he told her. "Are you ready for dinner with my family tonight?"

"I already know your uncle, and your sister is precious. I like her so much, William," she enthused. "You are right – she is very shy – but between Kitty and me, we were able to draw her out considerably while we were shopping. Although I will say she is quite stubborn and, between her and my aunt, we ordered far more than I would have done on my own. Surely, William, I do not need so much. We are immediately going to Pemberley and will not even be in company very often."

He smiled at her and lightly kissed her. "I am glad that you like my sister, and she is correct that you need much more than you are used to having. Derbyshire is much colder than Hertfordshire and London, and there will be many things you need there you did not need before. Now, let us sit and review the settlement, which I am sure you will find reasons to object to as well." He sighed dramatically and laughed at the face she made as he led her to a settee in the corner of the room.

Once they were settled, he handed her the documents. She immediately began to read over the document and barely made it through the first page when she first looked up at him. "William," she began slowly, "exactly how wealthy are you?"

He laughed before answering, and the two spent the next half hour in a spirited conversation about the settlements, his wealth, his estates, and the partnership he envisioned with her once they married. When Mr Gardiner joined them, Elizabeth shared a few of the suggestions they had discussed regarding the marriage settlement. Her uncle agreed, and the three continued to discuss the marriage settlements and investments until it was time for Elizabeth to dress for dinner at Darcy House.

Darcy escorted Georgiana home much later than he intended and had to rush to dress. He encouraged Georgiana to take her time to prepare as he would greet their guests when they arrived.

As planned, the Gardiners arrived first. Kitty sat with Georgiana and Mrs Annesley in the drawing room while Darcy showed the rest around the principal rooms on the first floor. He saved the library for last, and Elizabeth was in love – if one could be in love with a room. The library was large and likely occupied as much space, if not more, than the ballroom on the floor above. "Elizabeth," she heard Darcy's amused voice call as she looked around the room.

"It is wonderful, William," she exulted, then her voice became teasing. "If I did not already love you, I think I could fall in love with you for this room alone."

"I am thankful you fell in love with me first, although, if I had known you would react this way, I would have brought you here much earlier in our courtship," he teased back.

She laughed, a sound he had come to adore. The Gardiners were out of sight for the moment, and he pulled her into his embrace. "I adore you, Elizabeth," he whispered, leaning down to lightly kiss her.

"And I, you, William," she replied quietly. "Your house is stunning – I wonder if I will be able to live up to the expectations of it."

"I assure you, dearest, the house has no expectations of you," he replied. "And as for me, you absolutely meet any expectation I may have ever had for my wife. You make me happier than I have ever been. Rest assured, there is no one else I have ever wanted for my wife. You exceeded all expectations."

She sighed against him. "Thank you, William, although I confess you may have to remind me of that occasionally."

A sound at the door caused them to draw apart, and the butler announced that Lord and Lady Matlock, the Earl and Countess of Matlock, and their son, Colonel Fitzwilliam, had arrived and were in the drawing room with Georgiana.

Darcy and Elizabeth, accompanied by the Gardiners, entered the drawing room. Introductions were made between those who were unfamiliar with each other. Lord Matlock greeted Gardiner and Elizabeth enthusiastically.

"Gardiner," Lord Matlock greeted the man. "I confess that I am rather surprised to find you here tonight. And Miss Bennet, I am pleased to see you here. I did not know you knew Darcy and Georgiana."

"I met Miss Bennet in Hertfordshire while visiting Bingley, Uncle," Darcy informed him. "And I must tell you, Miss

Elizabeth has also defeated me in a game of chess, although I have won a game or two since."

"Ahh, so you have discovered Miss Bennet's talent for chess," Lord Matlock retorted. "We have played a few times, but I believe I have a slight edge over her in wins."

Elizabeth protested. "We are tied, sir," she challenged. "If I am not mistaken, we have played six times and have won an equal number of games."

Lord Matlock laughed. "You may be right, my dear," he replied. "Now, Darcy, your note said you had news to share with us tonight. Will you share it now, or must we wait for it?"

Darcy grinned at the Earl's impatience which alerted the company, almost as much as Elizabeth's entering the room on his arm and remaining there, to the type of news he had to share. Raising his free hand to rest on Elizabeth's, he looked at his family and proclaimed his happy news. "Congratulate me, Uncle, I am engaged. I asked Miss Elizabeth to marry me last week, and she has accepted me. We intend to marry at the end of the month in Meryton. Will you come?"

The three Fitzwilliams looked at each other in surprise. The Colonel was the first to recover and stand and offer his congratulations to the pair. Lord and Lady Matlock stood a little more slowly and offered slightly tepid congratulations, concerned for the match Darcy had made. As the night progressed, they slowly warmed to the connection as they saw the genuine affection displayed between the couple.

Following dinner, when the gentlemen separated from the ladies, the Earl pulled Darcy to the side to ask for more details.

"Darcy, you have been away from London for barely a

month, and yet you return engaged, ready to marry within the month. Are you sure you truly want to marry this woman? She is not your equal in consequence or society," he said. "I am concerned that you are rushing this decision."

Darcy sighed and sought to reassure his uncle. "I assure you I know what I am about, sir. I love her, and she returns the sentiment. We are well-matched in every way that matters; we will be very happy together," he said earnestly. "We have courted almost since the moment we met, and I am certain about my choice. Be happy for me."

The Earl looked at him and nodded. "I will support you, Darcy. I do believe you could have done better, as far as money and connections are concerned, but I also know you likely have little need for more money. And you already despise most of society, so her not bringing any notable connections into the relationship matters little to you. I do know Gardiner well, and he is a very good man, and Miss Bennet is a lively, pleasant girl who will likely help you in society. I will speak to your aunt, and we will support her in society for you."

"Thank you, Uncle. I appreciate your support," Darcy said earnestly.

Soon, the gentlemen joined the ladies. They were all having a pleasant conversation, and Lady Matlock appeared to have been making an effort to get to know Elizabeth. Darcy went to sit next to Elizabeth and joined the conversation.

"Darcy, I have enjoyed getting to know Miss Bennet in the last hour. Will you bring her to my house for tea while you are in town?" she asked.

Looking at Elizabeth, he saw her slight nod. "Will the day after tomorrow work, Aunt?"

"That will be fine, Darcy," Lady Matlock replied, then she reached over and patted Elizabeth's hands. "I look forward to getting to know you better, dear."

"Thank you, my lady," Elizabeth replied. "I look forward to the same."

The group conversed another hour before the Gardiners felt it was time to depart. Darcy escorted them out, disappointed not to have the chance of saying a private goodbye to Elizabeth, but knew he would see her again in the morning. He was beyond ready to claim her as his wife so she did not have to leave him at night. With this thought, he returned to his family.

The Fitzwilliams were all waiting for him when he returned to the drawing room. Georgiana had retired when the Gardiners departed, and only they remained. "Darcy," the Colonel cried, "Your betrothed is a delightful creature. How on earth did you manage to win her?" Darcy scowled in reply to his cousin's teasing.

"Darcy," Lady Matlock drawled, ignoring her son's observations. "I confess that we are rather surprised to meet your betrothed here tonight; none of us were expecting such news. I have never heard of Miss Bennet before – will you tell us more about her?"

Again, he nodded. "I met Miss Bennet, Elizabeth, at an assembly on the very day I arrived at Netherfield. I was in an ill humour – between being forced to attend an assembly and Miss Bingley's presence – and Elizabeth was kind. I was no doubt as rude and boorish as I normally am at parties where I know no one, but she pushed right past that and offered me a small kindness. I found a way to be introduced to her and then asked her to dance. I enjoyed her conversation, and we even danced a second time that night. Since then, we have met nearly every day, and I have grown to know her well. And her family.

"Her father has been indolent up to this point, and something his youngest did has spurred him into action. We have spoken many hours about how he might increase the profits on the estate, and he seems to be set upon this purpose to improve not only his estate but his family."

"How did the engagement come to be, Darcy?" Lady Matlock pressed. "Does she have a dowry? Her connections include a tradesman and who else? Mr and Mrs Gardiner are very genteel, and I know, James, that you know them well, but does she have any other connections?"

Lord Matlock interrupted. "Darcy does not need a dowry, nor does he need more connections than he presently has. Miss Bennet has neither, but after watching them together, you must admit that she is ideal for him. It is rather obvious that they care for one another deeply."

Lady Matlock sighed but agreed with her husband's observations. "I take it you have spoken with him already?" she inquired.

"Yes, and I have pledged our support for the match," he replied to his wife. From there, the conversation drifted into several different topics and plans, including the wedding. After a while, the Fitzwilliams departed and returned to their own home.

The rest of the week saw this same group gathered several more times, both at Darcy House and Matlock House, as the Earl and Countess threw their support behind their nephew and his betrothed with a promise to attend the wedding.

137

At Longbourn, Jane and Mary were coming to know one another better in the absence of the rest of their sisters. Bennet's dictate that Mary read something other than Fordyce nearly a month ago had led to her being less pedantic and less prone to sermonising and made her conversation more bearable by her sisters. She and Jane had discovered common ground in the still room as Mary desired to learn more about the use of herbs and flowers for healing. Mary had begun visiting Longbourn's tenants with Elizabeth and Jane and was now learning from Jane how to provide greater assistance to them.

Bingley visited almost every day during Darcy's absence, although with Bennet gone and Mrs Bennet confined to her room, the visits were naturally brief. Most often, Bingley immediately suggested they move into the gardens as the weather was still mild, and they walked together with Mary keeping a watch over them. Jane had come to like the gentleman very well but wondered what his intentions toward her might be. Mr Darcy had been in the neighbourhood the same length of time and had already proposed to Lizzy; they were to marry before the end of the month. She began to wonder if Mr Bingley was actually interested in her or if he was just occupying himself while he was alone at Netherfield. Jane spent a considerable amount of time pondering this while her sister was gone and there were fewer visitors at Longbourn.

When Bennet returned a few days later, he was surprised to find his two daughters were speaking about the relative merits of different herbal concoctions used for healing.

Rarely had he heard Mary speak so sensibly, and he was pleased with the change. Calling Mary into his book room, he began to quiz her on the books she had read in his absence. Although he had intended to begin instructing her sooner, all he had done before he left was take away Fordyce and suggest a handful of books to read. She had read them all and then had asked Lizzy for additional recommendations. He was pleasantly surprised at the change wrought in her with such little effort and quickly realised that had he made this effort sooner, he would have seen far more sense in Longbourn much sooner. As he had frequently in the last month, he felt heartily ashamed of himself and was determined to be a better father. Being a better husband seemed like the more difficult task, and he was uncertain how to even begin to approach that task.

Fourteen

Mr Collins Comes and Goes

Eight days after they had left Longbourn, Elizabeth and Mr Darcy returned, accompanied by Kitty, Georgiana, and Mrs Annesley. Elizabeth had enjoyed her time in London and was happy that her soon-to-be sister had joined them. She genuinely liked Georgiana Darcy, and Kitty and Georgiana had become fast friends. Since the day they met, the two girls had spent many hours together and found they had a number of things in common, including art, and they were loath to be parted. The engagement of Elizabeth and Darcy worked in the favour of both girls since it meant that they would be able to spend a significant amount of time together.

Mrs Gardiner had taken Elizabeth and Kitty shopping nearly every morning they were in London, and Georgiana had joined them frequently for these expeditions. Georgiana had introduced Elizabeth in many of the shops where she had accounts, and they purchased many items for Elizabeth's trousseau. Having spent time in Derbyshire, Mrs Gardiner was also aware of what Elizabeth would need for life in that district and so took Elizabeth to purchase warmer outerwear than she needed in Hertfordshire. Georgiana purchased a beautiful fur-lined cape for Elizabeth as a wedding gift.

Darcy had also taken Elizabeth to tea at Matlock House twice during the trip. The first time, the three had chatted about their mutual interests, but on the second visit, Lady Matlock had sent Darcy to visit with his uncle and cousin while she spoke to Elizabeth alone. This conversation had begun more awkwardly, with the countess quizzing Elizabeth about her accomplishments and her education, but slowly Elizabeth had won the lady's favour. The countess had been impressed by Elizabeth's wit and her ability to respond to her challenges. The entire conversation was meant to be a challenge, to see how Elizabeth would respond when faced with the tabbies of the *ton,* and she had been impressed with Elizabeth's performance. When Darcy was finally allowed to return, the countess had given her full support and approval for the match and was already making plans to introduce her into society in the spring. Elizabeth had felt pleased to have won this favour for herself, and Darcy was proud of her for doing so.

For Elizabeth, the highlight of the London trip had been the trip to the theatre on one of their last nights in that city. Accompanied by his relatives and hers, Darcy and Elizabeth had appeared together at Covent Garden for a performance of *Much Ado About Nothing.* Georgiana and Kitty had opted to stay together at Darcy House with Mrs Annesley for company, and the rest of the party joined them for a late supper after the play.

Darcy confessed to Elizabeth when he had arrived at the Gardiner home that night to escort them to the theatre that he had reread the play in preparation to watch it and that he often felt as Benedick did when he was with her. When she had asked why, he had replied that there was one particular line from the play that constantly ran through his mind since they had met. He would not tell her which line and begged her to guess after she had watched the play.

Throughout the play, Darcy and Elizabeth had held hands in the darkness of his theatre box. Their chaperones were likely conscious of this liberty but chose to ignore the relatively harmless gesture of their obvious affection for one another. In the last scene of the play, when Benedick spoke his line to Beatrice – "Peace! I will stop your mouth" – and then kissed her, Elizabeth grinned and squeezed his hand. He leaned into her slightly and whispered, "Every time you tease me, dearest."

She replied with an arched eyebrow. "So you think only to quiet me when I tease? Should I desist, sir?"

He had struggled not to laugh out loud as the play ended and the lights were raised. "Never, my Elizabeth," he whispered into her ear and then helped her to rise as a blush warmed her face. "I love your teases. No one has teased me before you, my love, and I find it addicting."

Elizabeth smiled gently at him and raised her hand toward him, thinking instinctively to caress his cheek. However, she became aware of the action and the audience and stopped, although he noticed it and smiled softly at her in response. Likewise conscious of the audience, he simply looked down at her affectionately before mouthing, "I love you."

Her own expression grew softer, and taking his arm, she squeezed it before he laid his free hand on top of hers, entwining their fingers for a moment before they made their way back out of the theatre. Darcy stiffened immediately upon seeing the attention on them when they exited the box. It had been the same when they had entered the theatre at the beginning of the night, and Elizabeth sought to reassure him somehow. When they had entered, Elizabeth had watched the transformation and worried about it but had inquired what wrought the change.

"I do not care for the attention, and the gossips are taking note of my attendance here with a stunningly beautiful woman on my arm. While I often attend the theatre, I rarely attend in the company of a woman other than my aunt or my sister. The fact that you are unknown makes the attention that much greater," he had told her. "Miss Bingley has attempted to take my arm before when I have invited Bingley to accompany me, but I have always managed to avoid her entering with me. She was a clinging vine when we would appear together in public, difficult to shake off, but I did what I could to avoid her presence and to prevent rumours from being spread about my connection to her."

"Whatever happened to Miss Bingley?" she asked then. "After the assembly, I do not think I ever really heard much about her other than she went to stay with an aunt."

Darcy scowled. "Ask me later, dearest," he replied. "It is not a story to share in such a public place."

She frowned at that. "I must say, that answer worries me, William," she answered.

"Do not be worried, Elizabeth," he said. "It was serious but did no lasting harm other than to firmly cement my dislike for her and further my desire to never again be in her company."

She arched her eyebrow at him and dropped the subject. The conversation had the impact she had desired – he was no longer stiff, but he did not have the pleased expression on his face that she would have liked to have seen.

As they made their way from the theatre, Elizabeth decided to tease him this time to see if she could coax a smile or even a laugh out of him as they made their way from the theatre.

"My sister is most anxious that we marry, sir," she began. "Since meeting your sister, I think that Kitty is even more excited about our wedding than you or me."

He barked a sharp laugh. "I cannot imagine anyone being more excited about our wedding than me, dearest Elizabeth," he replied, gazing at her wolfishly. "I find I am most anxious to claim you as my wife, and these next three weeks will feel interminably long."

She succeeded in making him smile and laugh, but she had not meant for his reaction to her tease to make her blush quite so violently. As they exited the theatre, she was very grateful for the cold air to cool her rapidly heating cheeks.

When the performance was done, the group made their way to Darcy House for a late supper, and Darcy managed to get Elizabeth alone for a few minutes by asking Gardiner for permission to show her something in the library. Permission was granted, provided the door remained open. Darcy showed her into the room, nearly shutting the door but leaving it cracked slightly before wrapping his arms around her and kissing her passionately.

"You, my love, are entirely too tempting and far too teasing. I foresee needing to employ Benedict's words and actions with you frequently once we are wed," he said before his lips crashed onto hers. When he released her several minutes later, both were nearly gasping for breath. As soon as he was able, he whispered into her ear, "I love you so much, Elizabeth. I cannot wait to make you mine. And no, Kitty cannot possibly be more excited about our wedding than me, and I hope you are equally looking forward to the event."

He wrapped her in his arms and kissed her again before finally handing her a book he had set aside for her earlier and then escorting her back to the family.

* * *

Elizabeth considered the trip and all that had been accomplished. Her wedding dress had been finished and was packed in her trunks, along with a ball gown for the ball to be held at Netherfield two nights before the wedding. Kitty also had a new gown, although it reflected her new status as not out, and the other dresses and items would be delivered to Darcy House in the weeks before the wedding. Mrs Gardiner had arranged for this to occur quietly without drawing unnecessary attention to the deliveries.

There was just over a fortnight remaining before the wedding, and, as yet, Mrs Bennet was still unaware of the imminent wedding in the family. Elizabeth still needed to speak to both her father and Jane about how they should inform her of the plans and intended to do so immediately upon arriving at Longbourn.

Darcy delivered Elizabeth and Kitty to Longbourn on a Tuesday two weeks before the ball was to be held. Bingley had visited that morning and introduced his maiden aunt, Miss Henrietta Bingley, to Jane, Mary, and Mr Bennet. Mr

Collins, a distant cousin of the Bennets, the heir presumptive to Longbourn upon Mr Bennet's death, was also in residence and was introduced to Bingley and his aunt. The Bingleys delivered the invitation to the ball, and Bingley requested the first set of the night from Jane. Jane was pleased to be singled out to open the ball with Mr Bingley, and she happily granted him the first set.

Since they were engaged, Darcy and Elizabeth had already discussed the dances they would share at the ball. They would dance the first, supper, and last sets, although Darcy had pled for more. He had reserved the second and third sets with Georgiana and Kitty, respectively and had reluctantly agreed to partner with others.

Upon entering Longbourn, Elizabeth and Darcy were surprised at the presence of a rector if his mode of dress was to be trusted. They began the introductions, but before Darcy's name could be completed, the man bowed low, nearly to the ground, and began to speak. "Mr Darcy, Mr Darcy," he nearly yelled in his eagerness. "I am William Collins, and I hold the living at Hunsford by Rosings. Your aunt, the noble Lady Catherine de Bourgh, is my patroness, and I am pleased to be able to tell you that I left her in very good health when I visited her yesterday. I am honoured by her patronage and her condescension in offering her advice. In fact, it is at her recommendation that I am here. She suggested I come to Longbourn to apologise for the entail that will leave Longbourn to me upon the sad day that my cousin passes from this world. I hope to make amends to my dear cousins by marrying one of them so they will not be forced from their home on the unfortunate day my cousin dies.

"I am amazed and honoured that someone of your conse-

146

quence would deign to visit my future home. Lady Catherine speaks so well of you and of the plans to connect Rosings and Pemberley through your marriage to her daughter."

Darcy, and all those in the room, were taken aback by this gush of words as the man continued to speak, especially when considering how incredibly insensitive and inappropriate his statements were. Uncertain how to respond, Darcy looked over at Elizabeth to see her reaction, and she looked at him, equally offended and aggravated by the man's words.

"Mr Collins," Darcy said sternly, interrupting the flow of words. "I cannot imagine that my aunt would approve of her rector gossiping so rudely and offensively as you have just done. You interrupted Mr Bennet as he was attempting to make introductions which would have explained why I am here. Not to mention you are spreading falsehoods about an imaginary engagement that neither party has ever desired." Darcy paused briefly to glance at his host. "Mr Bennet, perhaps you would like to finish your introductions so I might make mine? Collins, can you be silent long enough to permit him to do so?"

Bennet began the introductions over as Collins stood gaping at Darcy, unsure how to respond. He could not contradict such a personage as Mr Darcy, but he had contradicted Lady Catherine. Both could not be wrong, but for one to be right meant the other must be wrong. Lady Catherine could not be wrong, could she, Collins wondered, not listening to the introductions, thereby missing hearing of the engagement between Darcy and Elizabeth.

Darcy introduced his sister to those who had not travelled with them, and the group all took seats around the room. Collins moved toward where Darcy and Elizabeth sat and attempted to squeeze in between the couple.

"I say, Mr Collins, there is not enough room on this settee for three. Perhaps you had best sit over there," Elizabeth said, indicating a chair several feet away that was empty.

"Mr Darcy, perhaps you might move to another seat so that I might sit next to my cousin?" Collins requested.

"No," was all the reply Darcy gave, fixing the rector with a hard look.

Collins unhappily moved to the indicated chair, moving it closer to where Elizabeth sat and began to try to engage her in conversation, although his idea of engaging her in conversation was to speak incessantly of his patroness and his situation at his parsonage in Hunsford. Elizabeth listened patiently for a time before she interrupted and asked her father a question. "Papa," she began as Collins was speaking of Lady Catherine's suggestion to install shelves in the closets, "Mr Darcy has with him some papers for you to sign. Might we go to your study to review them?"

At Bennet's nod, the three stood and exited the room. Collins attempted to follow, but Bennet insisted he stay where he was.

"Papa, what is that man doing here?" she asked as soon as they were in the hallway.

"Exactly as he said," Bennet replied. "He has come to 'heal the breach' between our families and to look for a wife. All at the orders of your aunt, Mr Darcy. Since arriving yesterday, he has regaled us all with stories of his patroness." He nodded toward Darcy as he spoke.

"My aunt loves to share her 'expert' advice on all subjects. I am not, nor have I ever been, engaged to my cousin Anne. My aunt never mentioned that idea until after my father passed away, and I told her then, and have repeated it many times since, that I will not marry my cousin. My mother did not make any such arrangement, and my aunt has likely taken an idle comment and has been attempting to force her wishes on myself and my cousin. Anne does not wish to marry at all as her health has always been indifferent," Darcy explained.

"I was not worried, William, we have discussed this before," Elizabeth said, squeezing his hand.

He smiled at her before turning to her father to begin speaking. "I have the marriage articles with me ready for you to review, and I did acquire a special licence while I was in town," he told Bennet. "We can make any changes you feel are necessary, but it is rather comprehensive. I modelled it after my mother's settlement.

Bennet began to read the document while Elizabeth and Darcy quietly spoke. After a few minutes, Bennet signed all three copies of the document and handed them back to Darcy. "You have made arrangements for every contingency, sir; I am impressed at how complete this is. You will do well by my daughter. Now, let us join the others. We must begin to plan a wedding, and I suppose my wife will have to be told."

Elizabeth rolled her eyes. "How long will Mr Collins be our guest, Papa?"

"A fortnight, my dear," he replied. "He was disappointed that Bingley asked Jane for the first set when he arrived to bring the invitation, and I dare say he was not paying attention when I informed him the two of you were engaged. He is after a wife, and I am afraid Mary will not satisfy his vanity since you are engaged, and Jane has a suitor."

Elizabeth grimaced. "Can he or your aunt do anything to delay or prevent our wedding?" she asked.

"No, Elizabeth, my aunt can bluster but cannot actually do anything to prevent it," Darcy reassured her. "My uncle was the one who suggested I procure a special licence and aided me in obtaining it. They will be here the Monday before the wedding, and my uncle will prevent my aunt from doing anything."

"That is good to know, William," Elizabeth replied. "Let us go rescue the others from Mr Collins now. Is there any way we can send him back to Kent by saying we have too much to do to entertain him right now? Why did you not mention his visit before, Papa?"

"I received his letter announcing his intention to visit upon my return," Bennet answered. "There was not enough time to reply to him to let him know how inconvenient his visit was."

"That was inconsiderate of him, but based on what I have seen, I doubt he is able to comprehend that," Darcy replied dryly.

Bennet and Elizabeth laughed wryly at this as they all left the study and returned to the drawing room. Collins immediately approached Elizabeth when they returned and tried to draw her away from Darcy, whose arm she held.

"Cousin Elizabeth," said he, "it is inappropriate for you to be clinging onto Mr Darcy like that. He is an engaged man." He took her arm and attempted to pull her toward him. "Come, sit by me, cousin."

"Mr Collins, please desist from touching me," Elizabeth replied. "I am well aware that Mr Darcy is engaged, but since he is engaged to me, I believe that it is entirely appropriate for me to hold his arm."

"You cannot be engaged to Mr Darcy, Cousin," the man

cried out. "Lady Catherine has told me her nephew is engaged to her daughter. She and her sister, Mr Darcy's mother, planned for the union while the two were in their cradles. He cannot possibly be engaged to you."

Mr Darcy stepped toward Mr Collins, moving Elizabeth so she was slightly behind him. "Mr Collins, I told you earlier that I was not engaged to my cousin. Neither she nor I wish for it, and two sisters mentioning that it *might* be nice if their children grew up and married each other does not betroth the couple. No amount of wishing it to be true on my aunt's part will make it so, and I *am* happily and willingly engaged to Miss Elizabeth. She is my choice – the marriage contracts have been signed, and the licence purchased. My uncle, the Earl, is aware of my choice and heartily approves of her, and he and his wife will help introduce her into society in the coming season. My aunt's wishes do not weigh in my choice, and you will stop spreading lies to the contrary."

"But, Mr Bennet," Collins spluttered. "I came here to find a wife! I understood you had five daughters, but when I arrived, only two were present. One was away at school, and two others were in London. Now I find one is being courted, one is engaged to my patroness' nephew – which she will not let stand – and the other two are too plain or too young to marry. What is the meaning of this?"

"Mr Collins," Bennet began, his anger simmering, "you wrote to invite yourself here. You were not invited to Longbourn, and you have not been invited to take your pick of my daughters. I do not know who told you about my daughters, but the mere fact that I have five does not entitle you to one. You are not obligated to marry one of my daughters, and I would frankly be surprised if any of them

151

would have you after that speech. I believe it is in everyone's best interest if you depart from Longbourn today instead of staying the fortnight you had intended. Had you allowed me the privilege of responding to your request to visit, I would have informed you that now was a poor time for your visit. I will send a servant up right away to pack your things and will ask that a wagon be prepared to take you to the post station in town. If you hurry, you should be able to catch the post to London this afternoon." With that, Bennet rang for the housekeeper, who tasked a footman with packing for Collins and another to summon a wagon. Within half an hour, the rector was on his way, angry at the "mistreatment" he had received from his cousins and making threats about throwing anyone with the surname Bennet out of *his* house as soon as his cousin died.

All sighed in relief when he was gone, although Darcy felt the tiniest bit of worry in the back of his mind about what would happen once the man arrived in Kent. He determined he should write and send two messages by express riders, which he wrote in Bennet's study with Elizabeth sitting next to him. The first was to his uncle to inform him of the day's events related to his aunt's rector, and the second was to his aunt to inform her of his engagement. Two riders were engaged to deliver the messages and, with luck, Darcy's message would beat Mr Collins in delivering the news to Rosings.

Fifteen

Dealing with Wickham

I t was not until the next morning that the question of the wedding was finally addressed. Darcy and Elizabeth met once again at the top of Oakham Mount with Kitty and Georgiana in tow. The two girls chatted as Kitty was attempting a landscape of the view from that spot while Darcy and Elizabeth wandered off. Taking advantage of the inattention of the two girls, they found a place to exchange a few mostly-chaste kisses as they talked about what they both wanted from the wedding and the wedding breakfast. With their plans decided, they all returned to their separate homes until they would meet again at Longbourn later that morning.

Upon arriving back at Longbourn, Mr Bennet called for Mrs Bennet to join him in his study for a time. The companion had arrived the previous afternoon, and her first task would be to help her charge with planning a wedding breakfast in line with the wishes of the bride and groom.

"Mrs Bennet," Bennet began when she entered, "we have had many conversations about some of the changes that we will be undertaking. As you are aware, the companion who will assist you and our youngest daughters arrived yesterday afternoon. Lydia is at school and will not need her for now, but she will assist you, Mary, and Kitty gain a better understanding of the rules of propriety that govern our lives. For the next fortnight, she will be primarily assisting you. Just before I left to take Lydia to school, Mr Darcy proposed to Elizabeth. They will be married on November 28, two days after the ball at Netherfield. This ball is being given largely in their honour, although that is not the stated purpose. Tomorrow, Miss Bingley, the aunt of Mr Bingley, will pay you a call to speak about the ball and what may be needed from us to assist in the planning."

Mrs Bennet caught up with what Mr Bennet was saying. "Lizzy will wed Mr Darcy in a fortnight? Mr Bennet that is impossible. We cannot possibly arrange an appropriate wedding to a man of his stature in that amount of time," she cried while waving her handkerchief around her face in anxious fluttering.

"Enough, Mrs Bennet," Bennet stated calmly but decisively. "If you want to be involved in the planning, you will listen to me; otherwise, Jane and Elizabeth are entirely prepared to take on the responsibility of making the plans for themselves. Elizabeth and Darcy both prefer a small and simple ceremony and breakfast and do not want to wait months and months on fripperies and other such nonsense. They have discussed what they would like and what they are comfortable with for their wedding day, and that is the wedding they will have.

154

Do you understand?"

"No, I do not, sir," she said petulantly. "It is a mother's right to plan her daughter's wedding. It does not matter what she wants."

"But it does, and she and the groom are in agreement about this. Neither wants a large wedding nor do they want to wait months to wed. Darcy prefers to return to his estate before winter makes travel too difficult. They will marry on the date I have said, and, again, if you do not want to help with the planning, you may return to your room and to your lessons in comportment along with your daughters. If you ever wish to leave your rooms again and rejoin the company of your friends and neighbours, then you will listen to me and adjust your behaviour to what is suitable. If you cannot, then I will find a place for you to live where you will not be able to influence our daughters any further. I have lived with you for more than twenty years and done little to correct your poor behaviour, but now that I have seen my error, I am doing what I can to remedy it.

"You can choose to continue to behave as you always have and be exiled, or you can attempt to correct your behaviour and learn to behave as a gentlewoman. If you wish to go downstairs this morning to sit with Lizzy and her betrothed and discuss their plans for their wedding, you may, but there will be no mention of his wealth, carriages, pin money, or clothes. When Lizzy went to London last week, she went shopping with Mrs Gardiner and Mr Darcy's sister, and her trousseau has already been ordered."

"How can she have ordered her trousseau without me, for she does not know the best warehouses?" Mrs Bennet cried. "You have used me very ill, not telling me of our daughter's betrothal and of her going to London to purchase her trousseau. And how is it that Lizzy is to marry before Jane? Jane is ever so much more beautiful — she should have the wealthier suitor ....."

"Mrs Bennet," Bennet nearly shouted at his wife, stopping her before she could continue in that vein. "We have discussed this before. I see that you have no wish to help your daughter plan her wedding today. Remain in your room, and I will bring Mrs Higgins up to speak with you later this morning. Perhaps she will be able to persuade you to see sense."

With that, Bennet instructed Mrs Bennet to remain in his study and left the room, resisting the urge to slam the door behind him. He summoned the housekeeper to escort Mrs Bennet to her own rooms.

* * *

Several hours later, Darcy and Elizabeth walked to the Longbourn church to speak to the rector there to arrange their wedding. They had confirmed the date was free before leaving for London, but now that they had the licence and the wedding settlements completed, they were able to make more specific plans with the rector – deciding that they would marry at ten in the morning on Thursday, November 28.

After leaving the church, Elizabeth and Darcy walked into town accompanied by Georgiana, Kitty, Jane, and Bingley, who had called at Longbourn while Darcy was at the church. Mary had elected to stay behind with Mr Bennet to discuss their latest book.

The group walked in pairs: Kitty and Georgiana in the

front, followed by Jane and Bingley walking next to each other, and Elizabeth and Darcy lagging slightly behind the others. Their engagement was still not widely known, although many of those in Meryton had watched this courtship and anticipated it. The purpose of this visit to Meryton was to make the engagement public so the date of the wedding would not catch any off guard and avoid gossip that anything improper had occurred to force the marriage.

Darcy did take advantage of their slower steps as they walked into town, imitating his actions on the day they walked into town following his proposal. He pulled Elizabeth behind a tree, sheltering her from sight, and leaned in to kiss her. Their kisses were no longer hesitant, and she was a willing participant, having learned how to respond to his caress. Once again, they parted from each other breathlessly, and Elizabeth found it more and more difficult to stop when he kissed her in that way. She had a vague idea of what would follow, and her aunt had promised to speak with her before the wedding. Darcy pulled her back onto the path, distracting Elizabeth from her musings when he propelled her toward the village once again.

When they arrived in Meryton, they caught up with the rest of their party and were startled when Georgiana and Kitty stopped suddenly. Darcy heard his name whispered by his sister and caught the note of panic in her voice. He looked first at her and then to where she was looking and froze just as she had.

"Wickham," he muttered heatedly under his breath. He began to walk forward, but Elizabeth firmly grasped his arm.

"I do not mean to delay you, sir, but should we be worried? Should we return home?" Elizabeth whispered to him.

157

He stopped as abruptly as he had started and drew a deep breath. "Georgie, come here," he commanded, then placed a hand over Elizabeth's. "There is no real danger, dearest, not in public, but do you remember how I told you of my sister's heartbreak?" Seeing her nod, he continued. "The man standing over there is the reason for her heartbreak. I have more I need to tell you, but not here. Let us shop as we intended, but Georgie, Elizabeth, please remain very close to me until we return to Longbourn."

Both Georgiana and Elizabeth nodded at him, and, each taking an arm, the group continued on. Bingley, who was vaguely aware of Wickham's reputation, extended his arms for Jane and Kitty to take. Entering the milliner's shop first, they procured several ribbons to be utilised in Elizabeth's bouquet and decorating the church. This purpose was shared with the proprietor, Mrs Harris, a well-known gossip, who would ensure all of Meryton was aware of the engagement and the plans for the wedding before the day was out.

After the milliner, they went to the bookshop to peruse the shelves to see if there was anything new or that caught their attention. Darcy found a first edition he had been looking to acquire and bought each of the ladies a book. Georgiana and Kitty also selected some sheet music which Darcy also purchased. They visited the seamstress to order new ball gowns for Jane and Mary and promised to send the fabric they had obtained in London the next morning. Elizabeth had selected a fabric especially for Mary that would complement her sister, unlike the rather drab dresses she generally chose for herself. She intended Mary's dress to be a surprise and hoped to encourage her to dress her hair differently for the ball as well as to highlight Mary's many good qualities. Mrs Hudson had been making the Bennet ladies' dresses and gowns for years and did not need to take measurements.

While waiting for the order for the ball gowns to be settled, Darcy purchased a pale green silk shawl for Elizabeth that he observed complemented her very well. He had not seen her ball gown, but Elizabeth immediately recognized that it suited her ball gown very well and thanked him for his thoughtfulness. His purchase of a shawl for Elizabeth and their interactions also indicated the state of their relationship. This action was noted by several in the shop.

They visited a few other stores in town, including the cobbler and the tailor, although the ladies did not enter there. Instead, the ladies were safely occupied acquiring fabric for handkerchiefs and embroidery thread as Elizabeth intended to embroider a few handkerchiefs for Darcy as a wedding gift and was toying with decorating them with the sweet William flower. She wondered if he would carry a handkerchief decorated in such a way, then decided to make a few with the flowers and a few others with his initials. She had noted that his handkerchiefs all appeared rather plain and wondered if that was because Georgiana had not thought of embroidering them for him.

Their final stop was the small tea shop in the centre of the high street. The six of them sat between two tables, Darcy with his sister and Elizabeth at one table and Bingley, Kitty, and Jane at the other. These groupings caught the attention of the other patrons of the tea shop, and they heard whispers about the relationship between Jane and Bingley. Everyone knew he regularly called at Longbourn and, as there had been no news of any formal understanding between them, speculation was running rampant in the small town.

As they returned to Longbourn, the group paired off as they had on the way into Meryton. Darcy again lagged behind with Elizabeth and spoke quietly as soon as he could do so without being overheard. "Elizabeth, I know I briefly mentioned that Georgiana had been heartbroken, but it was more than that. The man we saw back there is George Wickham, and he preyed upon Georgiana. He pretended to be in love with her and convinced her to elope with him this summer. I arrived in time to put a stop to it and demanded he depart and never speak to us again. I threatened him with debtor's prison if he mentions my sister's name or does anything to harm her or her reputation. I hold a significant number of his debts – enough to imprison him for the rest of his days," he explained, then sighed deeply. "Georgiana reacted better to seeing him than I would have imagined. I did mention to a few of the shopkeepers that not all militia members are responsible about paying their debts. That may not have been his purpose in coming here, but since he was standing with a militia member, I felt that it would be prudent to warn them regardless."

"Is he a threat in other ways?" Elizabeth asked quietly.

"He is; it would be best if we speak to your father, and he can warn others to guard their daughters while the militia is in the area," Darcy replied gravely. "He is not the only one; my cousin has told me far too many stories of how militia units have wreaked havoc on areas where they are encamped."

Elizabeth grimaced. "I am thankful Lydia has been sent to school," she replied, equally grave. "She would have likely viewed the militia coming as an opportunity to flirt with the officers or worse. Kitty would have followed Lydia's example and would have acted similarly; Georgiana has been a good influence on her. I think both have benefited greatly from their friendship."

"They have done well together," Darcy agreed. "I think Kitty will greatly enjoy spending time with us in Derbyshire, and we will not have to worry about leaving Georgiana alone once we are wed."

"Returning to our original topic: did Mr Wickham see you in Meryton? Will all the gossip about our wedding force him to leave or encourage him to stay?" Elizabeth wondered.

"I do not know," he replied, sighing. "I will send someone to inquire of Colonel Forester to see if he has enlisted. If he has, I will send an express to Richard. He will be very interested to know where Wickham is regardless." He paused for a moment as if considering. "Dearest, I must ask you to cease rambling alone. I greatly relish our time together at Oakham Mount, and I am thankful Kitty has joined you on your walks to meet me in the morning, but if Wickham is aware that I am in Meryton and learns we are betrothed, it is likely he will attempt to injure me by injuring you in some way. That was his motivation behind trying to abscond with Georgiana, well, that and obtaining her dowry for himself. "

Elizabeth gazed into his eyes before reaching up to caress his cheek. "We have a fortnight remaining until we wed, William. I will stay indoors unless you are with me and forgo my walks for the present."

He brought her hands to his lips for a kiss. "Thank you, dearest. I cannot imagine what I would do if something happened to you. I love you so dearly."

"I love you as well, William," she replied gently, then her expression became arch. "I would not forgo my walks for any other reason than that."

Darcy laughed as she had intended. Upon arriving at Long-bourn, Darcy went directly to Bennet's study to warn him of the dangers of Wickham's presence in the neighbourhood and to relate a general warning about the militia based on what his cousin had said in the past. After several minutes of conversation, they left the study and joined the others in the drawing room where tea had just arrived.

Jane poured the tea while the other Bennet ladies helped to serve and when everyone was settled, Darcy warned the ladies to be careful around the militia officers and mentioned his acquaintance with Mr Wickham in particular. A servant was sent to Meryton to ascertain that Wickham had enlisted, and a letter had already been written to Colonel Fitzwilliam. If Wickham had enlisted, a rider would be dispatched to London with the note. With luck, Richard would arrive the following day and help resolve the Wickham issue. Since the incident in Ramsgate, Richard had wanted to find Wickham and mete out a punishment for the injury to his ward, and if Wickham had joined the militia, this would be the perfect opportunity for a reckoning.

After this general conversation, those present separated into smaller groups. Darcy and Elizabeth spoke quietly together of their plans for after the wedding – a brief wedding trip to London followed by the long journey to Pemberley, arriving no later than the fifteenth of the month. The Matlocks intended to arrive at Pemberley with Georgiana and Kitty by December twenty-second and would celebrate Christmas with them.

Jane and Bingley chatted together, their conversation mostly superficial. Jane often looked over at her sister and

162

her betrothed and wondered what was different about their relationship and why she and Mr Bingley could not get past the superficial. She was determined to ask Lizzy that night what topics she and Mr Darcy discussed and how she might persuade Charles to explore deeper topics together, allowing them to get to know each other better.

Mary, Kitty, and Georgiana eventually moved into the music room. Kitty expressed an interest in learning to play the pianoforte, and Mary and Georgiana were eager to share their knowledge with her. Mary had become less ponderous in her musical choices since her family was paying her more attention, although she admitted that part of the problem had been an unwillingness on her own part. She had begun to practise more with Lizzy and, taking her advice, had sought to add emotion to her playing, which made her playing more pleasing to those who listened to her. Mary and Georgiana began to teach Kitty some rudimentary skills on the instrument. Neither Mary nor Lizzy had ever had a true piano master, only having had some rather disjointed lessons from several women in the area, and Mary found she was learning from Georgiana as they introduced Kitty to the pianoforte.

Bennet retired to his book room to review his accounting books while the rest of the family was occupied. When the servant returned with the information from Colonel Forester that Wickham had indeed joined the militia, Bennet immediately sent the rider to London with the note Darcy had written earlier and then went back into the drawing room to inform Darcy. Darcy immediately tensed and spoke further to Bennet and Elizabeth about the potential for harm with Wickham nearby. After some time, Elizabeth suggested the group join the girls in the music room for some entertainment as she hoped to draw Darcy's attention away from his fear and frustration over Wickham.

Her gambit was moderately successful, although she noted that Darcy still lapsed into brief periods of introspection as the evening progressed. The Darcys and Mr Bingley remained for dinner with the family and finally returned to Netherfield late that evening.

* * *

Darcy rode to Longbourn early the following morning. An express from Richard had arrived just as the sun rose, stating his intention to arrive not long after the message. With that in mind, Darcy requested Bennet's permission for the ladies to join the party at Netherfield for the day as they developed plans to deal with Wickham. The ladies, other than Elizabeth, could help Miss Henrietta Bingley as she prepared for the ball. Bennet accepted the invitation, including himself in the party, and agreed the family would arrive mid-morning.

Elizabeth, who had yet to meet this new Miss Bingley, was rather looking forward to making her acquaintance, as Darcy had only positive things to say about his friend's aunt. She had been described as a rather outspoken lady, similar to Caroline Bingley in some ways but kinder and without the pretensions of her niece. Darcy had always liked her, and Elizabeth was predisposed to like her as well.

When the two ladies were introduced, they quickly found common ground despite their disparate interests. Miss Bingley had little use for books and walking but had an openness and a directness that Elizabeth appreciated and a broad knowledge of the world. She had remained unmarried by choice, not for lack of opportunity, and had travelled extensively in England and Ireland and had visited the Continent when she was younger. Elizabeth enjoyed the stories of her travels and excused herself to join the gentlemen to discuss Wickham with a small measure of reluctance.

Richard arrived after the ladies had been at Netherfield for nearly an hour and was introduced to Mr Bennet, Jane, and Mary. After greetings were exchanged, he made to exit the room. "Darcy, we have things we need to discuss," he began darkly. "Is there a room we might use, Bingley?"

Darcy answered, having already discussed this with Bingley. "I have already asked Bingley about using the library for our conversation. Mr Bennet, Elizabeth, will you join us for this discussion."

Richard and Bennet both raised their eyebrows at Elizabeth's inclusion in their discussion, but Darcy was insistent. "Elizabeth is aware of all the particulars, and I want her to join us for our discussion. You will merely have to temper your words, cousin." With little more than a shrug, Richard agreed, and Darcy helped Elizabeth to stand and lead her to join the others in leaving the room.

As soon as they were in the library, Richard offered his suggestion. "If you had let me run him through this summer, we would not even have a need for a conversation about the reprobate, Darcy. I always said you were too soft on Wickham. Your loyalty toward him has been misplaced, and regardless of how much your father loved him, you have protected him far more than he deserved. You have paid out hundreds of pounds to cover his debts, and although you say it was to protect your father's memory, it has just made him believe he will get away with anything."

"He left town this summer before anything could be done, Richard, as you should remember, but I still believe your solution is questionable at best," Darcy replied. "I have done little for him since he refused the living at Kympton, other than pay the debts in Ramsgate that he ran up in my name. I have refused every other request he has made."

"I agree with William, Colonel," Elizabeth interjected. "Granted, I am not an officer, but I would say few problems are truly resolved by 'running someone through' with a sword."

Richard grudgingly admitted they were likely correct, despite that being his overwhelming desire. "It could be a training 'accident,'" Richard suggested. "As an officer in the militia, he is obligated to follow any order given by a superior officer or face punishment for insubordination. I am certain I could find a way to make his death appear as an accident."

"Richard," Darcy barked at the same time as Elizabeth gasped, "Colonel!"

Darcy allowed Elizabeth to speak first. "I cannot imagine that murdering the man is an option whatsoever. Because what you are suggesting is nothing less. Can we not try to find a workable solution that does not risk you losing your life or facing murder charges?"

Richard grumbled but agreed. Darcy then shared how Wickham had amassed significant debts in both Lambton and Ramsgate, for which Darcy had paid. Richard brought with him the receipts held in Darcy's study in London, and the amount owed was enough to put him in debtors' prison for the rest of his life. Before Ramsgate, Darcy had been reluctant to take that step, although that had been his intention before

Wickham disappeared from the seaside town.

With Wickham in the militia, they might have a way to get rid of him permanently and legally. The militia had strict rules, although not always enforced, about the character of officers, and a man with as much debt as Wickham should not qualify to be an officer, Richard explained. "If Darcy or I present these receipts to Colonel Forester, Wickham could be expelled from the militia and thrown directly into debtors' prison," he told the group.

"Would exile be an option?" Elizabeth asked. "Could he be given the option of debtors' prison or transportation to New South Wales or a journey to America or Canada instead if he agrees never to return to England?"

"He deserves to be in prison," Richard objected. "He does not deserve the freedom offered in America, and he would fit too easily into the penal colony that is Van Diemen's Land. Both options seem far too kind for the ba … man."

Darcy sighed and nodded. "I agree with Elizabeth," he said. "While part of me would like to see Wickham thrown in a cell and the key lost, I feel we should at least offer him the option of transportation, but if he ever returns to England, I will not hesitate in the slightest to call in his debts and have him incarcerated at Marshalsea. I do not like it either, since he deserves to be thrown in prison, but at least in a penal colony such as Van Diemen's Land, at least he will not have the absolute freedom he would in the American colonies. He will still suffer, although perhaps not as much as he would at Marshalsea."

Bennet agreed with this suggestion, at least in principle, although his primary concern was in protecting his daughters from harm. For Darcy and Richard, any consideration of

Wickham was always far more emotional since Wickham had abused their trust again and again, first as children and far more seriously as adults. Richard always felt that Darcy was too soft on him, but he recognized the guilt and grief Darcy held for a childhood friend and much-loved godson of his father.

Finally, it was agreed Darcy and Richard would speak to Colonel Forester the following morning; however, it would be Bennet who invited the colonel to Longbourn for the conversation to keep Wickham from learning that Darcy and Richard were in Meryton. Once they had spoken with the Colonel, they would allow him time to summon Wickham to his office before arriving at the militia encampment to present Wickham with his options - transferring to a regiment in the Regulars in Portugal, debtors' prison, or transportation to Van Diemen's Land. Richard had suggested joining the Regulars to the other options discussed as yet another option, although neither he nor Darcy believed he would take it.

A note was quickly sent to Colonel Forester, and a time agreed upon for the meeting at Longbourn the following morning. With just two weeks remaining until the wedding, there was still much to be done, and dealing with Wickham added one more difficulty to be resolved for the couple. Little did they know, but there were two others determined to wreak havoc with their plans.

Sixteen

Lady Catherine Protests

L eft alone in the house while the rest of her family was at Netherfield, Mrs Bennet sat in her sitting room reflecting on the conversations she had with her husband in the last six weeks. Until the assembly last month, he had been content to ignore his wife and daughters and had not questioned anything they had done. She simply could not understand why, following the arrival of the Netherfield party and Mr Darcy's request to court Lizzy, her husband had changed so drastically. It rankled that he was now asserting his authority as the head of the family when he had left her to do as she wished for all these years. She would never forgive him for sending her favourite daughter away to school; she cried when she realised how much she missed her bright, lively Lydia, the daughter who had taken the most after her in both looks and personality. Jane was her next favourite because Jane also took after her in looks and she was the most beautiful girl in the neighbourhood.

Try as she might, Mrs Bennet could not understand why Lizzy was being courted and not Jane, nor could she understand how someone as rich and handsome as Mr Darcy would desire to marry Lizzy. Lizzy was nothing like her mother, not even in looks, since she took after the Bennet side of the family with her dark hair and petite stature. She was not interested in gossiping and talking endlessly about flirting and how to catch a husband as her mother was, and Mrs Bennet simply could not understand the girl. She could not forgive her second daughter for not being the son she wanted and nearly hated her for being so favoured by Mr Bennet. Mr Bennet had encouraged Lizzy in very unladylike studies, and Mrs Bennet resented not being able to follow some of Lizzy's conversations. Lizzy was always reading or walking, and Mrs Bennet thought it was unseemly that she spent so much time visiting the tenants and caring for the poor in Longbourn village. Jane helped with that as well, but she did not go as often as Lizzy did, and she also engaged in more ladylike pursuits. She did not read books, other than novels, and did not walk out as frequently as Lizzy.

The companion her husband had hired for her had just left her rooms after having instructed her on proper comportment for more than an hour. Mrs Higgins was rather snobby, in Mrs Bennet's opinion, and kept reprimanding Mrs Bennet for her words. Mrs Bennet did not care for the lady and was determined not to listen to her. She was not a gentlewoman; she was a servant, and Mrs Bennet was determined to treat her as such. No servant would tell the Mistress of Longbourn what to do and how to behave, she determined.

Lady Catherine Protests

* * *

In Kent, an entirely different conversation was taking place. The express from Hertfordshire had arrived and sent the house into chaos. More specifically, the reaction of one lady to the news contained within had led to the entire household walking on eggshells as they desperately tried to prepare for a rushed trip first to London and then Hertfordshire. Lady Catherine intended to collect her brother, the Earl, and have him condemn her nephew for his failure to do as she wished. She had spoken so frequently of the tacit engagement between Darcy and her daughter that surely everyone must agree with her and comply with her desire. If Darcy married Anne, he would take her away to Pemberley and leave her in control of Rosings.

Legally, Anne should already be mistress of Rosings but Lady Catherine had persuaded the solicitors that Anne was too weak for the responsibility and Lady Catherine ensured she remained weak by giving her the tonics that kept her in that state. She had done the same with her husband and he had died in that weakened state, unfortunately before she could convince him to change his will to leave everything to her and not Anne. Anne had inherited two years prior, on her twenty-fifth birthday, but Lady Catherine had ensured not even Anne knew of it. She so effectively convinced the solicitors Anne was too weak to manage her inheritance that they neglected to remind the trustees, originally Lord Matlock and George Darcy but now Fitzwilliam Darcy in his father's place, of the change in Anne's status.

Both men checked the estate's books each year – Darcy at Easter and Lord Matlock after the harvest. Lady Catherine allowed them access to the estate books but prevented them from learning much about the running of the estate beyond what she wanted them to know, and she *never* mentioned Lewis de Bourgh's will.

When Lady Catherine received the express early Thursday morning informing her of Darcy's intended marriage to some country nobody, she demanded her staff immediately begin preparations for her trip to bring an end to such a ridiculous idea. Darcy was to marry Anne, and nothing, not even Darcy himself, would prevent that. Her brother would accompany her to this insignificant estate in some out-of-the-way country town and would echo her demand that their nephew break the engagement. In fact, she would have him obtain a special licence for Darcy and Anne to marry, so they could marry immediately.

Just over an hour later the carriage was ready to depart with a determined Lady Catherine and a reluctant Anne who expected her mother would speak non-stop about the imagined engagement and spew her vitriol all the way to London. Anne was happy for her cousin, although she could not say so to her mother, and she made several attempts to inform her that she had no intention of marrying at all, much less marrying her cousin. All her protestations were ignored, and Lady Catherine insisted Anne would do as she was told, as would Darcy. Anne knew Darcy would resist as they had discussed their supposed engagement a time or two, and they were in agreement they would not marry. She was worried about how the enforced travel would affect her because of her general weakness. It also meant she would be forced to keep company with her mother in the enclosed carriage for hours on end.

Their carriage passed Mr Collins as he returned to Hunsford on the post coach that morning. He had travelled from Hertfordshire to London on Wednesday and, missing the connecting coach to Kent, had spent the night in the capital city before finding a post coach to Hunsford the following morning.

Arriving at Matlock House, Lady Catherine demanded entrance, and the noise she made quickly alerted the Earl and Countess to the identity of their visitor. "And so it begins," said the Earl. "I cannot imagine this will be pleasant. She will be livid when she learns she will not get her way."

The countess sighed. "How is it that your sister is the way she is while Anne was also such a kind, loving person? I have never understood how your sisters varied so widely in their characters."

"Catherine was the eldest and she was always jealous of Anne," Lord Matlock explained. "She was angry that she did not inherit the earldom as well, but there was little she could do about that. However, when Anne made a significantly better match than she had, despite George's lack of title, she became ever more hateful toward her sister and brother. I think she imagines that forcing Darcy to marry her daughter would somehow be retribution for all that Catherine 'suffered' when her sister married better than her."

"She married a man with a title, though," Lady Matlock protested.

"Yes, but Pemberley is far greater than Rosings and the Darcy name is older and carries more power," her husband replied. "I wonder … Catherine never let anyone else see her husband's will. I wonder who will inherit Rosings when

Catherine dies - will it be Anne or someone else entirely? Her solicitor is here in town; I may have to pay the man a call to learn more. I would like to imagine that concern for Anne is behind this, but I am uncertain ..."

"James, do you really believe Catherine could care for anyone besides herself," the countess asked sceptically. "I have always felt bad for Anne being left alone at Rosings with Catherine, but Catherine always insisted that Anne could not travel."

A knock sounded on the door and the butler entered. He attempted to announce the visitor, but before he could begin Lady Catherine pushed him out of the way and entered with Anne in her wake. Anne was pale and appeared to be exhausted and the Earl quickly stood and helped his niece to a seat. Cutting off his sister as she began a diatribe, he spoke to Anne. "Anne, dear, how are you? Do we need to call for a physician to attend you?"

"I need to lie down, Uncle," Anne replied weakly, sitting down heavily on the settee and stretching out as best she could. "I am afraid my tonic is not helping today; in fact, I believe it has made me feel worse today."

"Jennings," the countess said, addressing the butler, "send someone to summon the physician for my niece immediately and then have the housekeeper quickly prepare a room. Anne, dear, we will have someone see to you as soon as we can. Would you like a cup of tea?"

Anne was barely sitting up but nodded her agreement. Her companion sat next to her and supported her as she sat up enough to drink the sweetened tea. "I added extra sugar, Anne. Would you like to try to eat?"

"The tea will be enough for now," came the reply, in a voice so small it could scarcely be heard in the room.

"Catherine," the Earl boomed. "What is the meaning of this? Why have you dragged Anne to London in such a state? I cannot imagine what could have brought you here unannounced and with Anne so weak."

"Anne is merely upset because Darcy has been taken in by some harlot," Catherine replied arrogantly. "He sent an express stating that he was engaged to some … some nobody who must have used her wiles to seduce him and make him forget what he owes his family, what he owes to Anne. We will obtain a special licence, and he will marry Anne immediately."

"Darcy will not marry Anne, Catherine," the Earl said tiredly. "Darcy has told you this, I have told you this, and Anne has told you this. No one, other than you, has ever believed that Darcy and Anne should marry. Our sister, Darcy's mother, certainly did not wish it, nor did George, and I cannot imagine that Lewis would have recommended it either. There is no marriage contract, nothing that would bind the two, other than this delusion that you have carried for the last five years. There was no mention of such a match until after George Darcy died, which tells me as much as anything else that you are trying to take advantage of Darcy's honour and duty to his family.

"It may interest you to know that today's paper carries the announcement that *I* placed endorsing the match. I have met his betrothed and she is a lovely girl. She and Darcy are very much in love and, while it is not the match I would have expected him to make, he is extraordinarily pleased with his choice. I have never seen the man so happy as he is when he is with Elizabeth. They will marry - the contract has been signed, the licence has been acquired, and there is nothing

175

that you can do to prevent the match."

Catherine was nearly purple in her rage at this pronounce-
ment and began to yell all manner of invectives against her
brother, her nephew and the upstart to whom he had engaged
himself, her deceased sister, her deceased husband, and everyone else she believed stood in the way of Anne's marriage
to Darcy. Amid this diatribe, she revealed her scheme – that
of keeping Rosings for herself when it rightfully belonged to
Anne.

"Stop, Catherine!" the Earl bellowed once he processed
what she had said. "Did you just say that Anne was to inherit
Rosings when she turned twenty-five? Is that why you have
never allowed anyone to see Lewis's will?"

Catherine spluttered, "No, that is not what I said. Besides,
Anne is much too weak to be in charge of such a large estate
as Rosings. I am much better suited to be its mistress. Darcy
will marry Anne and take her to Pemberley so that I will
continue running Rosings."

"Do you honestly believe Darcy would have allowed you
to retain control of Rosings had he married Anne?" the
Earl laughed. "You are more delusional than I would have
believed." Calling for his butler, he had several footmen
escort Catherine into a bed chamber, still yelling, and lock
her inside. His wife escorted Anne to another bedchamber
well away from Catherine's room and helped her onto the bed
to rest. Her things were brought inside and a maid assisted
Anne into a nightgown to prepare for the physician's arrival.

A short time later, the physician arrived and was shown
into the room where Anne was lying down. "How are you
feeling, my dear?" he asked after briefly looking her over.
After the tea and a rest, Anne had begun to feel slightly better

but was still weak.

"My mother insisted we travel from Kent this morning and we only stopped briefly once. I drank my tonic before we left the house. Although I usually only take it once a day, I was so tired I took another dose when we stopped at the inn in Bromley to change the horses. When we arrived in London, my head ached, and I felt so ill I could barely stand. I was exhausted after walking from the carriage into the sitting room."

"What kind of tonic do you take?" he inquired, and Mrs Jenkinson, Anne's companion, handed him the bottle. "There is no label on this identifying it; where do you obtain it?"

"An apothecary in Hunsford provides it per my mother's instructions," Anne explained. "I do not know what is in it."

"Hmm," the physician said after smelling the contents and tasting a drop from his finger. "Do not take it for two full days, and let us see how you feel then. I will send a message to the apothecary to ask what is in it. Do you know his name?" Mrs Jenkinson provided the information he requested which he wrote in his notebook. "Thank you," he replied before exiting the room.

The physician went back downstairs to speak to the Earl. "My Lord, I believe your niece will recover, although she may continue to be weak for some time. I feel relatively certain that Miss de Bourgh's tonic is making her ill. I intend to request the receipt from the apothecary who prepares the tonic as it seems to contain arsenic, which would leave anyone feeling weak - not to mention other symptoms she is experiencing. She is likely weak because of an irregular heartbeat, which would be caused by the arsenic, and complains of shortness of breath and chest pains which can also be caused by arsenic. I observed white lines on her nails, which are additional symptoms of long-term arsenic use, and I expect her stomach often troubles her."

Lady Matlock entered while the doctor was explaining this and acknowledged the symptoms were those she had noted in Anne. "I do not know if her mother realises it, but the tonic Miss de Bourgh is drinking is slowly poisoning her. It affected her more strongly today because she took a second dose, thinking to counteract the effects of the travel, but it actually made her feel even worse because she received a greater dose of the poison," the physician concluded.

"Did not Lewis de Bourgh have similar symptoms before he died?" Lady Matlock inquired. "I remember how drawn he looked toward the end, and he complained of a sore throat constantly. He also struggled to breathe at times and coughed constantly. I believe he mentioned several times that he had a difficult time eating due to pain in his stomach when he did so."

"Is it possible that Catherine poisoned them both?" Lord Matlock wondered, struggling to give voice to such a terrible idea. "Would long-term exposure to arsenic in this tonic keep Anne weak? Perhaps that was her intention."

"I intend to inquire of the apothecary in Hunsford about what he includes in his tonic; however, if he is aware of what he has been doing, even if it is at Lady Catherine's orders, he may be unwilling to say anything that would incriminate him. It is unlikely Lady Catherine ever put anything in writing and if it went to trial and it was her word against his, her word as a peer would count far more heavily in the eyes of most," the physician warned. "Your sister may have only intended to keep them weak enough to control and not to kill them, and it is possible that like her daughter, her husband merely took too much one day, and that was what killed him.".

Both the earl and countess sat there in shock as they considered the implications of such a thing – if it were true. The earl requested that the physician examine Lady Catherine since she was still loudly and vociferously demanding her release. At the very least, he could dose her with laudanum and help them find a way to deal with her as they began to investigate further into the claims regarding the inheritance of Rosings and Anne's health.

Seventeen

Wickham is Finished

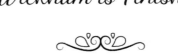

Those in were in Hertfordshire were unaware of the happenings in London on that day and were happily moving forward with the wedding planning. The meeting with Colonel Forester had gone well, and they agreed that it should be Colonel Fitzwilliam who met with Wickham first, suggesting a transfer to the regulars before Darcy came to offer passage to New South Wales in place of life spent in Marshalsea.

Wickham had been unhappy in the interview with Colonel Forester when it was discovered that he had already accumulated debts of honour to his fellow officers from losses at cards and had acquired debt in town as well. The amounts owed were not yet significant, but if he had already acquired this much debt, how much more would it be in a month? The debt he had run up in just a few days was the equivalent of at least a month's income as a militia lieutenant. Immediately following that conversation, Colonel Fitzwilliam entered the room, and Wickham nearly quivered in fear when he saw him.

"Wickham," Fitzwilliam nearly growled his name. "Fancy meeting you here." Fitzwilliam's mouth curved into a nearly feral grin, and Wickham was genuinely frightened of the man.

"Fitz … I mean, Colonel Fitzwilliam," Wickham stuttered out. "What are you doing here?"

"I heard you had joined the militia, and I had to come to see for myself," Fitzwilliam replied. "I have learned that in a matter of only a few days, you have already run up a stack of debts you cannot pay." Wickham was nearly ghostly pale, and Fitzwilliam felt almost gleeful to have been the cause. "You must not be aware that Darcy is here in Meryton, and as soon as he saw you, he notified me. He knew I would like little more than to run you through; however, so far, he has been able to convince me that it is not worth my freedom to murder you, though you deserve it."

Fitzwilliam paused as he watched the miscreant take in his words. "I have found a better option, I think, and Colonel Forester is inclined to agree with me. There is a regiment in Portugal, well, actually, there are many, but one in particular needs men like you. I could easily arrange for your transfer there, and then you could be cannon fodder. I could get my wish, and I would not even have to raise my sword to ensure you end up dead."

Wickham nearly collapsed into a chair, and Fitzwilliam attempted to restrain himself from grinning when he noticed a wet spot growing on the front of Wickham's breeches. He did laugh then, a sharp, joyless laugh. "I always knew you

181

were a coward, Wickham, or should I say Wickless, since that is what you are. You attempt to seduce fifteen-year-old girls because women can see through your false charm."

After a minute, Fitzwilliam went to open the door. "Cousin, I believe that Wickless here cannot find it in him to face joining a real regiment and facing the idea of Portugal. Would you like to present him with your option?"

Darcy walked in and took in Wickham's pallor, position, and the wet spot on his breeches. "Suddenly, Cousin, I believe your solution is truly the best option, but perhaps I should still put the others before him as a courtesy to my father's godson. My father cared for him once, although he did not truly see Wickham for what he was but for what he hoped he would have been. Nonetheless, Wickham, you have three options in front of you. Portugal, which Fitzwilliam explained to you; Marshalsea for your many debts; or Van Diemen's Land. I already hold a warrant from the Magistrate about your debts which would see you imprisoned for the rest of your life. They might offer you transportation instead, and I am willing to advocate for that, provided you never again return to England and never speak another word against me or my family. You have a minute to decide, or I will propose to Colonel Forester that we follow my cousin's plan for you." Darcy pulled out his pocket watch and examined it closely, watching the time pass.

Wickham remained pale and struggled to find his voice. Darcy had never before stood up to him in such a way; well, perhaps he had when he had refused him the living after Wickham had already received a payment for it. He could not stand; he could not speak. He had been utterly humiliated and did not know how to react.

Darcy closed his watch. "Time is up," he stated resolutely, waiting a moment for Wickham to speak. When he did not, he concluded: "Portugal it is."

Wickham began to protest, but Fitzwilliam cut him off. "The commanding officer is a friend of mine and will be sure to keep an eye on you, Wickham. I will send along a letter with a courier, and you will be accompanied every step of the way to ensure you do not disappear. Do not forget that the penalty for desertion is death. Those who will escort you will have very clear orders to shoot you if you attempt to escape. You *might* survive if you fight in Portugal, but you definitely will not if you make any attempt to escape. Part of me hopes you do, as being shot in the back would be a fitting death." Richard did not hold back his laugh this time. "Joining the militia was your best decision yet, Wickless. I am anxious to learn of your fate."

Wickham was escorted away, and orders were given to ensure he would not escape. He heard Colonel Forester order the men with him to shoot him if he attempted to escape. They all saw the new stain appear on his already wet breeches and barely contained their snicker. Utterly humiliated, Wickham realised he had been defeated by both Darcy and Fitzwilliam and knew he would never again be free. His dreams of becoming a true gentleman were over.

* * *

While Darcy was meeting with Colonel Forester in Meryton, Elizabeth and Jane were working in the still room at Long-bourn. They chatted comfortably and discussed Elizabeth's upcoming wedding when Elizabeth noted that Jane seemed troubled.

"Is everything well, Jane?" Elizabeth asked.

Jane sighed. "Yes, Lizzy, I am well," she replied, her tone sharper than usual.

"Are you certain?" Elizabeth tried again. "Is something worrying you?"

Jane huffed out a breath. "I am well, Lizzy. Let us finish our task here before the gentleman call. What was Mr Darcy doing this morning that prevented him from joining us for breakfast?"

"He and the Colonel went to meet with the colonel of the militia," Elizabeth replied, leaving out the details of the meeting. "The gentlemen, Miss Darcy, and Miss Bingley all intend to visit after luncheon."

Jane nodded and then continued working in silence. Elizabeth walked up behind her and hugged her back. "I will miss you, Jane," she said softly.

Turning, Jane embraced her sister. "I will miss you too, Lizzy. I do not know what I will do without you here."

Elizabeth pulled back and looked at her sister carefully. "We have not spoken of Mr Bingley in some time, sister. Have your feelings toward him changed? I admit, my preoccupation with William prevents me from paying you much attention."

"I like him, Lizzy, but no more than that. Our conversation rarely consists of anything of significance. I know little of him, and I do not know how to engage him in deeper conversation. I begin to wonder if he is truly interested in me or if he is simply occupying himself while he is here. Is he only capable of the type of superficial conversation we have had?"

Elizabeth considered this. "Would you like me to speak to William about his friend? I know he and I have seemingly rushed our courtship and engagement, but Jane, oh Jane, I knew almost from the moment I saw him that he was the one for me. Do you feel that way about Mr Bingley?"

"No," Jane replied diffidently. "I admit that I do like him well enough, but that is all I feel for him. We have never discussed anything of substance as you and Mr Darcy do."

"What do you know of my conversations with Mr Darcy?" Elizabeth teasingly asked.

"I know that he wears a smile when he speaks with you that he does not show any other time," Jane began. "Whereas Mr Bingley smiles at everyone. He speaks mostly with me, but I can detect no difference between how he looks at me and how he looks at anyone else. He seems equally pleased to speak with … with my father as he does with me."

Thoughtfully, Elizabeth remained silent for several heart-beats as she considered this information. "You did not answer my question about speaking to Mr Darcy. If nothing else, he can warn him that paying you too much attention, especially if he does not mean anything by it, could ultimately harm your reputation or give rise to expectations here in Hertfordshire. He has already requested your hand for the first dance, and I do not doubt that the neighbourhood has noticed that he visits Longbourn as often as William does."

"I would prefer you not speak to Mr Darcy about Mr Bingley; however, I do see the sense in warning him about not paying such dedicated attention to me if he does not have any intentions toward me. Perhaps it is our father who ought to be having such a conversation with Mr Bingley, but I do not know if it will occur to him, although I do appreciate how much more has been involved lately." Jane did not look at Elizabeth as she spoke, instead keeping her eyes firmly on her hands.

Nodding, Elizabeth replied simply that she would suggest Darcy remind his friend to be more cautious about paying such dedicated attention if he did not have any intentions toward her sister. The two continued to work on their tasks, and soon, they washed their hands to join the rest of the family.

Mrs Bennet and her companion joined the family for tea that afternoon. The matron was, frankly, bored of remaining in her room and had begged her husband to allow her downstairs to greet the gentlemen that afternoon. He had reluctantly given his approval while lecturing her on her behaviour and reminding her what would and would not be tolerated during this visit. She gave the appearance of listening to him but was considering the plot she intended to put into motion.

All the while, she was thinking that it was not right that Lizzy would marry Mr Darcy. She fully intended to do what she could to shift his attention from her least favourite daughter and place it firmly on her dearest Jane. Mrs Bennet was rather disappointed that she had not had the opportunity to meet Mr Collins, especially after hearing from one of the maids how he had intended to claim a wife from the Bennet daughters and that he had seemed to pay special attention to Lizzy. Mr Collins would have made a more suitable husband for that daughter, while Jane deserved all she would have as the wife of such a wealthy man as Mr Darcy.

Upon entering the drawing room, she was disappointed to find the gentlemen already in the room and seated. Elizabeth was next to Mr Darcy, and Jane was seated between Mr Bingley. Another gentleman, an officer from his red coat, and two ladies in the room were unknown to Mrs Bennet.

The gentlemen stood when she entered, and Bennet introduced her to the strangers. "Mrs Bennet, please meet Miss Georgiana Darcy, Mr Darcy's sister, and Colonel Richard Fitzwilliam, Miss Darcy's other guardian and their cousin. The lady there," he indicated a lady sitting near Mary, "is Miss Darcy's companion, Mrs Annesley." Greetings were exchanged, and everyone returned to their seats. Mrs Bennet immediately began to centre the conversation on Jane's desirability as a potential wife in an attempt to draw the attention of at least one of these single men to her most beautiful daughter.

As she sat down, Mrs Bennet smoothed her skirts and began to fan herself. "Oh, Miss Darcy and Colonel Fitzwilliam, it is such a pleasure to meet you both," she exclaimed, batting her eyelashes. "Mr Darcy, Mr Bingley, we have already had the pleasure of meeting you, and it is always a joy to see you again. I see my dear Jane has been doing an excellent job in taking care of you all. She is such a perfect hostess, and I have trained her so well. She will do a wonderful job of running a grand estate and will be the perfect wife for a truly great man. I dare say any gentleman would feel it a great privilege to have her on his arm."

Mr Darcy merely nodded in response as she continued on in this vein, speaking loudly and putting an end to all other conversations in the room. Mrs Bennet continued, "I must say, Miss Darcy, you are quite lovely. And Colonel Fitzwilliam, you cut such a dashing figure."

Colonel Fitzwilliam chuckled, "Thank you, Mrs Bennet.

You are too kind."

Seeming to ignore the reply and the red faces of their guests and her daughters, she continued. "Of course, Mr Darcy is quite the most handsome man we have ever seen here in Meryton, and his dark looks do so complement my beautiful Jane's fair hair and eyes. I think they would be quite the pair, do you not, Colonel?"

Darcy scowled at this comment but made no reply, instead cutting his eyes at his betrothed sitting next to him. Elizabeth lightly squeezed his hand and attempted to redirect the conversation to a safer topic, but her attempts were ignored. Mrs Bennet had not needed a reply from anyone, and she continued speaking of all of Jane's positive attributes, directing her conversation at Mr Darcy and preventing him from speaking as he struggled to hold back his anger.

Both the companion and Bennet attempted to direct the conversation to a safer topic but were unsuccessful. Bennet rose and went to his wife, forcibly helping her to her feet and leading her from the room while he made their excuses.

Once they were in the hallway, Bennet angrily addressed his wife. "Have you forgotten that Mr Darcy is engaged to Lizzy and that they will marry very soon? What are you attempting to do besides embarrass your daughters and anger your future son?"

"Lizzy does not deserve Mr Darcy. He would do much better to marry Jane." Mrs Bennet insisted.

"How foolish can you be, Mrs Bennet?" Bennet nearly exploded at her. "If he had wanted Jane, he would have pursued her, but he has chosen Elizabeth. He is engaged to Elizabeth – the marriage contract is signed, and all that remains to be done is for the actual ceremony to take place.

Nothing you can say or do will change that, but it will prevent Mr and Mrs Darcy from ever inviting you to any of their homes, and it may prevent them from ever desiring to return to Longbourn. I cannot imagine that he would want much to do with you after they are wed, especially if you continue to speak poorly of the daughter he had chosen."

"Why does he not want Jane? She is much prettier than Lizzy?" Mrs Bennet whined.

"What does that have to do with anything, Mrs Bennet?" Bennet replied, unable to comprehend her single-mindedness. "If the only thing Darcy sought was a pretty woman to adorn his arm, he would have chosen from amongst the *ton* long before he arrived in Meryton. Perhaps, just perhaps, there is something more that he was looking for, and perhaps Lizzy has exactly what it is he wanted. Have you ever considered that men want more than a pretty face to look at over the table?"

She frowned. "I do not understand, Mr Bennet," she replied after a moment.

"That much is obvious," he said before taking her by the elbow and escorting her back to her rooms. "I will send Mrs Higgins to you shortly." And then he was gone.

After Mr and Mrs Bennet had left the drawing room, no one spoke for a moment before Fitzwilliam broke the silence. "I propose a walk in the gardens to work off some of these treats we have been served. I have rarely had such a delightful afternoon tea."

Darcy and Elizabeth readily accepted, as did Jane and Bingley. The other girls hesitated, but after a moment of exchanging glances, all three agreed to accompany them. Mrs Higgins stayed behind, certain she would be called to attend Mrs Bennet soon. She had only been there a few days but was already uncertain if there was anything she could do that would have any impact on the lady she was there to help. Nothing she had said so far had made any sort of difference, and she began to despair of ever doing so with her recalcitrant charge.

Outside, the group soon separated. Mary, Kitty, and Georgiana walked together, while Jane walked with Bingley and Fitzwilliam. The engaged couple isolated themselves from the group and steadily moved to a location where they had some measure of privacy so Darcy could share the news of Wickham.

However, as soon as he had guaranteed their privacy, he pulled her into his arms and kissed her. "I love you, Elizabeth," Darcy told her.

Elizabeth reached up and smiled at him as she caressed his cheek. "How did it go today, William? I sense you are still troubled by the encounter."

He sighed. "He proved to be as much of a coward as we anticipated. However, he will go to Portugal as a member of the Regulars, and, with luck, that will be the end of him. I should not be glad to see him injured, but if he does die in battle, it will be the most honourable thing he ever does in his life."

She looked up at him, confusion written on her face. "Richard frightened him enough that he, um, released his bladder. Then, when I entered, and his options were presented to him, he seemed to be struck dumb. I gave him a moment to make his choice, and, when he said nothing, I told him his choice was made, and he was for Portugal."

Elizabeth continued to watch him. "You are certain of this?"

she asked.

He nodded. "I am. I believe it is for the best."

Elizabeth responded in kind. "And how do you feel?"

"Relieved, I think," he replied, feeling somewhat uncertain himself. "Does that make me terrible? He will be forced to leave the country and might even be killed, although I could see him deserting just as easily. But regardless, it removes him from my life and, I believe, renders him incapable of injuring anyone in my family ever again."

Reaching around his waist, she squeezed him tightly. "I do love you, William, not the least for the sense of honour with which you approach everything. I am certain that dealing with Wickham has been difficult for you if for no other reason than the man was loved by your father, and he would be disappointed that Wickham has turned out so poorly. You have acted honourably to protect those whom he would have otherwise injured."

"You paint my character in such a generous light, my love. I am not certain I deserve it," he replied, dropping a kiss onto her forehead as he held her. They remained that way for several minutes.

Finally, Elizabeth interrupted his reflection. "William?" she began, her voice full of question. He pulled back slightly to look down at her as she continued. "Is Mr Bingley interested in Jane? She is so confused about what his attention to her might mean and is, perhaps, a little jealous of how quickly you expressed your interest in me while Bingley has made no such overtures. She is worried that such marked attention may be misinterpreted by the neighbours."

Darcy considered her words. "He has visited as frequently as I, and I believe he even visited while we were in London, did he not?" She nodded at him. "I will confess that I had not really thought about Bingley's actions toward your sister, but I will suggest that he either make his intentions known or desist in paying such marked attention. They are to dance the first set at the ball, which will give rise to speculation, especially if he dances with her a second time."

Again, Elizabeth nodded. "Jane feels frustrated that their conversations remain … mostly superficial. I think she sees how open we are with one another and wonders why it is not the same between her and Mr Bingley. She is uncertain of how things stand between them."

It was Darcy's turn to nod. "I am no good at subtlety, Elizabeth, as you well know." He paused as Elizabeth's merry laugh rang out and smiled in return. "I will do my best to inquire without telling Bingley what he should do."

"Thank you, dearest," she replied. "I do enjoy your lack of subtlety, or should we call it your honesty. Shall we make it a virtue rather than a failing?"

His own laughter rang out. "Oh, please do, my dear Elizabeth. From now on, you shall be in charge of my character and do all you can to promote it so that I appear to the best advantage," he commanded her.

"And you shall do the same for me, sir?" she inquired.

He kissed her. "You always appear to the best advantage, dearest. I need do nothing to aid in that."

Eighteen

Married!

⟡⟡⟡

Several days passed before the news from London regarding Lady Catherine and Anne reached Hertfordshire. Colonel Fitzwilliam had left early on Saturday for London, accompanied by a small group of militia members whose responsibility was to guard Wickham until he boarded a ship for Portugal. That threat dealt with, both the Colonel and Darcy were content with his fate, believing it unlikely Wickham would ever return to England.

They were unaware of the letter that Wickham had sent while he waited to be escorted to London. Supposedly writing to his mother, who had died more than a decade before, he wrote a note to Lady Catherine informing her of Georgiana's ruin, embellishing the story, making a would-be elopement into something far more salacious. It was Wickham's final revenge, he thought, to ruin the sister Darcy had worked so hard to protect. Wickham was certain Darcy's aunt would use this information to force a marriage to her daughter. He had heard a rumour that Darcy was paying attention to a woman in Hertfordshire and believed this would put an end to that and ensure Darcy's misery.

As that letter made its way to Kent on Monday, a letter travelled from London to Hertfordshire, revealing Lady Catherine's presence in London and the suspicion that she had killed her husband and was poisoning her daughter. Lord Matlock had spoken to the solicitors who were responsible for executing the last will of Sir Lewis de Bourgh and learned much, including the fact that Lady Catherine had never legally been responsible for Rosings. According to the will, Anne should have inherited Rosings upon her twenty-fifth birthday; George Darcy and James Fitzwilliam were the trustees until Anne inherited. The explanation the solicitors gave for their failure to notify these men of this was insufficient, and Lord Matlock had hired additional solicitors to hold these gentlemen accountable. The situation was a mess, made all the more worse by the fact that Anne was presently too weak to take control of the estate as a direct result of the tonic her mother had forced upon her.

The physician had removed the source of the poison, but Anne was sufficiently weakened by the continued exposure for so many years that a complete recovery was unlikely. She had met briefly and privately with a solicitor to draft her will, the content of which was a secret to all but the one who wrote it. Anne was unwilling to tell Lord Matlock her intentions, preferring to wait until Darcy returned to London after his wedding to speak to both the trustees.

Lord and Lady Matlock remained concerned and were uncertain if they would be able to attend the wedding given

Anne's and Catherine's continued presence in their home. They felt less concerned about leaving Anne at home than they did leaving Catherine with just the servants in residence. Lord Matlock did not want the scandal that would arise if the news that his sister had murdered her husband and her daughter was on her deathbed due to her deliberate actions in poisoning them. In his letter, Lord Matlock asked Darcy for suggestions on what could be done with Lady Catherine without pressing formal charges. He dreaded the scandal that would come if they were to make her actions public.

Darcy brought this letter to Elizabeth almost as soon as he received it, seeking her advice and comfort after reading what was contained within. The moment she saw him riding toward Longbourn, she seemed to intuitively know something was wrong, and she went outside to greet him the moment he dismounted.

"My love, what is wrong?" she asked, leading him toward the garden and, seeing his ashen face, led him to sit on a bench hidden among the hedges. He handed her the letter from his uncle in response and watched her as she read. Her face grew white, matching his own pallor. "Is this the same Lady Catherine who my cousin praised so highly?"

Darcy merely nodded, still unable to speak. She wrapped her arms around him and cradled his head to her breast, caressing his hair as he held onto her. His grip on her was indicative of his turmoil. "Oh, love," she whispered as she continued to gently caress him.

Finally, he sat up, still holding tightly to her. "I need to return to London to see how I may help my uncle with this," he told her.

Elizabeth nodded her agreement. "I do understand,

William, I do. Do you think … will we need to delay the wedding until things are settled?"

He gazed at her. "I was thinking about this on the ride over from Netherfield. We have the licence, the settlement is signed, and there is nothing to stop us from marrying," he paused, taking a deep breath before continuing. "We could marry today or tomorrow morning if you prefer. If we were married, you would be able to accompany me to London to help me deal with whatever situation has arisen with my aunt and cousin. I feel certain that either my uncle or myself will be obligated to travel on to Kent very soon, especially if something happens to Anne."

"We should speak to my father." Elizabeth stood and took his hand in hers, pulling him up as well. "We can make it known that your cousin's ill health necessitated moving our marriage forward to avoid having to postpone it due to mourning."

After they explained the circumstances to Bennet, he sent a note to ask the rector if he was amenable to performing the ceremony the following morning. While they waited, they invited Jane into the room to make a plan for an abbreviated wedding breakfast. Before long, they received a positive reply stating that the church was available for the wedding the following morning. Notes were sent to a few families in the surrounding area announcing the change of plans and the reason behind the decision. These notes were judiciously sent, as they went to a few of the biggest gossips in the area to ensure the story that was spread about the rushed nuptials was the correct one. Neither Darcy nor Bennet wanted gossip to spread that accused either Darcy or Elizabeth of wrongdoing.

"Jane," Elizabeth said when she entered the kitchen where Jane was speaking to the housekeeper, "what should we do about Mama? She has been reluctant to help with the wedding under the original timeline; she will be certain something awful has occurred to cause it to be moved forward. I cannot imagine her not attending at all, but I am terrified of what she will say if she does attend. I do not know if Papa has considered what to do with Mama, although I do believe it is understood in Meryton that she has been ill."

"Papa has had Hill inform visitors that Mama has not been well, and I think the same excuse may work for your wedding," Jane answered. "Mayhap she can attend the ceremony or the breakfast, especially since the number of guests will be very limited now. The Netherfield party is invited, as are the Lucases and the Phillips." Seeing Elizabeth's expression, she sighed. "I know that Lady Lucas and Aunt Phillips are two of the biggest gossips in the area, but Papa had to invite them. I fear Mama will freely express her dismay if she is present at the breakfast."

Elizabeth looked miserable as she thought of Mama, un-certain which was worse. – offending Mama or offending her husband-to-be. She felt a bit like Hamlet, torn between two disparate choices. Since she would leave Longbourn to live with her husband, she thought excluding her mother was the better choice, but that would mean that those who remained at Longbourn would be subject to Mama's insistent complaints.

She soon found Darcy and asked him what he preferred, and he was equally at a loss for what to suggest.

"I think your father will have to make that decision, dearest, as he is the one who will have to live with it," he replied. "Our rushed wedding also means we will have to change our plans for after the wedding. Georgiana and Kitty will have to come with us to Darcy House. We will have to delay our travel to Pemberley until things are a little more certain. I also do not know if we will be able to attend Bingley's ball, depending on what happens with Anne. I think I mentioned I may have to travel to Kent, although if Catherine remains in London, we would at least be alone there. I promise, dearest, that I will make it up to you." He kissed both of her hands and looked at her, full of contrition.

"Do not worry, William, as it makes little difference to me where we go so long as we are together," she told him. "I am happy not to have to be separated from you as you work to resolve this crisis." She then repeated his own actions and kissed his knuckles, leading him to wrap her in his arms and kiss her deeply.

"As much as I hate this situation, I confess that I am nearly ecstatic that it means we are moving our wedding forward," he said after a moment. "Tomorrow, Elizabeth, tomorrow we will be man and wife. Tomorrow night, I will not have to leave you at the front door and make my way to Netherfield. Tomorrow, Elizabeth ... I am greatly looking forward to it, my love." His expression could nearly be called giddy, although delighted was also appropriate.

* * *

The following day dawned bright and clear. Mrs Bennet was to attend the wedding, accompanied closely by her companion. She had been given a small dose of laudanum, as she had been nearly hysterical the night before when told the wedding would occur the following day instead of the following week. She had begun to shriek about ruin and early babes and all manner of nonsense, none of it complementary toward either her daughter or Mr Darcy. Immediately following the wedding, she would be returned to her room and given a larger dose of the medicine so she would sleep through the wedding breakfast and the departure of the newly-wedded couple. It was necessary for her to appear at the wedding so their neighbours did not wonder about it. Still, her wan appearance lent credence to the rumour that Mrs Bennet was ill.

Bennet was seriously considering renting a cottage somewhere for Mrs Bennet since she seemed incapable of changing her behaviour in even the smallest ways. Despite her short tenure, her companion already despaired of making any progress with Mrs Bennet. She had gone so far as to suggest removing Mrs Bennet from Longbourn to see if that would have an impact on her disposition or behaviour.

Setting this issue aside for consideration later, Bennet met his second daughter in the hallway once she was dressed and ready for her wedding. She was beaming with joy and had rarely looked as lovely as she did that morning, and Bennet felt all the bittersweetness of this moment. He was sad to see her go, especially since she would be so far away, but glad that she had found such a man. Bennet had rarely met such a good man as Darcy, and he was inordinately pleased that following this ceremony this morning, he would call Darcy 'son'.

Kissing Elizabeth on the cheek, Bennet led her to the carriage, and they departed for the church. The rest of the family was already gathered at the church. Jane, Mary, and Kitty each kissed her cheek before entering the church. Finally, it was Elizabeth's turn, and she walked up the aisle on her father's arm. She was scarcely aware of anyone else in the room. She barely noticed her father or anyone else after she saw Darcy standing waiting for her. The whole of her attention was on him, and her eyes were locked with his.

Darcy had been distracted and nervous until the moment he saw Elizabeth enter the church. Then, everything else faded while his whole focus was firmly on Elizabeth. Bingley was standing up with him in Richard's absence and had to physically restrain him from leaving his spot at the altar and going to her. As soon as she was close enough, he reached for her hand, and she immediately dropped her father's arm and clasped his extended hand to the amusement of those gathered.

The ceremony passed in a blur. Darcy and Elizabeth must have answered as expected as soon they were declared husband and wife. They signed the register and walked outside, accepting the congratulations from those in attendance, although neither could have said who they spoke to or what was said. Finally, they entered the carriage and were blessedly alone, at least for the few minutes it would take to arrive at Longbourn. Not caring who saw, almost immediately their lips touched, and they remained entwined until a footman knocked several times to alert them that they had arrived at the house.

Much like the ceremony, the breakfast passed in a blur for the couple. They moved around the room, speaking to the blessedly small number of people who were in attendance. Soon enough, it was time to depart, and Darcy was excessively happy that he had two carriages in Meryton. He and Elizabeth would travel in one, while their sisters would travel in another along with Mrs Annesley. A third carriage had already begun its journey to London accompanied by Miss Darcy's maid, Mr Darcy's valet, and most of the luggage. That last carriage was an unnecessary extravagance – Darcy had hired an extra carriage just for that purpose – but Darcy had wanted to be alone with his wife for the four-hour journey to London. The last thing he wanted on the day of his wedding was to share a carriage with chaperones of any kind.

Nineteen

Honeymoon Interrupted

Elizabeth had seen Darcy House when they visited London at the beginning of November, but this time she was approaching it as the mistress. As they grew closer to Mayfair, she became unaccountably nervous. Darcy, who was sitting very close, noted when his new wife seemed to become tense.

"What is it, dearest?" he asked, looking at her with an expression of concern and squeezing her just a little bit closer.

She laughed at herself. "I am well, William, but it occurs to me that this time I am entering your home as its mistress, not as a visitor."

"*Our* home, Elizabeth Darcy, and you have already impressed the staff. *Our* butler and housekeeper liked you very much when you were here before; they are just as worried about making a good impression upon you as you are on them," he told her, dropping a light kiss onto her forehead.

She hugged him. "I hardly feel capable of being the mistress of your townhome. I have done more at Longbourn since Mama has been confined to her room, but this is not Longbourn. I have not even begun to contemplate what will happen when we finally go to Pemberley. You have not said much, but I anticipate that it is very grand. My aunt thinks very well of it."

"I have no doubt that you will be an excellent mistress of all our homes," he reassured her. "I have complete faith in you, and our staff will do everything to aid you as you learn what is necessary. Mrs Reynolds has run the house at Pemberley for years without a mistress, and Mrs Stewart has been at Darcy House nearly as long. They will provide whatever assistance you need; you will learn in due time what is required of you."

They remained entwined as they drove the last quarter-hour before the carriage slowed, indicating their arrival at Darcy House. Darcy stepped down from the carriage after the footman had placed the step and then reached inside to hand the new Mrs Darcy out of the carriage. The senior staff was waiting at the top of the steps to greet them and were pleased to see their master smiling so happily at the mistress. They had seen the change in him when he had come earlier that month and it was now even more marked – he was beaming his happiness for all to see.

She stepped down onto the kerb and began to walk up the stairs on her husband's arm. After acknowledging all those gathered, Darcy bent down as he reached the top stair and picked his wife up in his arms to carry her inside. He did not stop in the foyer but dismissed the servants and continued up the stairs with her in his arms all the way to their suite of rooms. Opening the door proved difficult, and, laughing, Elizabeth kindly assisted him by turning slightly in his embrace to reach the door and opening it herself.

Finally, he stood her on her feet but did not release her. "Welcome home, dearest," he whispered as he bent to kiss her. This kiss was different from any that had come before, even in the coach on their way here. All restraint between them was finally gone, and the kiss grew more passionate as both of them recognized that there was no longer any reason they must stop.

* * *

Darcy woke up sometime later, feeling his stomach rumbling, unaccountably hungry. He startled when he realised there was a woman in his bed, and then he remembered. His *wife* was nestled firmly within his arms. They had not eaten supper, having opted to go straight to bed upon arriving home earlier. Had they even greeted the staff? Had Georgiana and Kitty arrived?

His slight movements seemed to disturb Elizabeth, and he felt her move against him. She stiffened in his arms briefly. "William?" she whispered groggily.

"Yes, dearest," he replied. "Good morning or perhaps good evening. I do not know which it is."

"We ignored your staff," she whispered to him. "What will they think of us?"

He laughed. "They will think we are in love, dearest," he replied, smiling broadly despite the fact that she could not see his expression in the dark.

"I am hungry," she whispered after a minute.

He laughed, "I am, too," he replied. "My stomach woke

me. We can check the time and ring for a servant to bring us something to eat."

"I do not have a dressing gown or even a nightgown to put on, nor do I know where mine are," she whispered again.

"Elizabeth, dearest, why do you keep whispering?" he asked. "I can retrieve one of my dressing gowns for you, but you do not need one. I will get up and ring for my valet, and you can stay in my bed ... our bed."

She blushed. "Eventually, William, I will need something to put on, as I cannot stay naked in this bed for the rest of my life."

He growled and leaned over to kiss her deeply. "I certainly would not mind that."

She hit his arm lightly. "Eventually, I must leave this bed, William, and I prefer to don some clothing when I do."

"No," he replied gruffly, laughing at the expression on her face. "Not today and maybe not even tomorrow. In this room, clothing is entirely optional."

"You are being entirely too silly tonight, Will," she answered back.

"Will?" he repeated.

"You are acting like a child, so Will seemed appropriate. Has no one ever called you that?" she inquired.

"Never," he said, leaning to kiss her once again. "God, how I love you, woman."

She sat up, holding the sheet to her breasts, and leaned over to kiss him. "I love you, too, William, but I need food! Bring me a dressing gown, or one of your nightshirts, or, or something, and we can find some rolls or fruit to satisfy us. Dare we venture down to the kitchens?"

"You would scandalise the cook on your first night here?"

he asked her, his voice full of laughter.

"Do you never go into your kitchens, Mr Darcy?" she asked archly.

"Not since I was a child," he replied. "I drove the cook at Pemberley batty, constantly pilfering food from her counters. I was particularly fond of biscuits. She regularly threatened to quit if my governess did not do a better job of keeping me from her domain." He nibbled on her lips once again.

"Stop it, Will," she said after a few minutes. "I am hungry, and you keep distracting me."

"But it is such a wonderful distraction, my love, do you not agree?" he teased. "We can satisfy an entirely different kind of hunger here in our bed."

"Food, William. Focus," she laughed back. "You need to feed me real food before you nibble on me again." She laughed at the expression on his face.

"Now there is an idea," he said, taking her lips again with his and distracting her for another half hour or so.

Eventually, they did eat, requesting a cold collation brought to their sitting room when they rang for Darcy's valet. The man also confirmed that their sisters had arrived and were already in bed.

* * *

The following morning, William and Elizabeth rose late, enjoying breakfast in their rooms before sending a note to the Matlocks letting them know of their arrival in town. An hour later, the Earl and Countess arrived at Darcy House, where they found Darcy and Elizabeth seated together in his study.

"Congratulations, you two," the earl greeted the pair as he entered the room, not waiting for the butler to announce their arrival. Elizabeth and Darcy had stood upon the door opening and went to greet their guests. Lady Matlock greeted both with a kiss on the cheek while the Earl slapped Darcy on the shoulder and kissed Elizabeth. "I am proud of you, son," the earl whispered to Darcy.

"Thank you, Uncle," Darcy replied. "Now, what the devil has been happening at Rosings, sir? Is Lady Catherine insane?"

The jovial group immediately became very subdued. "Blast it all, Darcy," the earl exclaimed, "I do not know what to say about Catherine. I have been unable to speak to her since she arrived, as she has been even more difficult than normal. We have had to give her regular doses of laudanum to keep her from yelling the place down. Anne's health is beginning to improve slightly, but she remains weak."

"Is it certain that she killed her husband?" Darcy asked directly.

"She said as much during one of her rants," the earl acknowledged. "She blamed it on his valet, claiming the valet simply gave him too much of the tonic one day, but ultimately, it was she who ordered the tonic containing arsenic and insisted he take it daily. One of us needs to interview the apothecary to determine what he knew and what he was told."

"Do you really believe he will confess to knowingly poisoning someone?" Elizabeth asked incredulously.

"I do not know," the earl answered. "Not knowing the man, I cannot know how he will react. It will likely depend on what Catherine has said to him through all this because, obviously, this has been occurring for years. Does he know that a man died because of his 'tonic'? Does he realise that it has been making Anne sick?"

"There are too many unknowns, Uncle, but you are right in thinking that this cannot be made public. The resulting scandal would have so many potential consequences for all of us if this were to become public knowledge," Darcy replied.

The countess finally spoke. "Anne will never recover fully and will need full-time care if she is able to return to Rosings. I do not know what to do about Catherine at all. She needs to be sent somewhere far away where she cannot continue to harm others. She cannot be sane to have poisoned Lewis for so many years and then to do the same with Anne. Even if she is sane, she will never be able to return to Rosings after what she has done. Anne would like to meet with you, Darcy, and with your wife. She was very pleased to know about your wedding."

Darcy sighed deeply, and Elizabeth reached over to place her hand on his. "Would she be able to see us today, or should we wait? Will it disturb Lady Catherine if we are in the house?" Elizabeth asked softly.

"Catherine is kept far from Anne, and Anne would enjoy a visit as soon as you are willing. I know this is not the honeymoon you had intended," Lady Matlock apologised.

"Thank you, Lady Matlock," Elizabeth replied. "We would be happy to visit with Miss de Bourgh after luncheon this afternoon."

"Please, Elizabeth, call me Lady Susan or Aunt Susan when we are in private," Lady Matlock offered. "There is no need to stand on such formality."

Lord Matlock also invited Elizabeth to address him informally in private. The four of them discussed Rosings until Georgiana and Kitty arrived downstairs. The ladies then all withdrew to a drawing room while the gentlemen remained in the study, and Elizabeth ordered tea. Eventually, the younger girls drifted into another room for drawing practice, leaving Lady Matlock and Elizabeth all alone.

"How is the situation with your mother, Elizabeth?" Lady Matlock asked. "I know the wedding was pushed forward, and I will admit I was very glad it was. It will be very difficult for Catherine to insist that Darcy marry Anne as he is already married. I am also certain Darcy would have been very reluctant to leave you behind. He is very happy with you, my dear."

Elizabeth smiled softly. "I would have been reluctant to have been left behind. William shared his uncle's letter with me and then immediately suggested that we go ahead and marry so I might accompany him here and, if necessary, to Rosings. I am glad to be able to support him in this; I know how much it troubles him."

"Catherine is difficult at the best of times; I am sure William appreciates your support," Lady Matlock confirmed. "What are your plans for a honeymoon now?"

"We are not certain. William suggested a trip to the Lakes in the summer, and I think we will leave for Pemberley as soon as we are able," Elizabeth said. "We have discussed several ideas, but we will not decide until things are more settled here."

"I am truly sorry this has interrupted your plans. William intends to leave the knocker off the door while you are in town, so you will not have any callers. We will do our best not to interrupt you too much, and as soon as we can, we will invite both Georgiana and Miss Catherine to visit us at our home. Unless things change significantly with Lady Catherine or Anne, I know William still intends to take you to Pemberley for Christmas," Lady Matlock attempted to reassure Elizabeth.

"Aye, William said as much this morning," Elizabeth replied. "I know he is anxious about the possibility of a trip to Rosings and how that might affect our plans for the holiday. However, once we arrive at Pemberley, I know he does not intend to leave there again until at least Easter." She smiled as she remembered the conversation from the night before about how he would lock her into their chambers for at least a week once they arrived at his estate.

Lady Matlock correctly interpreted the look. "If you do not mind, Elizabeth, might I ask a question?" Seeing Elizabeth nod, she proceeded. "How are you finding married life, my dear? I know that is a rather personal question, but I do not know what your mother might have said to prepare you. Was … was William kind?"

Elizabeth blushed brightly. "Very," was all she could manage to say. Taking a deep breath, she attempted to continue. "I was not as well prepared as I would have liked, but William was very, umm, kind, and … well, I do not know what to say, but I have no complaints, nor do I have questions to ask. Might we leave it there?"

Lady Matlock smiled and patted her hand. "Yes, dear. Please understand I do not have a daughter of my own, and with Lady Anne gone, I have taken on the role of mother for William and Georgiana. Circumstances prevented us from attending your wedding, but I just wanted to be certain that all was well."

Elizabeth sighed. "It is, although I will admit, I am somewhat uncertain about my role as mistress. Darcy House is one thing, but based on all of what I have heard of Pemberley, I feel that house will be far more challenging. I feel unprepared for this role, although William reassures me the housekeeper will be a great help. My first challenge will be to redecorate my chambers. They are lovely but are in need of updating. I do not even know where to begin."

The countess made several suggestions to aid Elizabeth in this endeavour and promised to take her shopping the next week. There were several stores the countess regularly visited, and she intended to introduce Elizabeth to the proprietors. When Lord Matlock and Darcy entered the room, they found the two ladies happily conversing and making definite plans for a shopping trip the next week. Darcy was happy to see the ladies getting along so well and arranged to accompany them to establish accounts for his wife. Elizabeth then suggested they begin at her uncle's warehouses to see what they could find there. While she recognized the need for Mrs Darcy to be seen shopping on Bond Street, she also realised that purchasing from her uncle had greater advantages. The countess agreed, and their plans were complete.

"When will you announce your marriage, Darcy?" the earl asked. "I placed the engagement announcement as you requested, but how will you explain the change in the wedding date?"

"Could we explain that we advanced our wedding due to Anne's ill health and our wish to support and comfort her?" Darcy pondered. "It is well known amongst the *ton* that Anne has always been ill, but is that sufficient reason to have moved our wedding date forward a sennight? I suspect that regardless of what we say, there will be those who expect an early babe. There will be enough conjecture about my marrying someone unknown in society."

Both his aunt and uncle considered this for a moment. "It is not well known that Anne is in town with us, nor do many know of her illness. We can begin to make it quietly known that you married ahead of the intended date due to her illness and the possibility of your travelling to Rosings to help settle the estate that Anne has recently inherited. That will explain your early wedding date and announce that Anne has inherited Rosings, which will provide a reason for Catherine being deposed," the countess suggested.

Darcy and Elizabeth nodded in agreement. "Elizabeth, we will likely be travelling to Rosings late next week to arrange for the transfer to Anne and to ensure that all is well there. We have some questions for Anne in regard to this, but Uncle and I have agreed it is best that I handle Rosings while he deals with Aunt Catherine."

The earl agreed. "We think it best that Catherine goes to my estate in Ireland. There is already a skeleton staff in residence, and we will supplement it as necessary with people from the surrounding area. It is remote enough that she will have little society, and we will make it known that she has travelled there for her health. Without prosecuting her for murder, there is little we can do about what she has done other than to exile her in this way. The scandal would affect all of us if it were to become known, and I would prefer to avoid that if at all possible."

The others in the room agreed. With these things decided, all that was left was for Darcy and Elizabeth to meet with

Anne. Once that was done, they could make more definite plans for Anne's future and ensure that fulfilling Anne's wishes would be carried out.

* * *

Later that afternoon, Darcy and Elizabeth returned to Matlock House to meet with Anne. Anne had not been downstairs since arriving there herself but had felt well enough that afternoon to attempt it, with help from several footmen.

"Thank you for coming, Darcy," she greeted him, her face expressionless. "This is your Elizabeth?"

A smile transformed his face, and Anne nearly gasped. She had never seen her cousin as happy as he looked at that moment, and his obvious joy cheered her own heart.

"Aye, this is my Elizabeth," he replied, a broad smile on his face. Before he introduced the two women, he brought Elizabeth's hand to his lips and kissed it, keeping her hand within his. "Anne, I would like to introduce you to Mrs Elizabeth Darcy, Elizabeth, my cousin, Anne."

The two ladies acknowledged the introduction – Anne with her customary indifference, while Elizabeth smiled welcomingly at her new cousin. "I am so pleased to meet you, Miss de Bourgh," Elizabeth greeted the pale woman, who had not stood when the newcomers had entered.

Anne acknowledged her with a nod before turning to Darcy. "I understand you and Uncle have decided to exile my mother to Ireland for her role in my father's death and for hastening my own." Her voice was brittle and obviously weak.

Darcy replied with a nod. "That is what we intend. What

213

are your thoughts on the plan?"

Anne shrugged. "It is not enough, yet it is likely the best solution. A hue and cry would arise if the truth were known, and it would lead to scandal. I prefer to avoid that sort of attention."

"We all do," Darcy agreed.

"I have left Rosings to you," Anne said abruptly. "Although it would probably have been better to leave it to Richard, he refused the suggestion that I do so. I do not trust the Viscount, so you are the best option. I know you will manage it as diligently as you do things at Pemberley, and I know that it will do very well under your care. I have always known that I was not strong enough to manage Rosings, even with the support of the very responsible steward you would no doubt hire, so I would like for you and Uncle to take charge. However, you should be the one with the final say. I do not intend to ever return there."

"Are you certain, Anne?" Darcy said after a moment. He was rather surprised at this news and intended to discuss it with Richard. He agreed that it ought to be left to Richard, if for no other reason than to give him a way to leave his career in the military. Perhaps he could still persuade his cousin to take charge of the estate, even if it legally belonged to himself, Darcy thought. He would talk with Elizabeth about how he might convince Richard to give up his career and manage Rosings.

Elizabeth squeezed the hand she held. "I thank you, Anne," he spoke again. Anne had not spoken again and seemed to be struggling to breathe.

"Do you need anything, Miss de Bourgh?" Elizabeth interjected. "Perhaps I could call for some tea to soothe your lungs?"

Anne coughed and waved her hand in the air. Elizabeth went to the door to request tea and for the countess to be summoned. She was uncertain about what was needed.

The countess arrived quickly and, seeing Anne's struggle, immediately called for a servant to bring Anne's special tea and a tonic prescribed by the London physician. Soon, Anne was more comfortable, although obviously weakened. Darcy stood to help Anne to her room, offering to carry her. However, his offer was rejected, and a servant was summoned to do the task.

Darcy and Elizabeth were all but ignored while the countess and servants tended to Anne, settling her in her room. While they waited, they helped themselves to the tea that had arrived in the midst of the earlier chaos, and the couple discussed Anne's revelations.

"I have never wanted Rosings, Elizabeth," he said. "I have enough to do with managing Pemberley – I will need a man I trust implicitly in charge. Richard would be ideal, and I do confess to a deep desire for him to leave the army. Perhaps I can persuade him to act in my stead as the master of Rosings, at least until we have a second son old enough to take charge of the estate himself." He grinned at his wife as the image of her large with his child appeared in his mind. Unable to help himself, he leaned in and kissed her passionately.

A knock on the door interrupted them, and while he pulled away slightly, he continued to hold his wife in his arms. "I look forward to having you all to myself, my love," he whispered.

His cousin Richard entered and grinned when he saw Darcy with his arms around his wife. "Congratulations,

Darcy," Richard enthused. "I do not know how you managed to convince such a lovely lady to become your wife. I would offer my condolences to you, Elizabeth, but it appears that you rather like my reticent and dour cousin."

Elizabeth laughed at his antics while Darcy scowled and held his wife closer, making Richard laugh. "Come, cousin, I will not abscond with your wife," he cajoled.

With a scowl, Darcy greeted his cousin and sat more appropriately next to his wife, although he continued to hold her hand. "My wife already knows better than to listen to anything you say, Richard," Darcy retorted but could not hold back the large smile when the word "wife" slipped from his lips. How he loved the fact that she was his and he could claim her as his wife; his happiness was completely bound in hers. "We have spoken briefly with Anne. She is very weak and had to return to her room after just a short conversation. We are hoping we will be able to speak to her again. What is this nonsense about you refusing to accept Rosings upon Anne's death? She cannot run it on her own, so you would become master immediately and support Anne for the rest of her life. With Rosings as your inheritance, you could resign your commission and marry, should you choose to do so."

"That is not my path, Darcy," he said tiredly. "I do not want to inherit Rosings, nor do I want to be tied to any estate. Perhaps eventually, I may wish to marry, and then I can sit as caretaker of Rosings for you, at least until your second son comes of age."

Darcy glared at his cousin. "Why ever not, Richard?"

Richard sighed. "I do not want it, and I certainly do not want to sit and wait for our cousin to die."

"Neither do I," Darcy replied tersely.

"I know, but I also know that you are far better prepared to manage Rosings than I am. You will be one of the trustees until Anne dies. Now that you are married, you need to think ahead to what will happen when you have that houseful of children. Rosings will not be entailed and can go to a daughter if need be," Richard told his cousin.

"That does not answer my question about why you do not want Rosings, Richard," Darcy objected. "You have helped me during my visits all these years, and I know you have learned at least as much as the viscount in your youth. If Anne were to leave Rosings to you, it would mean you could sell your commission and be done with the military."

"But I do not want to leave the military, nor do I want Rosings," Richard said heatedly. "You may think I am prepared for it, but it has never been my intention to be the master of an estate. I do not want to live that lifestyle."

Neither man spoke for several minutes as they merely stared at each other as they considered the other's intractability in this matter.

Elizabeth felt the need to break the tension between the two and redirect the conversation to something else. "While neither of you wants the estate, Miss de Bourgh would like to give it to one of you. Perhaps this conversation would be best held at a later time. We should focus on ensuring that Miss de Bourgh is well. Colonel, has your father shared with you the plan for Lady Catherine?"

When Richard answered negatively, Darcy related to Richard their discussions from earlier that day. Lord Matlock would take Lady Catherine to his estate soon and then arrange for her to travel to Ireland at some point in the spring since travel in the winter could be difficult. "He may ask you to accompany him," Darcy warned his cousin.

"And what of Anne?" Richard asked.

Again, Darcy sighed. "She does not want to return to Rosings, and Matlock will not be an option with her mother in residence there. I am not certain she would be strong enough for the trip to either Matlock or Pemberley, so she will likely remain in London for a time. Nothing is definite yet; there are still a number of decisions to make. Elizabeth and I will be travelling to Rosings at the end of next week to settle things there."

"Lady Catherine appointed my cousin as the rector of Hunsford after Anne should have inherited," Elizabeth interjected as the thought occurred to her. "What will happen to him?"

Darcy's eyes grew hard as he thought of the obsequious man and thought for a moment. "She was not the mistress of the estate and did not have the authority to appoint Mr Collins to that position. The bishop will likely agree that he could be removed for that reason alone. However, I am uncomfortable making a decision about his living based on our conversation at Longbourn that day. We should consult my uncle and Anne to see what they would prefer to be done. If Anne would like him to stay, we can confirm his appointment; if she prefers to appoint a rector of her or our choosing, we could petition the archbishop and inform him what has taken place. He would then remove the man from the position. Perhaps, if he cannot toady to my aunt, he will become more tolerable. It should also depend on how he has treated the villagers of Hunsford and what they think of him."

Elizabeth grinned. "He was rather self-important, was he

not? I wonder if that is his usual character or if his actions reflected what he thought would please your aunt. I wonder if he would act in a more reasonable manner if he had a different patron."

Darcy grimaced in return. "Somehow, I doubt it, but Anne has far more experience with him. We will see what she wishes to do about him," he replied.

The earl and countess joined them, and Darcy informed them that Anne had said she had left Rosings to him and, although he did not want the responsibility, he would honour Anne's decision. Instead of protesting further, he explained the concerns relating to Mr Collins. Since Anne was too tired to see Darcy again that afternoon, Lady Matlock related her request that he and Elizabeth join her again the following day. They decided to speak with Anne to determine how she would like to handle Collins' situation before deciding on their next steps.

Their duty done, the newly-wed couple returned home, dining once again in their rooms before retiring for the night.

Twenty

Cleaning up at Rosings

For the next couple of days, things continued as they had. The Darcys slept late and retired early, eating most meals in their private rooms. Their sisters giggled together at this but left the couple to their own devices each time they disappeared into a room together.

Each afternoon, the couple visited Matlock House and met with Anne for short periods. After that first day, Anne remained within her rooms when they visited, only venturing as far as the sitting room attached to her bed chamber. Elizabeth always accompanied Darcy to Anne's bedchamber, and Anne liked the woman Darcy had chosen very much. She had laughed for several minutes, resulting in a coughing fit, when Elizabeth described the confrontation with Mr Collins in her home.

When Anne had recovered herself, she spoke, laughter still in her voice. "I apologise on my mother's behalf for sending

220

Mr Collins to your home to select his bride. It does not surprise me that the toad thought himself entitled to his choice from amongst his cousin's daughters. I remember that conversation, and my mother was quite appalled at your own mother's audacity to birth five daughters and no sons." Anne rolled her eyes at the remembrance of her mother's attitude. "Darcy, I am content to send the man packing – he is a terrible rector and spent more time visiting my mother to bring her the tittle-tattle from the neighbourhood than he did attending to his duties. I realise that neither of us will live at Rosings any time soon, but if I return, I would prefer not to deal with that toadying little man."

Soon after, Darcy left to write his petition to the bishop to remove Collins since Lady Catherine had usurped the authority of her daughter when granting him the living, and her daughter, the rightful owner, wished him removed. Elizabeth remained and continued to speak with Anne.

"Are you happy with Darcy?" Anne asked Elizabeth after several minutes of conversation.

"Extremely," Elizabeth answered immediately. "I love William very much, and he loves me in return. I have never felt as strongly about a person as I do about him. He is very dear to me."

"My mother always said that I would marry him, but I never wanted to marry anyone, much less William. He was always too silent and grave, and since I tend to be rather silent myself, I imagined marriage to him would have meant days of neither of us speaking to each other," Anne told her. "He is so much happier with you than he would have ever been with me. I have never seen him smile so often or so broadly and appear so … light as he appears to be now. I am

221

glad he met you."

"Thank you," Elizabeth answered, proud and pleased that his happiness was so evident. She had noted how different he seemed since they had first met and was glad to have that confirmed.

Anne continued. "I saw it the moment he called you his Elizabeth when he introduced you and the way he kissed your hand. That, more than anything else, made me want to leave Rosings to the two of you. I can imagine it finally becoming a true home as the two of you fill it with the noise of children. I doubt I will survive long enough to meet any of them, but I hope that a second son, or even a first daughter, will inherit Rosings one day. It seems only right for it to go to a daughter, although I am certain you and Darcy will do what is best."

"I thank you for this gift, Anne," Elizabeth replied. "I know William feels overwhelmed by your gift, but I will help him to see the meaning behind it as we honour your memory. I think that ultimately, he will be pleased by your faith in him to care for Rosings for a second son or a first daughter."

"He needs to fire the steward," Anne told her. "I feel certain that he has been stealing from my mother, but she would never listen to me. He will likely attempt to run when he discovers that Darcy and my uncle are now the trustees of Rosings, as he will not be able to hide what he has been doing from them. Tell Darcy to take some additional staff; I foresee several existing staff members disappearing as soon as the change in ownership is made known."

Elizabeth considered this for a moment. "I will be sure to let William know all this. May I ask, why are you telling me these things when you have not told William or Uncle

James?"

"I like you, and you are easy to talk to," she replied directly, shrugging at the observation. "Darcy would have listened to me, but I believe Uncle would have brushed it off. I know Darcy will do as you ask, plus, you seem intelligent and may have ideas that would not occur to the men." Anne began coughing once again, and Elizabeth assisted her to take a drink to calm it.

"I will speak to William about your concerns," Elizabeth told her as she sat back down. "Is there anything else we should know before we leave?"

"The butler and housekeeper will need to be replaced and will likely be difficult. The household accounts have seemed excessively high at times, and I have wondered if they were also taking advantage of Mother. Despite all the advice she freely shared with everyone, she was not a particularly proficient manager. Rosings' income has decreased over the last few years, and nothing I said would make her do anything differently. In fact, she regularly told me it was none of my concern."

"I do know a little of how you feel, Anne," Elizabeth said. "While my mother did not poison me or attempt to steal my inheritance, I am her least favourite daughter, and she constantly belittled me for, well, nearly everything about me. I am not as pretty as my older sister nor as lively and interesting as my youngest. I am too plain, too intelligent, too unladylike. I was not a son, which I believe was my greatest offence in her mind."

Anne shook her head. "Mr Collins is the heir presumptive to your father's estate, is he not?" At Elizabeth's nod, she continued. "I think my mother was glad to have a daughter,

223

for when my father died, a son would have automatically assumed control of the estate. I still have difficulty believing my mother has done what she has. She deserves far more punishment than she will get since she has created a dreadful mess that others will have to resolve. I am afraid Darcy and Uncle will spend a great amount of time and money to repair what she has ruined."

"William will do all he can to make Rosings successful," Elizabeth said assuredly. "I dare say he will work as hard to restore Rosings as he works for Pemberley. And we will do all we can to care for you. I do hope that when summer comes, your strength will have been restored, and you will be able to join us at Pemberley for the summer months."

Anne began coughing once again, and Mrs Jenkinson entered the room, aiding Anne in moving to a more comfortable position. Apologising, Anne told Elizabeth she needed to rest and invited her to continue the conversation the following day. "Thank you, Elizabeth," Anne whispered as her new cousin left the room.

* * *

On Sunday, Darcy and Elizabeth attended church and were the subject of much gossip since the wedding announcement had been in the paper on Saturday morning. Darcy had suggested sitting in the back instead of his usual pew to avoid the attention their attendance would garner, but Lady Matlock overruled him and invited the Darcys to sit with the Matlocks. This public demonstration of support was important, but Darcy was tense as he despised being the object of attention.

During the service, Elizabeth quietly cajoled Darcy into a much more pleasant frame of mind, and observers were surprised to see the normally dour gentleman smile softly at his new wife. Lady Matlock made introductions to a few of her friends, who gathered around the group, thus preventing some of the worst of the *ton* from approaching.

On Monday, the anticipated shopping excursion took place. They visited Mr Gardiner's warehouses and selected some of the fabrics and furnishings needed to decorate Elizabeth's rooms. They escaped Cheapside unscathed, but while shopping on Bond Street, they were approached for introductions to the young lady who had won Darcy's hand in marriage. Lady Matlock agreed to many of the requests, and before the day was out, Elizabeth had been introduced to a number of that lady's friends and acquaintances. Darcy remained with the ladies and was also inundated by requests for an introduction to his new wife. They received many invitations, which they declined, citing Lady Catherine's and Anne's ill health and the need to visit Rosings to assist in the management of the estate. They made a point of informing everyone that Darcy's wedding had been moved forward to allow the couple to honeymoon at Rosings as Darcy managed the estate for his relatives. They hoped this would be enough to satisfy even the worst of the gossips and prevent speculation about the "rushed" wedding or what was happening at Rosings.

Elizabeth met a variety of people that morning, some of whom were genuine friends of Darcy and the Matlocks and were pleased to see Darcy happily married. She also encountered disappointed mothers and daughters, who attempted to make Elizabeth feel small by asking subtle yet impudent questions regarding her fortune and connections since she was unknown to the *ton*.

When one particularly rude lady made a derogatory comment about Darcy's choice of bride within their party's hearing, Darcy bit back a retort. Elizabeth, seeing how unhappy he was with these comments yet uncertain of how to address them while adhering to proprietary, attempted to tease her husband and restore his humour.

In one store, however, Darcy found he could no longer be silent upon hearing two ladies making vile accusations against his wife.

"I heard he married his mistress," one lady stage-whispered to her friend. "I cannot imagine what else would have tempted him to marry such an unfashionable woman. She can barely be called pretty."

The other one whispered back. "I have heard she is already in an interesting state. Mr Darcy can expect an heir to arrive within just a few months."

Darcy stiffened and approached the women. "Lady Victoria, Miss Miller, I will have you know my wife may not be 'fashionable' as you put it, but I have rarely seen a more beautiful woman than she. She is everything I would desire in a wife, and I am certain she will be spectacular as the mistress of my homes. And as far as her being my mistress or being in 'an interesting state', such speculation is hardly befitting ladies such as yourselves. If either of your fathers desire to continue to do business with me or to be accepted into my presence, you had best find a way to apologise, and convincingly so, to my wife. Otherwise, I will cut off contact with them, and I assure you, neither of your fathers would appreciate hearing that."

The ladies paled as they had occasionally heard their fathers discussing that many of their investments were successful due solely to Mr Darcy's involvement. The fear that Darcy might also cut them socially if they continued to disparage his wife made them resolve to make certain they were seen as welcoming to Mrs Darcy, regardless of their true feelings on the matter. And they certainly did not want to be overheard gossiping about her again by that intimidating man. His scowl had been absolutely fearsome.

* * *

The newly-married couple appeared one other time in public during their brief stay in London. On Tuesday night, the day after their shopping excursion, they attended a play with their sisters, the Matlocks, Richard, and the Gardiners. The group of nine was spread across two adjacent boxes, with the Gardiners joining the Matlocks in their box and the younger set electing to sit together in the Darcy box.

There was much attention on the Darcy box that night as word spread that the new Mrs Darcy and the rarely-seen Miss Darcy were in attendance. Georgiana garnered some attention, but as she was not yet out, most of the attention – and nearly all the opera glasses – was focused on Darcy and Elizabeth as the gossip swirled about the wedding of one of the *ton's* most eligible bachelors.

Some had met Elizabeth when they had been out shopping the previous day, and the story about Lady Catherine had begun to spread and expand in their retelling. The few observers who were foolish or brave enough to speculate on the likelihood of an early babe or to suggest that the new

Mrs Darcy had compromised Darcy into marriage somehow were largely ignored when the obvious felicity between the couple was seen. They held hands during the performance, which was noted by many, and they appeared to constantly be in contact with each other. Darcy's hand was frequently seen on the small of his wife's back, clearly providing support and care. Some were jealous of the look in his eye when he observed his wife, and all took note of exactly how often his eye was on his lovely wife.

After that night, the gossip about the couple focused largely on the rather obvious fact that it was a love match between the two. Some remembered their attendance at the theatre earlier that month and remembered observing them then. A few of Darcy's friends had been privy to the story of how they fell in love, and when asked, they could verify that it was a love match between them. This was evident to Darcy's closest friends, if for no other reason than the fact that the man was smiling in public, something that had been rarely seen. Likewise, the obvious support of the Matlocks went far in assuring the *ton* that there was no scandal attached to the marriage, and the gossip about the two was largely silenced almost before it had begun.

* * *

Thursday morning saw Darcy and Elizabeth boarding a carriage for Rosings. A second carriage conveyed the new steward, butler, and housekeeper of Rosings. The Darcys' personal servants rode in this carriage as well. The new solicitor for Rosings travelled in a third carriage along with a magistrate who would ensure a peaceful transition. Letters had been sent ahead of their travel to the magistrate in Hunsford and to a few others who would assist the Darcys in taking control of the estate and arresting anyone who was discovered to be embezzling funds from the estate or otherwise harming it.

Darcy and Elizabeth took full advantage of their lack of company on the trip to Rosings. They snuggled together and talked and read and frequently exchanged kisses. It was the most enjoyable trip to Rosings Darcy had ever experienced.

Their bubble of happiness burst when they reached the estate, and immediately they began to meet with the problems created by Lady Catherine. The butler attempted to refuse them entry, and it took both the solicitor and magistrate to explain matters to the butler's satisfaction. He was immediately informed that he was removed from his position, and a Darcy footman accompanied him to his quarters, where he would be detained until questions about the estates' household funds were sorted. The same was done with the housekeeper and the estate steward, and the magistrates from Hunsford and London began to review the books to determine if there had been any wrongdoing.

The rest of the household staff was gathered and informed of the change in ownership. The new butler, Mr Jones, and his wife, who would become the housekeeper, were introduced, and the staff were given the choice to stay and transfer their loyalty to Anne de Bough and the estates' trustees or to seek positions elsewhere. All were warned that any servant who gossiped about the happenings at Rosings would be removed without a reference. The expectations of Miss de Bourgh and the trustees were outlined, and as Anne had predicted, those servants who had personally served

Lady Catherine chose to depart Rosings.

Mrs Jones immediately gathered her staff and requested a tour of the family and guest suites to begin preparations for the Darcys and their guests. While they waited, Darcy led Elizabeth to the steward's office to begin a review of the estate's books.

If the solicitor, Mr Edwards, was disturbed by Elizabeth's presence, he said nothing of it, and the three set to work reviewing the estate ledgers. It was she who discovered a second set of books kept hidden in that room just as Darcy exclaimed, "These are not the books that I saw when I visited at Easter!"

Elizabeth brought the ledgers she found to the table and said, "I found these in the corner of that bookcase. They appear to be an alternate set of ledgers and may help us determine what the steward has been doing."

Darcy took another minute to confirm what he was certain he was seeing. "In these ledgers you found, Rosings' annual income for the last few years has been nearly twenty per cent higher than the steward reported. In hindsight, I should have been suspicious when the steward never wanted me to visit his office but always came to me with the books. I assumed Lady Catherine insisted upon this; it never occurred to me there might be a nefarious reason for him not wanting me to visit his office."

All three began to examine the differences between the ledgers. "There is another ledger in the back that shows additional income," Elizabeth told him. "It looks like he began by taking small amounts each quarter and then gradually increasing it when it went unnoticed."

Given Darcy's familiarity with Lady Catherine's set of

books regarding the production and expenses for the estate, he quickly realised that the steward had been under-reporting the production of the estate while over-reporting expenses such as the cost of seed and supplies as well as the maintenance of the tenants' cottages, with the extra being recorded in the separate ledger that his wife had found.

"I do not understand how my aunt could have been so blind to what the steward has been doing unless she was collaborating with him somehow and knew of the missing funds. He was not exactly trying to hide that he has been stealing from the estate since he was keeping a ledger to record the amounts stolen. Mr Edwards, do you believe she could have been unaware of this theft? " He shook his head in disbelief at these words.

Edwards nodded in response. "I have dealt with Lady Catherine a few times through the years," he said, his tone resigned. "She has always considered herself superior to those around her, valuing flattery and deference far too highly. If someone showered her with enough flattery, it would distract her from their ulterior motives. And she would never believe that someone could take advantage of her, given her self-perceived 'exalted' position. Unfortunately, she seemed to have forgotten that her retaining the title of 'Lady' was merely a courtesy due to her position as the daughter of an Earl."

Elizabeth walked to stand behind her husband and gently rubbed his temples. "All will be well, my love," she reassured him. "We have the man here at the estate and under guard. We can ask him these questions, and ultimately, we can ensure that he is charged with the theft."

Before the following day was done, Anne's suspicions of the butler and housekeeper were also confirmed. They and the former steward were being held by the local magistrate and would be charged for their crimes; Lord Matlock, as a trustee of the estate, would ensure they were prosecuted fully. Whatever money could be discovered would be returned to Rosings' coffers, but Darcy held little hope that much of the embezzled funds would ever be recovered.

Darcy and Elizabeth agreed to ask Mr Gardiner's assistance with selling many of the expensive and overly ornate belongings that Lady Catherine had wasted estate funds upon. While the men were addressing legal issues, Elizabeth, with the assistance of the new housekeeper and a senior maid, began a list of those items which would be sold. The funds gained from the sale of these items would be used to better the lives of the estate's tenants, who had been neglected since Sir Lewis had died, and to replenish Rosings' coffers.

Twenty-One

The Bishop Investigates

On their third day in residence at Rosings, Darcy began to sort through Lady Catherine's correspondence. He opened every letter, quickly setting aside those of a personal nature for review later. However, when he came across a letter addressed in a familiar hand, he tore it open and immediately read what it contained.

> *Lady Catherine,*
>
> *I am certain you are unaware of the scandal your niece has nearly caused due to the lack of proper oversight by your nephew. This past summer, Darcy allowed Georgiana to almost be compromised by a fortune hunter, and the girl nearly eloped, which would have brought shame upon your entire family in the worst way. He has taken up with a trollop of the worst sort, and the little chit has coerced him into agreeing to*

marry her. You must act quickly, my lady, to prevent such a woman from becoming your niece and ruining your own plans for having your nephew as your son-in-law. You will find him staying at Netherfield Park in Hertfordshire, near Meryton. The chit is the cousin of your parson, and her presence would most definitely pollute the shades of Pemberley forever.

Sincerely,
  A concerned friend

Darcy cursed upon reading it, which drew Elizabeth to his side, and she read over his shoulder as he quickly wrote a note to Colonel Fitzwilliam, which he intended to send by express so it would arrive in London that very day.

"Are you sure of this course of action, William?" Elizabeth asked as she read over his shoulder. "Will the repercussions not potentially be worse if he remains in England?"

"The agreement Wickham signed in Meryton included his promise never to speak a word against the Darcy family again, and I have written proof that the cur has violated the agreement. If this letter reaches Richard before Wickham departs for Portugal, he will be imprisoned for debts he owes to me, although I do not doubt there will be others who will attach their own receipts to my claim," Darcy told her. "Anything he says about the Darcy family will be seen as revenge against my family and will not be believed. Besides, his society will be limited to those who are also imprisoned for their debts."

Elizabeth merely nodded, recognizing that Wickham clearly had earned whatever punishment he received after a lifetime of abusing the Darcys' trust and generosity.

* * *

A few days later, Bishop Allen responded to the letter he received from Darcy by arriving unannounced at the parsonage to meet Mr Collins and investigate the circumstances regarding his appointment and the request to have him removed. The bishop began his investigation by observing Mr Collins, getting to know some of his parishioners, and speaking to them about the cleric.

When the bishop presented himself at Rosings after two days of Mr Collins' company and speaking to parishioners, he was dismayed by what he found and astounded that a man such as Collins could ever have been granted a living. The man was clearly despised by those in his parish, both for his long-winded sermons written by his patroness, which Collins proudly showed him and for his tendency to share every detail he learned in the village with the same lady. The legitimate needs of the parish were ignored while Collins spent all his time at Rosings. Collins reportedly held Lady Catherine in higher regard than the Lord Himself and church officials. After having listened to Collins for these two days, Bishop Allen was in complete agreement with the parishioners' assessment of Collin's unsuitability to represent the church in any position of authority.

As soon as he was introduced to the Darcys, the bishop made his feelings for the rector known. "I have never met such a self-serving obsequious fool, and I question the decision-making ability of the person who granted him a living. I am amazed that he was able to pass his exams; I am interested in discovering who ordained him and pronounced him capable of becoming a minister," he said to Darcy and Elizabeth after they presented him with the will showing that Anne should have inherited Rosings on her twenty-fifth birthday, more than two years prior.

"You will inform him of this?" Darcy inquired. "I foresee a difficulty with either my wife or me speaking to him about any of this since my wife is a distant cousin, and we have already had a confrontation with him when he tried to prevent our marriage. He is also the heir-presumptive of my father-in-law's estate. He will likely view this as some type of retribution and might act in a way to get revenge upon her family."

"Why was he trying to prevent your marriage?" the bishop asked.

"My aunt, his supposed patroness, had sent him to his cousin's estate to find a wife from amongst Mr Bennet's five daughters. Immediately upon meeting her and after having been told of our engagement, Collins selected my betrothed as his future wife and would not listen to reason. My aunt had also convinced him that I was engaged to my cousin, despite the fact that neither my cousin nor I ever desired such, and I have never been engaged to another. The conversation my wife's father and I had with Mr Collins was heated, and the end result was him being thrown from the house on the day following his arrival," Darcy explained. "In the few conversations I have had with him, it seems that Collins believes anything my aunt has said is true, regardless of any other evidence presented to him."

"What will happen to him once he is removed from the living?" Elizabeth asked, trying to change the tone of the conversation.

Allen looked perplexed. "I cannot recommend him for another living – he is entirely unsuitable for a position as a clergyman. I am not certain he would even be competent as a curate, although perhaps with a rector who is sufficiently strong in character, he might be controllable." The bishop took a moment to consider, then shook his head. "I do not know what to do with him."

Darcy considered it as well. "Is there any position for which he might be suited?" he asked after a few minutes.

Neither Allen nor Elizabeth could think of anything the man was equipped to do. Finally, Allen spoke again. "I will speak to him tomorrow to let him know that he was improperly installed and that he will not be able to remain in his position. How he reacts to this news will determine what happens to him next."

"I am afraid he will view it as revenge for my father expelling him from Longbourn after he tried to convince William to forsake our betrothal," Elizabeth interjected.

"I will let him know in advance that how he responds will determine how or if the church assists him in finding a new position," Allen suggested. "If he responds as I suspect, he will have a difficult time of it."

Soon, the group was called into dinner and spoke of lighter topics during the meal. The confrontation with Collins would occur tomorrow; the bishop had already sent a note to Collins informing him they would meet at ten the following morning. The newly-weds did not remain downstairs long after dinner was complete since the bishop expressed a desire to entertain himself by reading in the library. He did so for several hours, laughing to himself at the couple's obvious desire for time alone and their less-than-subtle attempts to disguise their real reason for retiring early.

* * *

The confrontation with Collins was everything they had expected. Bishop Allen met Collins in the church and informed Collins that Lady Catherine had not the authority to award him the living and the new owner of Rosings wanted to appoint her own choice.

"This is ridiculous," Collins protested loudly. "A living is a lifetime appointment; you cannot take it away from me. Lady Catherine appointed me. Mr Darcy and my cousin are against me; they are doing this out of spite! Somehow they have persuaded Miss de Bourgh to displace her mother, and now they are trying to get rid of me!"

"Mr Collins, please calm yourself," Allen said placatingly. "Mr Darcy is one of the trustees for Miss de Bourgh, who inherited the estate more than two years before your appointment. Miss de Bourgh wishes to appoint a rector of her choosing. Lady Catherine has never been the owner of the estate and could not legally appoint you to this position. Your behaviour now is not what is expected of a man of God. We are willing to aid you in finding another position, but not if you continue as you are."

"But I have a living here," Collins irately insisted. "I do not intend to give it up."

"It was not Lady Catherine's living to grant. Miss de Bourgh intends to appoint her own choice, and I understand that she has someone else in mind for the position," Allen told him, speaking slowly and softly in an effort to calm the agitated man.

Collins continued to protest the bishop's decision, and the bishop eventually had the man physically removed from the church. Servants had been busy packing Mr Collins' belongings at the parsonage during the confrontation, so when he was escorted out, he was led to the cart containing his things and taken to London. The bishop sent letters withdrawing all support from Collins, not going quite as far as defrocking the man but making it very difficult for him to obtain any position of authority within the church in England.

Once he arrived in London, Collins used what funds he had to rent a small room. For months, he sent letters to Anne de Bourgh, the Darcys, and even Bennet, begging them to grant him a living or withdraw their objections to his being given one, not understanding it was the Bishop who ensured he would never again receive a position as a rector. After writing him back once to inform him it had been his own actions that resulted in him being unable to find a position, Darcy threw all letters directly into the fire. Bennet, however, chose to engage the man in a correspondence of a sort, responding sardonically to every four or five letters until they finally stopped.

* * *

Despite the business that frequently occupied them during their days at Rosings, Mr and Mrs Darcy spent their nights entwined with each other and learned much together about marriage and the marriage bed. They had no family to entertain, as Lady Matlock had remained in London with

Georgiana and Kitty while Lord Matlock conveyed Lady Catherine to the Matlock estate until she could travel to Ireland later in the spring. In many ways, their time at Rosings had been an ideal honeymoon for the couple as they learned much about and from each other. They found many things to do together and discovered a few things that irked them, such as Darcy's tendency to tap his pen when he was thinking about his words while writing letters and Elizabeth's tendency to hum as she went about her tasks. While at first Darcy had found this endearing, soon he realised it could be frustrating when he was trying to concentrate. There had been a few instances of hurt feelings in these early days of their marriage, but they quickly found a way to work together and solve these minor annoyances.

"At least we are discovering these traits early in our marriage, William," Elizabeth commented one afternoon after a heated discussion about some of those minor aggravations. They had already made up after the argument that had ensued, and Elizabeth now felt that she could tease her husband about them. "According to my aunt, it is good to learn how to argue early in a marriage so we might get all these little hurts out of the way."

Darcy laughed lightly before leaning over to kiss her. "Your aunt is very wise, my love," he replied. "My uncle said something similar when I first came to London after announcing our betrothal. He said that learning to communicate is one of the most important skills for a married couple; I do hope we will continue to improve on that as we learn to live together. I have become used to depending only on myself and making decisions that affect many people without consulting others. My steward, my housekeepers, my servants, and my tenants;

all of these have looked to me for the last five years as master. I have become rather used to that position, but that is not the relationship that I seek to have with a wife. You are in every way my equal, dearest, and you may have to nudge me occasionally to remind me of that fact.

"Please do let me know when I am being an insufferable arse."

"Fitzwilliam Darcy," she admonished teasingly. "You have already begun to curse in front of your wife of only three weeks? Is this how you show me that I am your equal?"

His only response was another kiss and a broad grin.

The two fell into a comfortable routine for dealing with estate matters. Elizabeth remarked to Darcy that it was good practice for when they arrived at Pemberley since Rosings was larger than Longbourn but still smaller than Pemberley, and determined the two weeks they were in residence was good practice for what she would need to do once she arrived in Derbyshire.

The Darcys remained at Rosings for a fortnight before they were finally able to leave the estate to return to London. Upon returning, they met with the Matlocks and Anne to discuss what they had found and done there. A new steward, a Mr Shaw, was in place, one who was trustworthy and would help restore the estate to what it had been. He would communicate with Darcy with all questions regarding the estate, and both Matlock and Darcy would continue to visit twice a year to ensure all was as it should be. Anne was pleased by this news and was confident that her estate would no longer be mismanaged. Although she had debated leaving the estate to her cousin Richard, she felt that Darcy was the better choice to continue her legacy. She wondered about leaving the estate to Darcy but entailing it along the female line to ensure the daughters in the family would always have a home.

Darcy also met with Richard after returning to London regarding Wickham. Unfortunately for Wickham, he had not yet sailed from England. Richard had confronted him about the letter he sent to Aunt Catherine, and since he violated the terms of the agreement through the letter, he had been thrown into Marshalsea for his debts, but not before Richard had enacted his own form of revenge on the cur.

"I will be surprised if he survives until Christmas," Richard informed Darcy. "I did beat him, but he would have survived from the damage I inflicted. Not surprisingly, he owed some rather significant debts to some others, and they caught up with him in Newgate, and that beating was far worse. Some of his wounds from that beating have festered, leaving him very ill."

"My father would be extremely disappointed in his godson," Darcy replied. "Wickham had a gentleman's education and far too many chances to correct his behaviour, and he has wasted every opportunity. He could have done well for himself in Portugal had he survived, but instead, he was determined to get his revenge by informing Lady Catherine of the events at Ramsgate and my engagement. She would have done nothing for him for the knowledge; he did not even sign the letter."

"He wanted revenge; he wanted to make your life as miserable as his was going to be. Had our aunt received his letter, she would have made things more difficult for you, even as vague as his information was," Richard countered. "Things have worked out as they should: Aunt Catherine is securely ensconced at Matlock for now, and Wickham will never bother you or yours again."

Darcy sighed. "You are correct, Richard; I should focus on what is, not what could have been. I am exceedingly happy with my wife, and although I still wish you would take Rosings, I am pleased that Anne will no longer be under our aunt's thumb and will have a measure of freedom for whatever time remains for her."

"I know you want me to take charge of Rosings, and I confess, it would probably be a good life," Richard owned. "But, I do not intend to marry, I like what I do in the army, and I cannot imagine a life like yours. I do not want to be tied down to an estate."

"And if you ever meet a woman you would like to marry?" Darcy inquired.

"Then perhaps I would take over Rosings and run it for you as long as you will let me. I know you will pay me enough to save a pile for the future when one of your dozen children takes the estate over," Richard retorted. "Or I can come live at Pemberley with you and your lovely wife and all those children you will make together."

Darcy reddened at this comment, allowing his thoughts to drift to an image of Elizabeth heavy with their child. When the silly grin appeared on Darcy's face, Richard nudged him with his foot to bring him back to the present, causing him to flush brighter. Darcy shifted the conversation to Christmas at Pemberley with the family and the plans for their arrival.

Richard's prediction did, in fact, come true, and Wickham did not survive long. When Richard arrived at Pemberley for Christmas, he brought with him the news that Wickham had succumbed to his injuries in prison. Wickham would trouble the Darcys no longer.

Twenty-Two

Pemberley

~~~⊰⊱~~~

Three weeks after their wedding, Darcy and Elizabeth were on their way to Pemberley. Once again, they were enjoying the time alone, as the Matlocks would join them in a sennight with Georgiana and Kitty. The Bennets had also been invited, but Mr Bennet decided his family would remain at home since he was uncertain of Mrs Bennet's ability to refrain from belittling Mrs Darcy. The matron remained frustrated that nothing yet had been settled between Mr Bingley and Jane, especially after the ball.

The ball had been a success, and Bingley had danced the first and supper sets with Jane. When he was not dancing, he was speaking with Jane, giving rise to more speculation within the community about the coming proposal. Mrs Bennet had been permitted to attend the ball along with Jane, Mary, and their companion, Mrs Higgins. If anyone noticed that the companion spent more time with Mrs Bennet than the girls, no one mentioned it.

While Mrs Bennet did crow about having a daughter married at the ball, she found she had little to say since she was not permitted to say anything negative about Lizzy or her rushed wedding. Several times, she had begun a sentence that was likely going to be disparaging of her second daughter, and each time the companion made a noise that caused her to fall silent. Usually, a few seconds later, she would begin again with what she had been trying to say, although without the slight to her second daughter. A few of the ladies made note of this and found it amusing to discover that Bennet had hired a companion in an attempt to govern his ungovernable wife.

Before the wedding, Darcy had spoken to Bingley of the need to be cautious in paying his attention to Jane if he had no intention of following through with them. However, Bingley seemed to have not heeded this advice since he indicated in his most recent letter that he was headed back to London, where he would remain through at least Twelfth Night. A letter from Jane indicated that he had departed without anyone being aware of it and without having taken any leave from the neighbourhood, including the Bennets.

On the way to Pemberley, the Darcys discussed the recent letters they had received from Meryton about the ball and the events that followed.

"What is he thinking?" Darcy muttered as he read Bingley's letter announcing his departure from Netherfield. "I warned him about this very thing."

"What?" Elizabeth asked, hearing her husband's low rumble.

"Bingley," he replied. "He is in town and writes to ask

246

what our plans are for the season. When he left, he intended to spend a few days with the Hursts but discovered they were not in town when he arrived. So, he will stay until at least Twelfth Night but may stay longer, depending on what amusements he finds in town. He does not intend to return to Netherfield for now."

"Jane was rather upset to realise he had left without a word to anyone," Elizabeth told him. " I received a letter from her today asking if we have heard anything from him since they learned he had left from neighbourhood gossip. Aunt Phillips was the one who brought the news to Mama, and of course, she complained loudly that he had deserted 'her dear Jane'. He did raise expectations in Meryton, and for him to have left without a word is exceedingly rude." She made no attempt to hide her aggravation with her husband's friend.

Darcy scowled. "I warned him about this very thing, that he needed to act the gentleman with your sister the very night before our wedding. He obviously did not listen to any of it, just like he did not listen to my advice regarding the management of Netherfield. As much as I like Bingley, he is a little too much like a puppy at times."

"Did he like Jane?" Elizabeth asked. "Was he merely toying with her?"

"He seemed to enjoy her company, and I thought he genuinely seemed to like her. However, I was rather busy courting you and did not pay much attention to his own attempts to court," Darcy countered. "The few times we spoke, he claimed to like her well enough or more than he had liked other women in the past. I have spoken to you about his tendency to fall in and out of love."

Elizabeth sighed. "You did," she admitted. "And I passed

that warning along to Jane. She liked him but was waiting for him to make his intentions known and guarded her heart. However, she is still hurt by his sudden desertion as she viewed him as a friend. Even if she did not have tender feelings toward him, he was a friend, and his lack of any notice of his leaving bothered her. It shows a lack of character on his part."

"It does, and I am disappointed with him," Darcy replied. "I will write and tell him that even if he had no intentions toward your sister, it was rather ungracious of him to disappear without a word. I wonder what his aunt did when he left; he does not say in his letter. When I write, I will let him know how displeased I am about his treatment of Jane. She is not just 'some angel' he met at a ball in London, but is *my* sister. He should know better than to toy with her."

"Did the Hursts change their plans so they were not in town, or did he simply arrive in town and expect them to still be there?" Elizabeth wondered.

"His letter is vague, at least the parts of it I can read," Darcy answered. "Bingley is not known for his handwriting – well, he is known for his rather poor handwriting. I can usually read about a third of what he writes to me."

"That does not speak well of him," Elizabeth replied. They discussed this a little longer, and then they moved to other topics.

* * *

The trip to Pemberley took five days rather than three due to poor weather along the way. They also travelled slowly because Elizabeth had never been this far north, which also extended their journey slightly. Elizabeth was enthralled with the sights as they travelled, especially as they grew closer to Derbyshire and the terrain became more rugged. Even though it was winter, there was much to see, and Elizabeth relished every new vista.

Around mid-afternoon on the fifth day, they rolled through Lambton, the closest village to Pemberley. Elizabeth began to look around more carefully, looking for landmarks or anything that might indicate they were approaching the place that would soon be her home.

They passed a gate that indicated they were entering Pemberley's grounds. From there, the path gradually rose until they reached a high point where the coachman brought the carriage to a stop. Darcy handed Elizabeth out of the carriage and led her to a particular spot. He wanted her first view of Pemberley to be special; this spot provided one of the best views of the manor house. It was there she got her first view of Pemberley. Her breath caught; the sight in front of her was simply stunning.

Nestled in the encompassing valley stood a magnificent stone structure, unlike anything Elizabeth had ever seen. The manor house blended seamlessly with its surroundings as if it had sprouted from the very earth upon which it stood. In stark contrast to Rosings, which, though beautiful, exuded an air of ostentation, Pemberley possessed a serene and unassuming elegance that harmonised effortlessly with its environment. The large lake in front of the house reflected the building, creating a mirror image of the grand building behind it. The lake itself sparkled in the winter sun, adding a touch of ethereal beauty to the scene.

Darcy watched Elizabeth as she first viewed their home,

a soft smile tugging at the corners of his lips. He knew the impact Pemberley had on those who beheld it for the first time and had a good idea of how Elizabeth would react; she did not disappoint.

"Elizabeth," Darcy spoke softly, breaking the silence that enveloped them as they stood there together. He wrapped his arms around her from behind as he whispered into her ear, "Welcome to Pemberley, dearest; welcome to our home." His voice carried a mix of reverence and anticipation as he regarded the estate with pride. His pride in his ancestral home was evident in his voice, reflecting the deep connection he had to the land and its history; however, that pride was nothing compared to the pride he felt in bringing his wife to their home where they would raise their family in the not-so-distant future.

Since meeting Elizabeth, Darcy's idea of a future had changed and expanded. Before her, he had envisioned a cold marriage for the sole purpose of getting an heir. However, with Elizabeth, he envisioned a partnership, a life he would share with someone who would help him carry the burdens of running Pemberley. He envisioned children running around, the dozen Richard had mentioned seemed ambitious, but he was willing to try.

He said as much to Elizabeth as they re-entered the carriage. "You know, before we left London, I spoke to Richard again about Rosings," Darcy began. "He suggested we begin soon working on the dozen or so children we are bound to have."

Elizabeth treated him to an arch look. "A dozen?" she questioned. "Is he insane? Or does he intend to help birth a few of those?"

Darcy let out a bark of laughter at her reply. "So, not a

dozen then?"

"Do you intend to keep me with child for the next two decades?" Elizabeth said. "I believe I will lock the door between our chambers after number eight. In fact, if we have that many, we may have to begin numbering them anyway. Otherwise, we will lose track."

He laughed uproariously at this response before pulling her closer and growling into her ear. "I look forward to seeing you carrying our child, Elizabeth. I have thought about it constantly since we met at that dratted assembly. Of course, I also was thinking frequently about the getting of them, but that was another thing altogether."

She pinched him in response to his rakish grin. "You are ambitious, sir. And may I remind you that I am the one who has to carry all of these children you are suggesting. As I understand it, the 'getting of them' is rather easy for you, but I am the one who will grow fat and ungainly, and I am the one to bear what I understand is considerable pain to birth them. Let us begin with one and see what we decide after that."

"Just one?" he pouted.

"Well, I did promise not to lock the door between our chambers until after number eight," Elizabeth rejoined, a small smile on her lips.

"Locking the door between our chambers seems rather pointless, my love, since you sleep in my bed every night," he retorted, grinning at her.

Her look became serious when she asked her next question: "Will you always want to share a bed with me? I know many married couples do not, and I have wondered if it was merely because we are newly married or if you will always want to share with me."

He pulled her close to him. "I do hope we will always share a bed, my dear," he told her. "Our suite at Pemberley will have two bedchambers, and we can use either, but I do hope you will always share the master's bedchambers with me."

She reached up to pull his face down to hers. "I do love you, Will, and I so enjoy waking in your arms each morning. I do hope that will never change, that neither of us will ever stop desiring the other's company, especially here," she whispered before she kissed him. They did not break the kiss until they felt the carriage stop at the front door. The footman had learned not to open the door until directed to do so, and it took a moment before Darcy indicated they were ready to alight. The staff was gathered on the steps of the large home, and it was clear they were cold as all could see the puffs of breath in the cool Derbyshire air. Darcy quickly greeted everyone and then indicated that introductions would take place inside.

Everyone quickly hurried into the warm manor house. Once inside, the staff gathered, and Darcy proudly introduced Mrs Darcy to them. He then escorted her down the line and introduced each servant to her by name before sending all but the most senior staff back to their tasks, indicating that additional introductions would take place as necessary. Elizabeth was then introduced more familiarly to the housekeeper, butler, and cook, along with a few others, exchanging a few words with each.

Mrs Reynolds was most enthusiastic in her greeting. "Welcome home, Mr Darcy, Mrs Darcy," she enthused. "We are so pleased to finally meet you, Mrs Darcy. We have heard much about you from the Master and from Miss Darcy, as well as the staff at the London House. We intended to celebrate your wedding tonight with a special dinner, if that is acceptable to you, Mistress?"

Elizabeth smiled at the eager lady. "Thank you, Mrs Reynolds, for the welcome and for your thoughtfulness in arranging a special dinner for us today. I have been looking forward to meeting you as well and am anxious to begin learning from you about how to run this magnificent manor."

Mrs Reynolds beamed at the praise. "Aye, Mistress," she said before curtsying.

Maids quickly took their outerwear and disappeared along the corridors, while Darcy requested tea be served in their private sitting room in an hour, allowing them a few minutes to change and for Darcy to show her around their rooms. He led his new wife up the stairs and down the hall into the family wing, where he showed her their suites. Instead of allowing her maid to assist her, Darcy helped Elizabeth to remove her travel clothes, and she helped him out of his before taking advantage of their relative privacy to test out both beds within their suite.

When the tea was brought up, their personal servants were unable to find them within their respective dressing rooms but blushed upon discovering the trail of clothing leading from the sitting room into the master's chambers. Despite looking for the couple in that room, Elizabeth's maid found them curled up together in the mistress' bed. Uncertain if she should wake the couple, she retreated to the sitting room, where she moved the hot water nearer to the fire so it would keep warm and then hurried to find the master's valet to ask him what to do.

Meanwhile, Mrs Reynolds, who had accompanied the

maids with the tea, observed the unfolding events with a knowing smile. She listened attentively as the maid anxiously whispered about her discovery of the newlyweds. The housekeeper's soft smile deepened, reflecting her genuine happiness for the master. He had been so sad and burdened following his parent's death, and she was pleased he had married a woman who seemed to love the man and not merely Pemberley. She could only hope that this obvious affection for each other would soon result in a new little Darcy.

A short while later, sounds within the suite caused Elizabeth to stir, which disturbed Darcy. He bolted upright and, upon recognizing where they were, broke into a broad grin. "Elizabeth," he whispered as he nudged her. "We fell asleep. I daresay tea is waiting for us, and we will be late for Mrs Reynolds' special dinner."

Elizabeth stirred and then stretched, smiling when she saw her husband looking down at her. "I am beginning to believe, sir, that you have remarkable stamina. Or are you merely working on that dozen children your cousin ordered?" She smiled up at him cheekily.

Darcy replied in a husky voice. " I assure you, my dear, that I will gladly work on that task as often as you will let me. We have not been married for a month, but I am beginning to believe I will never get enough of you. Now, do you have a preference for which bed we should share?"

She blushed at his question since, admittedly, she had noticed very little about either room or bed, given their occupation in them. "I think I will need to consider this question before I make a decision, Will." He laughed at her expression.

They quickly put on the robes that had been laid across the end of the bed, resulting in another blush. "I think we were discovered," she said bashfully. "They must have had to look for us when the tea arrived."

Darcy smiled softly at his blushing wife. "Dearest, no one will say a word. We are newly-wed, after all."

"That may be true, but I hate to think that the servants are speaking of what we do in private," Elizabeth replied, still blushing.

"Come, my dear, let us drink our tea, and then we might dress for dinner. I would like to show you a few important rooms before we dine," Darcy said to his wife, taking her hand and pulling her toward their sitting room.

Before too long, the couple were fed and dressed once again, and Darcy led Elizabeth from their chambers to the first floor, where many of the most frequently used rooms were. Of utmost importance were Darcy's study and the adjacent library. Darcy was quick to inform Elizabeth that if he were in the house, he would most likely be found in one of these two rooms if he were not with her or in their rooms. He also showed her the parlour he most preferred and the music room. After a cursory glance in these last two rooms, they returned to the library, where they remained until it was time for dinner.

Elizabeth was enthralled by Pemberley's library. The room was nearly as large as Netherfield's ballroom, with two full stories of books lining the walls. A catwalk hugged the upper walls of the room, granting access to the books on the upper levels of the room, accessible by a spiral stairwell in one corner of the room. On the lower floor, rolling ladders were strategically placed to allow access to volumes on the uppermost shelves. Thanks to large windows positioned along one wall, the room was blessed with ample natural light. During the day, sunlight would no doubt stream in, illuminating the literary treasures and casting a warm glow over the room. However, in the winter twilight, the room had a more intimate and cosy atmosphere, the sun casting its soft light throughout the room. In one corner, a massive fireplace warmed the room, radiating heat and adding to the inviting ambiance as its crackling fire filled the air with the comforting scent of burning wood.

Cosy chairs and plush couches were strategically placed throughout the library, creating a comfortable and contemplative atmosphere and encouraging readers to delve into the surrounding literary treasures and immerse themselves in the world of words. Elizabeth envisioned many pleasant hours in this room and was determined to ask the housekeeper to ensure that warm blankets were placed unobtrusively throughout the room to provide warmth for those within during the cold Derbyshire winter.

After looking around the room for several minutes, Elizabeth finally found her voice. "Your library is truly magnificent, William. I look forward to spending many hours with you in this room."

"*Our* library, dearest, and I look forward to it as well, as I have imagined you here with me for almost the entirety of our acquaintance," Darcy replied, then looked around and considered something. "Elizabeth, perhaps we could have our dinner here tomorrow night?"

She looked around and spotted a low table between two chairs that seemed the ideal location for such an intimate dinner. "I believe that could be arranged. Something simple?"

He nodded. "With a bottle of wine."

Elizabeth nodded again. "And blankets to keep us warm as we snuggle together by the fire?" She sighed, and he nodded. "That sounds absolutely lovely, my dear William."

Twenty-Three

Joyful News

The Darcys were alone at Pemberley for just over a sennight before their Fitzwilliam relatives arrived for Christmas. They were surprised and pleased that Anne was well enough to accompany them, as the last the Darcys knew, she had expected to have to remain in London for the winter. She arrived at Pemberley exhausted and given how difficult travel had been for her, she had determined to remain at Pemberley at least until spring. The Darcys intended to return to town for the season, and Anne would accompany them back to town then. In the meantime, she would get to know her female cousins better.

Christmas passed quietly despite the family in residence, and everyone enjoyed the relaxed holiday. On January second, the Fitzwilliams departed, leaving the three Darcys, Kitty Bennet, and Anne de Bourgh in residence. Fortunately for the newly-married couple, the three unmarried ladies

258

enjoyed occupying each other, allowing Elizabeth to begin to learn her duties as mistress of the grand estate. Darcy spent a considerable amount of time on business, and Elizabeth frequently was found in his study, writing her own letters or reviewing her books. Although he had shown her the private study that was designated for the mistress, both were content to share his space, and he loved being able to look up from his letters to see her there sitting in front of him.

The servants quickly learned to be careful about entering a room where both the master and mistress were together. No one entered the study without a clear indication that it was safe to enter, and their private rooms were never to be violated by anyone other than their personal servants, and even that was done with extreme caution. Many bets were placed among the footmen on how soon it would be before there was an announcement regarding an expected heir.

* * *

Winter in Derbyshire was quiet, and many letters were exchanged between Pemberley, Longbourn, Matlock, and London. Fewer letters were exchanged with Lydia in Northampton. Lydia did occasionally write to Kitty, and her letters conveyed how much she despised her school.

19 January 1812

Dear Kitty,

Father continues to leave me here in this terrible school while you go about having a good time with Georgiana Darcy. Lizzy and you have all the luck. I hate it here. The girls are rude, and the headmistress is very strict. I have absolutely no rights at all! They keep telling me I must earn privileges through "proper behaviour" and dedication to my lessons, but their lessons are no fun, and besides, what is the point of 'proper behaviour'? Ugh!

Please invite me to join you at Pemberley. I am certain that Lizzy would agree, and Papa would not say no to her if she were to ask. Besides, she is married now, so what does it matter how I behave? Shouldn't the headmistress have better things to do with her time than to worry about my behaviour? Anyway, they make me practise by writing letters to my family, and I much prefer to write to you. Mama rarely bothers to reply to my letters; all she does is complain. Perhaps you have something interesting to share? Did you meet any officers in London? Or other handsome gentlemen? I heard Lizzy's new cousin is a Colonel. Did you flirt with him?

Tell me all your news. Do not forget to ask Lizzy to invite me to Pemberley!

Lydia

Kitty was not at all willing to do as Lydia requested. She responded by telling Lydia what she was learning with Georgiana and encouraged Lydia to learn what was being taught. Kitty imagined that this was another reason Lydia did not write frequently – she did not give Lydia the sympathy she sought. After spending time with Georgiana, Lady Matlock, and even Anne, Kitty had begun to understand what Jane and Lizzy had so often told them about proper behaviour and why it was so important. Mrs Annesley was teaching them more than just proper behaviour, she taught them how to know one's self-worth and determine those who were trustworthy and those who were not.

In early March, those at Pemberley began to prepare for the return trip to London. It has been decided that Elizabeth and Darcy would leave sooner than the girls, so Elizabeth could begin working on her wardrobe for the Season. They would stop briefly in Meryton to pick up Jane and Charlotte, who would be joining them for the Season. Mary had been invited, but she found she was enjoying the time spent with her father learning about running the estate and with Hill learning to manage the house. She was content to allow Jane her opportunity for enjoyment, as she did not desire the excitement of a London Season.

Charlotte intended to participate in the Season, but she would also act as a companion to Anne. In an odd series of events, Charlotte and Anne had begun a correspondence over the winter. Anne had heard Elizabeth telling Darcy of something Charlotte had said in a letter one day, and that had spurred her into striking up her own correspondence with the lady, first through Elizabeth and then finally writing her own letters when Elizabeth tired of passing messages back and forth. Anne intended to accompany the Darcys to a few events, and Charlotte would be invited to go along with them. It took some convincing, and Elizabeth had been complicit in making this request before Charlotte was finally convinced to allow Anne to purchase her clothing for the Season.

Anne would travel to London a week after the Darcys with

Georgiana, Kitty, and Mrs Annesley. Mrs Jenkinson had not wanted to travel to Derbyshire and was given leave and had remained in London for the winter. Anne found she enjoyed the support and companionship of her new cousins and friends and no longer felt the need for a companion. She offered Mrs Jenkinson a pension sufficient for her to live independently, and that lady chose to spend her time with her daughters in Kent and London.

Elizabeth had exchanged letters diligently over the winter with Jane, Mary, and Charlotte. The few letters she had written to her mother had felt stilted, but she had continued occasionally out of a sense of duty; she had received no response. While she had written to her father, so had her husband, and his were the letters Bennet responded to, although he remained a dilatory correspondent despite his renewed interest in his estate. The letters between her father and her husband mainly consisted of the latter giving advice to the former, her father occasionally included responses to Elizabeth's questions in letters to her husband.

Letters between the other ladies in the neighbourhood elicited a more pleasing reaction. Mary and Jane shared with her what their father and housekeeper were teaching them about managing the estate and the home, although Mary had largely taken over the role as Mistress of the estate. Jane had received training from Mrs Bennet, Mrs Hill, and Mrs Gardiner and was a competent manager, but Mary needed the opportunity to develop confidence in her ability, especially as Jane would go to London in the spring. All three ladies shared the news from Meryton, although there was little new to share. Elizabeth enjoyed hearing from her sisters and friend, especially as neither of her parents had bothered to write.

Elizabeth and Darcy arrived at Longbourn after four days of travel, prepared to remain for a night or two, feeling mostly positive about their reception. Jane and Mary had expressed that Mrs Bennet was behaving more circumspectly and appeared to be resigned to Lydia's having been sent away to school and Mr Bingley's desertion. This expectation was quickly dashed as they arrived to find an angry Mrs Bennet meeting them in the drawing room.

"Lydia is miserable, and it is all your fault, Lizzy," Mrs Bennet lashed out as soon as she saw her daughter enter the room. "If that were not enough, I am confined to this house and barely allowed to speak. I receive few visitors, only those allowed by my husband, and I am even limited in what I am allowed to say in my own home. My plainest daughter has circumvented my role as its mistress; I am no longer even allowed that pleasure. All of this is because you sought to become Mrs Darcy, and now you think you are so much better than the rest of us." She was poised to continue, but at her husband's entrance, she abruptly halted.

"Enough, Mrs Bennet!" he bellowed as he entered the room. "I warned you what would happen if you disparaged your daughter when she arrived. She has written to you all winter and has made every effort to be kind to you, and you still insist she is to blame for *my* actions. I have been the one to insist on these changes because *I* saw the damage your lack of understanding was having upon our daughters. Lydia would have ruined the family had she followed your advice." Turning to the hallway, he called for Mr Hill and asked him to escort his wife to her rooms, where she would stay for the remainder of the Darcys' visit.

"I apologise, Darcy, Lizzy, for my wife's behaviour. I thought she was ready to accept what was in front of her, but apparently, she has the same complaints as always," Bennet said, shaking his head. "She has been warned, but instead of making an effort to change and adjust, she has allowed her bitterness to grow. The dower house has been cleaned, and she will take up residence there."

Elizabeth flinched when she recognized that despite the fact that her mother had insulted her, he had placed her husband first when offering his apologies. That, combined with the fact that her father had not replied to her own letters but to her husband's, made her wonder if her father had valued her before as a confidante because there had been no one better available. Now, his son-in-law garnered his attention, and according to Mary, he was teaching her as he had taught Lizzy. Perhaps she was not as important to her father as she had once believed.

They remained at Longbourn for only one night instead of the intended two due to the increased tension between Lizzy and Mrs Bennet after the attack on her daughter. While the matron was confined to her room, she was not silent, and her loud complaints could be heard throughout the house. Elizabeth had been feeling unwell, especially in the mornings, and they decided a hasty retreat to London was in order. The following morning, Darcy and Elizabeth boarded their carriage, accompanied by Jane and Charlotte, and departed for London.

Shortly after the Darcys pulled away from the house, Mrs Bennet boarded a carriage waiting at the front door with her trunks already loaded to carry her the short distance to the dower house. Her maid accompanied her, along with a cook and a chambermaid. She would essentially be confined to the dower house, since she did not like to walk, and she would not have access to the Bennet carriage unless it was permitted by Mr Bennet. Mary took charge of Longbourn, and their companion became her companion and friend. Mrs Higgins would accompany Mary when she went to Meryton and to evening entertainments since Mr Bennet did not like to attend.

* * *

The group travelling to London was subdued, partly due to Elizabeth feeling poorly and partly due to the reasons for their early departure. Jane had a difficult time reconciling herself to the action her father had taken, although she also censured her mother for her words to Elizabeth. Elizabeth was feeling unsettled as she considered her feelings about her father. She believed this was the reason for her feeling poorly and hoped that feeling would be relieved once they were in London and she could talk her feelings over with her husband.

Darcy had noted Elizabeth had been feeling poorly ever since they left Pemberley; actually, it may have begun before they left. He believed there were several causes for her anxiety – the meeting with her parents, the Season, Anne's health — all these weighed on her. However, he nearly became alarmed when Elizabeth fell asleep on his shoulder on the trip from Longbourn to London, as in all of their travels, Elizabeth had never slept in the carriage. She had always been rather insistent that she could not sleep while travelling, and the fact that she fell asleep within half an hour of leaving her family estate and remained that way nearly to London had him desirous of calling for a physician the moment they arrived at their townhouse.

It was Charlotte, however, who spoke a few words of reassurance and helped him to calm. "I do not doubt that it has been a stressful few days for Eliza, Mr Darcy. Dealing with her mother has always been difficult for her. Now that it is done, she simply needs the rest," Charlotte said quietly to him.

He was aware that Elizabeth had not slept well in the days they had been travelling, and perhaps she was simply more tired than usual. Elizabeth was unused to travelling for days at a time, and since they had married, there had been few nights that one of them had not woken the other at some point in the night. They had found it particularly interesting to engage in marital relations in hotels, as hotel walls were rarely as thick as might be desired. Both Darcys felt grateful not to have travelled with any of their sisters since their marriage, as the noises from their own rooms would have been hard to explain.

Neither Jane nor Charlotte had seen the London town-house before, and they were in awe when the carriage pulled up in front of the large townhome. It covered most of a block and was several stories tall, and included a ballroom on the second floor. That room had been utilised only as a *salle* in recent years, where Darcy and Colonel Fitzwilliam practised their fencing, and soon Georgiana and the other girls would have their dancing lessons. In the coming years, the Darcys would host a ball for Georgiana's coming out, and, with the addition of four more sisters, the ballroom would likely see more activity than it had in years, certainly in the years since

Darcy had become master.

After showing Jane and Charlotte their rooms, Elizabeth expressed a desire to bathe after the travel of the last several days. Instead of retreating to his study, Darcy accompanied his wife, leaving the others to rest for the afternoon.

"Is something bothering you, dearest?" Darcy asked as his wife prepared for her bath.

"Let me get into the bath, William, and then you can sit with me while we talk," she replied. "I would like to speak to you about something I realised yesterday, and I would like to see what you think about it."

He nodded and went to change into his own robe while he waited for his wife. Her maid helped her to wash her hair, and once she was done with that, she added hot water so Elizabeth could relax in the tub for a time. The maid left, and Darcy removed his robe before joining his wife in the hot water. Elizabeth helped him to wash before settling into his arms in the heated water.

"Something occurred to me yesterday, and it has left me unsettled," she began. "All winter, I have written to my father, approximately every fortnight, yet the only replies I received were messages in letters he had written to you. When we arrived at Longbourn yesterday, my father apologised to you before he apologised to me regarding my mother's words, despite the insults being slung at me, not you. I believed for most of my life that my father enjoyed speaking to me because he loved me – he always said all his girls were silly but praised me for my quickness of mind. Yesterday, I think I realised that he appreciated me not for myself but because there was no one better for him to speak to. Now that he has a son to share ideas with, he no longer has a purpose for me. Many of the suggestions you made to him in the autumn were suggestions I had made many times. Yet, it was not until you suggested that he take these steps that he actually did them. Ultimately, I only had value to my father as long as I was of use to him."

Darcy felt Elizabeth shudder in his arms and knew she was close to tears. As quickly as he could manage, he stepped out from the tub and wrapped his robe around himself before lifting Elizabeth out and towelling her dry as best he could before helping her into her own robe. He wrapped a towel around her hair to keep it from dripping and then carried her into the bedroom.

Gently, he placed her on the bed and then hurried to lay down beside her, wrapping her again in his arms as she began crying in earnest. He did not know what to say, as he had noticed what she mentioned without drawing the same conclusion. However, as soon as she said it, he realised that it was exactly the same conclusion he would have come to when presented with the same facts, and his heart ached for her. He held her as he mumbled soothing words into her ears, expressing over and over again how very much he loved her and how much she meant to him.

Darcy had no idea what to do to help Elizabeth through this but was amazed when her sobs stopped, and he realised she had fallen asleep again. He immediately dressed and sought out his housekeeper, explaining his wife's symptoms - mostly nausea and tiredness. That lady asked a few other questions, which Darcy did not fully understand, and recommended that he call for her again once Mrs Darcy was awake. She recommended waiting to call for a physician until after that discussion and attempted to reassure the master that all would be well.

That done, Darcy impatiently waited for Elizabeth to wake. Hurrying down to his study, he gathered the letters lying on his desk and brought them upstairs to read them sitting on the bed beside Elizabeth. He had found a rarely used lap desk, one that had likely only been used on the rare occasions when Darcy was sick in bed and used it to take notes and to jot down ideas that occurred to him as he read. He sat in this attitude for an hour before Elizabeth finally stirred.

She felt groggy and fairly surprised to find herself in bed when she woke. Vaguely recalling what had occurred, she looked sheepishly at her husband. "I do not know what overcame me earlier. I do not believe I have ever sobbed like that, and I cannot imagine what made me so sleepy," Elizabeth commented when she felt well enough to do so.

He offered her a glass of water. "I wanted to call for a physician, as I was worried about your sleeping so much, but Mrs Stewart suggested you speak with her first."

Elizabeth looked confused. "Does she believe something is wrong with me?" she asked.

"I could not tell. She almost looked pleased as I described what I have observed; the nausea and falling asleep so easily," Darcy replied.

"Well, call for her, and let us speak with her and see what she is thinking," Elizabeth suggested. She looked at him with the lap desk and his open ink bottles and commented. "Perhaps I should get up and ring the bell." She stood and removed the heavy towel from her head, brushing her fingers through her hair as she walked toward the bell pull. She had barely settled herself back upon the bed when Mrs Stewart rushed into the room.

The housekeeper asked Elizabeth several pointed questions, and one question in particular made understanding dawn. "Not since Christmas," she had replied when the housekeeper asked when was the last time she had had her courses. "Do you think…?"

Darcy watched the women as Elizabeth began to grin, and the housekeeper struggled to contain her own. "Oh, William!" Elizabeth cried. She began to launch herself into his arms but then realised that was unwise, given the open bottle of ink on his desk. "Put that down," she demanded.

"What is wrong, Elizabeth?" he asked sullenly, knowing he was missing something but uncertain of what it was."

"Put your ink pot down, William, and then I will tell you. But I do not want ink on these covers, nor do I want to bathe again today," Elizabeth said.

He scowled in frustration but did as she insisted. "Fine," he grumbled, capping the ink bottle and setting it and the lap desk on the floor. "Now, tell me."

"William," she said, her grin huge, "have you noticed that I have not had my courses since before Christmas?" He frowned but nodded as he reflected on the fact that she had not had to deny him since a very long week before their company arrived for the holiday.

He still did not recognize the importance of this fact. "Dearest, the lack of my courses, combined with my upset stomach and my sleepiness, are indications that I am very likely carrying our child." She thought for a moment. "He, or she, will likely be born sometime in September."

Darcy was struggling to hear her. "A child? Our child? You are carrying our child?" he cried. Suddenly, a broad grin broke out on his face, and he grabbed her around the waist and twirled her around. When she blanched, he sat her back on the ground apologetically. "I am sorry, my love," he said. However, his joy could not be contained, and as soon as his wife was sufficiently well, he captured her mouth in a passionate kiss. With that, the housekeeper let herself out of the room.

Twenty-Four

Charlotte meets the Colonel

This happy news was bound to change some of the couple's plans for the Season, although they would still likely attend more events than either truly desired to attend. Elizabeth was likely a little more than two months along, and after discussing matters more with the housekeeper, they believed she would probably feel the quickening in early May. At that point, they would decide if they would remain for the rest of the Season or return home to Pemberley early. Much of that would depend on how Elizabeth felt at that point and if Darcy could tolerate any more socialising.

Until the quickening, they would also keep their suspicions quiet. They would wait to tell others until the largest part of the danger had passed, and the child had made itself known.

The housekeeper, Mrs Stewart, was of great assistance in helping Elizabeth with the nausea that continued to plague her. It had grown steadily worse during their long days of travel, and while Elizabeth hoped it would grow better with them no longer in the carriage, it did not abate once they settled in at Darcy House. Mrs Stewart ensured that ginger or peppermint tea and dry toast were delivered to their rooms before Elizabeth woke each morning to help keep the nausea at bay. Elizabeth also began sleeping later in the mornings, and Darcy frequently escorted her to their rooms in the afternoons for a rest. Neither Charlotte nor Jane remarked on this habit of the couple, although Charlotte had her suspicions, which she kept to herself.

The ladies spent their first few days in London at the modiste, being fitted for dresses appropriate to the season. Elizabeth confided her suspicions to the dressmaker since her dresses would need to have room to expand soon. The modiste was accustomed to handling ladies in this condition and ensured that Elizabeth's dresses would have the room needed to allow her body to expand, although she reassured her that with a first babe, it was unlikely her waist would expand too much before she felt the quickening.

While the ladies were being fitted for new clothing, Darcy was handling business matters that had arisen while he was at Pemberley. He also met with his solicitor to review his will once again, making additional notations to include the child they suspected and any others they might have. While this task was likely redundant, Darcy's fastidious nature made him desire to ensure that all was as it should be. He met with Gardiner about his investments and extended an invitation from his wife for dinner in the next few days. Gardiner quickly accepted this invitation as he and Mrs Gardiner looked forward to visiting with their nieces.

Anne, Georgiana, and Kitty arrived in London a little over a week after the Darcys, and their days became even busier. All three of these ladies needed new dresses, although Georgiana and Kitty needed fewer and less ornate dresses since neither of them would be attending social events this spring.

The introduction of Anne to Charlotte and Jane had been interesting. "I thought you were older," Anne said to Charlotte after they were introduced. Charlotte raised an eyebrow and looked at Elizabeth, who was hiding a smile.

"I am old enough," Charlotte replied after a moment.

Anne seemed to realise that her blunt speech might offend. "That was not meant to be insulting, but from our letters, I just assumed you were somewhat older than you are. You appear to be barely older than Lizzy?"

Charlotte continued to look at Anne that same way, but her face appeared more pleased than it had a moment ago. "I believe it is the country air that makes me appear younger than my age."

Anne was nonplussed. It took her a few minutes before she seemed to gather her wits enough to try again. "I am grateful you have agreed to attend the Season with me. I heard from Lizzy that you have already been shopping. I hope to shop some this week, and I do hope you will accompany us. I look forward to seeing what you have chosen for yourself."

As this conversation seemed somewhat safer, they continued in this vein for several minutes until the camaraderie they established through their letters asserted itself, and they were speaking like the good friends they had become through their letters. They drew Jane into their conversation as they spoke about the clothes they had purchased or would purchase and the events they hoped to attend while in town.

A few weeks before Easter, everyone was well turned out and ready to take the *ton* by storm. Lady Matlock was often seen shopping with her nieces, Mrs Darcy and Miss de Bourgh, raising speculation about the relationship between the two. It had become well known that the Darcy wedding had been brought forward due to Lady Catherine's ill health and that the Darcys had aided Miss de Bourgh in taking over for her mother. Those who had heard the rumours that Darcy would marry Miss de Bourgh became convinced the rumour about that match had been merely idle talk since there was no obvious ill will between the two ladies who had lived together at Pemberley for a time and were even now living at Darcy House in London.

* * *

The entire party at Darcy House, except the two girls who were not out, were to attend the theatre now that all had appropriate clothing. Darcy felt a bit uncertain about escorting not only his wife but three unmarried ladies, so he implored his cousin to join them for the evening. Fitzwilliam was in town and easily agreed to the request. He had met Jane and Charlotte and was pleased with the idea of squiring either or both ladies around town.

Darcy had intended to invite Bingley along, but that man had all but dropped Darcy's acquaintance. Bingley had not responded to the last several letters he had sent, nor did anyone seem to know where to find that gentleman when the Darcys had arrived in town and inquired. Through the Bennets, Darcy knew Bingley was not at Netherfield, and he did not have the address of Bingley's relatives in Scarborough.

He was becoming concerned about his friend but did not want to take the chance that Miss Bingley would intercept a letter, so he left his card at the Hursts' townhouse and hoped Bingley would contact him.

When Fitzwilliam arrived at Darcy House to accompany them to the play that night, he was stunned by the ladies in residence. Anne, despite her still-fragile health, looked very well in a fashionable gown that made her appear more robust than usual, and of course, Jane was always lovely, but it was Charlotte whose loveliness struck Richard in a visceral way. Darcy had to nudge him when he appeared unable to speak.

"Good evening," Fitzwilliam said, bowing to all the ladies, although his attention remained fixed on Charlotte.

After winking at her husband, who was struggling not to laugh at his cousin, Elizabeth invited everyone to sit and partake in refreshments. They had a few minutes before they needed to depart for the theatre, and the group discussed the amusements they were looking forward to during the season until the butler notified Darcy that the carriage was waiting for them outside. They all stood and went into the hallway to don their outerwear, where Darcy helped Elizabeth with her cape, his fingers lingering to caress her shoulders and neck. He grinned when she shivered in response and had to catch back a laugh when he saw her cast a glare at him.

Fitzwilliam jealously watched this exchange and wished for something similar for himself. He settled for helping the unattached ladies into the carriage. Charlotte, Anne, and Jane took up the front-facing seat, so Fitzwilliam stepped inside to sit in the corner facing Charlotte. Darcy and Elizabeth were right behind the others, so Darcy helped his wife into the carriage and then sat beside her on the rear-facing seat. Although his carriage was large enough that it was not cramped, Darcy began to wish they had taken two, if for no other reason than it would have allowed him to travel alone with his wife, who was having some slight difficulty with the jerky nature of their travels.

Darcy did his best to curb his awareness of his wife pressed next to him in the carriage and attempted to concentrate on the lively conversation taking place inside the carriage but was not particularly successful. When they arrived at the theatre, Elizabeth became aware of Darcy's distraction and paused to allow the others to go ahead of them to ask about his distraction.

"You, my dear, are the cause of my distraction," Darcy growled into her ear. "You are utterly enchanting in that dress - too lovely, I am afraid, and I am ready to challenge every man who dares to look at you. I cannot stop thinking about your reaction when I helped you with your cloak, and now I wish I had taken advantage of the opportunity to kiss you before we left Darcy House. I am afraid I will be denied your kisses for far too long this evening."

She laughed at his admission. "Perhaps, dearest William, we can arrange our seats behind the others and take advantage of the darkness of the theatre."

"Minx," he breathed into her ear at her suggestive words. "You intend to scandalise all of London tonight, do you?"

"Perhaps," she replied archly, then laughingly pulled him forward to catch up with the rest of their group.

After this conversation, Darcy struggled to greet anyone civilly as they entered the theatre, all of his attention solely fixed on his lovely wife. Their marriage was still new enough to garner attention from many in attendance, and most who saw his distraction attributed it to his being besotted with his lovely wife. A few women, who were jealous or bitter that he had not chosen them, claimed his constant gaze on his wife was to find fault, but their suggestions were mostly dismissed and attributed to the proper motive; Darcy was besotted.

The play was interesting, and the plot entertaining for most of the party, but Elizabeth and Darcy saw little of the first act. As soon as the lights went down in the theatre and there were no more prying eyes on the couple, Darcy took advantage of the darkness to follow his wife's suggestion to engage in a more interesting occupation. When the lights were relit during the intermission, it was obvious to at least two members of their party that the couple had been engaged in activities other than watching the play. Jane and Anne asked Elizabeth if she was well since her face appeared flushed, and Darcy did not stand for several minutes until Fitzwilliam prodded him to help him retrieve drinks for the ladies.

Grinning, Fitzwilliam led Darcy into the corridor, where they remained just outside the box, as Darcy was unwilling to leave the ladies without a male protector. "You are determined to test the bounds of propriety tonight, are you not, Darcy?" Fitzwilliam inquired quietly. "Your sister and our cousin were unaware of what occupied you during the play, but it was obvious to Miss Lucas and me. If my mother were here, she would be extremely displeased with you."

"You will not say a word of this to your mother or anyone else, Fitzwilliam," Darcy hissed. "Notice that I neither confirmed nor denied your supposition about our occupation during the play, but I warn you, you will not mention this to anyone."

"Or what?" Fitzwilliam taunted, pleased to have caught his normally stoic cousin pushing, nay, ignoring entirely the bounds of propriety.

"No more drinking my port," Darcy warned his cousin, knowing exactly where to strike the biggest blow to his aggravating cousin.

"Hmm," he replied as he considered the threat. "I find that is a rather good inducement to keep silent. And you will be in town for the entire Season, which means I will have many opportunities to visit with you and drink your good wine. Now, do be a good cousin and tell me what you know about Miss Lucas."

Darcy shared with Richard what he knew, which was not much. He had met the Lucas family many times in Meryton, but his attention had been firmly fixed on Elizabeth, and most of the time, he had spoken with Miss Lucas in company with Elizabeth. She had shared with him most of what he knew about Miss Lucas, and he was pleased he could recall a few things that his wife had told him of her dearest friend.

The gentlemen were stopped several times as they made their way to obtain beverages, and the intermission was nearly at an end when they returned. Elizabeth's eyes sparkled at her husband, and he wondered if their conversation had mirrored his with his cousin. They handed the glasses of wine to the ladies and were already seated when the bell rang, signalling everyone to take their seats for the next act.

Darcy and Elizabeth whispered to each other during the next act and shared the conversations they had exchanged during the intermission. Charlotte had quizzed both Elizabeth and Anne about the Colonel, and Darcy shared that Fitzwilliam had asked what he knew about Charlotte. Elizabeth shared a few more details regarding Charlotte's dowry, which was small, but Darcy considered that if Fitzwilliam were serious about finally taking a bride, he might be persuaded to accept Rosings, or perhaps another small estate might be found.

When the second intermission came, they remained in the box, and many came by to speak to them or to be introduced to the unmarried ladies in the box. Jane, as Darcy's sister by marriage, received some attention, and Anne, as an heiress, received quite a bit more. Because Charlotte was unknown, she also garnered some attention, but the inquiries about her were largely met with silence. Fitzwilliam and a scowling Darcy both assumed a protective stance and only accepted visits and made introductions to a select few.

The entire party was grateful when the intermission ended; the men relaxed their guard, and the ladies no longer felt they were being measured and evaluated by nearly everyone who had come into the box. Elizabeth, who had experienced a bit of this in the autumn, was the least affected, but for Anne, Jane, and Charlotte, it had been exhausting and eye-opening. Anne understood that many of those seeking an introduction had only done so because of Rosings, but as she had no intention of marrying anyone, she had said little, choosing instead to observe. She was amused at the gentlemen who spoke to her yet stared at Jane. Few ladies were as striking as Jane Bennet, and Anne was well aware her only attraction was her estate, and she was angry again at her mother for making her so uninteresting and weak.

The final act of the play was interesting, and Elizabeth and Darcy enjoyed what they saw, whispering to each other that they would need to return so they could watch the entire play. Darcy suggested it might be more enjoyable to purchase a copy they could read snuggled together in Pemberley's library. Elizabeth wholeheartedly agreed, thinking of the hours they had spent together snuggled in front of the fire in that particular room.

Upon returning home, the group enjoyed a light supper. Fitzwilliam frequently spoke with Charlotte, while Elizabeth enjoyed watching their interest in each other. Charlotte brought Anne into the conversation often while Georgiana, Kitty, and Jane sat together and spoke quietly. Darcy moved to sit beside Elizabeth, and he lightly caressed her hand while they sat in companionable silence and observed the rest of the room. She moved to lean against him, and the two almost forgot there were others in the room as they snuggled together. After a while, Darcy looked down to see that Elizabeth had fallen asleep against him.

Garnering Fitzwilliam's attention, he indicated that the gentleman should depart as he could not remain with so many unmarried females in the house. Fitzwilliam reluctantly agreed, and Darcy made his excuses to the rest of the ladies before standing, pulling his wife up into his arms as he rose. He nodded to Mrs Annesley, who made it her business to see the Colonel out while also seeing the ladies toward the upper floors and their own rooms.

Charlotte and Jane retired to the former's bedchamber as they were eager to speak privately with each other. Jane told Charlotte she was concerned that Elizabeth was sleeping later than normal, and she had been very surprised to see her normally alert sister fall asleep on Darcy's shoulder several times lately while in company. Jane worried that her pace in town would make Elizabeth ill and suggested they attend fewer events until her sister felt better. Charlotte suspected the reason but did not want to say anything since the Darcys were obviously not sharing that news with anyone yet. She attempted to placate Jane as best she could and suggested ways they could all assist Elizabeth with her tasks while they were in London.

Jane asked Charlotte what she thought of the Colonel. They had all met in Hertfordshire in the autumn, but the Colonel had been busy dealing with the issue of Wickham and had not socialised much while there. Charlotte found him attractive, although obviously not as handsome as Darcy (for no man was as handsome as Darcy), but he was kind and interesting, and most of all, he seemed to be interested in her. It was late when these two ladies found their own beds and finally fell asleep.

Twenty-Five

An Easter Visit to Rosings

Following that first night out, the household fell into a routine. The ladies remained at Darcy House on their At Home Days to receive callers, and they returned calls one or two afternoons each week, an obligation that none enjoyed but that Lady Matlock assured them all was very necessary. For the first several weeks, she accompanied Elizabeth, Anne, Charlotte, and Jane as they made their calls before she felt comfortable allowing them to call on the ladies on their own. Anne was the least comfortable making these calls since she was the least used to the social routine and entirely too used to her mother's form of calling, which had included asking questions most would call impudent or intrusive, if not outright rude. Lady Matlock spent much time with her niece to try to correct this habit, and eventually, Anne began to learn that her mother's attitude had not been at all proper or correct.

While not exactly a revelation, it was interesting for Anne to realise what people thought of her mother's attitude. She became determined to do better and watched the Darcy House ladies learn how they acted. As a result, she was very quiet during calls, watching all the women and attempting to imitate Elizabeth's manner with others. This did not work for her as well as she had hoped, so she continued to watch until she discovered what worked for her. Although she struggled to make friends among the women of the *ton,* she grew closer to those within Darcy House.

Darcy's routine had not changed much since arriving in London, as he spent his mornings on business, meeting with gentlemen and tradesmen about investments and exchanging letters with his stewards at Pemberley, his other properties, and Rosings to prepare for the spring planting and to address issues with tenants. Easter was approaching, and Darcy would usually have travelled to Rosings, but the Darcys were uncertain about travelling right then. Darcy was tempted to travel to Kent on his own, although he did not want to spend even one night away from Elizabeth, and there was too much to be done to accomplish it in under a sennight.

Matlock was soon to travel to his own estate in Derbyshire and arrange for Lady Catherine's travel to Ireland. Before he left, Darcy met with him to discuss Rosings.

"According to Mr Shaw, all is going well at Rosings. I intend to travel there soon, but I have five unmarried females in my home, and I am not comfortable leaving them all in town. Anne does not want to go, and I do not intend to leave my wife in London while I go to Rosings," Darcy told his uncle.

"You have Georgiana's companion, and two of those ladies are over the age of twenty-five," Matlock replied. "You have any number of servants there to assure their welfare, so why can you not leave them? I realise that you have only been married for half a year, but surely your wife would not insist on travelling with you if it is not necessary."

"I am the one who does not want to be parted from her," Darcy asserted. "I love her deeply, and I do not wish to be apart from her for a sennight or more. The length of time we have been married has nothing to do with it."

"You will get over that, son, but go and take your wife with you. Your aunt and I will ensure all of those girls at your house are well. I do not doubt my wife will escort the elder three to every ball and party in town while you are gone," Lord Matlock commented.

When Darcy arrived home, he spoke to his wife about the need to travel to Kent. She expressed the desire not to be left behind, and so they decided to travel there in a few days. Arrangements were made for their travel, and Elizabeth spoke with Charlotte, Anne, and Jane about their plans. Charlotte suggested asking Mr Bennet to stay in Darcy House while the Darcys were away and inviting Sir William to accompany him, as Charlotte wanted her father to meet Colonel Fitzwilliam. After consulting with Darcy on this plan, the invitation was sent via express to Bennet and Sir William, with the information that the Darcy carriage would arrive the following morning to bring them to London if they were able to travel.

The party from Hertfordshire arrived as hoped, and Darcy and Elizabeth departed for Kent the day after their arrival. The journey from London to Kent was relatively easy, although it took the greater part of the day as they stopped frequently to allow Elizabeth to get out and walk. Long periods in the carriage still affected Elizabeth, and frequent stops for fresh air helped ease her nausea. They arrived at Rosings In the late afternoon, and Mrs Jones greeted them warmly at the door then they were quickly shown their rooms. The Darcys' personal servants had arrived earlier, as they had travelled ahead of the couple and stopped far less frequently. The couple elected to dine in the privacy of their sitting room that night and begin the necessary business in the morning.

Darcy woke early the next morning and rode out to view the estate on his own. When he returned, he found Elizabeth in the breakfast room and quickly sat next to her to join her for the meal, pleased to see her eating more that morning than she had on previous days. The nausea that had plagued her during her pregnancy had, at times, made it difficult for her to eat. While she did not often cast up her accounts, there had been a few mornings where she had seemed afraid to eat anything for fear she would, and there were a few foods that had aggravated her enough to send her rushing from the room as her senses protested.

As they ate, they discussed what needed to be done that morning, and then Elizabeth set off to meet with Mrs Jones, the housekeeper, while Darcy met with the steward. They came back together in the study in the early afternoon and discussed what each had learned. Darcy found that he needed to meet with several tenants over the next few mornings to address issues that required his personal attention and invited Elizabeth to accompany him on several of these. He momentarily considered that he would eventually need to convince Elizabeth to learn to ride, but right now, given her condition, was not the time for her to begin riding. For now, he would drive her himself in a gig, and perhaps they would pack a picnic and a blanket and enjoy a meal out of doors. Winter in Derbyshire would not have permitted such an escape as this, but they had enjoyed several indoor picnics in both the conservatory and the library. Darcy grew warm simply thinking about these interludes and began to anticipate these plans for tomorrow.

"My dear," he began. "I need to visit some tenants on the morrow to address some issues that have arisen. Shaw can handle most issues, but there are a few tenants that prefer to deal with me directly as Anne's representative. I think they just want some reassurance, and I am willing to give it. I was thinking that you might like to accompany me in the gig; we could take a picnic and I could show you around the estate. I know that we were here in the autumn, but Spring at Rosings is rather beautiful, and I think you would enjoy it."

"That is a wonderful idea, William," Elizabeth cried. "I would dearly love to spend the day out of doors with you, and a picnic sounds very pleasant."

He grinned rakishly at her. "I was thinking we could take advantage of our time out of doors, Elizabeth. I confess that I have had many dreams of you that involve seeing you in a grove or a meadow."

She blushed brightly. "Fitzwilliam Darcy!" she scolded. "Are you deliberately attempting to embarrass me?"

"Yes," he growled before standing and stalking toward her. Reaching out, he grasped her hands and pulled her up and into his arms. "You turn a lovely shade of pink when I tease you, my love, and I do love to see it. I wonder if there will ever come a day when you cease to blush."

She raised her eyebrow at him. "You enjoy making me

287

blush?"

"Aye," he said as he dipped his face toward hers. "Pink is very becoming on you." His lips captured his, and nothing else was said for quite some time. Darcy had locked the study door behind them when they had entered, as had become their habit both at Pemberley and Darcy House.

* * *

Later that afternoon, Elizabeth requested a picnic basket to be delivered to the stable at ten the following morning. She also informed the housekeeper of their intention to invite the new rector and his wife to dinner the following night, and another small dinner was planned for some of the neighbours two nights later. The cook was disappointed when the housekeeper informed her of the Darcys' intention to dine in their rooms once again and requested a menu with fewer rich foods than that lady would have preferred. Elizabeth's stomach had once again become unsettled that afternoon, and she found that plainer foods were less likely to cause difficulties for her. When she also requested peppermint tea to be served that afternoon and each morning, the housekeeper began to suspect Mrs Darcy's condition. This suspicion did much to placate the cook, who had been aggravated by the bland menus and the frequency with which the couple took their meals in their rooms.

Their sennight at Rosings passed pleasantly, and much business was accomplished. Darcy met with the tenants and authorised the needed repairs and improvements to their homes. He had spoken with many of the tenants in years past, and he now authorised their suggestions to increase the estate's overall profitability. He met with Mr Shaw and authorised an additional outlay of funds this year for seeds and supplies that would serve the estate well in the future. Tenants who had been unhappy under the reign of terror that was Lady Catherine began to feel much more hopeful with the new master of the estate. Rosings would profit under Darcy's management, and so would the tenants.

The Darcys' visit assured and placated nearly all of those who depended on Rosings for their livelihood. The tenants were pleased to see a member of the family in residence and felt reassured about the direction the estate was taking. Under Lady Catherine, little had been done to improve life for the tenants, resulting in many being discontent and a few empty farms. These currently had new tenants, as the steward had actively worked over the winter to find those willing to take over a farm or entice a former tenant to return. Darcy had authorised a reduction in rent for any willing to return and had authorised the same for those who had remained. Those who had been unhappy before soon began to feel more positive about their futures, as Darcy was willing to listen to them and even made suggestions to improve their lives. Despite his absence for most of the year, they felt they had an advocate in the new steward, and they trusted him to take their concerns seriously and address those that needed attention.

Rosings itself was a much happier place as well. Many of the more ornate furnishings had been sold as Elizabeth had requested, and the more frequently used rooms now reflected the tastes of both Anne de Bourgh and the Darcys, making the rooms more tasteful and far more comfortable. A number of rooms sat nearly empty, as the Darcys did not intend to decorate unused rooms in a house that would largely sit empty most of the year. There was also furniture in the attics that could be brought down as needed. Darcy considered the possibility of leasing Rosings and decided to speak of it to both Matlock and Anne after he and Elizabeth discussed the idea.

Mr Morris, the new rector at Hunsford, had been hired on the recommendation of Bishop Allen. He had been a curate in a local village for a few years, but the bishop knew him well and knew he would be a fine candidate for the position there. After a brief interview in London before the Darcys left for Pemberley, he was given the living at Hunsford, and he and his new wife had moved into the parsonage in January. Everywhere the Darcys had visited, they had heard good things about them both and were pleased to welcome them to Rosings.

"We are so happy you could join us for dinner tonight," Elizabeth greeted them happily as they entered the recently redecorated drawing room. "We have only been here for a short time, but we have heard much about your generosity and kindness to the residents of the area."

Darcy smiled cordially and welcomed them as well. Mr and Mrs Morris were appreciative of the invitation, slightly in awe of the room, and grateful for the condescension but not obsequious. They were anxious to learn more about this couple who were inhabiting the manor house.

"I wonder about the man whose place we took," Mr Morris asked nearly halfway through the meal. "We have heard much since we arrived, and none of it good regarding the former rector or about the lady who once inhabited this house. Forgive me if this is a topic you prefer not to discuss, but so much has been said, and we do wonder what is true."

They were dining informally at a small table, and Elizabeth was seated to the right of her husband instead of across from him. She reached over to touch his hand when he glanced at her as he spoke. "My Aunt, Lady Catherine de Bourgh, ruled this house, and yours, for many years, far beyond what she should have. We are aware there is much speculation about the recent changes at Rosings, but few are aware of the full story. Perhaps we can discuss it after dinner?"

Mr Morris seemed to understand his desire not to discuss this in front of the servants and nodded, changing the topic to something more innocuous. When the last course had been removed, the group chose not to separate, and they all returned to the drawing room where the Darcys had greeted the Morrises when they arrived. Once everyone had a drink, Darcy began to tell the story of Lady Catherine.

"This, of course, is known to only a few, and we are trusting that no part of it will be repeated," Darcy began, a note of warning in his voice. Both Mr and Mrs Morris nodded their agreement.

"Of course, sir," Mr Morris replied after exchanging a glance with his wife. "We would not want to create gossip. There is a considerable amount of speculation in the neighbourhood, however, so will you tell us how we should address that?"

Darcy nodded. "When my uncle, Sir Lewis de Bourgh, died, he left his estate to his daughter Anne and named my father and Lady Catherine's brother, the Earl of Matlock, as trustees of the estate. However, his wife convinced the solicitors that Anne was too weak and too young to take over the estate and somehow persuaded or bribed them not to inform the trustees of their role. She began to rule Rosings as a despot, far too involved in the lives of those who depended on the estate and surrounded herself with fools and thieves who flattered her excessively and who listened to her pronouncements. The worst part is that we believe she killed her husband and most certainly would have killed her daughter had it not been discovered quite by accident when she went to London to protest my marriage that she was poisoning Anne.

"After my father died, my aunt began to claim that she and my mother had arranged for me to marry my cousin, Lady Catherine's daughter, and regardless of how many times I denied this claim, she continued to believe that I would one day agree. When I announced my engagement, she set out to London with my cousin in tow to demand my uncle put a stop to it. While ranting at my uncle, she inadvertently confessed to poisoning her husband and her daughter to keep them in a weakened state so she could retain control of Rosings. The tonic she insisted they both drink daily contained arsenic, and we believe Uncle Lewis unintentionally overdosed on it one day, or perhaps it simply weakened him to the point that he could no longer survive. Regardless, Anne was clearly very ill when she arrived at my uncle's house, and it all came to light when Anne confessed to feeling poorly on the ride to London and taking a second dose, and the Earl called in a physician who recognized the symptoms of arsenic poisoning. Anne has been drinking it for years in a 'health tonic', and it has affected her greatly.

"Since this has been discovered, my uncle and I have taken our rightful roles as trustees of the estate, although Anne says she intends to leave it to my wife and me when she passes away. The physician believes that will happen within the year, although we hope she will grow stronger and live longer than the doctors believe. For now, my uncle and I will continue in our roles as trustees, ensuring the estate will thrive until Anne can take control or until someone else inherits."

Both of the Morrises sat for a moment in stunned silence at this account. "That is a terrible story," Mrs Morris finally said. "I cannot imagine a woman treating her husband and child in such a way, and all so she can retain control of something that is not even hers."

"How did Mr Collins fit into this story? And the servants who were fired - the steward, the housekeeper, and the butler?" Morris asked.

Elizabeth sighed. "Unfortunately, Mr Collins is a distant cousin of my family and the heir presumptive of my father's estate. He protested my engagement to Mr Darcy rather strongly, but we had little to do with his removal. It was Anne, Miss de Bourgh, who insisted that she be allowed to appoint the rector, and she despised Mr Collins. He was an obsequious toad who spent far more time kissing the slippers of Lady Catherine than doing anything to benefit his parishioners, and he informed Lady Catherine of everything he 'discovered' in the neighbourhood.

"When the bishop came to evaluate Collins to determine if he would assist him in finding another position as a curate, he concluded that the man should never have been ordained and was unqualified for any position of any authority within the church. The parishioners did not like or trust him, and he responded very aggressively when he was informed that he was being removed from the position here. He insisted that we did this out of revenge and had to be physically removed from the parsonage and escorted to London. I believe he has found a position in a rather remote part of England, although I understand he still writes to beg the assistance of both my father and my husband."

"On what grounds did he object to your engagement?" Mrs Morris asked.

Elizabeth chuckled. "Lady Catherine had proclaimed him engaged to his cousin since birth. As she could not possibly be wrong, he could not be engaged to me." Her eyes twinkled with mirth.

"Ahh," Morris replied. "His patroness was infallible, eh?"

"Something like that," Darcy replied wryly. "The others, the steward, housekeeper, and butler, were all caught stealing from Lady Catherine, proving that if one flattered her enough, she did not pay attention to what they were doing. They had become rather brazen in their efforts, and the three were found to be conspiring together in the scheme. Rosings' solicitors found an account with nearly twenty thousand pounds that were accounted for in ledgers found in the steward's office. Not only were they stealing, but they were keeping records of their theft. Lady Catherine had no idea of any of it. The money was returned to Rosings and used to make necessary improvements to the estate and for the tenants. The three conspirators were all hanged in January for their crimes."

"So not so infallible then," Morris commented. "What has happened to Lady Catherine? It was well known that Miss de Bourgh was sickly, and it is believed she is under a physician's care in London, but most people around here do not know what has happened to Lady Catherine. There are some interesting stories."

"I can imagine," Darcy replied dryly. "She is to travel to my uncle's estate in Ireland as soon as travel can be arranged. My uncle did not want her to risk her travelling in the winter, but she will be permanently installed at his estate, where she will have few servants and no visitors. It has been made known that she is ill, and the last time I saw her, she had to be dosed with laudanum to keep her from screaming about the injustice of it all. I do believe she lost her mind when all of this came to light, as she seems unable to cope with her new reality and broadcast to all what she had done in her mad rantings."

"If she has been poisoning people for decades, she cannot have been in her right mind," Morris agreed. "It seems she has gotten off far easier than she deserves, but I imagine the Earl did not want the scandal of prosecuting his sister for the murder of her husband or the attempted murder of her daughter."

Elizabeth agreed. "It would have hurt the entire family, but Anne in particular. She has endured enough and is finally able to participate in life, at least as much as she is able in her weakened state. She has improved from when she arrived in London but still cannot do as much as other women her age."

Darcy then informed the couple of the story known to the public regarding Lady Catherine and Rosings and again were assured by the Morrises of their discretion in these matters.

Soon, the conversation shifted to some of the issues in the parish, and it was late when the Morrises departed in the Darcy carriage.

* * *

The Morrises were again invited to join the gathering when a few other neighbours came over for dinner two nights later. This time, the conversation took on a more casual and general tone, covering various topics of mutual interest. As the evening unfolded, both Elizabeth and Darcy found themselves enjoying the company of their guests and felt a growing sense of kinship in this temporary residence.

Before bidding their guests farewell that night, both Elizabeth and Darcy expressed their appreciation for the pleasant evening. Elizabeth took a moment to approach Mrs Morris with her sincere interest in supporting the needs of the parish. She requested that Mrs Morris keep her informed of any specific needs or challenges that arose in the community and pledged her support. Mrs Morris, touched by Elizabeth's genuine concern, gratefully accepted her offer and promised to stay in touch.

Darcy made a similar request of Mr Morris. Although he would also communicate frequently with Mr Shaw, Darcy knew that the rector was often more aware of any needs in the community and felt this a good connection to maintain to keep an eye on what was going on at Rosings and in the area.

When Darcy and Elizabeth left two days later, they felt regret for leaving. Darcy had usually only remained at Rosings for the least amount of time possible and had never taken the time to get to know the people. He found that without Lady Catherine in residence, he could enjoy the estate and looked forward to the challenge of making it more profitable. Elizabeth laughed at this confession, and they had much to discuss on their return trip to London.

Twenty-Six

Bingley Makes a Reappearance

W hile Darcy and Elizabeth were at Rosings, Lord Matlock travelled to his estate in Derbyshire, where he collected his sister, transported her to Liverpool, and placed her on a ship to Wexford Harbour. From there, she would travel to his estate near Kilkenny. Lord Matlock could not accompany her, but he hired several footmen who could physically control Catherine and a maid who would try to keep her calm and dose her with laudanum if necessary. They were being well paid to remain in Ireland and ensure that Catherine was cared for in Ireland, as well as for their silence regarding the whole situation. They knew she had confessed to killing one person and had poisoned another; they would be wary of her.

Anne was relieved to learn that her mother had finally been removed to Ireland and that she would never have to encounter her again. Although she still felt her mother was not being adequately punished, she was relieved knowing her mother would be unable to return and rejoiced that she could freely move about in society, something that would not be possible if her mother's crimes were known.

Once the Darcys returned from Rosings, Bennet and Sir William departed for Hertfordshire, and Lady Matlock began preparing Anne and Elizabeth for their presentations to the queen. Although not really necessary for Anne, she wanted to experience the coming out she never had, which included a presentation. The practice was tiring for both women, but they made it through the event without mishap, although Anne very nearly tripped as she attempted to back out of the room after curtseying to the queen.

The night after their presentation, Matlock House hosted a ball to honour both women and celebrate the marriage of Elizabeth and Darcy. Elizabeth had met many women on her visits with Lady Matlock and at the heater and other entertainments, but this ball was an introduction to a much larger society. Darcy dreaded the event, as he dreaded all events that involved dancing, and was heard to bemoan the fact that society prevented him from dancing with his wife more than once. He intended to flaunt that rule by dancing with her at least twice - the first and the supper sets - and hoped for the opportunity to dance the last with her. He was grateful for all the women in his house, as he requested sets with Anne, Charlotte, and Jane, which meant he would dance enough that no one could complain.

Fitzwilliam had requested the first set with Anne since the ball was partly in celebration of her presentation and had requested the supper and last sets from Charlotte. While the Darcys were out of town, he had called at Darcy House nearly daily and spent most of his time speaking with Charlotte. He was well on his way to falling in love and was far enough along that he was contemplating requesting a courtship or even proposing marriage. He was uncertain how to go about this but also reluctant to ask Darcy for advice, given how much he had teased him when he was in the same situation just a few months before.

"You look stunning, my dear," Darcy said to Elizabeth when she entered his study the night of the ball. "I have never looked forward to a ball, but I am looking forward to dancing with you tonight. I fully intend to scandalise the *ton* by dancing frequently with my wife."

She leaned in to give him a kiss. "And I am looking forward to dancing with my husband, William."

They left his study and went into the hall just as Anne, Charlotte, and Jane descended the stairs. "You all look lovely," Darcy greeted them before they put on their outerwear and went outside to board the coach for the short trip to Matlock House.

When they arrived at Matlock House, Darcy exited first and then handed out the three unmarried ladies before helping his wife out of the coach. They met the Gardiners outside, and the entire party made their way inside, greeting Lord and Lady Matlock and both their sons in the receiving line. Elizabeth had met Viscount Fitzwilliam once before and, like Anne, did not trust him. He did his duty and requested a dance from each of his female cousins in attendance and then ignored the rest of their party.

Moving toward the ballroom, Darcy was surprised when he noticed Charles Bingley standing by one of the doors, apparently waiting for his party to enter.

"Darcy!" Bingley greeted his friend. "I am so glad to see you. I have just returned to town and found the invitation for this ball. I need to speak to you tomorrow if I can."

Darcy looked at his friend, confusion clearly on his face. "Bingley, I am surprised to see you here. I have not heard from you in months," he replied.

Bingley grimaced, a look Darcy had rarely seen on his face. "I know, Darcy. I have much to talk to you about, but I cannot do it here tonight. May I come by to visit in the morning?"

"That is acceptable, Bingley, but you have a great deal for which to account," Darcy replied. "Neither I nor the Bennets knew what to think when you disappeared from Netherfield without a word, and I received only one letter from you in all these months."

"I am sorry, Darcy, but it was necessary," Bingley insisted. "I will explain it to you tomorrow."

Darcy nodded and continued toward the ballroom. Bingley hung back and attempted to speak to Jane.

"Miss Bennet, might I have the honour of your company tonight? Will you grace me with a dance?" he asked that lady.

She looked unhappy at the request but knew propriety dictated that she could not refuse him, or she would have to forgo dancing for the evening. "You know the rules of a gathering such as this as well as I do," she hissed, her anger evident on her face. "I have little choice but to accept your request, or I must sit out all night, and you are taking advantage of this to force me to dance with you. You disappeared for nearly five months and did not even have the courtesy to say goodbye to my family or to send any word to anyone."

"I apologise, Miss Bennet," he replied. "I will withdraw my

request; I do not want to force you to accept my presence tonight or any other night. But I would like to speak to you and reassure you that, while perhaps poorly executed, the reason for my absence was unavoidable. I should not have attended tonight, but I desperately wished to see you."

Sighing, Jane relented. "No, Mr Bingley, I will accept the offer of a dance with you, as I know only a few of those in attendance, but you will need to account for your disappearance very soon," Jane replied.

"I have already arranged to speak with Darcy tomorrow," he informed. "I did have a good reason for leaving, but I could not say anything at the time. However, I should have informed your father and Darcy about my long absence. I do apologise and will seek the opportunity to explain further if you would allow me to do so."

Jane simply nodded, and the two exchanged a stilted conversation as they waited for the first dance to begin. They went through the forms perfunctorily, both having much they desired to say to the other but recognizing that the conversation would not be proper for a ballroom. After that first dance, Bingley had little opportunity to speak to Jane as her dance card filled quickly that evening, and she did her best to avoid Bingley.

* * *

When they arrived home that night, Darcy led his exhausted wife to their bedroom and helped her undress. She was asleep nearly as soon as he laid her down, and he followed soon after.

In another room, Jane and Charlotte sat in front of a fire and discussed the ball. Charlotte had danced twice with

301

Colonel Fitzwilliam and Jane just the once with Bingley, but he had remained close to her all night, giving every indication that he intended to continue as he had before he fled Netherfield without a word to anyone. The two women had much to say to the other about the dance; Charlotte was in the first throes of love, and Jane was ... well, she did not know what she was. She had been falling in love in the autumn, or at least she had thought so at the time, but then he disappeared. She had not forgotten him but no longer knew what she felt toward him.

"Listen to his explanation tomorrow," Charlotte advised, "and then you can determine if his reasons warrant your forgiveness."

"Is it really that simple, Charlotte?" Jane asked. "He did not say a word to anyone. He disappeared without a trace for months. How can I forgive that?"

"You will simply need to hear him out," Charlotte said. "Do not make a decision until then, that is all I am suggesting. If his reason is sufficient, then you can decide if it warrants your forgiveness. If not, then be done with him. Ask Mr Darcy to tell him to leave you alone."

Jane considered this. "I will listen to him, I suppose, and then decide from there. Now, tell me about you and the Colonel."

Charlotte began to tell Jane about her night and the two dances with Colonel Fitzwilliam. She had also spoken to Lady Matlock several times during the evening, and that lady had seemed to like her well enough. Charlotte thought she was not overly warm, as she was with Elizabeth, but seemed to be warming. "And, of course, I still have no idea what the Colonel is thinking, as he has not said anything. He does call nearly daily, but not on me, specifically, although he does tend to sit with me. I suppose I will not know what he intends until he says something to me." She sighed, as she did like the Colonel very well, but it was a woman's fate to wait until the gentleman made the first overture.

The Darcys had a similar conversation the following morning after they woke. Elizabeth had been very tired the night before, falling asleep almost before Darcy could remove her dress, but when she woke, the couple took advantage of their privacy to explore their ardour. As they lay together, Darcy caressed his hand over the small bump on Elizabeth's belly as he moved down her body to speak to their unborn child. Elizabeth laughed as she did every morning as he carried on this one-sided conversation. This morning they spoke of the ball the previous night and his utter delight in having danced with his wife four times. After pressing several tender kisses to the bump, he moved back up to the pillows and reclined with his wife, where the two of them took the opportunity to speak of Bingley and his sudden reappearance.

"He indicated, or rather insisted, that he needed to speak to me this morning," Darcy told his wife. "I do not know what he wants, although he stated he would explain it all today. I wonder what led to his departure and what kept him silent for so many months. Would you like to join me when I meet with him, love?"

She smiled and moved her hand on his chest to cover his still rapidly beating heart. "No, I dare say he will be more willing to tell you all if you and he are alone. You may tell me all later; I will speak with Jane about how she feels regarding Mr Bingley's sudden reappearance," she replied before moving to kiss him once more. "Now, what about your cousin and Charlotte? He danced with her twice last night, the supper and the last, which is indicative of a great regard for her. Charlotte does have a dowry, although it is small. If we can persuade Richard to at least live at Rosings as … as perhaps a caretaker if not the master, it would enable him to retire and marry."

"I wonder," Darcy began before drifting into his thoughts for a moment. "He claimed not to desire the lifestyle of a gentleman, but I wonder if he would run Rosings if I suggested I was considering raising horses there and would need someone to lead that venture. Then, he would not be running Rosings but managing a stud farm, which would perhaps hold more appeal to him. The house would be available for him, and then it is not charity. I will have to see if I can suggest the idea to him and if he would be willing to consider it."

"Is there a way you can have him make the suggestion?" Elizabeth mused. "Or we could plant the idea in Charlotte's head and allow her to direct him." She waggled her eyebrows at him, and he chuckled.

"You mean the way you direct me, dearest?" he asked, sitting up and then leaning over her to capture his lips with his own. It was sometime later before the couple went downstairs for breakfast, although they still were downstairs ahead of the ladies who attended the ball with them.

* * *

Not long after everyone had finished breaking their fast, Bingley and Fitzwilliam arrived on the doorstep of Darcy

House. Darcy and Elizabeth were in the study responding to letters when Bingley was announced into that room, while Fitzwilliam preferred to go directly to the drawing room where the ladies were gathered.

"Darcy," Bingley called out a greeting as soon as he entered the room. "I was very pleased to see you again last night. You and your lovely wife are looking very well."

"Thank you, Bingley," Darcy replied gravely. "Elizabeth, do you mind requesting coffee to be sent in? Bingley, would you like anything else?"

"No, thank you, Darcy. I do appreciate your willingness to meet with me today," Bingley responded, cheerful as always. Elizabeth left the study but not before asking the footman standing in the hall to have coffee sent up. She then went to join the ladies and Colonel Fitzwilliam.

"Good morning, Richard," she said as she entered the room. Georgiana and Kitty sat together on one side of the room with sketchbooks in their hands, while Richard sat with Anne, Charlotte, and Jane, entertaining them with his stories. She idly noted this as she moved to join them and participate in the conversation.

In the study, a much more tense conversation was taking place. Both men spoke only of trivialities until the coffee came, but after it arrived and the servant departed, Bingley began his explanation.

"Darcy, I do apologise for disappearing. I was at first uncertain how long I would be away, and then what I found was much worse than I could have imagined." Bingley paused and took a deep breath before he continued. "I received a letter from my aunt in Scarborough about Caroline. She had attracted a suitor, but my aunt was uncertain about his true

305

intentions and was wary of him. She wrote to beg my advice and my assistance, and foolishly, I believed I could return within a fortnight. I recalled what you said about not raising expectations and thought it would be best to simply leave the area and return when I could. I never expected I would be gone longer than a month and thought it likely to be far less.

"I was a fool, Darcy. I believed that whatever situation had arisen, I could deal with it quickly, and I also believed that Caroline would be reasonable. Likewise, I did not think that I would be nearly as heartbroken over leaving Hertfordshire as I was. I thought about Miss Bennet constantly while I was gone, but as I had left without taking my leave and was gone far longer than I expected, I did not know how I could write a letter to excuse my absence without revealing the whole of what kept me away, which I felt I could not do in writing."

"Blast it, Bingley, what happened and caused you to leave in the manner you did? It was foolish and ungentlemanly to depart in such a way," Darcy burst out angrily when Bingley paused and did not speak for several minutes. "No one knew where to find you. You said nothing to anyone, and not even your aunt remained at Netherfield."

"She ... she is with child," Bingley said, hanging his head in shame. "She was *enceinte* even before we came to Netherfield, and when her suitor discovered it, he became very angry and threatened to ruin her by announcing her situation to all and sundry. I was able to stop that from occurring, but something had to be done about Caroline. That was what took so long; settling Caroline and assisting her in finding a place where she could stay for her confinement. She could no longer stay with our aunt, nor in Scarborough, as all there knew she was unmarried – I had to take her somewhere she would not be known. I do not own as many properties or have as many connections as you, so it took some time. Caroline is residing in a cottage I leased near Leeds, and my aunt Bingley is currently with her. My aunt left Netherfield when I did, believing I had informed the neighbourhood, or at least the Bennets, of my plans. She journeyed to Bath but came when my other aunt sent a letter detailing the situation.

"After she arrived, I was sent away for Caroline's lying in, and I returned to London, hoping you would be here and could advise me. Fortunately, Caroline has been able to pass herself off as a widow, and she is presently known as Mrs Smith, an unimaginative name, but the best we could do in a moment."

"What do you think I would be able to do, Bingley? Was there no paper or ink where you were? You could have picked up a pen to let anyone know that business had taken you away for longer than you had intended," Darcy replied, his voice harsh. That Miss Bingley had attempted to compromise him while already with child caused him to reply more harshly than he might have otherwise. Darcy began to pace in his study as he attempted to find an outlet for his agitation.

"I am sorry, Darcy, and I do know that I disappeared without a word for nearly five months. It was wrong of me to do so, but I honestly did not know what to do, and I was too ashamed to think clearly," Bingley replied. He dropped his head into his hands. "Caroline cannot return to London, and I will have to turn her dowry over to her and help her establish her own household. I doubt she will ever marry now."

"You are likely correct, or at least not within the circles of society to which she aspired," Darcy agreed. He sighed.

"What do you need from me?"

Bingley rubbed his hands through his hair. "I do not even know, Darcy. I have been dealing with this for the last four months, and I still do not know what is best. When I consider that she attempted to compromise you in October and she was in this condition when she did so, it honestly scares me. I cannot imagine how you, or any man of the *ton,* would react had he found himself cuckolded. I cannot even get her to confess who the father of the babe is, so I cannot find that man and demand he marry her if he is even free to do so. I have failed my sister, both of them, although Louisa so far is unaware."

"She knows you have vanished since you left Netherfield. She wrote to me to ask if I knew your location," Darcy informed him. "I had to reply that I did not know where you were, and her letter in reply was nearly panicked."

"I apologise again," he replied. "I have handled this situation so poorly."

"You have handled it terribly; however, I do not believe that all is lost, Bingley," Darcy told his friend. "You have returned, and whatever you feel for Miss Bennet will need to wait until you redeem yourself in her eyes. She was rather upset that you left without a word, and when your absence continued, she was worried, as were we all. I think your appearing so suddenly has unsettled her, and she may not know how to react for a time. You will need to grovel."

"That I did know," Bingley replied, nearly laughing. "She was rather angry last night and expressed her displeasure with me quite clearly."

"She did?" Darcy looked surprised at serene Jane exhibiting anger, causing Bingley to bark a laugh.

"She did, much to my surprise," he confirmed, smiling for a moment before continuing with his tale. "Another reason I returned to London was to arrange to have Caroline's dowry turned over to her. I … I am not certain I will ever be willing to see her again. I also need to arrange for a cottage or something for her, but I do not know where. The child will be placed with a family somewhere, which is another issue I need to resolve."

"I can write to see if I have a tenant in need of a child once we discover if it is a girl or a boy," Darcy offered. "In a small town, a widow can live quietly without receiving much notice, and your sister will have to become comfortable with a quieter lifestyle than she once preferred. She must understand she cannot return to the life she once lived and will need to appear to live in mourning for some time. While she may one day marry, it will not be the marriage she expected."

"I do know that, and my aunt knows it, but Caroline seems unable to accept that fact. She hopes that once she has the child, she can return to London and find a husband from among the first circles. She has already forgotten that she is no longer welcome there and is unlikely to find a husband or anything but the cut direct."

The two gentlemen continued to discuss the situation until Elizabeth knocked on the door and, at her husband's call of 'enter', joined the gentlemen in the room. "Well, as both of you are still well, I must suppose that you have resolved your differences?" she teased pertly.

Darcy rose and greeted his wife with a broad grin. "Actually, dearest, you may have some suggestions to make about the topic we have been discussing." As he helped her to sit, he continued. "Bingley hopes to recover himself to Jane's good graces after being gone so long. He does have a good reason for his absence, although not for his leaving without a word. Will your sister forgive him when he explains his reasoning?"

"Am I to hear his reasoning?" Elizabeth asked, her brow arched.

"The short version is he had to do something about his unmarried sister, who is entering into her confinement in a remote cottage in Leeds," Darcy explained succinctly. "She still needs to be convinced of her new place in society, as she believes that all will return to what it once was. However, that is a problem for someone else to solve later on. For now, what can Bingley do about Jane?"

She looked over at Mr Bingley. "Could you not have sent a note to my father? To my husband? Certainly, you were not somewhere the post did not reach. You have turned this into a much more difficult situation with your silence. Nevertheless, Jane is very kind and will likely forgive you once you have explained your behaviour, although she may make you wait some time to be assured of your constancy toward her. In the autumn, she was rather uncertain of you. Now that you have returned, do you intend to continue as you did in Hertfordshire? My sister deserves far better." Elizabeth hesitated as though she would continue but snapped her mouth shut.

Darcy chuckled at his wife before fixing a glare on his friend. "I believe my wife is asking what I would also like to know, my friend. What exactly are your intentions toward my sister Jane? I will not allow you to continue hanging about without Jane's consent. She is staying in my house under my protection, and I expect you to treat her with respect."

Bingley looked taken aback at both the glare and the tone of his voice. "Darcy!" he cried, upset at the accusations and demands from his friend. "I ... I," he visibly deflated. "I have not behaved well in regard to Miss Bennet. I will strive to do better, and as soon as she will accept me, I will ask for a courtship." His head dropped.

"If Jane accepts you, I expect you to have a conversation with me as soon as possible, but if she refuses or indicates she does not wish you to call on her, you must accept that," Darcy warned.

"I will, Darcy," Bingley said seriously. "You know me, and you know that I would never do anything to dishonour a woman."

"I do, but I have also seen you fall in love many times and do not wish you to injure my sister," Darcy replied. "My wife and I will consult with her to see what she desires before we allow you to continue to spend time with her. She will have the final say, however, Bingley."

Darcy indicated the conversation was done and suggested they join the others in the drawing room.

Twenty-Seven

Planning a Dinner

J ane consented to Bingley's presence but not to his calling
on her. Elizabeth and Darcy gave them a small amount
of freedom to allow them to speak to each other privately
and were conscious of some rather tense conversations
between the two. Jane was understandably upset about his
abandonment in the autumn and needed to work through
her feelings about the man. In her typical fashion, she felt
compassion for both Mr and Miss Bingley, given that lady's
situation, and finally agreed to allow Bingley a chance to
redeem himself.

Jane slowly came around to become more accepting of
Bingley's suit, although she required many assurances that
he would never disappear without a word again. The two
spent hours speaking in one of the Darcys' sitting rooms as
Bingley explained the reason for his disappearance, the news
of Caroline's behaviour, and the steps he would take to ensure

Caroline would never be able to damage the reputation of the Bingleys. He found it necessary to also speak of the incidents that had occurred shortly after they arrived at Netherfield Park, which he had not disclosed to anyone outside those in the house that night. This level of honesty led to a new and deeper understanding between Jane and Bingley and while he did not ask for a courtship at this time, he did come around often to call on Jane, and she accepted his escort to various events while they remained in town.

They all noticed that Bingley seemed to have matured a great deal from the autumn until now. In addition to visiting with Jane, Bingley spent a great deal of time with Darcy asking questions about estate management and discussing items that Darcy had attempted to acquaint him with last autumn. Then, Bingley had been largely uninterested in learning anything, but now, he paid careful attention as Darcy discussed matters such as drainage concerns and the spring planting and even brought letters from the Netherfield steward to discuss with his friend. Darcy was pleased that Bingley was finally taking an interest in the management of his leased estate, and Bingley sought Darcy's opinion as he considered whether he should buy it or not.

"You would do well to wait before making any decisions on Netherfield just yet," Darcy advised. "Perhaps extend your lease for now, but you may yet decide you do not want to settle there permanently."

"Do you still think me so fickle, Darcy?" Bingley protested. "Do you still believe me capable of leaving Jane ... I mean, Miss Bennet, once again?"

"That is not why I am suggesting that you wait," Darcy told his friend. "Ahh, I forgot, you may not be aware of what all has been occurring at Longbourn. Mrs Bennet was sent to live in the dower house following her continued ill-treatment of my wife. Elizabeth continues to be injured by both her parents; Bennet has returned to his more indolent ways, and Elizabeth is now aware that the affection he showed for her was false. It is a long story, but I do not know if Jane would want to remain so close to Longbourn in the future. If she eventually accepts you, she may prefer you to find an estate elsewhere."

Bingley nodded, not fully understanding but realised this was something he would need to discuss with Jane when they took things further. Right now, he remained focused on ensuring that Jane realised his constancy and his devotion to her. He knew the Darcys did not intend to remain in town for the full season and intended to make the most of the time he had in town with the object of his affection. Gradually, Jane appeared to accept his attentions with a greater welcome as he proved his constancy.

Likewise, Fitzwilliam made no request of Charlotte, but it was evident to all that the gentleman had a specific woman in mind when he called at the house. This attention had been remarked upon by the ladies of the house, and Elizabeth was aware of the gentlemen's discussions over port in the study after dinners at both the Matlock and Darcy homes.

Jane and Charlotte were presently content with the situation, although both were aware that their time in London would soon come to an end. Charlotte, in particular, was uncertain of the outcome of the attention paid to her by the Colonel, and Jane only slightly more so. The harbinger of this time coming to an end arrived early in May. One morning Elizabeth gasped as Darcy was carrying on his daily conversation with their unborn child. Immediately, he reacted, concern evident in his eyes, which only grew when he noticed the tears springing up in Elizabeth's eyes. "What is the matter, dearest?" he asked.

"Oh, Will, I felt the fluttering my aunt told me about. Will, oh, my goodness, Will, it is true. I truly am with child," she said, her voice full of wonder as tears pooled in her eyes, and as he watched her, they sprung up in his as well.

"My Elizabeth, how I love you," he said before he leaned in and kissed her tenderly. "Our child is making itself known and is growing inside of you. Did … did your aunt say when I might feel it too?" he asked, his voice demonstrating the awe he felt at this moment, his hands moving back to her bared stomach as he caressed the bump that had grown somewhat but was still hidden beneath her gowns.

They remained this way for some moments, neither speaking as they gloried in the moment that confirmed they would, in fact, become parents, likely sometime in late September. Eventually, they both moved, and Elizabeth felt Darcy kiss her stomach and heard him once again speak to their child. "You will have a most wonderful mama, my child, and she and I look forward to meeting you in a few short months. We will do our best to raise you well and, if you are a son, to train you to be an excellent Master of Pemberley one day and, hopefully, the big brother to our brood. If you are a daughter, I hope you will have your mother's lovely eyes and lively personality. I will relish seeing your mother grow up through you, and I know you will one day break hearts wherever you go. I will love you, my child, no matter who you are, and your mother and I will raise you to respect others and to care for those around you as I see your mother do

315

daily. You have a wonderful example to look to in her."

Elizabeth placed her hands over his. "And you have an excellent Papa as well. He is such a good man, and he will teach you well, regardless of your sex," she whispered, never taking her eyes off her husband.

He removed his hands from her stomach and placed them on her cheeks, wiping the tears from her eyes. "I love you, Elizabeth," he said, kissing her tenderly once again. They celebrated their news and their love and arrived very late to breakfast with an unusual twinkle in their eyes that they could not hide from their house guests.

After breakfast, they met in the study, and Elizabeth wrote letters inviting the Gardiners and the Matlocks to dinner the following night. Another note and a carriage were dispatched to Hertfordshire, inviting Bennet and Mary to join them for dinner and a short visit. Darcy found he had an errand to complete that morning and set off to do just that.

His errand was to a jeweller and to commission some pieces of jewellery to commemorate the happy news. He had given Elizabeth the Darcy jewels and his mother's ring for their wedding, but he had not yet purchased a piece just for her. When he returned, he found the dinner invitations had been accepted by both the Gardiners and the Matlocks, and Elizabeth had already begun to make preparations for the dinner and for their hoped-for visitors. Elizabeth could not imagine that her father would refuse to come, but it was possible, so she had requested that Darcy write the note, believing that his request would be more successful than hers.

She shared her thoughts regarding this with her husband when she joined him in his study. "My dear William, I am torn about our decision to include my father in announcing our happy news. Part of me almost wishes he would not come but would send Mary by herself.

"I no longer know how to react to my father. For years, I pled with him to do something to increase the profit of the estate and to do more to educate his daughters. I could not ask him to censure his wife, although I would have dearly loved to since her behaviour regularly mortified both Jane and myself. Instead, he teased and belittled us, calling us all silly, although he would appear to favour me by stating that I had a little more quickness than the rest of my sisters, and I viewed that as his praise for me rather than the cut it truly was.

"However, nearly the moment you began to speak to him of these same things, he acted, and I am frankly surprised at his willingness to continue on this path for more than a month or two. My begging him to take a more active role in the running of Longbourn fell on deaf ears, but as soon as you suggested it, he acted immediately."

He stood and plucked Elizabeth from her chair and sat again in his chair, pulling her down onto his lap. "I know you love your father, dearest, and have been disillusioned by his actions and attitude toward you since our marriage. I know you have felt ... perhaps, used by him since he has chosen to ignore you to seek my company and has all but replaced your company with Mary's at Longbourn. It is hurtful for you to believe that his love for you was based entirely upon the fact that you were convenient. Instead of finding companionship with his wife, he trained you to provide that, and when he found it somewhere else, he ignored you. I want you to know, Elizabeth, that I will never treat you in such a way.

You are my chosen companion for my life, and I have chosen you not because it was convenient but because I love you so very dearly." He caressed her back as he spoke, and her head rested in the crook of his neck. He felt her tears as they wet his cravat and felt her shudder in his arms, so he held her until her tears subsided. Finally, he felt her breathing slow and lightly chuckled when he realised she had fallen asleep.

Darcy remained as he was for several minutes, caressing his wife's back as she slept as he considered their brief conversation. The injuries to his dear wife by her parents went deep, far deeper than even she realised at times, and the evidence of these appeared at the most unexpected of times. Darcy knew he would need to reassure her when these matters erupted, as he knew she would do for him when his own insecurities rose to the surface. Pemberley was one of those—he was constantly worried if he was doing enough for the people who relied on him. He knew he needed to prepare for his own children, but what of the children of his tenants, who would not have the advantages of wealth and education? He was aware of the changing world, with industrialization moving more people into the cities and away from farms such as Pemberley, but also very conscious of those who were resisting these changes. As he sat there holding his wife, contemplating their future and the new life they would soon bring into the world, his hand moved to cover the slight bump on her abdomen. He rested his head on hers and remained that way, lost in his thoughts, for some time.

* * *

Later that evening, a messenger arrived with word that both Mr Bennet and Mary had accepted their invitation and would arrive the following noon and stay for several days. Darcy, to whom this note was directed, shared its contents with his wife. She had recovered from their time in the study. After allowing her to rest in his arms for a time, he eventually stood and laid her upon the settee and covered her with a blanket he had kept for that purpose since learning she was with child. She often fell asleep in that room or in the library when they sat together in the afternoons, so he had prepared for them by keeping light coverlets easily accessible.

When she had awoken nearly an hour later, he was sitting at his desk working and keeping frequent watch over her. He immediately noticed when her eyes opened and quietly moved toward her, and they spoke again about her parents. That had turned into a conversation about Darcy's concerns for all of his holdings, particularly Pemberley, and they discussed changes they could implement to improve the lives of their tenants in the future. While nothing was definitely decided, both felt lighter for having confessed their worries and, in so doing, were reassured of the love of their spouse.

The Darcys remained home that night while Richard and Bingley escorted all the ladies to the opera, accompanied by Mrs Annesley and Lady Matlock. It was the first night in some time that the Darcys were alone at Darcy House, and they took the opportunity to enjoy a private dinner in their sitting room and play a game of chess before retiring early. They had dismissed their personal servants long ago and helped each other into their nightwear, although it soon proved to have been a pointless effort.

In the morning, following Darcy's daily conversation with

the babe, which was continuing to make its presence known to its mother, they continued the preparations for their visitors. Darcy spent most of the morning in his study with his correspondence before leaving for a previously scheduled meeting at his club. Elizabeth met with the housekeeper, ensuring that all would be ready when their visitors arrived and confirming details about the dinner for that night. Afterwards, she found her sisters, cousin, and friend and acquainted them with all the details that had been decided the night before. The women sat comfortably in the drawing room, chatting lightly as they worked on various tasks.

Occupied as they were, they were surprised at the sounds that drifted down from an upper floor of the house — a distinct metallic clang echoing through the corridors. Intrigued, Elizabeth rose from her seat, and Charlotte and Jane, equally intrigued, swiftly followed suit, their inquisitive gazes fixed on Elizabeth's determined form.

Approaching the door to the ballroom, Elizabeth noticed it stood slightly ajar and discovered the source of the sounds. She cautiously peered inside, her eyes widening at the scene before her. To her astonishment, she beheld her beloved husband engrossed in a lively fencing match with none other than his cousin, the Colonel. Bingley, a silent observer, stood at a distance, observing the action. All three gentlemen were clad in shirtsleeves and breeches, their brows glistening with sweat from their exertions. Elizabeth's breath caught in her throat as she watched her husband, his form exuding strength and grace, a sight that sent shivers of excitement through her being.

The enjoyment of such a spectacle was short-lived, interrupted by the realisation that Charlotte and Jane had also followed her to the ballroom door and were likewise enjoying the scene, disregarding the impropriety of their actions. Elizabeth swiftly took charge, urging her sister and friend to retreat from the room and closing the door behind her.

A slight noise caused Bingley to glance toward the door and see the ladies as they made their exit. Calling out to the others, he drew their attention to Elizabeth's hurried efforts to usher her companions away. As their gazes converged on the door, Elizabeth locked eyes with her husband, mischief twinkling within her own. With a bold and playful wink, she conveyed a silent message of shared excitement and anticipation before deftly closing the door behind her, concealing the scene from maiden eyes.

Elizabeth was waiting for Darcy in their rooms when he returned there to wash and dress before the arrival of their guests. "What were you doing in the ballroom earlier, Elizabeth?" he inquired as he removed his sweat-soaked clothing.

"We heard noises and came to investigate. I did not know the gentlemen had arrived or of your plans to use the ballroom as a *salle* for fencing. Although I confess that it was a scene I could eagerly hope to see repeated, I am uncertain how to achieve that without the addition of the other gentlemen as well. What I witnessed was rather … enticing and … alluring," Elizabeth replied, dropping her voice to a near whisper. "It is a scene I would like played out just for me sometime in the future."

Darcy growled deep within his throat and crossed the room quickly to take Elizabeth into his arms. The couple was not heard from until they arrived downstairs just in time to meet the arriving carriage.

Twenty-Eight

Sharing the News

Mr Bennet and Mary arrived mid-afternoon, later than intended, as Mrs Bennet had arrived at Longbourn and attempted to inveigle herself into the trip before they could depart. That lady had noted the arrival of the Darcy carriage the day before and had seen activity that heralded a departure. She had high expectations of Darcy's influence and was convinced Lizzy could not be doing enough to secure rich suitors for Jane and Kitty, as neither had sent news of an engagement or really any news at all.

It took a significant amount of effort, mostly from Mary, to persuade Mrs Bennet to return to the dower house, as she did not seem to understand that she would not be welcome at Darcy House as a result of her behaviour toward Elizabeth. It was shocking to the matron that the invitation did not include her, nor would it likely ever do so. It took a considerable amount of time to return Mrs Bennet to the dower house and to unload the trunks she had somehow managed to get loaded onto the carriage. She was told then, in no uncertain terms, that she was not to leave the vicinity of the dower house. A footman from the main house was assigned to accompany her whenever she left the house and ensure she did not approach Longbourn while the master was gone.

Bennet was still in an agitated frame of mind when he arrived at Darcy House, agitated both at the need to travel and at the need to deal with his foolish wife. He had not missed his wife in the months since she had been in the dower house, in fact, he had found life far more peaceful and regretted the need to deal with her at all. He had enjoyed the relative peace to be found in a house empty of all except Mary. Mary had responded well to his training and, with very little effort on his part, had taken on the dual roles of master and mistress of the estate. He did not realise how much advice she received from Elizabeth and Darcy, as well as Mrs Gardiner. All he knew was that Mary bothered him little and was a good companion when he wanted some conversation.

His agitation increased when he saw his daughter and her husband rushing down the steps to greet them and noted the blush on his daughter's face and the smugly pleased look on her husband's, making it obvious what had delayed the couple. For some reason, their obvious happiness with each other irritated rather than pleased, perhaps because he had never had such felicity in his own marriage.

"Thank you for coming on such short notice, Bennet," Darcy greeted the man solemnly while Elizabeth greeted her sister, who had entered quietly behind him.

Bennet greeted him gruffly and asked to be shown to his

room directly, ignoring his daughter entirely as he followed the housekeeper to his room. Elizabeth's face fell as he walked by without so much as a glance or word, an action that did not go unnoticed by either her husband or Mary. Mary allowed her sister to escort her to greet the others in the drawing room as she quietly explained the events with their mother that morning.

"He has not been himself the entire way from Longbourn," Mary told them. "I believe Mama upset him more than he has realised, if only because he has not had to deal with her since she was sent to the dower house. He has relished the quiet that presently exists at Longbourn and has retreated into his study once again, leaving most of the work of the estate to the steward or to me. Longbourn is becoming more profitable with the improvements that have been made, but I am concerned that Papa will completely lose his interest in the estate again soon."

Neither Darcy nor Elizabeth looked pleased to hear this, and Darcy determined to speak with him while he was in town about Longbourn and also about the pain his treatment of his daughter inflicted. Elizabeth had been deeply hurt by his indifference, and while it may not accomplish anything to mention it, Darcy would make certain that Bennet was aware of it.

Upon entering the drawing room, Mary spoke to all of those in the room before realising there was one person there she did not know. Darcy introduced her to his cousin Anne and the two spoke briefly before the conversation turned to the day's travel and the many entertainments the group in London had attended over the last few weeks. Mary found herself feeling a bit envious and wished she could attend

325

some of these events.

"Lizzy," Mary began, "do you think I might stay for a few weeks instead of hurrying home to Longbourn with Papa? I find myself wishing I might attend some of these events, at least the theatre and the opera. I do not care about the balls or dinner parties, but I would like to see and hear some of these performances my sisters have been describing."

Elizabeth beamed at her sister. "I would love to have you stay with us. We will likely be departing for Pemberley soon and could take you home to Longbourn on our way. I do not know if Jane intends to join us at Pemberley, as we have not yet discussed our plans, but you would be welcome there if you wanted to accompany us."

Mary seemed to consider the idea. "I am not certain who would help Papa with Longbourn if I am not there. Jane mentioned that Mr Bingley has returned and has been visiting often and escorting her everywhere, so I wonder if they will marry soon. With Kitty remaining with you and Lydia away at school, Papa would be by himself if I went away. No, I think it is likely best that I remain with him."

"If you change your mind, just know that you will always be welcome to join us wherever we are. If you send word, we will ensure you are escorted to wherever you would like to be," Elizabeth reassured Mary. "Papa should not expect you to be with him always – eventually, you may desire to marry and have a life of your own."

Mary shook her head sadly. "I do not think so, Lizzy. I will be quite content on my own, and I consider it my responsibility to remain with Papa to care for him."

Patting her hand, Elizabeth simply reiterated the invitation to visit them at Pemberley before offering to escort her to her room to dress for dinner. The entire party stood to return to their rooms to prepare for the meal, and Jane took charge of Mary, allowing Elizabeth to speak with the housekeeper for a few minutes to ensure all was in readiness for dinner.

In reasonably short order, the party from Darcy House, excepting Mr Bennet, was gathered in the drawing room awaiting the other guests. When the Gardiners arrived, Darcy quietly asked a servant to locate his absent father-in-law, suggesting he first look in the library. Bennet grudgingly joined the party, going to speak with his son-in-law but not bothering to acknowledge any of his daughters whom he had not seen in many months.

Before Darcy could do much more than to take note of the slight, the Matlocks were announced together with Fitzwilliam and Bingley. The necessary introductions were performed, and the group separated into smaller groupings as they conversed. As the host and hostess, Darcy and Elizabeth circulated the room, taking the time to speak to everyone. Only Darcy noted the tension in his wife's face when they deliberately moved to her father to speak to him, and Bennet only barely acknowledged his daughter, directing his attention to Darcy as he spoke of the books he had discovered.

"You have a rather exceptional library, which I am certain you already know. I believe I could spend weeks in such a wonderful room," Bennet remarked to his host.

"We do rather enjoy that room," Elizabeth commented. "But the library at Pemberley surpasses even this one," Darcy noted that she did not extend an invitation to her father but merely commented on the room itself.

"Ahh," Bennet replied. turning toward Darcy. "Perhaps one

day I will see it for myself. I am rather fond of a good book, as you know, Darcy, and your relations have had much to say of Pemberley's library."

"Well, sir," Darcy said wryly, "my wife is responsible for invitations to join us at our estate. Perhaps you should speak to her."

Bennet chuckled. "It may be a wife's responsibility to invite, but she does so at the bidding of her husband. Besides, my daughter would never expect me to stand on such formality as to wait for a written invitation to visit her at your estate."

"Again, it is my wife who is responsible for inviting people to Pemberley, and I would never demand that she does so unwillingly. I reiterate my earlier words, I suggest you speak to your daughter," Darcy replied before escorting his wife to speak to the Matlocks.

"I say, Darcy," Fitzwilliam whispered to his cousin, "what was that exchange about? Bennet looked rather flummoxed after you left him, and I noticed undertones in the conversation that indicated you were upset with the man. He did as well but is uncertain about why."

"He has injured my wife," Darcy said in the same low tone. "I held her as she cried yesterday when she realised how little her father valued her. All winter, she has written him weekly without ever receiving so much as a note in reply. He replied to my letters and only occasionally included a word or two for his daughter. It was not about saving postage or paper. She has realised he only valued her as a companion when there was no alternative and how little respect or real love he carries for his daughters. Before he returns to Longbourn, I intend to express my displeasure, and I will not let him use her or me for our libraries while he ignores his daughters."

Fitzwilliam looked angry on his cousin's behalf. "I thought he had improved," he stated.

"Perhaps for a time, although according to Mary, he is returning to his indolent ways. Before, it was Elizabeth who ran Longbourn, now, it is Mary, and Bennet is content to sit and read his books. The only change is the house is quieter now since three of his daughters presently reside in my house, one is all but forgotten by him at school, and his wife has been banished to the dower house where he no longer has to deal with her. Only Mary is left at home, and she keeps herself occupied except for when he wants conservation. He treats her in the same way he treated Elizabeth," Darcy finished. "I had liked the man when we first met, and he seemed to be making the necessary changes to make the estate profitable again. However, he is already losing interest in that endeavour and is returning to the man he was before I married my wife."

"That is too bad," Fitzwilliam agreed. "I will tease him with your library this evening, especially as it appears he will never see it for himself as long as he is upsetting your wife."

Darcy merely nodded at his cousin, and they moved to where his wife stood speaking to Lord and Lady Matlock. After a few more minutes of conversation, dinner was announced. Darcy offered his arm to his wife and announced: "This is a family dinner; therefore, we will not stand on formality. I intend to sit beside my wife tonight, so please, sit where you wish in the dining room."

That said, he escorted his wife into the dining room, waving off the footman as he helped his wife into her seat to his right. As arranged, the countess sat at the other end of the table with the earl to her right, and everyone else filled in around the table with the married and courting couples sitting next to each other and the single ladies seated together near the middle of the table. Bennet came in last and, looking around the table, finally took the last open seat between Anne and Mrs Gardiner.

Elizabeth had arranged for four courses, including at least one of the favourites of nearly everyone gathered at the table. Conversation around the table was lively, with nearly everyone participating. Bennet, seated as he was, found little to say to either lady and frequently found himself left out of the conversation.

When the last course was removed, and before the ladies could separate from the gentlemen, Darcy stood, commanding everyone's attention. "We are so pleased to have all our family here tonight; my wife and I are thankful that all of you could attend tonight's dinner as we have news we would like to share." He took his wife's hand and bent to kiss it lightly before continuing. "My wife has informed me that we are expecting an addition to our household, and we expect him or her just after the harvest in September. I am extraordinarily pleased with this news - we both are - and wanted to invite you all here to share in our joy. I have never been so happy as I have been in these last few months, and I am beyond pleased that our family will expand. Please, all of you, raise your glass in honour of my dear wife and our happy news."

As soon as he finished speaking, the table erupted in congratulations, and those gathered raised their glasses to celebrate the future heir of Pemberley. Before long, the party separated, allowing the ladies to go into the drawing room to discuss this development further while the gentlemen spent the next few minutes slapping Darcy's back and teasing him about his accomplishment in impregnating his wife.

"Given the looks that pass between the two, and their constant disappearances, I am not the least bit surprised that she is already expecting," Fitzwilliam remarked to his father a few minutes later. "I am frankly amazed that the announcement took as long as it did. Char..., I mean, Miss Lucas told me she has suspected it the entire time they have been in London."

"We have suspected it for some time but have only recently had our suspicions confirmed. We wanted to wait until things were more certain before we made an announcement," Darcy offered.

Fitzwilliam and Bingley teased him a little more while Gardiner and Bennet attempted not to hear. Matlock occasionally laughed at the younger men since it was not his daughter or niece they were speaking of, but eventually engaged the two older gentlemen in conversation and attempted to block out the comments made by the younger, unmarried men.

The conversation in the drawing room was very different. There was little teasing, and the unmarried ladies, beyond offering their congratulations, soon drifted away to discuss other topics. Mary asked Georgiana to show her the music room, and those two, along with Kitty, retreated to practise on the pianoforte. Jane and Charlotte remained in the room but sat quietly discussing their beaux, leaving Mrs Gardiner and Lady Matlock to speak to Elizabeth.

"I have suspected this for the last several weeks, Lizzy," Aunt Gardiner began. "You have appeared wan at times, but you have had an unmistakable glow about you that made me wonder. Have you felt the quickening?"

331

Elizabeth nodded. "Yesterday morning," she acknowledged. "We arranged this little party so we might tell you all at once. I am grateful everyone was able to attend on such short notice."

The three married ladies spoke a while longer as Elizabeth's aunts told her about what to expect in the days and weeks to come. Both women offered to come to Pemberley for her lying in if she desired it, although Elizabeth hesitated as she was uncertain what she would desire when her time came. She hoped her husband would attend her, but if he followed the custom of the day and did not remain, he would need another gentleman there to keep him company. She pondered this as she continued speaking with the ladies and saved this question, and a few other comments of her aunts, to discuss with her husband later.

The gentlemen returned to the drawing room, and the jovial mood persisted for most of the party. Bennet did not remain with the party for long, excusing himself to retire, although Elizabeth and Darcy believed he would retreat to the library rather than his room. Elizabeth once again shrugged off her father's indifference, focusing instead on those who did rejoice in their news. The party continued for another hour or two, with Georgiana, Mary, and Kitty amusing them all with performances on the piano. Anne even sang, which surprised all but Georgiana, who had dedicated a considerable amount of time in practice with her over the last few months. Everyone considered the night a great success, and congratulations were offered once again as they departed.

It was late when Elizabeth and Darcy crawled into bed, once again forgoing the assistance of their personal servants and assisting each other in their preparations for bed. Although tired, they had enough energy to slowly reaffirm their own joy in the news of their coming child and then lay together, entwined as they spoke together quietly.

"There was one thing our aunts told me that you might find particularly interesting, William," Elizabeth told her husband, her tone arch, and he knew if he could see her in the darkness, she would have arched that one eyebrow as she always did when she teased him.

"And what is that, my love?" he asked as she clearly intended.

"Well, she told me that as the pregnancy progresses, my stomach will grow, which I knew, but apparently, so will my, ummm, desire for you," she replied, her voice notable for its lack of emotion as she attempted to hold it in. "My aunt Gardiner said in the final few months of her confinements, she was nearly insatiable at times."

Darcy's arms tightened around her reflexively. "Do you mean to say," he began, pausing for effect, his voice dry, "that you will want to engage with me even more frequently than we already do? That you will become even more insatiable than you already are, my love?"

"That is what she said," Elizabeth replied, a hint of laughter creeping into her voice. "When she began to speak of positions, I did divert the topic, but she indicated that we would need to be more creative as I grow larger."

"That nearly sounds like a challenge, my love," Darcy replied wryly. "One that I happily accept. I will be sure to give you whatever you desire, you temptress, and if that means that all business must fall by the wayside as I keep you satisfied, I will have to tolerate it."

She laughed at that, and the laughter he attempted to hold

in burst forth. They soon calmed and fell asleep tightly wrapped in each other's arms.

Twenty-Nine

Bennet is Set Down

Now that Elizabeth had felt the quickening, They began to make plans for their return to Pemberley in a few weeks. Georgiana and Kitty would accompany the Darcys to Derbyshire, and Anne, Charlotte, and Jane were given a choice about what to do. Jane was determined to return to Longbourn, as Bingley had expressed a desire to return to Netherfield after so many months away from his leased estate. He attempted to convince Darcy to spend a few weeks at his estate with him, but Darcy and Elizabeth had exchanged a glance. Darcy determinedly refused on the grounds that Elizabeth needed to be settled at Pemberley as early as possible.

Anne and Charlotte decided to remain together and spent many hours in conversation about the choices offered to them. Finally, they accepted the invitation to move to Matlock House and remain with Anne's aunt and uncle until the end of the season. When he heard this plan, Darcy offered Fitzwilliam the use of Darcy House if he ever made up his mind about courting Charlotte. He knew his cousin was interested in the lady but was uncertain what was preventing the relationship from moving forward.

Although Darcy had little desire to intrude upon his cousin's business, he did take the opportunity one afternoon when his cousin visited to ask him about it. "So, Richard, Miss Lucas and Anne are to remain in London for the season. What will you do?"

Richard looked taken aback. "What do you mean, cousin?"

"What will you do about Miss Lucas? It is clear the two of you have formed some sort of relationship, and Elizabeth is convinced that Charlotte likes you quite well," Darcy replied.

Richard groaned. "I did not realise that she was affected as well. I, uh, well, it is possible that I am in love with her, but I cannot offer for her. I did not … I had not considered that her heart might be affected. I do not know what to do."

"Why not?" Darcy demanded.

"I have no home, no fortune, nothing to offer her," Richard complained. "I cannot ask Anne for Rosings now, nor do I want the estate. All my objections remain, although I do realise now that I wish I had something to offer to Charlotte other than a life of following the drum."

"Allow me to help you," Darcy offered cautiously. "Even if you do not want to own Rosings, you could take up residence there and run the estate. I have been considering expanding the horse farm in Kent, using the pasture land at Rosings, since the farm is less than thirty miles away. You could oversee the expansion of the barns while living at Rosings and ensuring that all there is well."

336

"And I would be what, a steward, or your employee?" Richard said bitterly.

"No, I was hoping you would be willing to accept a partnership," Darcy replied. "I know that you have some substantial savings, and Miss Lucas does have a dowry, though smaller than you might have sought in the past. My financial investment would be larger since your investment would include not only a financial investment but your expertise in the area and your actual oversight of the enterprise."

"This feels a bit like charity," Richard protested lightly.

"Not really," Darcy said nonchalantly. "I have been considering the expansion of the horse farm for some time, but managing Rosings has added to my responsibilities of late. I have excellent stewards at both properties, but I need someone I trust to manage the expansion, as it will require working with both stewards. Having you near to manage this and help oversee Rosings would be of a substantial benefit to me. I do hope to spend less time on business once our child arrives. I anticipate hiring a secretary soon to assist me, although I believe I might struggle to find one I can trust implicitly."

"I would like to throw an absolute fit since this definitely stinks of a scheme devised just for my benefit," Richard began. "However, if I agree, it will enable me to make an offer for Miss Lucas. As long as this is a true partnership and you will allow me to invest my funds as well as my 'expertise', I will agree. I want legal documents drawn up that will clearly outline each of our contributions as well as how any profits will be split. And I will agree to live at Rosings since I have seen the house on that horse farm and cannot imagine living there myself. If I, who have slept in tents for weeks on end, cannot fathom staying in that house, I cannot imagine that Charlotte would ever desire to do so."

"Wonderful," Darcy replied. "One other matter, Miss Lucas is moving to Matlock House to finish the season when we depart for Pemberley. You will need other accommodations, so Darcy House will be open to you as usual for the duration. Do know that once we are settled in at Pemberley, we will not intend to remove until after the child is born. I apologise if this will interfere with any plans the two of you will make."

Richard waved off the apology. "I do not know if it will matter. It will ask Miss Lucas for a courtship in the next few days. I do not need to ask her father for permission, but I will still ride to Hertfordshire to speak with him. You have met him; what is he like?"

Darcy began to tell him some of what he knew about Sir William Lucas before the conversation returned to their joint venture. A rough draft of the agreement was made, and Darcy stated his intent to take it to his solicitor on the morrow to have him begin work on it. They expected the agreement would be ready before the Darcys intended to depart, and they would not have to alter their plans for their return to Pemberley.

* * *

A similar conversation took place between Darcy and Bingley about the latter's attention toward the eldest Miss Bennet. This conversation should have occurred between Bennet and Bingley, but despite Darcy's prodding, Bennet remained unconcerned about the relationship between his eldest daughter and the leaseholder of Netherfield. Bennet and Mary were still in London, having decided to remain until the Darcys departed so Bennet might take advantage of their library.

It seemed to Elizabeth that Jane had forgiven Bingley, and while she was not certain her sister should have given in so easily, it was in Jane's nature to forgive quickly. Bingley had courted Jane assiduously in the month since he returned and appeared to have developed a consistency that allowed Jane to feel more certain of him. She would return to Longbourn, and Bingley would follow. Darcy felt it was his business to determine Bingley's intentions and to warn him, again, not to toy with her.

The conversation went easily enough, and Bingley expressed his intention to ask for a courtship upon their return to Hertfordshire, believing that six weeks was enough time to assure Jane and her father of his consistency. After a few weeks of courting, Bingley would propose, and he had already purchased a betrothal gift for the lady. All of this assured Darcy that Bingley was in earnest, which enabled Darcy to reassure his wife of the same.

One more confrontation occurred in the last weeks the Darcys remained in London, but Darcy himself had little part of it. Elizabeth entered the library one morning and, finding her father there, sighed loudly. "Good morning, Papa," she greeted when she noticed him and then waited for a response that did not come.

"Papa?" she called again after a moment went by without him responding. Just then, Darcy walked into the room from the study, and that drew her father's attention from his book.

"Darcy, good morning. I know I have told you before, but I will reiterate; you have a magnificent library here," Bennet said and then, taking a note of his daughter, spoke again.

"Ahh, Lizzy, I did not see you come in."

"I spoke to you twice, Papa, but apparently, the noise of my husband's silent entry garnered your attention more easily than the sound of your 'beloved daughter's' voice," Elizabeth dryly remarked, her tone laced with sarcasm.

Both gentlemen looked at her, one with concern, one with mocking indifference.

"Well, you know how engrossed I become when I am reading a good book, my child," he replied dismissively.

"Perhaps we should restrict your access to books in our home, and then you might take more notice of your daughters," Elizabeth began. "You have certainly spent far more time in this room than you have with any of your daughters who are residing under my husband's roof. My husband has borne the cost of dressing two of your daughters for the last few months, not to mention their room and board. I wonder, how much money have you saved toward their dowries while they have been cared for elsewhere? You have only had the care of Mary at home, and with Mama in the dower house, you should have been able to save a considerable sum." She stood there quietly, staring at her father for several minutes while he squirmed slightly under her direct gaze.

He chose to try to put her on the defensive in an effort to unsettle her. "You are being quite impertinent, daughter. I can imagine how Mary would chastise you were she to hear you speak in such a way," he remarked.

His attempt to rattle her composure failed. Elizabeth laughed. "So you would delegate the task of reprimanding me to my younger sister. Even in this, you cannot be bothered to take a real stand. Not that it would matter, as I am no longer under your dominion. My husband will not chastise me for

340

my direct words, as he is aware they are well-earned."

"What can you mean by that?" Bennet protested, his anger beginning to rise in earnest.

"Since you entered this home, you have ignored me and the rest of your daughters, barely speaking to anyone except at dinner. Afterwards, you retire to your rooms or the library. If this were an isolated incident, I might think little of it, but the truth is that it has always been this way. Since leaving Longbourn, I have written you countless letters without receiving a single reply of my own. Any response to my questions came through a letter written to my husband, to whom you have deigned to respond, mostly seeking his advice," Elizabeth coldly explained.

"The same was true at Longbourn, although I did not see it until I had left. You taught me, you spoke to me only because you needed *someone* to speak to since you could not do so with your wife. I was educated as you would a son, not because of any true love for me or desire for my company, but simply because I was the best option. Jane was not interested, and I was, so you used me as a companion. You trained me to keep you occupied or take over roles you did not wish to do on the estate. Where I believed you sought my company out of a desire to spend time with me, I have realised that you desired a companion and formed me in a way to keep you entertained. Even I, your supposed favourite, did not escape your censure, as you lumped us all together as 'the silliest girls in all England', although you owned that I 'had a bit more quickness than the rest'. You never once considered how these words affected any of us, and you mocked our mother until you finally realised the danger she was creating by allowing her youngest daughters to run wild.

341

"I appreciate your efforts in addressing Lydia's poor behaviour, although all that has been accomplished is her languishing in a school she despises. As far as I know, she hasn't received a single letter from you during this time, and she still does not understand why she was taken from her home and placed in that school. You have banished Mrs Bennet to the dower house, but does she understand the reasons behind it? I commend your initial effort, although I have begun to question your motives, but are you taking any initiative to ensure that the lesson is learned, or are you simply removing obstacles to your own peace of mind without considering what it means for those who are supposed to be learning something?"

Elizabeth paused and looked at her father, who, in turn, looked at her husband as if waiting for him to take charge. This additional evidence of her father's lack of respect for her prompted her to make one final statement. "I hope you enjoyed your visit to our library, Father. It will be the last time you set foot in this room or any of our homes. As my husband has informed you, *I* am responsible for issuing invitations to our home, and I do not anticipate sending you one anytime soon. However, my sisters will always be welcome if they seek respite from your indifference. Consider our libraries closed to you from this moment on."

Having said her piece, Elizabeth turned and started walking towards the exit. She paused at the doorway, casting a glance back at her father before calling a footman over and informing him the library was closed to Mr Bennet. She requested that he escort Mr Bennet to either the drawing room or his chambers upon his exit.

"Are you going to allow your wife to speak to her father

in such a manner?" Bennet asked Darcy, expecting him to intervene.

"Aye," Darcy replied simply before exiting through the same door he had entered, locking it behind him.

* * *

The time between that confrontation and Bennet's departure was tense within the house. Bennet kept to his room, but the entire household was aware of the conflict, and he scarcely spoke a word to anyone. His departure came as a surprise to the entire house – he had planned to remain another week but had sent for his carriage on the day of the confrontation and rose early, intending to depart before anyone else was awake in the house.

On that particular morning, Darcy had risen early and was downstairs when he noticed Bennet slipping into his greatcoat, obviously attempting to leave unnoticed and approached him.

"You are leaving?" Darcy inquired neutrally.

"Yes," Bennet replied shortly, his manner still brusque. "I prefer not to be where I am not welcome. Should I assume that my letters are no longer welcome?"

"You may write, and I will continue to advise you; however, I suggest you implement the strategies we have discussed and take a more active role in the management of Longbourn. My wife heard from Mary that you have begun hiding yourself in your book room once again and are leaving the estate management to her and your steward. She also asked about the dowries for your daughters - are you still putting money aside for this purpose, as we discussed?"

343

Bennet could not respond to this inquiry and felt chastened once again, although he was less sure that he cared enough to put his money into dowries. Books interested him, while his daughters and the responsibilities of the estate did not. The steward Darcy had helped him find was competent enough and did not require much guidance as long as Darcy's advice sufficed. Although he would have liked to retain access to the library at Darcy House and wondered about the library at Pemberley, he did not like travelling well enough to make the effort required to gain access to these rooms.

By the time he arrived home, he had almost convinced himself that his daughter's words had been unreasonable and that he needed to make no changes to what he was presently doing. Mary would return home eventually, and then all would be well, as she would take care of what was needed.

Thirty

Returning to Pemberley

D arcy House stood empty in the first week of June except for servants, as all the occupants departed. Anne and Charlotte had relocated to Matlock House a few days prior, and after asking Charlotte for a courtship and going to Hertfordshire to obtain the permission of Sir William Lucas, Fitzwilliam had relocated into his own bachelors quarters, choosing not to take advantage of Darcy's hospitality and reside at Darcy House. Fitzwilliam was in the process of selling his commission, and the paperwork had been signed regarding the partnership between himself and Darcy for the horse farm in Kent. He would relocate to Rosings after the summer, hopefully as an engaged man, if not already wed. While he had assured Darcy he was in no hurry to marry, he became increasingly anxious to claim his wife and take her to their home once Charlotte had accepted his courtship.

The men had agreed that the manor house at the original horse farm would be repaired for the manager's use. It was a large manor house, similar to the size of Longbourn, and some wings were in better condition than others. Fitzwilliam hoped the repairs to the house could be done quickly, and he would be able to bring Charlotte home to live with him there instead of at Rosings.

Bingley escorted Jane and Mary to Longbourn, his carriage accompanying the Darcy carriages until they left the Great North Road to go toward Meryton. Mary had been invited to accompany the Darcys to Pemberley but, ultimately, had chosen to return home to Longbourn to help her father through the summer. She promised to let the Darcys know if things with her father improved, but it was uncertain if that would be the case. Elizabeth had told her sisters about the confrontation with her father and had received mixed responses. Jane did not understand Elizabeth's ire toward the patriarch, nor did Kitty, although she appreciated that she was no longer called silly while living with the Darcys. Mary, however, did understand, having felt the same treatment since taking over Elizabeth's role in the household. So long as Mary was useful, she was respected, but when someone or something better was available, her significance to her father decreased significantly. It was an odd feeling, but Mary knew what she was doing at Longbourn was valuable and necessary, and that alone made her want to stay.

While Elizabeth was no longer nauseous as frequently as she had been, the Darcys still took the journey slowly, travelling for six days instead of the usual three. They stopped often to allow for walks and visits to interesting spots along the way, taking in many sights and touring homes as they made their way home to Pemberley. They arrived late on Saturday, and everyone immediately made their way to their rooms, where warm baths waited while their dinner trays were prepared.

Sunday was spent recovering from the journey, as six days in a carriage, no matter how few miles were travelled each day, was enough to leave them all feeling stiff and exhausted. All that is, except for Darcy, who arose early, left his sleeping wife in his bed as he dressed, and rode out to survey some of the issues the steward had previously brought to his attention in preparation for their discussions the following day. After a long ride, he returned to his rooms to find his wife in their sitting room, breaking her fast.

"Good morning, dearest," he said as he entered. "Give me a moment to change, and I will join you to break our fasts."

She nodded her agreement as she sipped the peppermint tea she still drank each morning before she could eat breakfast. Her nausea was nearly gone, but she found that upon waking, she still sometimes struggled with the feeling, and drinking the tea helped her to be able to eat breakfast.

"You were up and about early this morning," she commented when he re-entered the room, dressed in his robe as he had not wanted to take the time to summon his valet or to dress more formally.

"Aye, I wanted to take a ride during the cool of the morning to see how things were going. I did not see any obvious issues, but I am sure the steward will have much he will want to discuss, despite his frequent letters," Darcy replied.

Their discussion continued along this way for several more minutes as they discussed the estate and its tenants, and Darcy offered to accompany Elizabeth on her visits to the tenants later in the week. "In your condition, I think it better if you allow someone to accompany you on your visits, and I would like to escort you as time allows. I know that you have met all the tenants, and I do not fear you in that way, but I would be more comfortable if you waited for me to be able to go with you. I also ask that you allow a footman to accompany you any time you venture out for a walk on the estate – you do not yet know it well, and I do not want you to take any risks."

Elizabeth smiled gently at her husband before leaning against his chest. "As much as I want to refuse your request, I know that it is best that I not wander alone, however much I might like to. I have not yet begun to show, but according to our aunts, that will happen soon, and as I increase, I will become more ungainly, and the danger of a fall will become greater. I would appreciate your accompanying me as I visit the tenants – you knew I would desire to do so without my ever mentioning it to you. I have not seen many of them since the first of the year since it was too cold before we left for me to venture out much."

Darcy hugged her to himself. "Although we have not been married even a year yet, I know your sense of responsibility dictates that you visit our tenants as soon as you are able. I imagine when you meet with Mrs Reynolds tomorrow, you will begin discussing their needs and start arranging for baskets to take with us as we go on our visits." Darcy paused, and as he lightly caressed her back, he considered his next words. "Dearest, after you are no longer carrying this precious little one, I hope you will allow me to teach you to ride. I know you are not particularly fond of horses, but as the mistress of an estate, it would be beneficial if you knew how to ride. I do intend to take you on many drives this summer and into the autumn, as long as you are able, but there are also places that I want to take you that can only be reached on horseback. Do you think, perhaps, you would be willing to let me try to teach you? We can begin now by acquainting you with our steadiest saddle horses, so you can choose your own mount. You could ride double with me, but I think you would prefer your own mount."

She sighed before moving slightly so she could look up at him. "I had already been considering this before we discovered I was with child. Part of me wishes to refuse and allow my fear to guide me, but I agree that it is a skill that I need to learn, and I would enjoy the freedom riding would allow me. Pemberley is simply too large for me to tramp around as I did in Hertfordshire, and I am no longer a plain miss; I am now Mrs Darcy of Pemberley. Aunt Matlock impressed the importance of that upon me while we were in London, and I have had time to consider what being Mrs Darcy means. The Mistress of Pemberley rides, and you will not allow me to come to harm. I realize that I must trust you in this; therefore, I will bow to your wishes, my dear William."

They remained snuggled together for a while longer after this, talking of little things. Darcy gently caressed Elizabeth's growing bulge and spent a few minutes conversing with their child, speaking of the estate and its legacy before they eventually rose regretfully to dress and go downstairs to find their sisters. They found both girls in the music room practising on the piano, and they spoke about their plans for the coming weeks.

Georgiana and Kitty would Mrs Darcy in some of her

meetings with the housekeeper and others around the estate as they began to learn the duties of the mistress of an estate. They decided they would go into Lambton later in the week to purchase cloth for sewing, as the three of them wanted to sew items for Elizabeth's child, the tenants' children, and as donations to the poor house. Darcy had received a letter from the rector in Kymptom just before they returned home about several significant needs there, and he intended to inquire of the rector in Lambton about similar needs. Along with their lessons, these projects would give the girls plenty to do while they remained at Pemberley.

Elizabeth and Darcy were much occupied as they settled into their roles at Pemberley, but they made time to discuss their expectations for the birth, care, and parenting of this child and any future children. Elizabeth wanted the support of Aunt Matlock and Aunt Gardiner during her labour and for at least a short while after the child was born. Although it was not considered fashionable for women of their station to nurse their children themselves, Elizabeth was adamant that she wanted this experience with her children. Aunt Gardiner had shared her experiences nursing her own children, and after discussing this with Darcy, he agreed they would hire a wet nurse only if it was necessary for the health of the child or if Elizabeth needed the relief to rest and recover from the birth.

Following these discussions, she sent letters to both aunts asking if they would visit in September when they expected the babe would be born. She also informed them that they might be assisting Darcy, as her husband intended to break with convention and remain by her side throughout her labours.

Mrs Reynolds had been absolutely ecstatic when she learned of Mrs Darcy's condition and began to watch over her mistress carefully. At times, Elizabeth felt her housekeeper was nearly as smothering as her husband, but she chose to laugh at both of them and attempted not to be too aggravated by it. Elizabeth found that her housekeeper was more responsive to her gentle suggestions to take a step back than her husband was, and the couple had a few spats that resulted in ears that Elizabeth was quick to blame on her condition.

Of particular concern to Darcy were Elizabeth's quick swings from anger to tears to joy. At times, he struggled to understand her, especially as her mood shifted so rapidly that it often left him shaking his head. However, both his uncles and a few married friends reassured him that this was normal during this stage of her pregnancy and he would simply have to learn how to deal with these temperamental swings and the tears that would appear for seemingly no reason.

One of these temperamental times was the day Elizabeth received two letters, one from Jane and the other from Charlotte, announcing their engagements and weddings scheduled to occur in August and September in Hertfordshire. Elizabeth had cried tears of joy at the happiness conveyed in the letters and then, immediately after, tears of sadness that she would not be able to attend either of their weddings. She cried again when she realised Darcy would not be able to attend and encouraged him to go, but he refused to leave her in her condition for any reason, and certainly not for a wedding. Instead, he suggested she invite them both to Pemberley for Christmas or sooner if she preferred. She cried again at his suggestion, and while he was tempted to throw up his hands, he elected instead to hug her and hold her as she cried.

"I am so sorry, Will," she sobbed. "I am... I am completely irrational, and I know I must be driving you mad."

He gently caressed her hair. "I love you, Elizabeth, and you may be as irrational as you like as you are carrying our child. We will endure this, and I will do whatever I can to be of aid to you," he whispered into her ear.

She held him as she cried until finally, exhausted, she fell asleep in his arms. Darcy looked down at her and shook his head, feeling confused and off-kilter but desperately in love with his wife and child. Chuckling, he remarked quietly to himself, "You drive me mad, my love, but I have a feeling you are equally confused with the wealth of emotions you are currently feeling. You are carrying our child, my dearest Elizabeth, and I cannot imagine that I could love you more than I do right now. However, given that I felt the same when we married seven months ago, I imagine that love will only continue to grow. Sleep now, my dearest. Sleep, and perhaps you will wake feeling a little more yourself than you do at present."

* * *

Charlotte and Fitzwilliam's wedding day came at the beginning of August. Fitzwilliam had managed to get a considerable amount of work accomplished towards expanding the horse farm and, utilising the stables at Rosings, had made a good start on their goal to double their breeding stock. Using Darcy's funds as a start, Fitzwilliam had purchased a stallion and half a dozen mares with impeccable bloodlines to add to their existing stock, and they now had a solid foundation for their breeding programme. Fitzwilliam had also hired a former cavalry officer to aid in their endeavours and was able to move his wedding date forward a few weeks. The Fitzwilliams would travel directly to Kent after the wedding and visit Pemberley for Christmas.

Jane's wedding was scheduled for the end of August. When informed of the plans, Mrs Bennet had desired to be involved in the planning. Jane, being far too forgiving and too unwilling to risk anyone's displeasure, had allowed her to participate, but after a week of her mother's raptures, she regretted it. Bingley held firm on the wedding date when Mrs Bennet insisted it be pushed back several months. Mr Bennet had likewise taken a stand when Mrs Bennet demanded she accompany Jane to London to obtain her trousseau, claiming that Jane had already received many beautiful dresses from the Darcys that spring and did not need many more. He informed her that Jane would go to London for only a sennight, accompanied by her aunt Gardiner to shop for a few necessary things, but Mrs Bennet was expressly ordered to remain at the dower house.

When the Hursts left Netherfield the previous autumn with Caroline, they had delivered her to her aunt in Scarborough and then retreated to his father's estate near Bath. They had cut off all contact with Caroline, given the verbal abuse she had meted out on their travels to Scarborough, and had not received any replies to their letters to Bingley. Bingley had finally written to Louisa after his return to Netherfield Park and shared the details of Caroline's behaviour and his actions to protect the Hursts and himself from the consequences. Louisa had replied with a scathing letter to her brother for his lack of communication and for not asking for help in dealing with Caroline. Eventually, the relationship was repaired, although brother and sister were firmly resolved to have no further association with Caroline. When the Hursts received the wedding invitation from Bingley, Louisa sent their regrets and invited her brother and new sister to visit with them sometime in the new year.

Despite Mrs Bennet's involvement, the wedding did occur, and things did go smoothly, but it was Mrs Gardiner's assistance that made it work out as well as it did. Jane was too complying and went along with many suggestions that her mother made, regardless of her feelings about them. While Mr Bingley did well in standing up to Mrs Bennet on occasion, it was not until a fortnight before the wedding that Mrs Gardiner arrived, and Jane was finally encouraged to put a stop to some of the unnecessary decorations and other such nonsense and take charge of her wedding.

"You will be a married woman in a matter of days, Jane," Mrs Gardiner had admonished after just an hour of listening to Mrs Bennet and seeing her niece interact with her betrothed. "These plans are obviously not what you want, and you need to speak to your mother to express your wishes. How will you ever be able to deal with servants or tradesmen who want to cheat you if you cannot express your desires and wishes?"

Jane hung her head as she considered her aunt's words. "I know, but Mama has been so disappointed, and this seems like such a small thing to allow her."

"But it is *your* wedding, Jane, and you should be happy with the plans. Your mother will be miserable regardless of what you permit, and you should have what you want for your wedding. I can tell already that Mr Bingley is not pleased by how easily you allow yourself to be pushed around by your mother," Mrs Gardiner replied.

Jane considered these words that night, and the next morning, she took a stand against her mother. It was difficult, and she nearly fainted afterwards, but both her aunt and her betrothed looked at her proudly for having done it. It was a turning point for Jane, making her feel more confident. That new-found confidence was tested frequently in the days leading up to the wedding, but with her aunt's support at home as well as support from her betrothed, the wedding met all her desires and not those of her mother. The breakfast, too, was far less grand than her mother would have desired, but it suited Jane and Bingley, and they were content. Through conversations with her aunt, Jane realised that this experience of standing up to her mother was significant for her as it would aid her as she became the mistress of her home, wherever that would be, and in managing her relationship with her mother. As long as they remained at Netherfield, her mother would be a problem, and now Jane knew she would be able to stand up to her.

Following the wedding, the Bingleys travelled south to the sea for their wedding trip and visited with the Fitzwilliams in Kent on their return journey. They were home for only a few days before they departed Netherfield once again, this time going north to Scarborough to meet some of Bingley's family. While there, Bingley made arrangements for Caroline, who was now sufficiently recovered from the birth, to move to a cottage in Scotland that Bingley had purchased for his sister. Before accepting Bingley's proposal, Jane required his promise that Miss Bingley would never live with them, and she was very pleased that Bingley never wavered in his determination to remove Caroline from society and cut ties with her. Once Caroline was on her way to her new future, Jane invited Bingley's aunt to stay with them at Netherfield, as she liked the woman very well when she had been Bingley's hostess in the autumn. Slowly, they made their way home, stopping briefly to visit with the Darcys as they made their way south.

Thirty-One

New Life

ᗦ᎒᎒᎒᎒ᗣ

Summer at Pemberley advanced, as did Elizabeth's condition. By the middle of August, Elizabeth was utterly miserable, feeling huge and ungainly, and as her abdomen increased, so did her misery. Although she attempted to bear it as much as she could without complaint, still the entire household was aware of her growing discomfort. She could often be found wandering the halls, although she tired easily, and at least one footman was tasked with following Elizabeth through the house and grounds to assist her as needed. She had bristled at first, but when she had nearly fallen one day out walking in the garden, she became more accepting of the need for the footman to follow her.

Around the first of September, visitors began to converge at Pemberley. Lord and Lady Matlock arrived first, accompanied by Anne, and they greeted the entire family gathered in the front drawing room. Lady Matlock exclaimed over Elizabeth's size and commiserated with her for the general discomfort she was feeling, recommending that Elizabeth would be more comfortable sitting with her feet up instead of constantly moving about.

"But I cannot sit still," Elizabeth complained when Lady Matlock made the suggestion. "I ache when I sit for too long, and I ache if I move about. William is very kind and does all he can to help, but I have been so unsettled the last few days."

"Your time is approaching, and your body is getting itself ready," Lady Matlock reassured her. "What does the midwife say?"

"The same as you," Elizabeth admitted. "She was here the day before yesterday and examined me and told me to take it easy and try to relax. She also insists that the room be kept dark, the fire raging and that I am to remain in bed and not move for a month following the birth. I assure you that none of this will be occurring when I give birth if I can prevent it. William had arranged for the accoucheur to arrive in the next few days, along with a monthly nurse, but we have spoken of hiring a wet nurse only for the night feedings. I have spoken with my aunt Gardiner, who has given birth four times within the last twelve years, and she did not follow any of the practices the midwife believes are necessary for me." When Lady Matlock began to object, Elizabeth held up her hand. "William agrees with me on this. My feeding the baby will likely prevent me from becoming with child again as quickly, and neither of us intends to be like many of those in society who only bring their children down on occasion to show them off."

"I do understand a few of your points, but I do urge you

358

against feeding the child yourself. That is not something a woman of your station does," Lady Matlock replied.

"My aunt fed her children, and there were no ill effects. She also did not fall with child immediately after like many women do," Elizabeth said. "William and I have discussed this and are in agreement about what is best for our family. I understand and appreciate your objection, but we intend to act in a manner that suits us, regardless of what 'society' thinks."

Lady Matlock simply nodded before changing the topic to something else.

Several days later, the Gardiners arrived, along with their children. Darcy had made a second carriage available for the children and their nurse to travel in, making the trip much easier on that family. Mrs Gardiner took a look at Elizabeth as was surprised at how large her petite niece had grown. "If superstition is to be believed, you are carrying a boy, as you are all in front, and I imagine you will deliver very soon."

Lady Matlock agreed with this statement. "The accoucheur and monthly nurse have arrived and agree that it will not be long. Does Darcy still intend to remain with you through the birth?"

Elizabeth nodded. "He does, and again, we know that it is not the norm. However, I want him with me through this, and we have discussed it with the accoucheur, who reluctantly agreed to say nothing. We have also discussed some other concerns with him; we insist that all tools be cleaned and kept separate ahead of the birth, as William has read that helps to prevent infection. The birthing room has been prepared, and everything within has been scrubbed very well. We are as prepared as we can be, as the accoucheur also believes my time will be soon, and the babe will not wait until the end of the month."

Over the next few days, the atmosphere at Pemberley grew more expectant as the rooms were abuzz with activity, as they worked to be certain that all was in readiness for the arrival of the heir. Darcy, always fastidious, took a keen interest in the arrangements and ensured that the birthing room was properly cleaned and remained that way as they waited.

Likewise, the accoucheur and monthly nurse were well settled at Pemberley and were ready to assist Elizabeth as she gave birth and were reluctantly willing to follow all the strictures laid down by the couple. They both recognized that the wealthiest members of society often had odd habits and simply went along with what they believed to be odd behaviours.

Elizabeth continued to experience pains, which eventually turned into true labour pains. The true indication of Elizabeth's labour beginning was her waters breaking, which occurred one morning as the family sat at breakfast. After a particularly intense pain, Elizabeth felt her dress become damp and immediately stood, drawing attention to herself. Lady Matlock and Mrs Gardiner noticed the condition of her dress and encouraged Darcy to accompany her upstairs to the birthing room adjacent to their suite. The accoucheur was called to the room, and Elizabeth's maid helped her to change and prepare for the birth. Through it all, her husband remained at her side, offering encouragement and soothing words whenever needed.

Her labour was intense, and with Darcy's help, Elizabeth walked around the room as long as she could to help the babe move into position for the birth. Finally, the accoucheur encouraged her to move into position on the bed set up for that purpose. Before long, Elizabeth's cries grew in intensity and volume, and her grip on Darcy's hand threatened his own well-being. However, his presence brought Elizabeth comfort, and he had no desire to be anywhere else.

Likewise, their two aunts were nearby, their faces a mix of concern and anticipation. They watched the couple, knowing there was little for them to do but wait. As Elizabeth's breathing grew more rapid and shallow, Mrs Gardiner approached with a cool towel to wipe the perspiration from her face.

Through it all, William offered words of encouragement. "You are doing well, my dearest Elizabeth, my love," he murmured. "I am here. Just a little longer, dearest, and we will meet our child. I love you so very much."

Elizabeth's gaze met Darcy's, her eyes filled with a mixture of pain, determination, and love. "Thank you, William," she breathed, her voice strained. "Your presence means more to me than words can express. I love you too." His words encouraged her, and her determination grew. She began to focus all of her energy on the task and, using her husband's words, found the strength to push through the pain.

Finally, Elizabeth pushed again at the direction of the accoucheur, and everyone held their breath as they heard the cry of a newborn fill the air. The child was quickly taken by the month nurse and cleaned and wrapped in a clean blanket before being laid on Elizabeth's chest.

"It is not quite over, Mrs Darcy," the accoucheur told her. "There is one more yet to come. It appears this little one will have a sibling very soon."

Elizabeth and William looked at each other in surprise and

361

then looked down at the child in her arms. "How soon?" he asked.

"A few more minutes," the accoucheur told them. "Mrs Darcy, you will need to push again in a few minutes, but you have a moment or two to rest."

The joyous couple caressed the face of the babe in Elizabeth's arms, although the child was quickly taken up by Lady Matlock as another pain struck Elizabeth, making her incapable of holding her child at that moment. Lady Matlock and Mrs Gardiner helped clean the child further and dressed it in a little gown that Elizabeth had sewn as she had waited.

In a little more than half an hour, a second child was brought into this world, and the steps with the first repeated. The accoucheur and monthly nurse helped Elizabeth deliver the afterbirth, and finally, the little family was washed and dressed in clean clothing. Darcy carried an exhausted Elizabeth into her room and laid on her the bed, and sat down beside her. Lady Matlock brought in their firstborn while Mrs Gardiner held the second, and the two children were presented to their exhausted parents.

"You have a son, Darcy," Lady Matlock said as she presented the child to his father. "Already, he looks like you – look at that scowl." Darcy, too happy with the outcome, ignored the tease and took the babe in his arms.

Mrs Gardiner brought the second child and handed it to Elizabeth. "And this one takes after you, Lizzy. You have a daughter, and I can discern your own impish look upon her face."

Both new parents laughed at this comment as they stared down upon their children. "One of each, William," Elizabeth said quietly to her husband. "We never considered the idea of twins, but I guess that means we can use both of the names we selected."

Darcy nodded. "This is William James Alexander," he said, indicating the child in his arms. "Elizabeth wanted to name him after me, but I did not want to saddle another generation with the name Fitzwilliam. We settled on William." He grinned broadly. "And the little lady there," he continued, indicating the child Elizabeth held, "is Roseanne Elizabeth, named for her exceptionally beautiful mother."

Elizabeth smiled at her husband and reached over to caress his cheek, forgetting the presence of others in the room. He leaned down to press a lingering kiss to her lips, which caused the others in the room to blush. However, it was obvious to those in the room that the new parents were extraordinarily happy with each other and their children, and soon, they left them in the room alone.

When the child Elizabeth held began to fuss, she moved to bring her to her breast to feed her. It took a few minutes, but the two of them, mother and daughter, soon figured it out, and William looked down on her in awe. "How does that feel?" he asked.

She laughed. "It is a rather interesting feeling, and it does not feel at all like it does when you suckle me," she teased. "I believe the wet nurse may be more needed than we had planned, as I believe feeding two children will be substantially more demanding than feeding one."

Darcy agreed. "You are likely right, my dear, and I would have suggested it, but I was not certain if I should approach it just yet," he told her honestly. "You will be a wonderful mother, my dear, and I love our children so very much already."

"Has anyone told our sisters or Anne of our news yet?" Elizabeth wondered sleepily.

"I am certain our aunts have mentioned it, as I believe they were nearly as excited as we. I am somewhat astounded that none of them has arrived at our door and attempted to demand entry yet," Darcy replied.

"What time is it, Will?" she asked when they traded babies so Elizabeth could feed baby William.

He took his watch from his pocket before standing with his daughter in his arms and moved to look out a window. "Good Lord, Elizabeth, it is two in the morning. I was unaware of how long you had laboured, and I would guess that is why our sisters have not banged on our door. They will likely do so in the morning."

Elizabeth chuckled. "It has been an eventful day," she said wryly as her son finished eating, and she adjusted her nightgown to cover herself.

Darcy returned to his position next to Elizabeth and wrapped the arm not holding his daughter around her shoulders. The four of them sat together on the bed, the two new parents staring down at their children. Soon, Darcy felt Elizabeth sag against him and realised she had fallen asleep. He could not sleep yet; his heart was too full of what the day had held. He was a father, not to one but to two perfect, tiny little babies. An heir to teach, and a daughter to spoil, although, by rights, little Roseanne would be heir to Rosings. Anne had shared her desire to ensure that Rosings would be inherited by Darcy's eldest daughter, so she could ensure that the women of the family always had a place as well.

Basking in the peacefulness of the moment, Darcy contin-

364

ued just to sit there awake as his mind wandered through a whirlwind of emotions and thoughts. He reflected on the weight of responsibility that now rested on his shoulders as a father and the legacy he would pass down to his children. He was determined to do his best for his children to ensure they would be prepared for whatever life brought to them.

With a tender gaze, he looked at his daughter, Roseanne, cradled in his arms. She stirred slightly, and he watched her delicate features, so like her mother's. Darcy felt a surge of protectiveness and vowed to be the best father he could be, guiding her with love and instilling in her the values that had been passed down through generations.

Turning his attention to William, held in his mother's arms, Darcy could not help but feel a swell of pride. His son, the heir to Pemberley, would one day carry on the family name and all that it represented. It was a weighty role, but Darcy was determined to be a supportive and nurturing father, guiding William in the ways of honour, integrity, and compassion. He prayed he would be there when it was time to turn it all over to his son and that his son would not be saddled with Pemberley so abruptly as he had been. He had been prepared to take it over, yes, but the weight was very heavy on such a young man, and he felt he had failed often in those first few years. He would have much preferred to have had his father's guidance as he began the running of the estate and hoped he would be there in that role for his son.

In the midst of his contemplation, Darcy felt Elizabeth stir against him, her drowsy voice breaking through the silence. "Will," she murmured softly, her eyes still heavy with sleep. "We are parents, love, twice over."

A tender smile graced Darcy's lips as he placed a gentle kiss on Elizabeth's forehead. "Aye, we are, my love," he replied in a hushed tone. "We are parents to these precious babes entrusted to our care. It is a heavy weight but a welcome one."

Elizabeth's e fluttered open, and she looked at her husband with a mixture of exhaustion and contentment. "I cannot believe how blessed we are, William," she whispered, her voice filled with awe. "Twins, a boy, and a girl!"

Darcy pressed his cheek against Elizabeth's, revelling in the warmth of their connection. "Indeed, Elizabeth," he whispered, his voice filled with happiness and awe. "I am filled with gratitude for the love we share and the beautiful family we have created together."

As the night slowly gave way to the soft light of dawn, Darcy held his wife and children close, cherishing the stillness of the moment. He knew that soon the bustling chaos of life would resume, with their sisters and extended family clamouring to meet the newest additions to the family. But for now, in the peaceful embrace of his family, he allowed himself to be absorbed in the profound joy and love that filled his heart.

* * *

Georgiana and Kitty were delighted to meet their new niece and nephew the following morning. The new parents had slept late, and Elizabeth remained in their rooms, although she refused to remain in bed all day, defying convention and her husband in standing and carrying their babes to and from the nursery. She sat in a rocking chair several times throughout the day as she fed her children. A temporary wet nurse from the village was quickly found and brought to the house to assist with the feedings since Elizabeth had not been expecting Elizabeth to give birth quite so soon or to twins.

When their sisters finally visited the nursery, they were surprised to find both their sister and brother there. "Lizzy," Kitty cried reproachfully, "Lady Matlock indicated you should not be out of bed yet."

"Kitty, you know there is little that can convince me to remain abed for days upon end, and now I have these two amazing babes to tend. I certainly will not stay abed for a month, and my husband will ensure that I do not overtax myself," Elizabeth explained. "Our aunt Gardiner certainly never remained in bed any longer than necessary. I was with her in her last confinement, and she was up the next day as well. I will be fine."

"What are their names, William?" Georgiana asked. "Two babies; We were so surprised when we heard the news."

Each of the new parents was holding a child as Darcy began the introduction. "This lovely lady in my arms is Roseanne Elizabeth, and her brother over there is William James Alexander. Would you like to hold them?" he asked the girls. At their eager nods, Darcy transferred his daughter into Kitty's arms, retrieved his son from his mother, and gently handed William to his younger sister. "I remember holding you when you were this small, Georgie," he said affectionately. "You were so tiny, yet so noisy." He grinned at the memory. "Just like with these two, I loved you from the moment I saw you."

He went and stood next to his wife, laying his hand on her shoulder and speaking quietly, only for her. "As I loved you from almost that first moment. It took me a day or two to recognize the feeling, and I am more in love with you than ever. I am so grateful for the gift you have given me this day."

She reached to squeeze his hand. "I love you too, William," she whispered back. They stood there and watched as their sisters held the babies and laughed when they attempted to exchange them. They were unsuccessful until Darcy plucked baby William from his sister and handed him to Kitty once she had released Roseanne to Georgiana.

A few moments later, Anne joined the group in the nursery. "I could not believe it when Aunt Matlock told me that you had twins, Lizzy," she said loudly upon entering, startling both children, who jerked in the arms of their aunts. "Oh, I do apologise," she said much more quietly, seeing the reaction her entry had caused. Both children required some effort to settle, and Georgiana was unsuccessful with Roseanne, who began to cry in her arms.

"Let me take her, Georgie," Elizabeth said gently. "I was going to feed her before you all arrived, and I do not believe she will calm until she has had something to eat."

"Do we need to leave?" the girl asked, uncertain of what to do since she had never heard of such behaviour before.

"No, just give me a moment to get her settled, but you are welcome to stay if you are comfortable," Elizabeth replied, taking Roseanne and accepting a blanket from her husband, who stood in front of her, blocking the others' view, as he introduced Anne to his son and shared the name they had selected for their daughter. Elizabeth smiled softly. She appreciated her husband's protection of her modesty even though she knew it was unnecessary as she and her sisters had frequently darted into each other's rooms regardless of their state of dress. Once she had Roseanne settled at her breast, she indicated that her husband could move. He moved

368

slightly and sat down directly beside her in a chair he had moved there for just this purpose. From this spot, he watched his wife as she fed their babes and reached over to caress his wife's cheek before dropping his hand to caress his daughter's downy head, forgetting the others in the room.

The three unmarried ladies watched the connection between the couple, and two of them felt a longing to find the same one day. Anne was content, pleased to know that her legacy would be continued at Rosings through the daughter of her cousin Darcy.

Thirty-Two

Settling In

T he extended family remained at Pemberley for a fortnight after the birth, long enough for the new family to settle into a sort of routine. An additional nurse was hired for the nursery, but the twins remained in the nursery adjacent to the mistress's chambers for now, and Elizabeth and Darcy remained determined to provide much of their care. Elizabeth nursed her children as much as she could and was hopeful that she would only need the assistance of the wet nurse for the first few months. That lady was grateful for the income but would be happy to return home with her young child when her services were no longer needed.

In spite of all of the help from family and servants, the couple was still exhausted, as might be expected of new parents to not just one but two healthy babies. And so far, mother and babies were healthy, which pleased everyone greatly, as both parents knew it was far too common for children not to survive to adulthood. They did not allow this thought to consume them; instead, they ensured their children had the best of care, and Darcy cared for his wife. Over the next few months, William and Roseanne grew and delighted their parents, aunts, and others who cared for them. Although both Elizabeth and Darcy spent considerable time with their children, Elizabeth resumed her walks and some of her duties as mistress of Pemberley, and Darcy returned to his duties managing their estates and business interests. They had established a routine with the nursery maid and wet nurse, although Elizabeth wanted to be very engaged in the rearing of their children and was often up with one or both of them at night. One day, not long after the children had been christened and Elizabeth churched, Darcy found her in tears over some minor issue and, recognizing that his wife was exhausted, insisted she rest. After she woke from her nap, he led her into their sitting room and pulled her into his arms as he sat on a settee.

"Dearest, I know you want to take an active role with our children; however, you are running yourself ragged," he gently told her. "You cannot continue in this way; you are the mistress of the estate, nursing two children almost exclusively, and getting only a few hours of sleep each night. The wet nurse and nursery maid have very little to do because you will not allow them to ensure you rest. They are there to aid us, not to take over, but Elizabeth, you must let them."

"I do not want someone else to raise my children," she replied heatedly, her face defiant.

He sighed deeply and continued to reason with her. "But you would not be allowing someone else to raise your children, Elizabeth," he said. "You need to find a balance, to find time for yourself, the children, and me, along with fulfilling your role as mistress of this estate. You cannot do it all, and you need to allow others to help you."

"Dearest, I know that you want to take an active role with our children; however, you are running yourself ragged," he gently told her. "You cannot continue in this way; you are the mistress of the estate, nursing two children almost exclusively, and getting only a few hours of sleep each night. The wet nurse and nursery maid have very little to do because you will not allow them to ensure you rest. They are there to aid us, not to take over, but Elizabeth, you must let them."

"I do not want someone else to raise my children," she replied heatedly, her face defiant.

He sighed deeply and continued to reason with her. "But you would not be allowing someone else to raise your children, Elizabeth," he said. "You need to find a balance, to find time for yourself, the children, and me, along with fulfilling your role as mistress of this estate. You cannot do it all, and you need to allow others to help you."

Elizabeth turned to him with tears in her eyes. "I am exhausted, Will," she admitted after a moment, nearly wilting in his arms. "I cannot seem to keep up with all that needs to be done, and I am constantly forgetting things. I almost feel as I did in the last few months of pregnancy; my mind is so foggy."

"You are too tired, dearest," Darcy said reassuringly. "Do you know how quickly you fell asleep this afternoon? Nearly as soon as your head found its pillow. Our children were fine as you slept, and the nursemaid had something to do. I propose you allow our servants to do their job for the rest of this evening so we might dine together in our sitting room. We have spent little time alone in the weeks since the children were born, and I would love an evening with just you. The wet nurse can handle the feedings tonight, and tomorrow we will find a way for you to do what is required of you while not exhausting yourself. Have you not taught Kitty and Georgiana what they need to know to manage the estate? Could they not help in some ways?"

Elizabeth considered her husband's words. "I have neglected you as well, have I not? I am so sorry, William." She began to cry again.

"No, Elizabeth, I did not intend to make you feel badly about anything. We have both been tired, but you are attempting to do too much, my dear. I simply want you to begin to take some time for yourself and to allow those we have hired to assist you to do their jobs," Darcy insisted. "If you continue as you are, I worry you will make yourself ill, and we cannot have that, dearest."

Elizabeth sighed deeply. "We will dine in here tonight, William, and then I will strive not to wake in the night to tend to the children and bring them to me only if necessary. I do need to feed the children soon, though, or I will ache from being too full. Can you please see if one or both are hungry now so that I might feed them?"

He nodded, understanding her discomfort. "I might assist with that as well if you would like," he replied salaciously, looking at her with the rakish smile she had not seen in some time.

She grinned. "That would be something new," she replied, surprised when he shook his head. She lifted an inquiring eyebrow at him.

"We made love a day or two before you gave birth, do you remember?" At her nod, he continued. "You fed me then, although I did not speak of it, and I found I quite enjoyed the taste. It was sweet." He licked his lips, and she coloured even as she smiled at him.

He pulled her face to his for a slow, lingering kiss that made Elizabeth desire more. She hesitated. "I ... I am uncertain if I am ready to continue," she told him.

Darcy continued to kiss her. "I just needed to kiss you, dearest. I will not press for anything you do not want. Although, I will help you ease your pain tonight or any other time you may need my assistance." They kissed for several more minutes before he felt her milk let down and soak her dress. She coloured deeply, but he merely laughed. "Come, my darling wife, let us find our children so you can feed them and relieve the pressure so that we will both enjoy our dinner together."

* * *

Following that conversation, Elizabeth did accept additional assistance from the nurse and wet nurse. Georgiana and Kitty, under the watchful eye of Elizabeth, Mrs Reynolds, and Mrs Annesley, took on additional duties to aid the mistress of the estate, learning much in the process. The girls finalised plans for the annual harvest celebration for the tenants and staff of Pemberley, which Elizabeth had begun planning, had been delayed due to the birth of the twins. It was scheduled for the third week in October, and Georgiana and Kitty were to finish preparing the baskets for the tenants, arranging the games for the children, and overseeing the arrangements for the dance. Elizabeth was very grateful for their help and for her husband helping her realise how much help she really needed, while Darcy was just grateful she was asking for the help she needed.

With this additional assistance, the Harvest Celebration went off incredibly well, and despite Elizabeth thinking it was far less than she would have liked, it was still the best celebration in recent memory. Darcy had continued this tradition since inheriting, but the festival had been subdued without a mistress. The tenants were delighted to see the master looking so obviously happy with his wife and to see the new heir and his sister when the twins were brought out to their parents briefly during the afternoon.

In addition to congratulating the new parents, many of the women had brought little gifts, trinkets, which were received gladly by the master and mistress. They understood how vital these two children were to those who lived on and earned their livelihood from the estate. Darcy's annual speech thanked everyone for yet another exceptional year and alluded to the future that slept in the manor house. The gifts from Pemberley were well received, and the tenants danced as they celebrated along with the master and his beautiful wife.

* * *

Once the Harvest Celebration was done, the family turned their attention toward Christmas, when they would once again host a number of visitors. The two other newly-wedded couples, the Bingleys and the Fitzwilliams, would join them, as would the Matlocks and the Gardiners. Mary would accompany the Gardiners, leaving Mr and Mrs Bennet at Longbourn, as neither had been invited to spend the holiday with them. Elizabeth and Kitty debated asking Lydia to join them, as neither had seen her in more than a year, although both received frequent letters from her and were almost certain that her behaviour and attitude were significantly improved. This was primarily due to an incident she had related to Kitty.

> *15 November 1812*
> *Kitty,*
> *I believe I finally understand why I was sent to school. As you know, I have not made many friends here, which I have complained about often enough, but I have finally come to realise that this was due to my own attitude and behaviour. I have been determined to 'inflict my misery' on those who were here with me, or at least that is what a girl named Jessica told me. At first, I was rather offended, but as she explained all that was wrong with me and my attitude, I came to wonder if she was correct.*
> *This discussion occurred after an event that nearly shook me to my core and pointed out just how wrong my behaviour was. Another girl, Mary, arrived at the school in July, and she felt the same as I did about all the ridiculous rules and the constant reminders for 'proper behaviour.' We mocked the other girls, and please do not be angry at me, but we even snuck out one afternoon to visit a militia encampment a few miles away to flirt with the officers. We were nearly caught, and I was sufficiently afraid not to do that again. However, that*

did not stop Mary, and she was caught and punished. The headmistress notified her family, and they were set to come to pick her up but were delayed for some reason. Before they could arrive, Mary snuck out one more time, and this time, she intended to elope with a captain. She left me a note explaining her plans, and as soon as I discovered it, I told the headmistress because I thought that is what Lizzy and Jane would tell me to do.

A hue and cry was sent up, and Mary was discovered. The captain did not intend to marry or take her to Gretna Green. When they were found, he said his only intention was 'to take what she was offering' and called us both light skirts. I have never been so mortified. They questioned him about how he knew me since he called me by name when he saw me, and I had to confess that I had snuck out once before. I was punished, and they wrote Papa a letter, although they did not tell him to come and pick me up since 'I had seen the error of my ways' and not done it a second time, as Mary had.

Papa wrote back and told them they were stuck with me regardless and to punish me in the way they saw fit. He wrote a similar letter to me, telling me not to embarrass him more than I already had and that if I intended to misbehave, I ought to find someone who would actually take me to Gretna Green so he could be done with me. He said that with Jane and Lizzy married so well, the actions of one silly girl would not impact the rest and that Mama would be taken care of by them no matter what happened.

I have always known that Papa cared little about his

daughters, myself in particular, but this has made it much more clear. Kitty, could you please ask Elizabeth to let me come to Pemberley for Christmas? I know many girls stay here year-round, as I did this last year, but I would like to see my family again. I realise I have not always acted as I should, but I understand now and am doing much better. Mary was sent away to live with someone she did not know since her family could not allow her to return home as her eloping had become too well known. There was also concern about possible consequences of her actions since she was found alone with the captain in an inn after three or four days. The headmistress sat me down and talked to me about these consequences – diseases or a child – and quite frankly, she terrified me. Please ask Lizzy for me. I miss my sisters. I have written to all of them to apologise, and to Maria Lucas as well, since I was a terrible example to her.

Your penitent sister,
Lydia

Upon receiving this letter, Kitty immediately took it to her elder sister, who was sitting in the nursery feeding Roseanne. "Lizzy, have you received a letter from Lydia lately?"

Elizabeth nodded. "A few days ago. She begs for an invitation to Pemberley for Christmas; I must own I had already been considering inviting her. I would like for her to meet her niece and nephew, and her letters have become more positive. In this one, she actually apologised to me for her previous behaviour. I hope she is sincere."

"I believe she is," Kitty replied. "Read the letter she sent me." Elizabeth did as asked, reading it carefully once before reading it a second time, clearly upset.

"I am uncertain who to be angrier with, this girl Mary, the captain, or Papa," Elizabeth replied after several long minutes. "Clearly, this Mary was taught just as poorly as Lydia was, and the captain took advantage of her brazenness. However, I am completely taken aback by Papa's response. Perhaps he meant it sardonically as he usually does, but to put that into writing ... I am astounded." Elizabeth sat there for a moment, considering. "Might I keep this? I would like to show it to William and discuss it with him before we decide if we will invite Lydia."

At Kitty's nod, Elizabeth stood and handed her daughter to Kitty. She took the letter and went directly to William's study.

"William, you should read this letter from Lydia," she said immediately upon entering the room. He did so, his expression steadily growing stormy. Finally, he stood, marched to the window, and took several deep breaths before finally returning to where she waited.

"Every time I think your father cannot do worse by his daughters, he manages to surprise me. I do not understand the man at all," he stated.

"When Mary arrives," Elizabeth began, her voice filled with determination, "I will try my utmost to persuade her to stay. It has become apparent from the letters she has sent us that Papa, in an astonishing act of negligence, has relinquished all responsibility for the estate. He has abandoned all pretence of advising or managing, leaving Mary solely in charge. His correspondence with you, my dear husband, has ceased altogether, leading me to wonder if this is something more dire than mere neglect."

Elizabeth's tone shifted, tinged with a hint of disappointment. "For a fleeting moment last autumn, I dared to believe that Papa would finally prioritise his family's welfare. But alas, within a matter of months, his interest waned completely. Now, it falls upon us to do what he refuses to do — to ensure that my sisters have a chance at some semblance of a meaningful life. If Lydia accompanies Mary here, together we can provide the support and guidance he fails to provide."

Worry laced Elizabeth's words as she voiced her concerns. "I fear for Mary's well-being if she remains in that environment. The weight of the estate's responsibilities, combined with Papa's abandonment, places an immense burden upon her shoulders.."

"I worry as well," he replied. "She still has the companion, Mrs Higgins, with her, but she is nearly entirely on her own, and neither her mother nor father are interested in improving her situation. Perhaps if she were to marry, she and her husband could take charge of Longbourn together, but I worry for her in that situation."

Elizabeth's eyes took on a teasing glint. "Do you intend to matchmake my sister, William?"

He flushed. "No, but you must admit, it would solve several problems."

"You are right, William, but Mary has always said she did not wish to marry," Elizabeth replied, no longer teasing. "It would also provide some companionship for her, and she might be happier with someone to love and love her in return. Someone local would be good for her, perhaps one of the Lucases? Or there might be someone new?"

"Now you are matchmaking, dearest," William replied dryly. "Let us speak to Mary first and see what she desires before we make plans to marry her off."

Thirty-Three

Christmas at Pemberley

The invitation to Lydia was issued, and letters flew between London and Pemberley to arrange for the Gardiners to retrieve her along the way. The Darcys offered a carriage from Darcy House to help transport those coming from London and points along the way, and that offer was readily accepted.

The anticipation for Christmas at Pemberley grew as the invited guests began to arrive at the grand estate. Lord and Lady Matlock arrived first. As Lady Matlock intended to help Elizabeth with the plans for the holiday, assuming that she would be feeling the burden of so many guests arriving so soon after the birth of the twins.

The Bingleys collected Mary Bennet from Longbourn and the sisters enjoyed visiting with each other during the days in the carriage. Jane and Mary had not spent much time together since the former's marriage, and they took the opportunity to discuss their parents and their very different reactions to the events of the last year.

Elizabeth had continued to try to persuade Mary in letters to remain at Pemberley after Christmas. However, Mary remained adamant that she would return to Longbourn, as she enjoyed the work she was doing at Longbourn and having complete control over the estate. Mrs Higgins was a great help to her, both in instructing her and as a companion, escorting her to social events within the community. Despite the disinterest of both of her parents, Mary really had found her place at Longbourn.

In another carriage, the Gardiners, having collected Lydia from the in Northampton, were on the way to Derbyshire. Considering the events that led to Lydia's reformation, Mrs Gardiner had taken Lydia under her wing and utilised the time in the carriage to speak to her about what she had learned at school and how she would use that information in the future.

When their paths finally merged, the two groups arrived at Pemberley together. When the doors swung open, revealing the breathtaking sight of Pemberley adorned with festive decorations, a collective gasp of awe escaped the lips of Mary and Lydia. These two, who had only heard tales of Pemberley's grandeur, were amazed at the grandeur of the large manor house and lovely grounds and the fact that their sister was the mistress of it all.

Darcy and Elizabeth, ever the attentive hosts, stood at the entrance to welcome them with warm smiles. They welcomed the groups into the opulent halls of Pemberley, where the flickering glow of roaring fireplaces cast a cosy ambiance. The air was filled with the sound of laughter as the guests all greeted each other, creating an atmosphere of joy and camaraderie. Elizabeth, ever the gracious mistress of Pemberley, radiated warmth and hospitality and immediately eased the minds of Mary and Lydia, who felt a sense of belonging and acceptance in her presence. Elizabeth's genuine affection for her sisters and her easy charm put them at ease, erasing any lingering nervousness they may have felt, especially Lydia, who had been uncertain about her welcome.

Lydia, lingering in the background, watched the warm exchanges with curiosity. Elizabeth turned her attention to her younger sisters.

"Lydia, Mary, how wonderful to finally have you both here," Elizabeth greeted her sisters, her voice filled with warmth.

Lydia's eyes widened, her uncertainty fading away. "Truly, Lizzy? I was not sure how I would be received. Pemberley is utterly breathtaking, Lizzy. I am so excited to spend Christmas here."

Elizabeth embraced Lydia, her voice gentle yet firm. "You are always welcome here, dear sister. We are family, and nothing could change that. I have also been pleased to learn of the changes in your life and behaviour."

The group moved into a cosy drawing room and tea was ordered. After everyone had some refreshments, the twins were brought down and sparked an immediate burst of delight from the family. Their cherubic faces and innocent expressions captured the hearts of all who laid eyes upon them. Her sisters surrounded Elizabeth and Darcy, eagerly vying for a glimpse of the precious babies, showering them with affectionate smiles, coos, and gentle touches.

Lydia, unable to contain her excitement, leaned in closer to get a better view of the twins. "Oh, Lizzy, they are absolutely precious! Look at those tiny little noses and those chubby cheeks!"

Elizabeth smiled, her eyes filled with adoration for her children. "They truly are a blessing, Lydia. We could not be happier with our precious blessings."

Mary, standing beside Lydia, observed the twins with a gentle gaze. "They're so small and delicate. It's fascinating to see how they bring such joy to everyone around them."

Lydia, her impulsive nature taking over, reached out her hand to touch one of the twins' tiny fingers. "Can I hold one, Lizzy?" Elizabeth nodded and handed baby William over to her

More reserved but equally captivated, Mary watched Lydia with a soft smile. She approached Elizabeth hesitantly. "May I…may I hold one, Lizzy?"

Elizabeth's eyes filled with warmth. "Of course, Mary. They would love to meet their aunt." With gentle hands, Elizabeth carefully placed Roseanne in Mary's arms. As the baby settled against her, a wave of tenderness washed over Mary. Her eyes filled with tears, and a radiant smile spread across her face.

"Oh, my little darling," Mary whispered softly, her voice filled with affection. "You are simply perfect. Welcome to our family." The room fell into a hushed silence as everyone watched Mary, captivated by the love that emanated from her.

* * *

Two days later, on the twenty-first of December, the last of the guests arrived. Darcy and Elizabeth warmly welcomed the Fitzwilliams to Pemberley. Their joyous smiles reflected their happiness in hosting such a gathering, and their hearts swelled with gratitude for the presence of their loved ones.

In the days leading up to Christmas, Pemberley came alive with the spirit of celebration that permeated their guests. The grand rooms echoed with the sound of lively conversations as they gathered in small groups, exchanging stories while laughter filled the air. The crackling fireplaces provided a cosy backdrop for cheerful banter while the scent of pine and cinnamon wafted through the halls, enhancing the festive atmosphere. The twins were often present, adding much to the celebration as they were passed from guest to guest.

Amidst the joyful ambiance, the guests engaged in various activities, each bringing their unique talents and interests to the forefront. Games of charades became a favourite pastime, with laughter echoing through the hallways as players eagerly acted out clues and guessed the answers. Lady Matlock initially held back but eventually began to become more comfortable with the lively displays. Likewise, Lord Matlock found enjoyment in the lively debates and discussions that took place by the fireside, where differing opinions were met with respect and intellectual curiosity.

The sprawling gardens of Pemberley, now transformed by a glistening blanket of snow, beckoned the guests to venture outdoors. They explored the enchanting winter wonderland, the crunch of snow beneath their boots accompanying their delighted footsteps. Snowball fights ensued, and even the formerly staid Darcy joined in, frequently targeting his cousin, and shrieks of laughter echoing through the serene landscape. Some guests, particularly the newly wedded couples, bundled up in warm coats and scarves strolled hand-in-hand, enjoying the peacefulness of the season.

On Christmas Eve, the guests at Pemberley gathered in the drawing room for traditional holiday games. Snapdragon, a game of daring and excitement, took centre stage as a large shallow dish filled with raisins was placed on a table, and brandy was poured over it. The room was dimmed and the guests gathered around the table, anticipation in their eyes.

As the host, Darcy ignited the brandy, creating blue flames that danced atop the dish. One by one, the guests reached into the fiery depths, snatching a raisin while trying to avoid the flames. The crackling of the fire, the scent of warm brandy, and the sound of laughter filled the room.

With the flickering blue flames of the Snapdragon game dying down, Darcy stepped back, his eyes gleaming mischievously. "Well, my friends, I must say, that was an impressive display of bravery and nimble fingers. I hope you all managed to snatch a raisin without getting singed!"

The guests laughed as they exchanged stories of their daring attempts. Charles Bingley chuckled, his eyes alight with mirth. "I must admit, Darcy; it was quite a sight to see everyone diving into the flames like a pack of hungry wolves. But we emerged victorious!"

Elizabeth joined in the laughter, her voice filled with amusement. "Indeed, Charles. Snapdragon is always a spirited tradition; you all embraced it with enthusiasm. Now, is anyone interested in a game of spillikins?"

Delicate wooden sticks, intricately carved and coloured, were quickly scattered on a table. The goal was to carefully remove one stick at a time without disturbing the others. Each player's steady hand and strategic thinking were put to the test as they delicately manoeuvred the sticks, trying not to cause a cascade of movement. It was a game of patience, concentration, and friendly competition, bringing both moments of triumph and light-hearted laughter.

Lord Matlock delicately plucked a stick from the pile, her brow furrowing in concentration. "I used to play this game when I was younger. It requires steady hands and a keen eye for balance."

Fitzwilliam nodded, reaching for a stick of his own. "Indeed, Father. It tests our patience and strategic thinking. Let us see who among us has the most delicate touch," he replied as he not-so-subtly nudged him off balance.

The room fell into a peaceful hush as the guests focused on their task, their faces illuminated by the soft glow of candlelight. Each player gingerly removed a stick, trying not to disrupt the delicate equilibrium of the remaining sticks. Concentration etched their brows, and friendly banter filled the air as they shared tips and tricks.

Lydia, always eager for a challenge, playfully teased Charlotte. "Careful, Charlotte! One wrong move and the whole table might come crashing down. Don't let the sticks defeat you!"

Charlotte smirked, her eyes narrowing in mock seriousness. "Oh, Lydia, I shall not be defeated by a bunch of sticks. Watch and learn."

As the game progressed, a chorus of laughter erupted whenever a stick wobbled or a player's hand slipped, causing a cascade of movement. It was a delightful blend of skill and chance, creating moments of triumph and light-hearted laughter.

As the clock struck midnight, signalling the arrival of Christmas Day, the guests set aside the spillikins, their faces flushed with merriment. Darcy called for their attention. "My friends, it is time for us to make our way to Kympton for the midnight services. Let us bundle up warmly for the ride to the chapel; I have arranged for sleighs to transport us all."

The guests donned their coats and scarves, the frosty air invigorating their spirits. They stepped out into the night, guided by the soft glow of lanterns, their laughter and chatter blending harmoniously with the sound of crunching snow underfoot.

As they settled into the cosy sleighs, Elizabeth leaned toward Mary with a glimmer of excitement in her eyes. "Mary, I do hope you will enjoy the midnight services. There is something quite magical about attending them on Christmas Eve."

Mary smiled warmly, her heart filled with anticipation. "Thank you, Lizzy. I am looking forward to experiencing this beautiful tradition with our family."

Inside the cosy sanctuary, the air was filled with hushed reverence. Candlelight flickered, casting a warm glow over the wooden pews and stained-glass windows. The choir sang angelic hymns, their voices intertwining in melodic harmony, and the congregation joined in, their voices rising in unison to celebrate the birth of Christ. Prayers were whispered, and the timeless story of hope and love unfolded through scripture readings.

In that sacred space, surrounded by loved ones and fellow believers, a sense of peace settled over the hearts of the guests. The midnight services in Kympton served as a gentle reminder of the more profound significance of Christmas—the message of faith, love, and hope that resides in the birth of Christ. The serenity of the moment enveloped them, allowing them to reflect on the blessings in their lives and the joy of being in each other's company during this special time of year.

After the services, the guests returned to Pemberley, their hearts brimming with a renewed sense of peace and goodwill. They gathered in the grand drawing room, where the soft glow of the fireplaces welcomed them back. With cups of hot cocoa and eggnog in hand, they exchanged stories of their experiences at the midnight services, relishing in the beauty of the traditions that bound them together.

The family slept late on Christmas Day, and gathered in the breakfast room mid-morning. After a sumptuous breakfast, they moved to a drawing room for games and laughter. The twins were present for much of this gaiety and spent much time looking around at their family. A few small gifts were exchanged, and the twins received several gifts – some simple toys, a few children's books, and little gowns embroidered by the ladies.

A grand Christmas dinner with all manner of delicacies and holiday favourites lasted more than three hours and was thoroughly enjoyed by the company, both for the quality of food and of conversation. Everyone shared stories and traditions from past Christmases and remembered those who were no longer present. Despite this one melancholic note, the dinner was a delicious and happy affair, and everyone left the table having eaten their fill.

Elizabeth and Darcy woke early the next day and set out to visit their tenants and deliver baskets to each, a tradition they had revived the previous year. These baskets contained items needed by each family, a few coins, and treats for the children, and were well appreciated by the recipients.

At Rosings, the Morrises assisted the steward, Mr Shaw, in ensuring the baskets contained needed items for each household and delivering them to the tenants, who received them gratefully..

The week after Christmas passed in a similar fashion to the week before. A hunt occupied the men for a day or two, and they provided meat for many on the estate. Elizabeth and the other ladies sewed and chatted and generally enjoyed each other's company. The sisters were aware that this time together was unique, and Charlotte, Georgiana, and Anne had become a part of that sisterhood in the last year or so. Along with Lady Matlock and Mrs Gardiner, they had many conversations as a whole group and in smaller groupings. The twins and the Gardiner children were often with them, and they provided much entertainment for them all.

Elizabeth took the time to speak with each of her sisters individually, focusing particular attention on Mary and Lydia. In particular, she had several serious conversations with Mary about remaining at Longbourn. However, Mary was determined and reiterated the reasons she had already given for staying. In a quiet corner away from the rest of the guests, Elizabeth was finally able to coax the real reason from her reticent sister.

"I like Robert Goulding," she blurted out. "And I think he likes me too. He has begun visiting, and while he says he is there to speak with Papa, he spends most of his visits with me. We speak about Longbourn and books that we have both read. He just finished at Oxford in the spring and has been working with his father to learn about their estate, although his older brother will inherit it."

Surprise and curiosity filled Elizabeth's eyes as Mary

admitted her feelings. She could not help but be genuinely interested in her sister's admission; however, she felt she needed to raise some concerns, delicately reminding Mary of the entailment and the financial matters at hand.

"Mary," Elizabeth began gently, "I do not want to dissuade you at all, but Robert does know that you will not inherit Longbourn and the estate is entailed to Mr Collins, does he not? You have not spoken of the money you are investing with our uncle?"

"No, Lizzy, I have not. Uncle warned me most carefully not to speak of that to anyone, including our parents. Papa does not know that I have significantly cut the costs of the estate and that the profits are up. William's and the steward's suggestions have allowed us to save a large part of Longbourn's profits, and that money is invested with Uncle Gardiner for a ten percent return. It is not a significant amount yet, but it is far more than Papa has ever managed to save," Mary told her proudly.

"It is significant, Mary, and I hope you know that we are proud of you and what you have accomplished," Elizabeth replied, the pride evident in her voice. "You have done an excellent job with little help from our father. I am glad for you – how serious are things between you and Robert?"

"He has asked for a courtship, and I told him I would answer once I returned from this trip. I ... I wanted to talk it over with my sisters, mostly with you, before I replied," Mary said, seeking advice from her sister on this matter, a matter she had not wanted to commit to paper.

"Do you love him? Or do you think you could love him?" Elizabeth asked.

"I do," Mary replied. "He is so very kind and cares for

me as well. He has not said as much, but it is in his look and the way he treats me. He asked to speak to our uncle Gardiner about investing a small legacy he received from his paternal grandfather; it was unexpected, but he says it will make it easier for us to marry. He wants to purchase a small home nearby, but I was wondering... do you think we could remain at Longbourn after we marry? We could continue to run the estate, and Robert has many ideas about increasing the profits."

"As long as Papa does not mind, I cannot think of any objections to the plan. Of course, he would have to approve, and you realise he will likely do to you what he did to me once you are married. And you will be living with him," Elizabeth warned.

"I do realise that, and I do not mind because, well, I expect nothing less from him," Mary confessed. "I have never thought Papa cared for me beyond what I could do for him. He never favoured me as he favoured you, and it was obvious I was just someone to occupy him."

Elizabeth hugged her sister, pleased at the evident admiration that lit her face as she spoke of her beau. The two spent a few more minutes discussing Longbourn and their father before Elizabeth was called away to feed the twins in the nursery. Mary went with her, but since there were several others in the room, the conversation shifted to something far lighter.

Mrs Gardiner likewise spoke with each of her nieces but spent significantly more time with Lydia. In these conversations, Lydia disclosed that she did not want to return to school, but neither did she want to return to Longbourn, as she worried if she would be able to resist the influence of her mother. Recognising that Lydia needed guidance, something she would not receive at Longbourn, her aunt invited her to accompany her to London and to stay with them for a while, as Elizabeth and Jane had done. This invitation was eagerly accepted; she had been invited to remain at Pemberley as well, but she did not want to add to Elizabeth's burden since she already had two children to care for, along with Anne, Georgiana, and Kitty. No, Lydia would return to London with the Gardiners to learn to care for their children and to learn from Mrs Gardiner how to be a lady.

* * *

The day after the new year began, the Gardiners, Mary, and Lydia began their trek toward London, intending to stop for a night or two at Longbourn along the way. Lydia had not liked this plan initially but had been convinced that it was necessary for her to let her parents know of her plans. The Gardiners assured Lydia they would not let Mrs Bennet dissuade her from her purpose and would provide the support she needed to break away from her mother.

Mary was glad that the Gardiners were accompanying them, as she wanted her Uncle Gardiner to speak with her suitor as he had requested. While her father would be the one to ultimately give his consent, there were things that Mr Gardiner was aware of that Papa was not. Another consideration for Mary was that she believed her aunt and uncle truly cared for her and her happiness, unlike her parents. Her mother would be unconcerned that Mary was marrying, especially to one as 'low' as Robert Goulding. Likewise, her father would likely care little so long as Mary continued to run Longbourn. After speaking to Elizabeth, Mary had finally shared her thoughts with her uncle, and the two had discussed what would likely take place after her marriage. With the savings she had amassed, they could create a second master suite for the couple in a separate wing of the house, enabling them to have some privacy in their marriage. Of course, they would have to seek Bennet's permission, but given his lack of interest, Gardiner felt certain he would agree. After all, it would make little difference in Bennet's life if another man occupied his place instead of a daughter.

The Matlocks, Fitzwilliams, and Anne departed next to visit the Matlock estate for a fortnight. Anne accompanied Fitzwilliam and Charlotte to their newly renovated manor house nearly thirty miles from Rosings. While Anne had no desire to live there again, after all she had heard from her cousins, she wanted to view the estate again and was even willing to spend a night or two in the home while she was in the area.

Finally, the Bingleys departed to visit the Hursts at their estate near Bath. Louisa had not been able to attend the wedding as she had been entering the final months of her confinement and could not travel. However, the Hursts had invited their brother and new sister to visit after the new year and to meet their new niece. The couple would remain there for a few weeks before returning home to Netherfield. Bingley had extended the lease for an additional year, as he and Jane needed to stay there for a few months before they decided if they would remain or search for another estate to purchase.

Thirty-Four

The Season

∼⬮⬯⬮∼

S pring was slow to arrive, although the family residing at Pemberley was well entertained watching the twins grow. When it was time to travel to London for the season in the middle of March, they were six months old and were able to sit up with help and attempt to crawl or at least push up onto their arms. They babbled and gurgled, and these noises provided ample amusement to the two girls, who loved making noises and encouraging the babies to imitate them.

Although the accepted behaviour would have been to leave the children behind with their nurse, the Darcys, who were determined to defy convention whenever it went against their beliefs, intended to have their children accompany them. To that end, they planned to travel in three carriages, with several outriders for protection. Elizabeth and Darcy would travel in one, Georgiana, Kitty, and Mrs Annesley would travel in a second, and their personal servants, along with the nursemaid and wet nurse, would travel in the third. By travelling this way, the babies would be able to travel in all three at different times throughout the day, allowing all the travellers to help with their care.

This proved to be a good plan, as the children were not good travellers and, as they had made additional stops, the trip would take longer than planned. In each carriage, at least one person had become very adept at changing a wet or dirty napkin while the carriage was in motion. Unfortunately, the baskets in each carriage to hold these had everyone seeking fresh air on a regular basis, and the windows were constantly open regardless of the dust that made its way into the carriage. The entire group was tired that night and retired early. Each day followed the same pattern – frequent stops, crying babies, and exhausted adults.

Late on the fourth afternoon of travel, they arrived at Darcy House. After taking a day to rest and recover, the adults attended church on Sunday at St. George's and then gathered at Matlock House for lunch and an extended visit. The twins joined the family at Matlock House, where their great-aunt fussed over them. The next day, Lady Matlock accompanied the ladies to their appointment at the modiste. She was there to assist and advise, as Georgiana was to be presented to society that spring and Kitty would experience her first season in London society. Kitty, who was two years older than Georgiana's seventeen, had attended assemblies in Meryton but had not attended any London events beyond the theatre in her time with the Darcys.

Georgiana was now 'out' in society and felt a considerable amount of anticipation and fear of the season. Her coming out ball was planned for after Easter and promised to be quite the occasion, especially since it was the first of its kind at Darcy House in anyone's memory. The ballroom, which in recent years had been a space for exercise and dance lessons, would be put to its proper use.

Kitty was equally nervous and was glad that she did not have to endure the court presentation. She watched Lady Matlock work with Georgiana, as she had done with Elizabeth the previous spring, to prepare for being presented at court. The dress she was required to wear was very formal and cumbersome, and Georgiana practised for hours, learning how to walk backwards while carrying the heavy train attached to the dress.

"Georgiana, I must confess, I am grateful to be spared the ordeal of a presentation," Kitty admitted to her friend in the privacy of their shared sitting room, her voice tinged with a mixture of gratitude and amusement. "Watching what you have to endure, I realise how fortunate I am to merely be the sister of Mrs Darcy and not the granddaughter of an earl."

Georgiana's gentle laughter filled the room. "Oh, Kitty, you would do extremely well, and I do so wish I had someone to endure this with me. It has been so tedious. However, as Lizzy likes to remind us, each of us has our own path to navigate. Unfortunately, this is mine, but at least we will be together at the ball."

* * *

Far too quickly, the day of the presentation arrived. Georgiana presented herself well, managing not to trip or to embarrass herself in any way, for which she was very grateful.

The ball was scheduled for the following day, and both girls would make their debuts to London Society.

The day of the ball, the excitement surrounding the ball came to a crescendo, and the halls of Darcy House buzzed with activity as servants rushed about making final preparations for the event. Elizabeth, Lady Matlock, and the dedicated staff worked tirelessly to transform the home and ballroom into something spectacular.

That evening, Darcy House shimmered under the soft glow of countless candles. Guests adorned in their finest attire began to gather in the opulent ballroom, and Elizabeth and Darcy stood to receive them all while Georgiana and Kitty waited upstairs.

Georgiana and Kitty made their entry into the ballroom on the arms of Lord Matlock and Darcy respectively. Both felt a little anxious when they noted all the eyes on them and kept in mind the warnings from both Elizabeth and Lady Matlock that not everyone who would attempt to befriend or court them that night would do so with the right intentions. They had been warned, and Georgiana had learned the hard lesson of the danger of those who offered a false friendship. With Georgiana's dowry, she would likely be sought by fortune hunters, while some would pursue Kitty solely for her connection to the Darcys.

Both girls had discussed this many times and were determined to escape the season unengaged. Neither wanted to accept anything less than the example they had lived with for the last year and a half and wanted to find a man to marry who loved them as much as Darcy loved Elizabeth. Fortune and connections mattered far less than a good character, mutual respect, and genuine love.

However, this determination did not prevent either from dancing. They danced their first sets with their escort, but the two gentlemen switched partners midway through, enabling Darcy to dance the second dance of the first set with his sister. He appreciated this gesture from his uncle, as Darcy often felt more like a father to Georgiana than an elder brother. He had struggled with this whole event, because of these feelings and did not like the fact that Georgiana was now considered to be of marriageable age.

The ball was a success, and Darcy expected suitors for both girls to begin arriving that day. Quite a few flowers had arrived that morning for both girls, although a majority of the offerings were for Georgiana, as she was a Darcy and had a significant dowry. Since neither girl was serious about marrying that year, they were both planning to enjoy the season to the best of their ability. Even Lydia had enjoyed being allowed to attend, although she had chosen not to participate in the dancing except with her brothers.

* * *

The day after the ball, the entire family — all the Bennet sisters, the Matlocks, Gardiners, Bingleys, and Fitzwilliams — gathered at Darcy House in the mid-afternoon to discuss the previous night. Mary had accompanied the Bingleys from Hertfordshire and was staying at Darcy House. Robert Goulding had accompanied them to London as well, having finally proposed to Mary, and the two had enjoyed the opportunity to dance at the ball the previous night. Bingley had kindly extended an invitation for him to stay in their leased townhouse, and the gentlemen in the family had found him to be a pleasant young man, intelligent and willing to work hard. Darcy had been impressed by the man when they met, as had Elizabeth, who believed him to be an ideal match for her serious sister.

As the family discussed the events from the night before, they also spoke about their plans for the rest of the season. Mary would only remain for a few more days before she and Goulding would return to Longbourn, accompanied by the Gardiners. Mary and Goulding would marry in less than a month, as soon as the banns were called, and Mrs Gardiner would help plan the wedding with Mary. The entire family would join them in Hertfordshire in a fortnight and would be housed between Longbourn and Netherfield Park, where they would remain until the wedding. While Darcy preferred to return to Pemberley after the wedding, Lady Matlock impressed upon him the necessity for Georgiana to experience a full season, so after a sennight in Hertfordshire, they would return to London. The Fitzwilliams would accompany them to the wedding to visit with Charlotte's parents and remain an additional sennight after the wedding, although they would remain at Netherfield for their entire stay.

Bingley and Jane would not return to London, as Jane suspected she was with child, although no announcement would be made until they were certain. The couple were looking for an estate to purchase nearer to Pemberley, and hoped to be settled before Jane's lying in, which they estimated to be late October. Despite her lack of a carriage, Mrs Bennet had proved to be a pest over the months they had lived at Netherfield. When she did visit, she would stay far longer than anyone desired, and she wrote nearly every day to beg a carriage to bring her to visit. Mrs Bennet had managed to convince several ladies in town to provide a way for her to get to Netherfield, but then she would encourage them to leave without her, so the Bingleys were obligated to allow her to stay longer or to send her home in their own carriage.

While Jane had made several attempts to restrict her mother's visits, Mrs Bennet simply ignored her and still arrived unwanted and unwelcome. Bingley had likewise spoken to her about visiting less frequently, which also had little impact on her showing up whenever she could manage. Finally deciding it was enough and the only way to stop these visits was to move away, they sought Darcy's aid in finding an estate in the North. They would travel north after Mary's wedding to view an available estate the Darcy recommended, and if all was as advertised, they would purchase it and would be settled in the house before Jane's time of confinement.

The weeks before the wedding passed quickly, and the Darcys again travelled in several carriages with the twins. With the Bingleys and the Fitzwilliams, they made for a rather large caravan travelling together. Although this journey was far shorter, they still broke it into several smaller increments to make the journey easier for everyone, and it worked this time. It was a much happier group that arrived at Netherfield Park that afternoon than the group that had arrived in London.

Mrs Gardiner and Mary were awaiting their arrival at Netherfield and immediately offered the tea and refreshments they had arranged. Mary greeted the adults but quickly demanded to hold one of the children, having enjoyed the few days with them in London earlier that month. Mrs Gardiner took her turn with Roseanne while Mary held William, and after some time, they switched.

After much deliberation, they decided to invite Mr and Mrs Bennet to Netherfield Park for dinner two nights after the arrival of the party from London. The invitation was accepted, but everyone remained uneasy about the seeing the Bennets. Mrs Gardiner had been in favour of the invitation, but after the invitation had been sent, she saw a significant decline in Mrs Bennet's behaviour and began to dread the event.

The Bennets, including Mary, arrived at Netherfield together with Robert Goulding. Goulding stepped down after Bennet and grimaced at his hosts before turning to help the ladies down. As had become his wont, Bennet barely acknowledged anyone and simply walking into Netherfield to sit. Goulding handed down first his betrothed and then his future mother-in-law. From the moment her foot touched the ground, Mrs Bennet was loud and obnoxious. She praised Jane for her marriage to Bingley and proclaimed him her favourite son. Elizabeth she ignored, although that was likely because the one time she attempted to approach her, Darcy glared at her hard enough to make even her hesitate to speak.

Other than a few distasteful comments and a few slights to her least favourite daughter, she did behave fairly well. She complained several times about Lydia not being 'out' in London and not being allowed to attend the parties that Kitty had attended. She also made several loud comments about her youngest daughters remaining unmarried. Darcy and Bingley attempted to tune out any conversions related to introducing her youngest daughters to wealthy men, and they only rolled their eyes when she suggested Lydia would surely marry into the peerage. When Lydia protested this claim and stated she intended to wait several more years before she even considered marriage, Mrs Bennet replied, "Nonsense," and continued speaking of the events and parties that Lydia ought to be permitted to attend as the sister of Mr Darcy.

After dinner, when the sexes separated, the night took a decided turn for the worse. Once all the ladies were gathered in the drawing room drinking tea, Mrs Bennet asked Jane when she would become with child and complained about the Bingleys' plans to leave Netherfield soon and their unwillingness to host her as often as she would like. At no point in these diatribes did she ask about Elizabeth's children or speak to either her or Kitty, neither of whom she had seen in many months. Her loud speech ensured everyone heard every word she uttered and made it difficult for others to converse.

The men returned far sooner than the ladies expected, and it was obvious when he walked into the room that Darcy was irritated. Elizabeth looked at him inquiringly, but Darcy merely shook his head at her, silently indicating they would speak of it later.

Bennet barely spoke to anyone after the men joined the ladies, and the hour after their return passed very slowly for everyone in the room. Finally, the carriages were ordered. The Gardiners boarded the first carriage with Goulding, who they would drop at his home before returning to Longbourn. Mary boarded the Bennet carriage and felt the heaviness that hung about the carriage from the apparent pique of the others with her.

Following the departure, all of those remaining at Netherfield agreed to retire. As soon as Elizabeth and Darcy reached their chambers, Elizabeth whirled around to ask, "William, what happened with Papa after dinner?"

"He was his usual self and, I believe, insulted nearly everyone in the room in some way or another. He insulted his daughters, although at this point, I believe it is so second nature for him that he does not even realise it. Goulding would have punched him for some of his comments related to Mary had I not prevented him," Darcy explained. "He does not know what she has done for the estate and how she has made it more prosperous than it was before; he simply does not care to view his daughters in any other way than he always has. I am sorry, dearest, but it seems that he has retreated even further into his books since we saw him in London. We already knew he is even less interested in the estate and Mary is in complete control, but now it seems his tongue has become even sharper, perhaps from the lack of its use."

Elizabeth shook her head, having no words to say for several minutes. "It appears evident that he will never change, William, and it is useless to believe he ever will. His daughters will always be silly in his mind, regardless of the fact that I worked with the steward from my fourteenth year to my twentieth, and after only a few months of his taking an interest, Mary has acted as both mistress and master. Mama was a little better, although I suppose I should appreciate that she did not speak to me all evening."

He hugged her to his chest. "We will likely encounter them periodically because I cannot imagine you will ever forsake Mary, who is content both with her chosen husband and remaining at Longbourn. She is in charge, as your father largely ignores her, and has been able to do much for Longbourn. Do you know she has saved two thousand pounds for her dowry and has another fifteen hundred invested toward each of your youngest sister's dowries? It is invested with Gardiner, and I have committed to adding another two thousand pounds toward each. Goulding is aware of my gift and asked that it continue to be invested for now. At some point, Collins will inherit, and they will have to find another place to live. He believes that between his legacy, Mary's dowry, and their savings from Longbourn's profits, they will be able to purchase a home or cottage somewhere."

"You are so good, William," she replied, kissing him hard. All conversation was forgotten after that.

* * *

Despite the rather inauspicious start to the wedding celebration, the wedding of Mary and Robert Goulding went off without a hitch. Mrs Gardiner was hostess for the wedding breakfast, and Mrs Bennet was only permitted to attend if she held her tongue. She made it through the entire ceremony and a portion of the wedding breakfast without disparaging any of her less favoured daughters. However, when she made an unkind comment about the bride's poor appearance – her dress had too little lace – she was quickly removed from the main house and escorted to the dower house. Gardiner had arranged in advance for Mrs Higgins to remove the matron should she not behave with proper decorum during the wedding breakfast.

By early afternoon, the happy couple were ready to depart for their wedding trip. Darcy had arranged for the couple to first travel to London to spend a night at Darcy House before travelling to the coast the following day. When the couple left, so did the rest of the guests. Only Bennet remained at Longbourn, and, for a moment, he almost felt lonely that evening. He briefly considered seeking out the company of his wife, but then his book captured his attention once again. Had Mary not ensured that meals would be served to her Papa at regular intervals, it is unlikely he would have seen another soul while the Gouldings were away.

The following day, the Darcys returned to London to complete the season. As expected, Georgiana was a tremendous success in the eyes of the *ton* and had received several marriage proposals, which had all been promptly rejected. Kitty had received two proposals, but since she did not really care for either man, these were also kindly refused, and both escaped the season with their hearts untouched. Soon enough, the family fled the city for Pemberley, where they intended to remain for some time. They travelled slowly, taking the time to ensure the now nine-month-old twins were comfortable. After four days of travel, they happily returned to life at Pemberley.

Elizabeth and Darcy quickly settled into their routines and enjoyed the increased intimacy afforded to them at Pemberley. With fewer social demands, they found more time for themselves, despite the many demands of Pemberley. They resumed their habit of daily walks throughout the park each morning and used this time to discuss anything of interest or to simply be together. This time was precious to both of them, and it was a habit they protected fiercely, ensuring they had time together, no matter if it were merely a quarter of an hour of privacy.

Elizabeth finally began her riding lessons with Darcy. One of her arguments against learning to ride was that women were expected to ride sidesaddle, which had always appeared extremely unsafe to her, so Darcy had agreed to teach her to ride astride. He hoped that she would learn to ride sidesaddle once she was comfortable riding astride, but it was not necessary at Pemberley. To this end, Elizabeth worked with the dressmaker in Lambton to create a riding habit with a split skirt so she could ride astride while protecting her modesty. The lessons went well, and before long, Elizabeth was often found riding the estate with Darcy, particularly in the mornings before the rest of the house awoke.

Their sisters also found much to occupy them at Pemberley. Georgiana continued to immerse herself in her music while Kitty pursued the arts. They often met to peruse the vast library under the guidance of Mrs Annesley, who guided them through the world of literature to continue to expand their knowledge. They also worked with both Elizabeth and Mrs Reynolds to learn more about managing the house, and dedicated hours to their charitable pursuits, mainly sewing clothing for the children of the tenants and the poor house, and accompanying Elizabeth on visits to the tenants and preparing baskets for those who were sick.

Word spread that the Darcys were in residence at Pemberley and the ladies began receiving and returning visits. As more of the landed gentry and aristocracy arrived at their country homes, the Darcys were occasionally invited to dinners and hunts, especially as summer transformed into autumn. Georgiana and Kitty accompanied the Darcys to these events and were introduced to young gentlemen they had not met during the season.

The only time the Darcys left Pemberley for more than an afternoon or an evening was when they visited the Bingleys' new estate, called Windermere Grange. The estate was located just twenty miles away and was easily reached by carriage in just a few hours. When they arrived in late October for Jane's lying in, they admired the charming Georgian-style manor house made of both brick and stone and surrounded by lovely gardens, which displayed well even in the late autumn. Elizabeth looked forward to walking through these during her visit.

As Jane was too large to move much beyond her rooms, Bingley welcomed the family to the manor. The housekeeper showed the ladies to their rooms while Bingley took Darcy around the estate. Darcy would have preferred to rest with his wife, but he had grudgingly agreed after Elizabeth smiled and encouraged him to go. "I will refresh myself and then go to check on Jane, dearest," she told him. "You go with Bingley; he is rather pleased to be showing you his estate. Go now, and we will take a walk later."

With those words, he had agreed, and the two set off to ride the estate. Overall, the estate was modest, slightly smaller than Netherfield, but it appeared to be well-maintained. Bingley proudly guided Darcy through the grounds, showing him the freshly ploughed fields that would soon be sown with winter wheat and the pastures where sheep grazed. The air was slightly crisp and Darcy found himself refreshed with the exertion.

When they returned from their ride, Bingley enthusiastically described the plans he and Jane had for the manor house and grounds. They planned to create a garden for the herbs and other medicinal plants Jane had frequently worked with at Longbourn and add a still room for her to dry these herbs and prepare medicines and the like. She and Elizabeth had frequently worked in the still room at Longbourn to create medicines, lotions, and scented toilet waters using flowers gathered from the gardens there. Elizabeth continued this practice at Pemberley, where she was teaching Georgiana and Kitty. Bingley had other more grandiose ideas, such as adding a glass house, although Darcy did try to dissuade him from doing that for at least a year or two to see if the estate could support such a structure.

He was still speaking of the glass house when they arrived at the manor to find everyone in turmoil. Upon entering Jane's rooms, Elizabeth had quickly realised Jane was quietly in labour and had called for the midwife, but this request had sent the largely new and still untrained staff into confusion. Elizabeth quickly took charge and called for clean cloths and towels to be prepared, water to be heated, and Jane to be moved into the birthing chambers. The monthly nurse had already arrived, as Jane had been uncertain about when the baby would arrive. The midwife arrived within the hour and took charge, with Elizabeth assisting as she could, along with the monthly nurse and housekeeper.

Jane's labour lasted the rest of the afternoon and into the night. While Elizabeth stayed with Jane, Darcy remained with his friend in his study, doing his best to prevent him from getting too far into his cups while keeping him distracted from what was happening upstairs within his chambers. Finally, the two gentlemen succumbed to sleep in the wee hours of the morning, and the sun was just peeking over the horizon when Elizabeth gently shook her husband awake.

"William," she said quietly as she shook his arm. "William, wake up. I need your help to wake Bingley so that he might meet his son."

Darcy jerked awake and slowly opened his eyes, blinking against the sun shining through the windows. "This is a terrible location for a study," he groaned. "Too much sun in the mornings." He blinked and looked up at his wife, realisation dawning. "Did you say Bingley has a son?"

She smiled. "Yes, and I need your assistance in waking him. My speaking to him has not worked," she said.

"I am afraid he drank rather more than he should have last night," Darcy said dryly. "I will wake him, dearest." He stood and, walking over to Bingley, shook him violently until he woke. "Bingley!" he called loudly.

Bingley's eyes blinked, and he blearily looked up at his friend. "Wha… Why am I sleeping in my study?" He looked around again. "And why are you here with me?"

"We waited in here for your wife to give birth and apparently fell asleep – although your nap was likely aided by the quantity of brandy you consumed," Darcy replied. "And now, your wife is waiting for you so she might introduce you to your child."

Bingley gaped for a moment but could not speak. He flew to the door, slung it open, and dashed toward the stairs. The door slammed behind him, causing Darcy and Elizabeth to look at it and laugh. "So, dearest," Darcy began, walking up behind her to embrace her from behind, "was it difficult to watch your sister give birth after experiencing it for yourself?"

She laughed. "No, not really difficult, but very tiring. I will say that giving birth is considerably more so. I was

411

unaware of how many periods of inactivity were involved in the process, given that the last time I was in pain throughout the event. I have heard the next time will likely be easier, and I believe it might occur in about seven months if the signs are to be believed."

Darcy looked at her incredulously. "The next time?" he asked.

Elizabeth smiled gently and turned in his arms. "The next time, my love," she replied, reaching up to caress his face. "Although I must say, I hope for just one this time around."

He leaned down to kiss her, tightening his arms around her. "I love you, Elizabeth," he said. "Thank you."

Almost The END ...

Thirty-Five

Epilogue

J ane and Bingley were very happy together at Windermere Grange. Both had learned how to stand up for
themselves and what they wanted as they dealt with
troublesome family members, although they remained far
too generous with much of their family and even their
servants. One area where he never wavered was in dealing
with Caroline. Although she was settled in Scotland, she did
not cease sending letters to her brother asking him to arrange
for her to travel to London. Bingley steadily refused these
requests, reminding her that she was ruined, even though
few knew of it. No one in London would believe that she had
been married anywhere but in London, and he attempted to
convince his sister that she should find someone there or live
as a spinster since he had no intention of ever returning her
to England.

Their first son had been named after Bingley and was

christened Charles Edward Bingley before the Darcys departed the estate. The Darcys were named the child's godparents at that ceremony, and the families remained close. After little Charley, Jane and Bingley went on to have three more children, all girls. Bingley eventually added a small conservatory at his estate, and Darcy had aided his friend significantly in this endeavour. The path between the two estates was well travelled, and the cousins spent much time together as children.

* * *

Anne shocked everyone by surviving longer than anyone would have anticipated on the day she first arrived at Matlock House following Darcy's wedding. She allowed Darcy and Lord Matlock to continue to run the estate, and she saw two more sons born to the Darcys in the years before her death.

For the most part, Anne resided with the Darcys, feeling the closest to them, although she did frequently visit the Matlocks and even, on occasion, Charlotte and Fitzwilliam at Deerwood Stables. Darcy remained a largely silent partner in the enterprise, which became very successful. After more than two years of marriage, the Fitzwilliams finally had a son, followed quickly by a daughter. Several years later, Charlotte gave birth to a second son, much to everyone's surprise.

Her mother, Lady Catherine, never left Ireland and only survived for another two years after her banishment. Ironically, Lady Catherine's death was hastened by a tonic made for her by the local apothecary, which contained opium to keep her calm and subdued. Her addiction to the laudanum eventually reached a point where she consistently needed more, and she was finally given too much of the drug, dying of an overdose of the medicine. Her maid ended up marrying one of the footmen hired to protect her. After Lady Catherine's death, Lord Matlock installed them as the caretakers for that estate, as they had discovered they enjoyed living there.

* * *

Mrs Bennet remained in the dower house for the rest of her life. Elizabeth attempted to visit with her mother when Darcys returned to the area for the first year or two of their marriage, but her overtures were rejected. Mrs Bennet could not see her least favourite daughter without becoming greatly distressed and continued to belittle her second child at every opportunity. Finally, Elizabeth ceased all attempts to visit. Mary had attempted to visit her mother weekly when that lady was first banished to the dower house but her mother refused to see her until finally, after her marriage, she quit visiting as well. Mrs Bennet wanted nothing to do with Mary; she only wanted her most beautiful daughters, Jane and Lydia, to come and see her. However, when Jane visited, her mother only bemoaned her isolation in the dower house, and any suggestions Jane offered about improving her life were ignored. After moving away, Jane's rare visits caused even greater agitation in the matron, and eventually, Jane also gave up the attempt.

When Lydia first returned home from school, a much wiser girl than the one who had left, she also visited with her mother. Mrs Bennet welcomed her eagerly but became very upset when Lydia shared what she had learned with her mother and spoke of her newfound desire to follow her sisters in proper behaviour. She told Lydia she was no longer as lively as she had been and complained about her dresses, which were far more modest than Mrs Bennet had tended to purchase for her daughters. Likewise, Mrs Bennet could not persuade her to speak of beaux and flirtations, as Lydia had sworn to give both up until she felt she was ready for marriage. Her mother became irate when Lydia shared how she was learning to manage a household from Mrs Gardiner and that she intended to remain in London with her aunt and uncle for some time. The final straw was when Lydia praised all that Elizabeth had accomplished at Pemberley and how well all the Bennet daughters had been doing since Elizabeth and Darcy had married. Mrs Bennet began to berate Lydia for forsaking her own mother and choosing instead to listen to Mary and Lizzy until Lydia finally ran from the house in tears. This poor treatment further cemented Lydia's desire to be nothing like her mother, and Lydia did not revisit her mother for many years.

Mrs Bennet remained isolated in the dower house with no daughters willing to visit her. During his lifetime, her husband visited monthly to ensure that all was well in the home; after he died, Goulding took on that role. Few others bothered with the matron. The ladies of the village had grown tired of her boasting and simply ignored her existence after learning of the calumny that had led to her banishment. Only rarely did Mrs Phillips stop by or, on the rare occasion, did a daughter visit, but Mrs Bennet was far too unhappy with her life for anyone to remain long in her company.

* * *

Four years after Anne took over the ownership of Rosings, the Darcys once again encountered Bishop Allen. They learned from him that Collins had been granted a position as a curate in a parish on the Isles of Scilly, a remote archipelago in the Southwest corner of England, and he had died there. There were few parishioners, and the patron was only accessible by boat, which meant that Collins had been forced to work in the interests of those he was there to help instead of fawning over one of higher rank. Life was difficult for him in his less-exalted position, and his corpulent frame was unsuited for hard work. It took no one by surprise that within just two years of arriving, Collins suffered an apoplexy and died – alone and miserable, cursing both the Bennets and Darcys. However, his death ended the entailment upon Longbourn, enabling Bennet to leave Longbourn to whoever he chose.

When this information was shared with Bennet, he shrugged, as it mattered little to him who inherited his estate upon his death. However, his brother Mr Phillips, the local solicitor, hounded him to update his will to make it clear who would inherit after him. Without giving it much thought, he named Darcy as his successor since, in his mind, it was Darcy whose efforts had made the estate more profitable.

Despite this, Mr Bennet allowed Mary and her husband to continue the estate management. He occasionally sought out his son-in-law's company, and he continued writing the rare letter to Darcy or the even more occasional letter to Bingley. He did not, however, write to his daughters and as a result, they rarely bothered to visit with him, even when they visited the area, which they did frequently.

Bennet did not live long after he learned of Collins' death. When his will was read naming Darcy the owner of the estate, all the Bennet sisters felt the slight. After a brief conversation with Elizabeth and another equally brief conversation with Phillips, they deeded the estate to Robert and Mary Goulding since they had done much since Mary had taken on its administration. This was handled with surprisingly little fanfare, and in a very short period of time, the paperwork was handled and all documents were signed to hand the estate over to its caretakers. In the six years since Mary had fully taken over the responsibilities from Bennet, she had improved the estate, and its profits had increased to nearly one and a half times what it had been generating when Bennet was in charge.

Since marrying, the Gouldings had invested the profits from the estate with Gardiner and had amassed in their savings several times its annual profits, giving them a comfortable nest egg and the ability to provide for whatever children they were blessed with. They offered a portion of the interest and income from their investments as annual gifts to both Kitty and Lydia when they married, but both declined it, stating that Mary had made the estate profitable and she deserved most to benefit from what she had been able to raise. They each had dowries of five thousand pounds from the estate's profits and contributions from both Darcy and Bingley.

* * *

Georgiana and the remaining Bennet sisters all married within the next few years. All three girls attended the following season, staying at the home of Lord and Lady Matlock most of that time since Elizabeth was too far along in her confinement to risk travelling to London. Kitty had a suitor that year who frequently danced with her and escorted her to various events and parties. He did not propose, but at the end of the season, he requested permission from Lord Matlock to visit Kitty at Pemberley to meet her guardians. The Matlocks knew the family, who lived in a neighbouring county, and agreed to forward the request to Darcy for his decision. This young man was the second son of a viscount with good prospects and was presently studying to become a barrister.

Darcy eventually extended an invitation to the young man to a house party they hosted that autumn, following Elizabeth's giving birth to their second son the previous April. He carefully observed the young man, Arthur Kingsley, and spoke with him frequently during his visit. In the end, he was amenable to his suit for his sister-in-law; however, he required that the two court for a time, including sending letters back and forth during the time they would of necessity be apart. Kitty had just reached her twentieth birthday, and young Kingsley was not yet capable of supporting a wife. The couple reluctantly agreed to this and frequently corresponded for the next six months. In the following season, Kingsley was called to the bar, and with Kitty's dowry and his father's gifting them a small house in London, they married at the end of the season. The wedding was held at Pemberley, and Darcy gave his sister away since her father had abdicated this role to his eldest son-in-law.

Georgiana and Lydia met their future husbands at the celebrations surrounding Kitty's wedding. Lydia met the curate at Pemberley and fell madly in love at first sight. She elected to stay at Pemberley that summer and led the young man on a merry chase. Philip Harrington took much convincing to get to the point, as he believed that as just a curate, he had little to offer the young lady who lived at Pemberley, but get there he did. To help the young man he knew to be a good man from his service to the church in Kympton, Darcy aided Harrington in finding a living in nearby Staffordshire. That done, Harrington proposed immediately to Lydia and the two were married as soon as the banns could be called.

Georgiana was not struck by love at first sight. Instead, she developed a sudden antipathy for the man who insulted her at the ball celebrating Kitty's engagement held at Pemberley two days before the wedding. Viscount Sebastian Ashford, son of the Earl of ____, was overheard calling Georgiana 'merely tolerable' when a friend suggested he ask the young lady to dance. Georgiana was standing next to Elizabeth when he said it, and she begged her sister to say nothing to Darcy, choosing instead to laugh off the insult. However, Elizabeth could not let such a comment slide and soon informed her husband about it. Ashford, not knowing who he insulted, found himself unpleasantly surprised when he was pulled aside a little later by Darcy and severely reprimanded for his rude comments regarding his sister. He apologised profusely to Darcy, stating that he avoided dancing whenever possible and had not been really paying attention to who his friend recommended for dancing.

When he was introduced to the beautiful young woman he had so rudely insulted, he nearly kicked himself when he recognised her as the woman he had been interested in since he had seen her during the season but had never been near enough for an introduction. He apologised to Georgiana, but it took months of the gentleman pursuing her before she finally allowed him close enough to get to know him better and several more months before she agreed to a courtship. Nearly a year after Kitty's wedding and after his dogged pursuit, she finally accepted his proposal of marriage the second time it was offered. The two married from Pemberley that autumn, the wedding having to be delayed somewhat to allow for Elizabeth's third confinement, which produced another healthy son born in June.

* * *

After Mary inherited Longbourn, Darcy and Elizabeth purchased Netherfield Park, which remained empty and had been largely neglected since the Bingleys moved north. With a capable steward appointed to oversee the day-to-day operations, Netherfield Park thrived under the Darcys' careful management. Its profitability ensured a steady stream of income, but more importantly, it became a cherished gathering place for the entire family.

Throughout the year, Netherfield Park buzzed with the presence of the Darcy sisters, their husbands, their many children, and other family members, including the Fitzwilliams visited the estate when they visited Charlotte's family. The estate also served as a welcoming retreat, particularly during the midst of the hectic London season when one or more of the Bennet sisters and their families would escape to the tranquillity of Netherfield for a week or two of respite from the social whirl.

A Different Impression

At the end of the bustling London Season, the entire extended family convened at Netherfield Park for a brief but joyous reunion. Laughter echoed through the halls of both Netherfield and Longbourn as the Bennet sisters and their families shared stories and created lasting memories before they dispersed to their own homes scattered across the country.

* * *

Elizabeth and Darcy were incandescently happy with each other. That did not mean they never argued – for they most certainly did. However, these infrequent events were nearly always resolved to everyone's satisfaction and the passion with which they made up usually equalled or surpassed the passion of the argument itself. It was evident to all that the Darcys were deeply in love, and only rarely was the witty repartee that passed between them misinterpreted as discord. Darcy had fallen in love with Elizabeth in part because of her ability to challenge him, and this remained true throughout their marriage. Darcy relied on his wife's judgement, and they frequently made decisions together, shocking those who did not know them well and could not understand how a man could view his wife as an equal and not a chattel.

It came as no surprise to anyone when the Darcys gave birth to several more children. In fact, when Anne passed away more than four years after the twins were born, the Darcys had two more children, and Elizabeth was increasing again, although she had not realised it yet. When their last child was born, the Darcy clan numbered ten in all: Darcy and Elizabeth, five boys, and three girls.

Roseanne became the owner of Rosings at the age of 21. Although she had already married at that time, Darcy ensured she retained ownership of the estate in the marriage settlements. Anne had ensured that the daughters of the family would always have a home by entailing it along the female line. Darcy taught all of his children about estate matters as he wanted to ensure they were well-prepared for whatever the future would bring. Whether they inherited Pemberley, Rosings, or one of the other estates spread throughout the country or made their own way in the world, he wanted to ensure they were prepared and could support each other and none would struggle as he had.

Following the excellent example of their parents, each of the Darcys' eight children made a love match, worried less about connections and dowry than about character and respect – not to mention a deep, abiding love for their spouse. As each child married, they passed down the secret to a long, healthy marriage – a willingness to communicate with their partner and a fair bit of passion go a long way toward a happy life. On their fortieth wedding anniversary, their eight children, each of their spouses, thirty-something grandchildren and a great-grandchild or two, and a myriad of extended family gathered together at Pemberley and raised a toast to the extraordinary couple who set the example for felicity in marriage.

The END

About the Author

I first read Pride and Prejudice in high school and, in the last few years, have discovered the world of JAFF. After reading quite a few, I thought that perhaps I could do that, and these are my attempts. I write under the pen name Melissa Anne.

I began my career as a newspaper reporter before becoming a middle school English teacher and then moved to high school to teach Literature. I presently live and work in Georgia, although I grew up in East Tennessee and claim that as home. I have been married to a rather wonderful man (a cross between Darcy and Bingley, perhaps) for nearly two decades, and we have three children.

Also by Melissa Anne

What Happened After Lambton

Darcy and Elizabeth meet at Pemberley months after the disastrous proposal in Kent. A frank conversation and several apologies lead to the couple getting engaged much sooner than in canon.

After Kent, Darcy had confessed all to his cousin Colonel Fitzwilliam, including Wickham's presence in the militia in Meryton. Fitzwilliam keeps an eye on Wickham and prevents the elopement, meaning that Elizabeth's stay in Derbyshire is not interrupted. That does not keep Wickham from creating problems for the couple, even after Wickham is tried for desertion. Mr Bennet is unhappy about the engagement, and Jane is … too easily led by those who do not have her best interests at heart. Mrs Bennet and Lydia are foolish and remain so.

Printed in Great Britain
by Amazon